THE FOG LINE

THE *fog* LINE

CAROL BIRCH

BLOOMSBURY

First published 1989
Copyright © 1989 by Carol Birch

Bloomsbury Publishing Ltd, 2 Soho Square, London W1V 5DE

A CIP catalogue record for this book
is available from the British Library.

ISBN: 0 7475 0453 9

Typeset by Cambrian Typesetters, Frimley, Surrey
Printed in Great Britain by Butler & Tanner Ltd, Frome and London

'It was like freefalling. Nothing lasted. There was never a time when
I could look forward and say Yes, one year from now I will
be . . . because I never knew.'

Gloria's childhood ended the day she was raped and made pregnant – the
day she came face to face with the devil. That's when the voices started
inside her head; that's when the fog descended and the drifting began.
Caught between the guilty secret of her past and the void of her present,
Gloria struggles to hang on to her dreams. She meets David – charming,
romantic, an aspiring poet, but weak in a way that is to prove fatal.

With Gloria's daughter Kit they wander the country: a few months here, a
year there, making do, just making out. Over the years the uneasy
triangle stretches to breaking point. David drinks, his poetry goes
unpublished, and he clings to Gloria with a cloying dependency. Kit has
found some measure of security in Scotland and doesn't want to leave.

Tired of living on the edge, of clinging to the fringes of other people's
lives, Gloria moves on, alone. But a flat, a job, and another boyfriend are
not enough to make for a new beginning. The voices become insistent, and
further, more terrifying action must be taken before Gloria can start to be
free of her past.

Carol Birch draws us into Gloria's world with an engaging frankness
and a subtle eye. Passionate, unsentimental, *The Fog Line* is a powerful
re-creation of the texture of young life on the margins. Her first novel,
Life In The Palace, won the 1988 David Higham Prize.

FOR VALERIE COUMONT

PART ONE

1

Gloria plays in the mushroom field, a boggy place full of strange fungi, like tongues, trumpets, showers of bells, sprouting on and under tree stumps that loom here and there like lopped torsos. Round and round the edge of the field she runs with her invisible twin, playing out some desperate adventure.

Evil vampire hordes hover in the clouds over England, waiting to attack. She's riding to Africa to find the only antidote to their bite, a plant that grows on the lip of a boiling lake of molten lava on top of a massive rain-forested peak, rising like a needle from endless miles of jungle. Stopping beneath the wide spreading boughs of a tall old tree on the road side of the field, she looks up, sees monkeys and parrots, turns her lucky fish in the pocket of her tartan pinafore, pauses for a second then climbs, swift but clumsy, breathing hard. This is the Africa tree. Her invisible twin, whose name is Michael, waits below, as ever the weaker. When she returns he is gone and the bells are pealing. They always ring on Sundays. It's time to go home but she stands awhile, a tough stocky girl with capable filthy hands, thin legs with scraped knobbly knees, feet shod in scuffed red sandals, the straps gone thick and hairy and curling up with age.

You can't see any houses from here, only high rough hedges and a wire fence with a scrawny copse beyond. Many things are forbidden: certain places, certain people, certain shops, certain words, certain feelings. Everything beyond the mushroom field is forbidden: the filthy brook, the wreck of a factory, the gravel pits, the mile of cracked khaki-coloured mud where people get murdered, sink screaming into quicksand, fall into holes in the earth.

She listens to the trees soughing mysteriously, slowly waving against the grey sky. She's hungry. By the gate that stands open to the road an elder tree stands, heavily laden with sprays of creamy must-scented blossom called Motherdie. If you bring Motherdie into the house your mother dies. Her mother told her that. She pauses beneath the sprays to collect her stick from where it always waits in the hedge, a good strong green stick with a graceful serpentine twist around the middle; wields it this way and that lovingly for a while then canoes home whistling through her teeth, using the stick as a paddle.

The place where she lives is not town nor country nor village. It's housing estates and little green bits, a big brash pub with a car park, a cluster of shops, an old sandstone church and a pool where ducks and swans and moorhens swim. It seems from all this that there should be open countryside somewhere near, but there isn't. She runs along by the pool, past the corner where a great hole like an open mouth sucks all the water down to roar and gargle like some demon under the road, crosses the narrow plank bridge that spans the stream and rattles as you walk over it. She runs up the hill to her house, a solid brick square with a scruffy little garden at the front, a concrete path down one side and a high-walled yard at the back.

Under the dense three-foot-width of the front hedge, never tended, there is a damp, dark, hallowed space where she hides things – some threepenny bits, two tortoiseshell combs, a big pink and grey shell and a little blue soap dish set into the soft earth. Her father's moped, never used and untouchable, blue-grey and rusty with a dent in the front, leans up against the side of the house. A spattering of tiny, silent drops of rain appears on the concrete and she shivers pleasantly as it touches the back of her neck. She ducks through a doorflap into her den and sits cross-legged with the green stick across her knees, listening to the whisper of moisture on tarpaulin and smelling the familiar mingling of slightly damp carpet and eroding brick. She can't remember a time before the den. It houses an insect colony, leaves, bones, lollipop sticks, toy cars, milk bottle tops, jewellery, plastic cups and saucers, and a withered, half-eaten apple with a weevil inside.

She waits until her belly is gurgling with hunger before going inside to stand on tiptoe and drink water from the tap in the kitchen. Her mother stands with her back to her at the stove, banging a bent silver spoon against the rim of a pan. Everything smells of cauliflower. Gloria climbs under the sink and lies on her back amongst the floor cloths and scrubbing brushes and dirty rubber gloves, looking up at the spiders and meditating. A great big grey one hangs motionless in the corner, poised with ballerina legs. Ancient black festoons of cobweb quiver finely every time she breathes out. Out there in the kitchen white steam billows about her tall, gaunt, harried mother, whose thin, slightly bowed bare legs are sallow and downy. Her mother is whipping something in a bowl, frowning grimly, hands red and cracked. The skin under her eyes is pale. She looks up with a dissatisfied, self-conscious air, pushes her hair back and sighs, and for a moment her eyes become unfocused and bewildered. Then she sees Gloria under the sink.

"Get out from under there!" she snaps, banging the bowl down. "How many times have I told you?"

Gloria comes scrambling out. Her mother grips her shoulders, brushes her down roughly, puts her hair back behind her ears, hugs her, pushes her away. "I'm sick to death of this!" she scolds, her face crumpling up as if she might sneeze or cry. "Sick to bloody death! Look at the state of you! Look at your socks!"

Gloria looks down at the mud all up her legs, all over her shoes and socks. "I fell in this puddle," she says. "This boy pushed me."

"You make me want to scream," her mother says through gritted teeth. "Do you know that? You make me want to scream." Her hair is brown and sits on top of her head a bit crooked, as if someone's just stuck it on without much thought. Gloria just looks at her, deadpan, a little afraid. "Sometimes," her mother says, shaking her, "sometimes . . ." Her fingers dig in hard and tickle as they hurt. Gloria wants to laugh but daren't. "I don't know why I bother," says her mother, suddenly careless, letting go and flapping her hands dismissively. "I try and get you nice clothes and what do you do? Ungrateful, that's what you are. I'm finished with you."

Gloria wants to cry. "I didn't do it on purpose," she protests. "Honest. I got pushed."

"Pushed!" says her mother, seizing her again, pulling her about capably, inspecting, making sure her clothes aren't snagged or ripped anywhere. "Anyway, you shouldn't be playing with boys. What do you expect? And where've you been? I hope you haven't been hanging round the edge of that pool, it's dangerous."

"No," says Gloria, "I haven't. I was in that big field at the back of the shops."

5

"Well, what were you doing there?" Her mother shoves her in the direction of the door. "Your dad'll go mad if he sees you like that. Go upstairs and have a wash. Go on!" She points, gestures imperiously with her hand, turning back to the stove.

Gloria goes out into the hall. A staircase runs up to a dark landing where all the food smells gather in a thick, swampy soup. A bottle garden stands on a small table, a huge onion-shaped jar of cloudy green glass through which you can just make out a miniature landscape of water and pebbles and different kinds of moss – smooth emerald, dark starry, pale, ragged, spiry. The front door windows are reflected on an elongated curve. The TV babbles in the back room. She peeps around the open door to see what's on but it's just some old film flickering away, her father sitting before it in a big brown swallowing chair with wide arms, his eyes half closed, chin all podgy because his head's sunk upon his chest. He glances round briefly, a short, thickset man with growing stomach, small, squashed, bad-tempered face, thick bushy moustache, sees her but gives no acknowledgement before looking back at the screen. He doesn't speak to her often, though sometimes he communicates through her mother, like God through a priest, issuing commandments.

Gloria runs upstairs, careful not to make a noise – he hates noise – goes into the bathroom and climbs on a stool to wash her hands at the sink. The bar of soap is yellow with hard edges and keeps jumping out of her hands because it's too big. A green plastic frog sits in a soap dish in a pool of slimy water like egg white. She sings under her breath, looking in the mirror at herself with the room behind, bright turquoise walls and crooked yellow towel hanging on the back of the door. Gloria is the best singer in her class. She sings a song about a meeting between a bunch of birds, forgetting and growing louder till her mother comes in and hisses, "Shsh! For God's sake, shut up – your dad's in one of his moods."

Gloria sneers.

"Take your socks off," her mother says. "You might as well wash your feet while you're at it."

Gloria sits on the floor and peels the wet, clinging socks off her filthy feet.

"God's truth!" her mother says, scowling and running water into the bowl then looking down at her with a great weary sigh. She makes Gloria sit on the closed lid of the toilet, washes her feet roughly then scrubs her face with a hot flannel.

"It burns!" cries Gloria.

Her mother laughs and launches into baby talk. "Aw! Was Mummy rough? Poor little bucket! Horrible Mummy! Oh, my poor little girl!" She throws the flannel in the sink and is brisk and serious again. "Right, you'd better put something clean on. Go on – in my room – and *don't make a noise.*"

Gloria's parents' bedroom always smells musty because they hardly ever open the window. There is a pee pot under the bed that gets emptied once a day, a sideboard with photographs of her parents' wedding and Gloria as a baby, a small framed picture of Jesus with a cherub over the fireplace, a great brown slab of a wardrobe and a double bed with a cream-coloured candlewick bedspread. The bed takes up most of the room. It's a terrible thing that her parents have to sleep together there even though they can't stand one another. She doesn't really understand why they have to sleep together. It's just one of those things people have to do whether they like it or not. There are a lot of things like that.

"*Your* hateful father's in a terrible mood, so watch it," her mother whispers as she comes in. "He's driving me bloody mad." Her fists are clenched; she gestures with them, a slow, curious, pounding motion. "He just drives me so – bloody – mad. I *hate* him. Stand there!"

Gloria stands there. "What's up with him?" she asks.

"The stupid fool!" her mother whispers fiercely. "Looking for the dictionary! I don't know. He's had all the stuff out of all the cupboards in the hall looking for that old dictionary. It's probably been thrown out, for all I know; he probably threw it out himself, and he's gone and put everything back all wrong, of course. I'll have to sort it all out myself later. Sulking now, of course. I suppose we'll have to put up with his sulks all day. Sometimes I think he's not right in the head."

She stoops and pulls open the drawer at the bottom of the wardrobe where Gloria's things are kept, yanks out bits and pieces of slightly rumpled clothing and throws them on the bed. "Let's try this one," she says, briskly pulling Gloria's sweater over her head, hurting her ears. "Stand still. Good girl." She dresses Gloria up in skirt and T-shirt, changes her mind, tries a green smock that Gloria

7

hates, decides it looks too – I don't know – scruffy, somehow; tries something else and something else, prodding, pushing gently. "Keep your shoulders back. You'll go all bowed and horrible like a hunchback if you stand like that. I don't know, nothing looks right on you today, sometimes I don't know what you look like."

Gloria stands still, glazing over a little and staring at the picture of Jesus and the cherub on the wall. Jesus is pale browny-yellow all over and has lovely waving hair and big hollows under his eyes. The cherub leans over the edge of a small pink cloud in the sky above, all dimpled fat and bloated cheeks. "That's our Michael," her mother used to say, and occasionally still does, pointing to the picture. "He's with Jesus." Her mother still weeps about Michael sometimes. "I wonder what he'd have been like now," she says, "six years old." Gloria doesn't really know what happened about Michael, except that it was terrible and awesome, lost in the mists of time. He was her twin but he died when they were being born. She feels she must have had something to do with it and sometimes has a vision of one baby strangling another, locked in a death struggle in some weird, pink, feverish dream.

Her mother settles on a yellow dress with a green cardigan, then gets playful, putting hats on Gloria's head and taking them off again, laughing silently as she marches her up and down in front of the mirror. She sits down on the bed and looks at Gloria, her eyes moist and desperate, lips drawn back, mute, laughing and laughing. Gloria laughs too (Oh no, oh no, here she goes again), never sure if it's she herself who's being laughed at, obliged to join in so that her mother won't feel lonely laughing alone. After all, she can't help it. Her mother falls sideways across the bed as if shot. Agonised by the effort of silence, she puts her hands in front of her face, then rolls on her back and screams soundlessly with tight closed weeping eyes. Gloria laughs too. It's a club for two, this silent, screaming laughter.

After a while her mother sits up and dries her eyes. "Oh. Oh, dear. Oh, dear," she sighs, pulling a tissue from her sleeve and blowing her nose. "There. I think you'll do now." She stands and grips Gloria's shoulders, turning her to face herself in the mirror, a stocky child with a block of thick brown hair, big lips in a wide face. "Wait," she says, "your hair," and picks up a hairbrush.

8

Gloria closes her eyes as the bristles stroke the back of her neck, sending pleasure through her scalp and down her spine.

Downstairs, they eat in silence for a while. The old film has violin music and lots of shouting. Her father's face is stern as he looks from his plate to his paper to the TV screen, turn and turn about. Finally he says to her mother that it looks as if the rain might keep off now, after all, and she peers disapprovingly at the window where the grey sky lours.

"Eat your cauliflower," she says to Gloria. A crowd roars on the TV. Gloria eats slowly. "Tell her she's got to eat her cauliflower, Pete," her mother says to her father.

He looks at her, his eyes mildly amused. "Of course she has," he says.

"I don't like cauliflower," Gloria says. It comes out too loud because she's nervous.

"Of course you do," her mother says.

"Eat it," her father says, turning back to his paper.

She eats, grimacing extravagantly as if it were dirt.

Her father stares at her coldly. "Your face is exaggerated," he says in a blank voice, then goes on eating his dinner.

She looks at the mess on her plate, her face red. The rain begins quite suddenly, sparkling in the yard beyond the window. He makes a sound of resignation, pushes his plate away and his chair back and goes out of the room wiping his mouth with his hand. They hear him open the back door and stomp about at the side of the house.

"Oh, what's he up to now?" her mother scowls. "Here, give me your plate quick, while he's out."

Gloria slides down under the table and stays there till her father has returned and fallen asleep in front of the TV and her mother is in the kitchen washing up, then emerges and crosses to the window to look out. The sky is quite bright and the rain's turned steady and fine and soft.

Something is terribly wrong with the yard. She feels sick, her heart pounds; she runs outside and stands in the rain looking at the bit of wall where her den used to be. The tarpaulin is gone. The carpet is rucked up and soaked, the green stick's rolled away, and a jumble of anonymous bits lie scattered here and there, bereft of all significance. She sinks to her knees in the mess, gingerly

9

overturning an old withered apple. The weevil is gone, either burrowed in deeper till the earthquake is over, or fled for good, maybe killed by an uncomprehending shoe.

She dashes round to the side of the house and sees her orange tarpaulin covering her father's hateful moped; runs to it and kicks it as hard as she can, starting to cry.

Her mother's voice calls from somewhere, "Gloria! You come in out of the rain in that dress!"

Gloria kicks, hates, hates the stupid moped sitting there useless, just another stupid whim of her stupid, stupid father's, just because he used to have one hundreds of years ago when he was young and thought it'd be cheaper than getting the bus to town where he works in the Post Office building. He's ridden it once in a year.

She's still crying as she runs in the back door. Her mother starts to tell her off, but seeing her face gets down on one knee instead and hugs her quickly. "What's the matter?" she asks, holding her away and staring into her face. "What's the matter, my little bucket?"

"He's smashed my den up," Gloria sobs. "He's smashed it all to pieces. He's taken my roof and put it on his horrible bike. I *hate* that bike, I'd like to *kill* it." She gasps for breath, clenching her teeth till they feel like breaking.

"Shsh!" her mother hisses, shaking her. "Now stop crying. We'll get you something else for your den; your dad doesn't realise." She sighs long and weary, stands and looks out of the window and goes all limp. "He is a thoughtless swine," she says quietly to herself. Then she turns back to Gloria. "I tell you what, love," she says kindly. "I'll take you out on Monday, after school, and we'll go up to town and you can have a posh ice-cream. How about that?"

Gloria's father comes in suddenly. Her mother turns away and pretends to be doing something at the sink. Gloria stands very still, afraid, trying not to cry and hoping he won't notice her blotchy face. He mumbles, peers into a little mirror that hangs to one side of the sink, strokes his moustache, sticks his fat red tongue out at himself to see if he's got an ulcer on the end of it. "What's the matter with Gloria?" he asks her mother, turning to go out again.

"She's upset because you took that old tarpaulin for your bike," her mother says, wiping her hands on a dish cloth. "She had a little den out there." And she gives a silly, betraying little laugh.

He stops in the doorway, looking down. Gloria feels herself weak and withered. Then he sniggers offhandedly and says, "That old ripped tarpaulin? You don't want that. That's not for playing with."

"I had my things under it," she says.

"Oh, well," says her father, "never mind."

She starts crying again quietly, sniffing and dripping.

"Well, there's nothing to cry about," he says, half stern, half smiling. "It wasn't yours to play with, anyway."

But she can't stop. "I had my things under it," she says again.

"Well," he says, "now I've got mine under it."

She smears her face.

"Now stop!" he orders, all humour gone.

Her mother makes sympathetic faces at her behind his back, then laughs nervously. "You know what she's like," she says lightly. "She takes things so seriously."

"Well, she'll have to learn not to," he says. "I can't stand whingeing kids." And he goes out into the hall, her mother following. At the door she turns and whispers to Gloria, "Come on, now, that's enough. Let it go now."

Gloria stands for a long time listening to the soft rain and the louder dripping of the tap. She hears the two of them laughing about something in the back room and wonders if they're laughing at her. She'll never understand why her mother says she hates her father then laughs with him while she stands crying in the kitchen. She looks down at the yellow dress and wants to get it dirty, absolutely filthy; wants to run down to the pool and roll in mud like a hippopotamus. When she's big, she'll have a house of her own where no one can ever take anything from her. She'll sit inside it with all her things around her and listen to the rain on the roof. And she becomes aware of the rain still drumming on the tarpaulin that covers her father's bike, of a strange old weariness inside, of the excitement of rebellion rising through her like silver in a thermometer.

Smiling wickedly and starting to shiver, she runs out, goes madly down the road with her feet spraying water off the paving slabs every time they hit the ground. No one is around. The church bells peal, the rain soaks through the green cardigan, the yellow dress.

Reaching the pool she slows down to walk over the rattling wooden bridge, watching white and grey water swirl angrily beneath the slats. The pool is misty, not a bird in sight. The rain eases, the world sighs peacefully. She walks along the edge of the pool getting her feet wet, soaking up dirt, comes to the big hole that sucks all the water tumbling and roaring into underground darkness, stands for some while watching the endless shimmer of its endless fall, deafened entirely by the sound, and imagines going down with it like Alice, down and down through darkness and sound till she's in some other world.

Another world. *How would you ever know if you never jumped?*

She feels strange. She isn't sure how long she's been here. The rain still falls and the water still roars, but for a moment the only sound she hears is a humming on the edge of the world, and for a second she wonders where she is. But the moment passes and, looking up, shivering, she sees through the clearing mist a woman in a long dark gown walk proudly and seriously, with measured steps and head held high, across the wooden planks of the narrow bridge that crosses the stream some hundred yards away. The woman is in profile; Gloria can't make out her face. She reaches firm ground and never pauses, turns swiftly and walks away along the quiet street. Gloria's teeth chatter, the hairs at the back of her neck stand on end. The woman is walking to her execution, a beheading. The woman is a ghost. Gloria knows.

Terrified, she runs all the way round the other side of the pool so that she won't have to go near the bridge, then home by a long unfamiliar route. When she gets there the sky is just beginning to go dark and the back door still stands open. All rebellion has sunk down into the pit of her stomach. She stands and listens but all seems peaceful, so she rescues her green stick from where it lies wet by the wall, creeps in and closes the door and tiptoes upstairs. She lays her stick across the end of her bed in the box room, pulls off her clothes and gets into her pyjamas, then goes into the bathroom, runs a flannel over her dirty feet and rubs her hair with a towel. Her face is flushed. Picking up a toy owl from her room, she goes downstairs and looks in the back room. Her mother is knitting and watching TV, her father is reading the paper.

Gloria sits on the stairs and swings the owl lightly by his wings, watching the movement reflected in the green glass of the bottle garden. She begins to play that the owl and she are sworn comrades on a dangerous mission that involves going up and down the stairs on their hands and knees. She talks to the owl and talks back to herself in the owl's voice.

Her mother comes out into the hall. "Shsh!" she says angrily. "Your father's trying to read the paper. Now be good or you'll get me into trouble. Why is your hair wet? Have you been outside again?"

"I saw a ghost," Gloria says.

"Oh, don't be silly," says her mother, turning to go into the kitchen to put the kettle on.

"I did," says Gloria, "I saw a ghost."

"Oh, shut up," says her mother, disappearing into the kitchen.

I am not silly. I am *not*.

Her ears go funny, as if something shatteringly loud has just crashed on either side of her. The strange feeling comes swooping – *It's coming*, says a voice in her head, *it's coming, it's coming again* – and on it comes, the strangeness, like the beginning of falling asleep or the end of feeling sick: solemn, terrifying, like stepping off a cliff in a dream and finding endless invisible air below. She falls into a dark hole inside her head, where she turns into a momentous bubble being blown out of a vast soapy wand.

The green bottle lifts itself from the table and dashes itself in one glorious moment to death upon the wall opposite, a world exploding. Thick green shards burst from the wall. Gloria sits on the stairs with her owl and trembles, looking down at the mess of old moss and earth, pebbles, broken glass. A wet stain spreads. Her father comes lurching from the back room, her mother from the kitchen. For a moment they stand bewildered, looking down with hanging lips and troubled eyes. They look at each other, then at Gloria.

"What the hell's going on?" thunders her father.

"What have you been doing?" her mother says. "Have you been running up and down?"

"No, honest; I was just sitting here and it just fell off the table. Honest." Her voice is unconvinced.

Her father's face is white. He doesn't look at her. "We have had that for – ten years!" he says incredulously. She freezes with horror.

"You've been running about in the hall!" her mother accuses. "Don't tell lies!"

"I'm not!" cries Gloria. "Honest! Honest! I didn't do anything!"

"You'll get such a crack in a minute if you shout at me like that!"

"We have had that for *ten years*," says her father. "Ten years for some kid to come along and break it like that."

Gloria can't find any more words. She goes sullen, wide-eyed, staring. Her father looks her straight in the eyes with his own weak, bloodshot ones, and they are angry, puzzled, hurt, fierce. It seems to her that he is always looking at her in this way and she never knows why.

"She's an idiot," he says coldly. "She's our daughter but she's an idiot." His lips are thin and stiff and he doesn't take his eyes away. A burning sensation rises from her chest up through her neck and face. "You'd better keep her out of my sight," he says, turning abruptly and walking into the back room.

"What are you doing?" her mother hisses, darting towards her like a snake. The line between her eyes is so deep it looks painful.

"Nothing." Gloria runs upstairs with tears starting in her eyes, into her room to crouch under the bedcovers and wait for her mother to appear in the doorway.

"Now, listen," says her mother furiously, bending over her and gripping the covers on either side with white knuckles, "I've had about enough of you denying things. Lying. And stop crying!"

"I can't."

"I said stop it!"

"I can't."

"I'm going to have to clear all that mess up because of you. And you've put him in a terrible mood for the rest of the night. Oh, it's all right for you, you can just disappear off up to bed. *I'm* the one that's got to sit down there all night with him sulking and bloody sport on the TV."

"I swear on the Bible I wasn't anywhere near it. I didn't do anything."

"You *must* have," her mother says, and her face suddenly distorts into something dreadful, something helpless, worse than rage. It hurts to look at her. "You *must* have, you *must* have!"

"I didn't!" cries Gloria straight into her mother's face. "I didn't! I didn't!"

Her mother clouts her hard across the top of the head and stands back. "I don't want to hear any more out of you tonight," she says furiously, and walks out, turning the light off and closing the door smartly.

Terrified in the sudden dark, Gloria claws frantically for her green stick, her protector, and pulls it under the covers with her. She lies holding it, sweating with fear and crying, her head ringing a little from the blow, her heart pounding like a gong. She hates the dark, but a light isn't allowed. She just has to grow out of it. She lies with eyes wide open waiting for something unknown: a sound, a touch, a movement in the dark; begins to see shapes: the big cardboard box her toys are kept in, an old nightdress of her mother's hanging on the back of the door. Never in a million years could she get up and cross the darkness to put the light on, even if she could reach it. She is trapped.

Five minutes later the door opens quietly and her mother steals in and turns on the light and sits on the edge of the bed. Gloria blinks in the sudden glare, her face hot and damp, burning.

"Poor Gloria!" her mother whispers, taking her face between her hands and kissing her on the cheek. "Oh, my poor little girl."

"I'm sorry," says Gloria. "I'm sorry, I'm sorry, I'm sorry."

Her mother pats her shoulder. "Yes, well, you're a good girl now, aren't you? Never mind. I'll leave the light on for you for a little bit and you can look at your books, if you like." Smiling wearily, she goes and fetches a handful of slim, well-thumbed books from the toy box and places them on the bed, telling her not to worry any more. Everything'll be all right. "Shsh!" she says softly, finger to her lips as she leaves, closing the door like a whisper.

Gloria sits dazed for a little while, her mouth open because her nose is full of snot, then finds an old tissue down the side of the bed and blows her nose, reaching up to the windowsill for her lucky fish. Tonight she'll sleep with it under the pillow. She found it a long time ago on the edge of the mushroom field and loved it instantly. She's comforted now as it lies on her palm, a fat scaly silver fish with its tail in its mouth and a great wise benevolent eye. She places the green stick on top of the covers, across her feet, the fish beneath the pillow, leans back and leafs slowly and lethargically through her books. She has loads. She likes the fairy stories best.

She knows all the pictures and all the stories by heart and, if anything moves her, she becomes it. She is the lady in the tower letting down her hair, she is Fallada's head; she is the little girl who walked on and walked on and walked on, barefoot in the snow. She's nearly asleep when her mother returns to turn off the light.

"Oh, throw that old stick away!" her mother says.

"Aw, no!" cries Gloria. "That's my green stick. I want it there."

"It's dirty," her mother says. "It's all right, I'll just put it in the yard. It doesn't belong in the house." She picks it up, kisses Gloria goodnight and tells her to say her prayers, then goes out, leaving darkness. The fear returns, cold and silent. But after a while the rain comes softly whispering at the window and makes her less afraid. She thinks of her stick out there in the rain and feels sorry for it, then thinks about the weevil, what a strange, lonely creature it was, living all alone in an apple like that.

Then she thinks about a big picture book she used to have once about a little wild girl who lives in an endless tangled forest full of bears and wolves and moose and all kinds of other, smaller creatures. The book has long since gone, but Gloria still sees the pictures. The wild girl is the only human being in the forest. She loves all the animals and they love her with a solemn, peaceful, wordless kind of love. She rides around on a gentle moose, whose tremendous prehistoric antlers, lined with flowers and moss, form a wide bowl that sways majestically ahead through the forest ways. Sometimes she climbs into the fragrant bowl and lies down and sleeps under blankets of moss.

Gloria is the little girl in the moose's antlers. Every night she lies down and the great beast carries her away, pacing sure and steady, deeper and deeper into the vast primeval forest. She is perfectly content there alone with the animals. Nothing more is required.

2

Most people don't like to come to Gloria's house because you have to keep quiet there. She passes her time playing in the mushroom field, knowing she's a changeling, walking there waiting for discovery. But nothing happens. The green stick vanishes but the lucky fish remains.

Finally, when she's eight, she gets a friend, Mary, a fair, solid girl with round glasses and shapeless jumpers. Now she can go to Mary's house, which is bewildering and much more fun than her own. There's a big brother called John, lots of little brothers and sisters, big messy rooms, a long passageway at the side where you can run up and down and yell and scream and shout, a hall with a long wooden table where cages line the wall and mice live. The hall smells excitingly of sawdust. The mice are bright, clean, brisk little creatures, brown and white and cream, with pink paper-thin ears of enormous dimensions. They potter about, go round and round in wheels, sleep curled up in little straw nests.

Gloria gets one when Mary's mother says four's too many.

"The poor little thing!" says Gloria's mother, bending down to look at it as it whittles away at a sunflower seed with its two long orange teeth. "What a life! I hope you're going to make sure and feed this properly and clean it out without me having to tell you all the time."

"Course I will," says Gloria.

Her father comes and looks at it. "Hello there," he says to it through the bars, and chuckles. "Look at it go!" he says as it dashes away miles on its wheel.

Pearly the Mouse is cream-coloured with a very faint smudge of chocolate on her flank. Her nose, her great veined ears, her tiny cold feet are pink, her eyes are bright and dark and wear a look of serious concern as she runs from nestbox to food pot to toilet corner time and time again. That's all she can do if she doesn't want to go

17

round in the wheel, which goes drub, drub, drub, drub, round and round, hour after hour, on and on and on as she paces the miles with her palms. She looks up as she runs, always upwards, as if she expects to get somewhere. Then she gets tired and sleeps in her nest. Gloria peeks in the top and sees her lying with her belly exposed and her front paws limp, the big front teeth showing and the breath so big in her frail body that you can watch it coming and going as if she were a bellows. She's all Gloria's. She lives on top of the chest of drawers and keeps Gloria awake at nights with all her busy rustling and working away at the wheel. She doesn't think much of cheese but loves Milky bars. Of an evening Gloria blocks the door and opens the cage on the floor, and Pearly comes out and scurries about the room, discovering everything, eating any crumbs she happens to find, gnawing the wooden feet of the bed.

Pearly is beautiful but she's never a friend. She'll never stay when you want her to and she doesn't really seem to like Gloria, who begins to feel sad whenever she looks at the cage and sees the anxious whiskers twitching at the bars. Through winter Gloria plays with her nearly every night, but as the evenings grow lighter and warmer Gloria stays out late, forgetful. She plays out with Mary and Mary's brother John, walking on forbidden territory, round the old disused factory with its broken windows and weed-clogged walls, across the mile of cracked khaki mud. Sometimes she forgets to check the feeding bowls and clean the cage, sees with a shock of guilt and discomfort the mess of soggy straw in the water bowl, husks in the food bowl, a rotten smelly patch in the toilet corner. She never knows she's forgotten until it's too late. Her mother nags about the smell. Pearly gets harder to catch, and summer comes. She lies awake at nights listening to Pearly gnaw the bars of her cage and wondering how it all went wrong.

Gloria goes to the seaside for a week with her mother and father. The weather's hot, the sand fine. There's a funfair, seafood and ice-cream and hot-dogs, country lanes, a stream, salt marshes, tall cliffs and miles of rock, boats in the bay.

She makes friends with a small, dark-haired, elfin boy called Steven whose parents are staying in one of the other guest houses down the road. For four days they clamber about in the lower reaches of the cliffs, play on the beach and push each other into the

18

waves, run around the woods and the funfair. On the fifth day, while her mother sulks and reads books and her father plays Patience, she plays with Steven on a grass slope in the lane at the back of all the guest houses. Over and over again they run to the top and roll down, giggling, out of breath; then they start to fight playfully, pushing and grappling and rolling. She gets him on his back then he gets her on hers and sits astride bouncing up and down. The breath catches and gurgles in their throats.

Suddenly an old woman with white hair and a flowered apron comes running out of one of the houses.

"You clear off!" she yells. "You *dirty* little sod! You clear off! Not you!" The last words are for Gloria, whose shoulder she clutches with a strong, wrinkled hand that smells of soap. Steven backs away uncertainly, his face blazing and his mouth all stiff and embarrassed. "Go on!" the woman shrills, waving him away with her other hand. "I know you! I know your mum and dad! You *dirty* little sod! Don't let me see you round here again!"

He turns and walks away trying to look nonchalant. His shorts are too long and his knees are wobbly. Gloria feels sorry for him. Her heart thumps and she feels guilty and doesn't know why.

The woman releases her and gives her a little push backwards. "You keep away from that boy," she says, appearing to lose interest, not even looking at her as she turns to go back into her house. "Go home now. Don't let me see you round here again."

Gloria runs till she finds her parents sitting at a table outside a café, her father drinking Seven Up and smoking a cigarette, her mother in an orange dress and white high heels, looking out across the bay. They don't speak. Gloria sits down on a white metal chair that burns the back of her legs.

"A woman shouted at me," she says to her mother.

"What woman?"

"This old woman in the back lane."

"What did she say?"

"She told me to go and play somewhere else. She was horrible."

"Well, what were you doing?"

"Nothing. Just playing. I was with Steven."

"Oh," says her mother, rubbing her long freckled arms. "Well, maybe you were making a noise. Or maybe she was just some nowty old woman. Anyway, don't worry about it."

19

Later, Gloria sees her mother and father talking very seriously, their heads close together, her father's face hard and stern. She turns cold. It's something to do with that horrible old woman, she knows it. She's in the wrong again somehow, God knows how she keeps doing it. She washes her face and hands in the first-floor bathroom and goes down to the dining-room where her parents are already sitting at their usual table, eating in silence. Her father doesn't look at her and when her mother does, the look is awkward. Afterwards he goes for a drink with the man from Room 2B, and her mother lies with her legs crossed on the big bed, leafing through a women's magazine.

"There's some comics in that bag," she says. "You go and get on that bed and read them nice and quietly. Or there's some crayons in that drawer." Then, after a while, she says, "Your dad doesn't want you playing with that lad any more. Just you stay with your dad and me from now on . . . And don't you pull that face at me." After that there is silence for a long time.

On the last day, Gloria's parents argue about whether or not to go for a cliff walk. In the end her mother says she's sick of walking about looking at the sea, she's bored stiff and has been all week if you must know and can't wait to get home.

"Oh! Right then!" her father says. "Right then! I'll take the kid. Come on!"

Gloria glances once at her mother, who is settling on the bed and bending her head over a book, her mouth tight and sulky, then follows her father's offended back out on to the landing and down to the hall. She feels guilty about leaving her mother all alone on the last day of the holiday.

Her father walks fast and she has to trot to keep up with him, but soon gets into a rhythm and starts to enjoy herself. They come to a place where you have to cross the stream by stepping stones, and her father keeps looking back and telling her to be careful. "If you get your socks wet," he says, "your mum'll go mad. Mad."

Reaching the other side, they start up the path that leads to the top of the cliffs and continues right along one arm of the bay to where the sea birds nest in their thousands, chattering and cackling. The heat is intense. A wall of rock rears on their right and the salt marsh lies below, a variegated plain of rank green, mustard-

20

yellow and grey, shot through with pools and streams where the blue of the sky glimmers, stretching for miles to the shimmering silver haze of the horizon.

"It's dangerous down there," her father says, pointing. "Don't you ever go wandering around down there on your own – you never know what might happen. Treacherous." He's panting with the exertion of their climb by now; his face runs like a joint of meat just out of the oven.

Gloria looks down on all this wild treachery, exhilarated, wishing she were down there hopping from island to island across the crude, dark, forbidden wasteland. On and on they go, further and further out along the outflung arm of land, till the sea is crashing on the rocks below, gulls with savage eyes cruising on their level, everything so big and blue and shiny that she is afraid in a way she would not miss for anything. Her father stops frequently to mop his brow and admire the scenery and tell her off for running on ahead. The path grows narrower and narrower and boulders lie in the track so that you have to keep walking close to the edge and glimpsing – too sudden, too near – waves that explode upon dark grey rocks below. She clutches her lucky fish in her fist.

"Don't run on," her father says, one hand steadying himself against a rock. "You don't know what the path's like ahead; it might be dangerous."

"It's all right," she says. "I've already been round the corner. It gets better."

"Don't run on," he repeats.

She stands and waits for him, not tired at all. When he's ready to move on she gives up all pretence of waiting, runs ahead nimbly, whistling through her teeth, clambering over rocks, skirting dangerous bits with panache, looking back now and then to see if he's keeping up.

He waves at her at the turn of a corner. "That's enough!" he calls in his stern voice. "Get back here!"

Triumphant, she comes to heel. Her fat little father sits sweating and panting on a rock, rubbing his moustache. She shows off, doing handstands against the rock face.

"Stop it!" he barks, and she stops immediately. "Stupid!" he says darkly. "You don't cavort about like that on top of a cliff."

She stands quietly while he gets his breath back, wiping his face

21

again and again, till he's ready for the descent. Back on the prom he buys two ice-creams and eats his in silence, sitting on a wall and reading the midday paper till it's time to go back to the guest house.

All through dinner both her parents sulk. Lighting his cigarette, her father starts to complain in a low voice to her mother, "Ham or chicken! Ham or chicken! They think that's all anybody eats. I suppose they think we're impressed. Ham or chicken. What about people who don't like ham or chicken? That's what I'd like to know."

Her mother says, "Mmm," and turns away from him, playing with a charm bracelet that hangs loose about her wrist. She notices Gloria looking at it and holds out her arm, smiling. "Do you like it? It's nice, isn't it? I got it at that little shop next to the café with the shells."

Her father sucks his front teeth, sour-faced. He's funny about food. Her mother scratches her ear and sighs. Silver charms jingle delicately, falling down her arm, a shoe, a dog, a bird, a key, a pig. "Are we going to the beach or what?" she says.

"Of course we're going to the beach," says her father as if he were speaking to a fool.

"Well, we might as well get going then."

"Are you ready?"

"*I'm* ready. Gloria, do you want to go to the toilet?"

"No."

"Have you left anything upstairs?"

"Well, *I've* got to go up anyway," says her father, "so say now if there's anything you want." He stands up clumsily, jogging the table and causing a slop of cold tea to drip into her mother's lap.

Her mother's face turns wounded and defiant as she slaps at her skirt, a clean, bright-yellow one fresh on this morning. Her eyebrows gather childlike, as if she might cry. "Oh, watch what you're doing!" she says, but he doesn't notice anything and goes on striding importantly out of the dining-room.

Gloria and her mother go out into the hall and sit on a bench and wait. Her mother's hands are curled on top of her handbag and her eyes are unhappy. "I hate your father," she says to Gloria, looking away. "I do. I really hate him."

The beach is hot and crowded, the sea is so far out it's scarcely

22

visible. Her parents, still sulky, get two deck chairs and park them side by side in a little gap in the crowd.

"Can I go over on the rocks?" Gloria asks.

"No," says her mother.

Gloria messes about in the sand. Little hot prawn-like creatures leap out at her from time to time. The sand is too dry to do much with and the sea is too far away. "I wish we didn't have to go home," she says.

"All good things come to an end," says her father pompously.

"No, they don't." Gloria speaks sharply and instantly, full of faith, surprised at herself.

"Course they do!" He is dismissive and faintly annoyed.

"No, they don't."

Her mother smiles at her with a strange air of apology and embarrassment.

"Don't be pert," says her father.

She pauses for a second, her face goes red, then she says in a flat, nervous, defiant tone, "Well, they don't." She feels stupid but is somehow sure this is too important to let go.

"Oh, well, if you want to argue!" says her father scornfully. "Name me one example of a good thing that doesn't come to an end, Miss Know-all. Go on."

She thinks. Her brain is blank.

"You can't," he says, his voice edged with disgust. "You can't."

All good things come to an end. No, they don't. They don't. It can't be true, it can't all be like they say it is, like they make it.

"We could move," she says. "We could come and live here. Then it wouldn't have to come to an end, would it?"

Both her parents laugh. "You can't just pack up and move," says her mother. "Your dad has to go to work."

Her father looks sideways at her with a derogatory smirk, triumphant. His nose is peeling, a stupid bit of skin sticks up on the end of it. He is hateful, hateful, hateful. A terrible rage rears up inside her, making her feel stretched and shaken even though she knows she still appears quite normal. Her eyes fill with tears.

All good things come to an end, says a voice like doom.

She is seized by a fear so much greater than any other she's ever experienced that she turns cold as ice upon the hot beach.

"Gloria," says her mother, "Gloria. Are you all right?"

23

She nods.

"What are you crying for?"

"I'm not."

"Yes, you are."

"No, I'm not," she says. "I'm not really crying. Not really."

"Whingeing again," says her father.

She sits in the back room waiting for Mary to call for her, feeling funny in her gymslip and white blouse and a bit sick as she always does on the first day back at school in September. Her mother scrubs away at a stain on the lapel of her school blazer.

"Now, you're sure you've got everything?"

"Sure."

"Because there's no running back at dinner time . . ."

"I'm sure."

"And don't you go giving half your KitKat to Mary."

"OK."

"Oh, by the way," her mother says, standing up and shaking out the blazer by the shoulders, "you know that little fish of yours? The one on your windowsill? It really goes lovely on that little bracelet I got on holiday. Do you mind if I borrow it, love? It's just been stuck on your windowsill for ages."

At first Gloria cannot speak. She cannot believe this. "That's my fish!" she croaks. "You can't have that. It's my lucky fish."

"Well, it's not as if it's going out of the family," her mother says. "It'll be on my bracelet, you'll be able to see it. I mean, it's not as if you ever wear it or anything, is it?"

"It's mine," says Gloria. "I've had it ages. It brings me luck."

"Aw, go on," her mother says. "Don't be mean."

"You're not having it."

"But that's what it is. A charm. A charm for a charm bracelet. It's perfect for it."

"I don't care," says Gloria. "It's mine and you're not having it."

"Oh, you are mean," her mother says, going out into the hall. Her voice continues. "I've never known anyone as possessive as you, the way you are with your things."

Her father comes in, chomping toast greasily and breathing loudly down his nose. He's always in a bad mood in the mornings and his nose is always full.

"After all," says her mother, coming back in, "it's not as if *you* want it. It's just sitting up there on your windowsill."

"What?" says her father peevishly.

"Not you. I was talking to her."

"I know," says Gloria. "That's where it's supposed to be. That's where I keep it. Except sometimes when I take it out with me. For luck."

"Oh, silly!" her mother says. "Aren't you acting a bit like a baby?"

"No." Gloria fumes helplessly in the unfamiliar, uncomfortable clothes.

"Anyway," says her mother, "it's not meant for children, a charm like that. It's proper silver. You shouldn't have had it really. It was me that found it in the first place."

"You did not!" cries Gloria. "I found it! I found it!"

"Keep your voice down!" raps her father.

"You don't half make a fuss about little things," her mother says.

"What's all this about?" asks her father in the tone of one who'll sort it all out instantly.

"Oh, nothing," her mother says, offhand and martyred, pushing her hair behind her ears and turning towards the door. "I wanted to wear that little fish charm she's got on my bracelet, but she won't let me." She goes out.

Gloria and her father sit without speaking to each other, her father reading the paper till it's time to walk down to the church where he catches his bus into town. Rage keeps her motionless for fear she should scream and cry and yell, a feeling like a sea exploding in her chest. They'd win. They'd always win. They are stronger than she is.

Her mother comes back in. "It was me that found it," she says. "I remember, I was walking down Chapel Lane with Mrs Eccles, coming back from the market, and it was lying on the pavement. I remember because . . ."

"You didn't," Gloria says, tears of rage burning the backs of her eyes. She found the fish on the edge of the mushroom field. She loved it instantly. It lay in the grass, a wonderful, sudden, magic thing, glinting like a jewel. It had always been waiting for her.

"People are supposed to share things," her mother says. "People are supposed to be generous."

25

"Of course they are," says her father from behind his paper.

Gloria jumps up and grabs her schoolbag. "Have it!" she cries, storming into the hall. "Have it!" She runs out into the front garden, slamming the door, freezing with terror when she realises what she's done.

Her father comes after her and catches her by the arm and pulls her back inside, twisting her shoulder and pushing her against the wall. "Who do you think you are?" he thunders, his face serious, appalled. "You're lucky I don't crack you right across the face. It's all I can do now not to hit you. Who do you think you are? Making a scene like that, slamming doors, sulking, arguing! Who do you think you are?"

"I didn't mean it," she whispers, her throat dry.

Her mother stands behind her father. "I don't think she meant to slam the door that hard. Did you?" she says timidly.

"I don't care!" snaps her father. "I don't care whether she meant it or not. I can do without all this melodrama first thing in the morning. I don't care what's the matter, I'm not having you flouncing about slamming doors. Is that understood?"

"Yes," she says.

He turns and walks furiously into the back room. Her mother touches her shoulder. "You get off to school now," she whispers. "He'll have forgotten all about it by tonight."

She turns Gloria and pushes her towards the door, and she goes obediently and starts walking round to Mary's house, even though it's out of her way and she'll only have to walk all the way back again. She tries not to cry. Old Mrs Eccles, with frizzy grey permed hair and flowered pinny, is looking out of her window and waves at Gloria as she passes. Gloria waves back. Her mother's friend. Stupid old bag. It begins to spot with rain. Soon she meets Mary coming along, steady and solid under a pink and orange striped umbrella, which she swirls and swirls as she stomps between the paving cracks. They share the umbrella as they walk the mile to school.

"I hate my mum and dad," Gloria says glumly.

Mary gasps in horror. "Oh, Gloria, that's a terrible thing to say! Oh, you shouldn't say that! Have they been horrible to you? You should *never* say a thing like that about your parents. It says in the Bible."

26

All day she is nagged by a little pain in her heart, which feels faint and weak and fluttery. The teacher tells her to wake up, she's usually so good, what's the matter? She cannot say. She's always been one of the best in the class, first in reading, first in composition, first in sums, but now she doesn't care. She can think of nothing but the lies of adults. They lie, she decides, they lie to keep children down.

When she gets home she sees her lucky fish dangling on her mother's wrist, calling to her with its great round eye. She goes behind the kitchen door and turns into a demon, grinding her teeth and shaking, scaring herself. She could kill. She daren't speak all through tea time. The evening advances. Her father lights his cigarette and her mother counts stitches. On the TV a naked man stands on a raft on a jungle river. He is like a reed, spear poised.

"Marvellous-looking, really, some of them, aren't they?" her father says.

"Oh, yes!" says her mother. The man throws the spear and catches a fish, a silver fish with a great round eye. It's like ballet. It must be beautiful to live naked on a raft on a jungle river. Some people do. Not like here. Why not me? She'd go there one day.

"They're like children, really," her mother says wistfully.

"What's the matter with her?" her father asks her mother.

"I think she's still sulking about the fish," replies her mother softly.

"Fish? What are you talking about? What fish?"

"Oh, never mind. It's not important."

Gloria slips out and goes upstairs and seizes the orange towelling curtain in her bedroom between her teeth and rips as hard as she can, all her strength rushing into the attack in cold, shaking fury. Her teeth must surely break and come flying out of her head. Tears burst from her closed eyes. She opens them and sees a big ragged hole in the curtain, stares at it in horror, sits back on her bed and cries very hard and very quietly.

They'll never keep me here. Never. I'll get away. Somehow. Some day.

She jumps up and draws the curtains but the hole only looks worse with the dark blue night peering through. There's no way she can hide it, pointless even to try. So she gives up and sighs and gazes around the room, messy because everything from her big

27

cardboard box is scattered all over the floor. Her mother will tell her to clear it all away later.

Her eye falls on Pearly's cage and sticks: something's moving there, something not Pearly. Instinctively afraid, she draws near. Her blood runs cold. A clot of maggots pulses obscenely on the floor of the cage. For a moment she stands amazed, sick, then sinks slowly to one knee and stares in awful fascination. Pearly's head is still there: great pink ears and long orange teeth, eyes a little open but dull. Gloria stares at the film that covers her eyes. The maggots heave their grey slimy bodies about in the sac of Pearly's belly.

She backs away and sits against the wall, her two hands crawling against her arms. She doesn't know what to do, her brain reels. It isn't possible. Oh, my God, she thinks, they'll go mad. She runs out on to the landing and listens. No sound but the TV. It's too much, too much, a hole in the curtain and a cage full of maggots. Pearly. Pearly the Mouse with her perfect ears and the little smudge of chocolate on her flank. Her mind runs this way and that. Finally she goes back into her room and picks up the cage by its metal handle, holding it at arm's length with every nerve recoiling, steals silently along the landing and down the stairs, out through the kitchen into the dark yard. Here she stands again to listen, but there's nothing, so she runs around to the front to the secret place in the hedge where she keeps her hidden things, scrunches down and pushes the cage as far away under it as it will go, then stands back, shuddering all over: unclean, frozen, faint. The dense, untended, drooping hedge covers everything, damp and dripping above the vile atrocity. The end of her hidden place. Everything gets spoiled. She'll never go there again. Whenever she passes the spot, a sadness will fall upon her.

Inside, undetected, she takes off all her clothes, washes herself all over, scratches her head all over, gets into her pyjamas and sits at the top of the stairs. She is breathless, disembodied, as if she's just come out of a nightmare. Pearly's dead, she thinks, she's dead. What does it mean? How can she suddenly be like that? Suddenly? Her mind pushes back, a dreadful chill sinks through her heart, falls through her stomach. Yesterday: there is no real memory of Gloria opening Pearly's cage, feeding her, slopping out the water dish. The day before: there is no real memory. The day before: surely everything was normal then? No memory. The day before:

28

no memory. I have to feed my mouse and clean her out regularly. Oh, Mistress Mouse, are you within? Not any more. The maggots crawl in her belly, she feels them, eating away with their little mouths.

She sits with her face cupped in her hands, staring straight ahead. She can't remember the last time she fed Pearly the Mouse. She puts her fingers in her mouth and stares and rocks. In her mind she gives Pearly a proper burial with a good strong cigar box-coffin and a lolly stick-cross.

"Your dad'll go *mad*," says her mother when she sees the hole in the curtain. "*Mad. Mad.*"

3

Gloria makes up her face, striking a pose before the mirror. She feels the silky straps of a slip on her bare shoulders and is pleased, smells talcum powder, stares into her round brown eyes as she brushes away at the lashes. She's sixteen but looks older, slim and muscular and breastless with a blunt-nosed, wide-mouthed face and dark, reddish-brown hair that hangs long and straight and symmetrical. She is fascinated by the things she can do with her face. She's made it beautiful in an unearthly, slightly frog-like way, the eyes huge and startling, the lips pale. She sings along with the radio that always plays quietly in her tiny room which is faintly rose-scented from the pot-pourri that sits on her dressing table in a jar of carved rose-coloured soapstone. She is a rose-coloured study, girl in a mirror, the toilet of Venus: Gloria knows her classical allusions, she reads everything.

She watches herself put on a red dress and floppy jacket, then goes downstairs and out through the kitchen where her mother sits at the table rubbing the sallow dry skin of her arms and yawning, stretching the tendons of her long thin neck.

"Have you got everything?" her mother asks automatically. "If you want to borrow my Amplex it's in the table drawer. Have you got your key? – Oh, God, I'm all achy, I do feel tired – Don't forget to ring if you're going to be late. Stay with Mary. I wish you'd do something about your hair . . ."

"See you later," Gloria says, and steps out jauntily into the mild night, saunters proudly down the road, past nosy old Mrs Eccles at her window, to the church where she's meeting Mary to get the bus into town. Gloria and Mary are a team: they're cynical, read a lot, hate school but do well, go dancing, ice-skating, drinking, walk for miles, talk about life, death and everything. Every weekend they go out and spend all their pocket and Saturday job money. Tonight they start off in a pub called the Feathers, full of friends from school, drink cider with Mary's brother, John, and some of his mates, then detach themselves and go up to the poly and gatecrash the Saturday night dance.

The lights are low and take some getting used to. The crowd swarms the long glittering bar, sits at tables hazy with smoke, stands drinking, dances to crashing deafening waves of music played by a bored DJ bathed in red light on a plinth, while on the stage a band prepares itself to play. Gloria and Mary drink Martini and lemonade then dance together with their bags at their feet, Gloria sinuous and effortless but playing it down a bit because she doesn't want to look flash, Mary graceless but cheerful, big and confident with her ample breasts and fuzzy hair, her face glowing pale with the make-up she wears to tone down her hearty complexion and hide the spots that sprinkle the lower part of her face. Boys ask them to dance and they separate briefly from time to time but keep coming back together. When they are tired and starting to sweat they yank their bags up on to their shoulders, get another drink and sit away from the loudspeakers at a table on the outskirts of the room.

The band plays now – old muffled rhythm and blues. Gloria and Mary talk, light with drink, high-spirited, watching the dancers and tapping their fingers on the sides of their glasses. After a while a tall, emaciated boy with a fine downy beard appears and asks Mary to dance, and she rises, smiling apologetically at Gloria who smiles in return to let her know it's all right, walks with the boy out on to the floor, weaves into the crowd and vanishes.

Alone, Gloria plays idly with her long red nails, looking around at all the people. She feels a sweet mixture of elation and melancholy: elation because she's here, out in the world getting drunk against the flashing lights and loud music; melancholy because she knows that in all of it nothing compares with the fantasies of romance that run through her brain when she daydreams on the bus or in the classroom, or lies at night waiting for sleep. She's been kissed in the pictures, kissed at the bus stop, had her breasts groped in the park, had a valentine, walked hand in hand in the rain through the lights of town at night. She's always two or three steps removed. But in her mind there is passion and pain, an obsessive yearning for a faceless someone who'll look at her one day and recognise her.

A man in a beige suit and trilby hat comes to her table and stands looking down with a pint of beer in his hand. "Do you mind if I sit here?" he asks. He looks older than most of the people here, strangely formal and out of place amongst the students, like a bank clerk or something.

Just my luck, she thinks, and says quickly, "My friend's sitting there."

"Ah," he says, hovering for a moment while she ignores him, then walks away.

"He's awful! He's such a beanpole. He looks like he's just got in from Biafra." Mary reappears, flushed and smiling, not meeting Gloria's eyes, sits down at the table and finishes the drink she's abandoned. "Want another?" she asks, getting up all eager and tipsy and nearly spilling her purse. "He's just gone to the toilet. I think he might be coming over – do you mind?" She goes to the bar and comes back with two more drinks. "He's a student," she says. "His name's Tony. He's awful-looking."

"Go on," says Gloria, smiling. "You know you like him." It's obvious from the way she's slagging him off.

The boy comes and sits with them and holds Mary's hand and talks about Buckminster Fuller. Gloria's head swims delightfully. She hears her own voice, low and throaty when she speaks, her own earthy laugh. A strobe light flickers on the dance floor, then stops and gives way to ultra-violet. Everyone starts laughing at each other's teeth. She thinks she might leave Mary to it and go down to the Feathers and try and get a lift home; is about to do this when another drink appears in front of her, so she has to drink it while Mary and Tony dance once more. Greasy boys ask her to dance but she refuses, leaning back and crossing her legs as she surveys the dance floor. There is really nothing here for her.

Someone stands in her light and doesn't move away: the man in the beige suit, a misfit of the wrong kind, looking at her so that she has to look back. He is like a podgy schoolboy. Oh no, she thinks, and tightens up and drinks her drink. Who does he think he is with that stupid hat on?

"You look lonely," he says.

"I'm not." She looks away.

He sits down opposite her and puts his beer on the table. "I won't ask you to dance because I can't dance," he says smoothly. "Don't

32

get me wrong. I'm just being friendly." He leans casually back in the chair and flicks open a packet of cigarettes with an air of studied aplomb that doesn't fit his face, which is small and round with a receding mouth. He offers her a cigarette.

Suddenly she is depressed. Why him? Why is it that no one interesting ever sits down and offers me a cigarette? But she takes it anyway because she's drunk and feels like holding one. The room, the lights, oscillate gently.

"Look," she says, holding the cigarette with an air of experience she doesn't really have, playing the part of the frank, mature woman, "I'd better say this now. When someone sits down and offers me a cigarette in a situation like this, it usually means they want to dance with me or take me home or . . . something . . . so I'm just letting you know, OK? It's not on. No offence, it's just not on." Christ, she thinks, I sound completely sloshed. Keep your mouth shut.

He smiles, his tiny mouth vanishing, his eyes slitty, leans forward and lights her cigarette. There are little wrinkles round his eyes and his collar is very white. "What an honest young lady you are," he says.

She thinks he's slimy. She looks for Mary but can't see her anywhere.

"Well," he says, looking amused, "I'm honest too. I'm afraid I'm very boring and straightforward. I'm in town for the night and I don't know anyone and I'd like very much to sit for a while and chat. Nothing more. And anyway, your friends will be back soon, so you're hardly likely to be stuck with me, are you?" He grins. "Don't worry, I'm harmless."

Gloria sighs inwardly. She isn't good at telling people to bugger off, in spite of her worldly air. She shrugs. Where the hell's Mary?

"So, what's your name?" he asks.

"Gloria."

"Gloria," he says, "I see you've finished your drink. Would you like another?"

Oh, what the hell. She has to wait for Mary anyway, might as well; it's a long way to the Feathers. The night is done for. "OK," she says.

He stands and goes to the bar without asking her what she wants. He's a bit overweight and the suit fits badly, she notices, as he

33

walks back carrying a pint of beer for himself and a glass of something cloudy for her.

"What's that?" she asks.

"Pernod," he says.

She sips carefully. She's never tasted it before and thinks it's lovely, goes down fast and smooth like ginger beer.

He talks while she drinks, says he does a lot of travelling. Sells things. Someone in a pub told him to come in here and see a man at the bar about getting a room in the college for the night, but there's nothing doing. He's been all over the place. "Don't suppose you know of anywhere?" he asks.

"Why don't you try bed and breakfast?" she says.

"I might just do that," he says, but smiles knowingly at the same time and looks away, so that she feels as if she's just said something very naïve. She feels confused.

"Oh, well," he says, "I've always got my trusty car. I suppose I might just press on. The long and winding road and all that."

Then he asks her what she does for a living. Gloria tells him she's doing A levels, and looks round for Mary who's nowhere to be seen. What's she playing at? Talk about all's fair in love and war. When tall students appear, loyalty goes out the door. Her glass is empty. She feels tearful.

"Let me buy you another," the man says, and soon she is sipping wilfully, not caring that she's more drunk than she's ever been in her life before. He says the firm he works for is quite a large concern, you know, office blocks everywhere. He seems very much at ease though he looks so different from everyone else in the place, opens a wallet and lets her see that there's a lot of money in it. "We ought to get danger money," he says, his face shining in the sickly light, "driving through the night, tired, matchsticks propping the old eyes open. Sometimes you have to work a very tight schedule, and it's all commission-based, of course. I used to give lifts to hitchhikers for company, but you can't trust anyone any more. Not these days. I once picked up this bloke on the A4 . . ."

Gloria feels her own eyes wanting to close. Music and light blur, jag, grate. I hate this, she thinks, I want to be at home, in bed, falling asleep. It's not fair. She tosses back the last of the drink and says she has to go to the toilet, then goes and stands in a different part of the room, looking for Mary. Oh, sod her. She dances alone

34

and then with a boy, starts to feel sick and slips into the Ladies and stands looking into the mirror with her fists clenched round a couple of taps. Her face is strange and lurid and staring, the bright lights over the mirror lurch gently. A hot swell of sickness rises up inside her. Quelling it, she keeps her head down till the spasm has passed.

I am so lonely, she thinks, so awfully lonely. Why? Why? I can't wait any longer. She goes and gets her jacket from the checkout, goes outside into the chill, desperate for air. If she walks quickly up to the High Street she can get a cab, her parents will pay for it when she gets back. She's much too ill to go back in there. For a moment she stands on the steps of the poly waiting for her head to clear, but it doesn't. The sickness comes swelling again. She sits down on the steps: This is awful, awful, it gets worse, oh Lord, don't let me be sick, please God, not here, not here. She wants to cry.

Someone comes and sits a little way away from her, but she can't look because if she moves she'll be sick.

"Where do you live?" the man in the suit asks. "I'll take you home. My car's only round the corner."

She's breathing strangely. "No thanks," she says, "I'll get a cab." She's amazed she can say it without exploding.

There's a short pause.

"Fair enough," he says. "Are you all right?"

"Dizzy," she says shortly, putting her hand to the wall and standing awkwardly.

"Careful," he says.

She walks down a few steps then turns an ankle and falls in a silly heap on the pavement and bursts into tears because everything is just so stupid. "Oh, get off!" she says as he tries to help her up. "I'm going home." She sets off down the street, her ankle twinges and her knees shake. Nervous, confused by all the lights, she stops at a crossing.

"Here," he says, coming up behind her, "it's just down here. You're going the wrong way."

"What?"

"My car. That's it, the black one. Come on, don't be silly, you need a lift. You'll wait ages for a cab at this time on a Saturday night, and anyway it's not safe."

"It's not late."

35

"Where do you live?"

She tells him.

"Oh, I know. Oh sure, I can have you there in ten minutes."

Gloria gives up. She sits in the front of the car with her head loose against the headrest. "I feel so sick," she says weakly. The car is comfortable and clean and has a fluffy brown steering-wheel cover and an intricate dashboard full of green lights. He drives smoothly.

"Open the window," he says, "for the air."

Out of town with its queasy lights, through the endless suburbs they go. She closes her eyes and tries to will away the nausea, feels intensely sad about the whole night, wants nothing more than to be home in bed with a night light flickering on the windowsill, not these awful staccato yellow lights that pierce her closed lids. He doesn't speak. She falls into uneasy sleep, wakes afraid, disoriented, the air rushing through the window like a slap on the face.

Where am I, where am I? Lost, lost, somewhere in the dark, some dark lane with big houses set far away from the road behind sinister trees. But then she sees that it's only the long avenue that passes the mushroom field and comes out by the pool. Her heart stops racing.

"You'll have to tell me where," the man says. The houses fade. The headlights show an empty road with a high wall on one side and hedges on the other.

She is suddenly afraid, and her voice, when she speaks, is hoarse. "You go right to the end of this road," she says, "then turn left at the pool." Turning her head, she thinks his face in profile is the face of a priggish middle-aged boy of six, the kind that doesn't change from one end of life to the other. His lower lip is hardly there at all.

In a dark stretch of road by the mushroom field he stops the car.

"Why have you stopped?" she asks sharply. Her insides heave. He says nothing, tapping his blunt fingers on the wheel, smiling vaguely. "Why?"

He turns his face towards her and giggles foolishly. "Kiss," he says wheedlingly, "kiss."

She can't believe this. She goes limp, turns away. "No," she says, "no. I told you." Her head aches and her knees tremble; she can't hold it much longer, tears sting her eyes.

36

He reaches over and takes her hand, touching her leg as he does so. She jerks away. "No!" she cries, furious. "I told you, no!"

"Why?" he says, soft and insistent. "Why, eh? Why?"

"Because I said so!" She lifts her hand to her hair and shivers, feels sweat on her forehead. "I'm going to be sick! You said you'd take me home. I just want to go home." She starts to cry.

"Oh, what a little girl," he says in the same soft tone. "I didn't realise what a little girl you were. Little girls shouldn't drink more than's good for them."

His soft cold hand squeezes her knee, revolting. Something breaks and she slaps the hand hard, grapples with the door, gets it open and scrambles out, staggers a few steps then sinks to a crouch and is violently sick in the grass by the dark open mouth of the mushroom field. She feels as if her head will burst. He comes behind her and holds her head. "Leave me alone!" she moans, too weak to push him away.

"Now, now," he says, "now, now. There, there, there, there, there," and his thumbs dig into the back of her neck.

"Leave me alone!" she moans, panting, wiping her mouth, tears streaming from her eyes.

"Better now," he says. "Better."

She wants to die. "It's your fault," she says, struggling to rise against waves of nausea. "You said you'd take me home. If you hadn't stopped."

Waves hold her down, sickness, weakness, pain in the head; more than this holds her down, on her knees with her head hanging, the night's indulgence sinking steaming into the earth before her eyes. The man holds her there, his hands bigger than they should be, clamps on either side of her head, the pressure of his fattish body growing on her back, rocking against her with a slight, disturbing rhythm.

Oh, dear God, she panics, ice-cold, strikes backward with her elbows, lurches to her feet and weaves about ridiculously. He stands solid, sensible, a respectable businessman with a silly young girl. She notices he's not wearing his hat.

"What's the matter?" he says innocently. "Why all the fuss?"

"I want to go home," she weeps, six years old again. "I want to go home."

"Oh, dear, dear, dear, dear, dear," he says softly, "such a fuss.

Come on, then, home it is." He comes towards her with one hand outstretched as if to usher her helpfully back to the car. But instead he takes her by the shoulders and tries to kiss her on the mouth.

He can't, he can't! He can't do this! She's only just been sick, it's preposterous. She pushes him away. She has no strength. He comes back, an automaton: there is nothing there she can appeal to. He pushes her through the gate into the mushroom field and there knocks her to the ground as if she were made merely of paper, sits on her legs and holds her wrists, his face unclear. He chuckles.

"Get off me, get off me!" she weeps, struggling and shuddering in this horrible parody of children playing, but he just sits there, faceless, chuckling. He's very heavy, like a mountain, shiny knees and plump thighs on either side of her body. Suddenly he drops his face on to hers and kisses her grossly with a fat, vicious tongue. His breath has some faint unpleasantness that she can't place. She moves her head this way and that, her hair caught underneath her and yanked at the roots. Escape, escape, please, get my mouth away from his tongue, but it wriggles all over her face like a great, wet, scaly slug. The earth sticks into her in ridges, her wrists burn in his grip, she's going mad.

"You're hurting me," she tries to say, but he sticks the fat slug in her mouth. She spits it out. "You're hurting me, you're hurting me," she gasps, and knows as she says it that he knows he's hurting her and doesn't care. Oh, dear God, she thinks, don't let him rape me, please don't let him rape me, please, please, please, make him go away, please God, please God, I'll do anything only take him off me, please God, don't let this be happening, please don't let it be happening. She sees the Plough in the sky above. He's hurting her bones.

"Leave me alone," she whimpers, "*please* leave me alone, I don't want to."

It's as if she doesn't exist. He puts her arms behind her back, pulls her legs apart and lies with all his weight at length on top of her. She can't breathe. She's made of rags, wrung out, sick, feeble. She tries not to *be* any more. Lie still, lie still, soon it will be over.

Tears run into her ears and her face is slimy and cold. She isn't sure what's happening any more, what he's doing, what's moving down there. Her skin crawls, sickness heaves, the stars twinkle, twinkle; there's the cold of air on her legs, on her belly where no air should be.

He heaves and grunts and groans, his great weight unendurable; her thighs burn with pain, and then more pain but this time inside, impossible, she is torn, stabbed with a bludgeon that rips through flesh, batters up through her middle, burning and searing as it goes. She can't stand it. It goes on and on and on and she can't stand it and still it goes on, and on, and on, and on, till he gives up and takes a break, sitting up on her and panting for a while, visible now in the moonlight, grinning like a happy football player at half-time. He flicks his thing around with one hand. In this light it looks grey and soft, like a lazy grub.

She tries to move but nothing happens. Then he leans down over her and it starts again, his bad breath in her nostrils, the swollen stick scraping her insides, butting the boundaries. This will never end. This is for ever and ever and ever. This is real. The rag doll is all used up, dying; little cries escape from her lips but she has no breath, no voice. She closes her eyes and hopes to die.

The man lunges, lunges, forcing her to open her eyes in horror. His face hovers above, all pinched up, ridiculous, as if he's going to sneeze. Then his face opens wide and he groans and goes limp all over her, lying like a dead weight that she'll never shift as long as she lives. She turns her head on one side and waits, begins to think dimly that a still, scattered audience of people are watching, but then realises with a swift, strange little jerk back to some kind of reality that it's only the old tree stumps that cover the mushroom field, the old familiar lopped torsos. She's a lopped torso now, too: her arms are nowhere.

The man gets up and walks a few feet away, fiddling with his clothes. Her arms return to her slowly, crying out to her with pain so that she is sorry for them and rubs them soothingly: poor arms, poor arms that never did anyone any harm. She sits up, amazed that she can, retches dryly and feels between her legs to see if she's bleeding. It's all wet but she can't tell if it's blood. Yes, says her brain, crawling through sludge, sticking and faltering, get up now, run away, run out into the road, get away from here. But the rest of her won't move.

He comes back. "Lie down," he orders, and she does. He

spreads her thighs wide, places a hand on each and presses down hard. She screams. "Shut up!" he hisses. "Shut up! Shut up!" Gloria starts to cry, to choke on her own breath. He holds her open, crouching there and looking down into her with a curious, emotionless kind of interest.

After a long time he says softly, "Who's a naughty little girl, then?"

She sobs hopelessly.

"I said, who's a naughty little girl, then?" he says, pressing harder. "Say I am."

"I am," she whispers.

"Who?" he says, pressing.

"I am."

"Who?"

She cries out.

"Who? Who?"

"I am. I am."

"What? What are you? What are you?"

"I don't know."

"A naughty little girl. What are you?"

"A naughty little girl."

"Again!"

"A naughty little girl."

"Again!"

"A naughty little girl."

He lets go of her suddenly, stands clumsily and walks out of the mushroom field. She hears the slamming of the door, the revving of the engine, the car moving smoothly away, in no hurry. She rolls on to her side and curls up and puts her fist in her mouth and waits to die from some rupture, shivering with cold and watching the faint movement of the leaves of the old elder tree by the gate, dim against the starry sky. The blossom gives a vague mustiness to the air. Motherdie. If you bring Motherdie into the house, your mother dies.

For a time she lies paralysed, but then rises slowly, a ghost in the ghostly dark field, and wanders on hands and knees looking for her knickers. She can't find them anywhere; it seems a catastrophe beyond belief and she searches and searches growing more and more frantic till she's forgotten what it is she's lost and seems in

40

some dim dreaming way to be looking for her old green stick in the shadows under the elder tree.

Then a calm, sensible voice inside her head says: What are you doing? Don't be ridiculous. Go home.

"Gloria," says her mother outside the door, "what are you doing?"

"Having a bath."

"What, at this time of night?"

"I fell over," she says. "I fell over. Getting off the bus. Got myself all dirty."

"Are you all right?"

"Oh, yes! I just got a bit dirty."

The phone rings and her mother goes away. Gloria hauls herself from the scalding water and lies steaming on the bath mat, staring at the lightbulb in its turquoise shade. She's changed. She's empty. What has happened could not have happened and therefore has not happened; she will not allow it to have happened. She will not have it. She will throw it out, press the automatic reject, snip off every shoot of memory as it tries to unfurl, and soon it will not exist, will never have existed. But she's changed. She feels like an intruder inside her own skin.

"Gloria," her mother calls through the door.

Gloria sucks her fingers.

"Gloria."

"What?"

"That was Mary wanting to know if you'd got home safe. I thought you were coming home with Mary?"

"Oh. Oh, I was, but I got a lift, you know, from this girl at school, her dad, you know – so I came on without Mary because she was dancing with some boy."

"Are you sure you're telling me the truth?" says her mother after a slight pause. "I know you. I can tell when you're not telling the truth. The way you sneaked in and came straight up here."

Gloria sits up, pulls a towel tight and draws herself into as small a space as possible. She'd had her key in her pocket, thank God. Her bag was in the front of the car. The car. She closes her eyes and heaves. Vomit and petrol fumes. Never again.

"You said you got the bus!" her mother says accusingly.

She thinks fast. "They were only going as far as the Red Lion," she says. "They put me on the bus there. It was OK. There were a few of us from school. Sandra and Dawn were there."

"I know what it is," her mother says. "You got drunk, didn't you? That's why you fell. Falling about drunk like some old tramp. You ought to be careful getting out of the bath."

"It's all right," says Gloria, "I'm out. I'm coming out now." Her voice trembles a little.

"Are you all right?" her mother asks. "I'm not really angry with you, you know. Are you all right?"

"I'm all right," she says, her voice controlled, though her heart's begun to throb rather sickeningly in her chest. A great well of loneliness is opening somewhere and she's falling into it.

"Would you like some cocoa?" her mother asks. "I'll bring it up to you in bed, if you like."

"Yes, please," she says. "Thanks."

When her mother's gone she cries fiercely, stuffing the towel in her mouth. "Oh Mummy, Mummy, Mummy," she says. Then she pulls the plug, gets her nightie off the back of the door, puts it on and stands looking at herself in the mirror. Funny to see that she's still there. Funny. When she'd first come into the bathroom her face had frightened her. Now it's pink and scrubbed and damp-haired, forlorn. It's all right, she tells it, really, it's all right now. Everything's back to normal now.

She wipes her face and goes into her parents' bedroom to borrow her mother's hairbrush, sees Jesus and the cherub that used to be Michael and is glad it isn't Michael. It's so dimpled it's deformed. But she stands looking at the old picture for a while as she brushes her hair. When she hears her mother coming up the stairs she goes into her own room and gets under the bedclothes and pulls the blankets right up to her eyes.

"I don't feel very well," she says when her mother brings in the cocoa.

"I'm not surprised," her mother says. "Anyway, never mind now. You get some sleep and you'll feel much better in the morning." Her mother kisses her on the forehead and leaves her. The cocoa comforts her and makes her feel sick all at the same time. She looks at her room and that's changed too, the mirror where she'd got ready to go out so long ago, the little carved rose-coloured jar of pot-pourri, some clothes drooping on the back of a chair as if tired.

She lies down and grows warm, curls up holding herself tight. Outside, rain comes softly, long-awaited. She goes away into some half-real place where nothing exists unless she wants it to. She lies in the moose's antlers. The primeval forest soars above her head like a cathedral, hallowed, inviolable. But, even here, pictures flash on a screen to disturb her – a middle-aged schoolboy, her own filthy face startling itself in the mirror, Mary dancing with the tall student, a crowd of jerking puppets in a strobe light. She wakes time and time again with pounding heart, weeping or sick, chiding herself.

Let it go, let it go, how can you survive if you don't let it go?

The last time she wakes the house is dark and quiet, the rain whispers, the street light shines on the wall telling her not to worry, nightmares pass. She lies in the moose's antlers and the great, gentle beast carries her away.

4

Gloria dyes her hair blonde, then copper chestnut, then mahogany, goes to school but nowhere else, stays in her room and sleeps a lot, feels silly and vague and loses track of time.

She's late with her homework, gets lousy marks, doesn't care anyway. She sits in class doodling in the margin of *Othello*, feels fat and heavy and achy because her period's coming, falls asleep with her eyes open and wakes with a start. Mary's leaning across and pointing out something on the page. "That one," she's saying.

"What?" says Gloria stupidly.

"Gloria, *will* you wake up," the teacher says. "Now, really!"

"That one," says Mary gently. "Othello's speech, the one about the Anthropophagi."

"What?"

The teacher tosses her head in disgust and turns away.

"What?" whispers Gloria.

"Oh, nothing," whispers Mary.

Gloria feels a fool and wants to cry. She looks down at the page and reads "She swore 'twas strange; 'twas passing strange . . ." She doesn't see the point of coming here any more, just seems like time's wasting. She looks round at her classmates and thinks they're all aliens, even Mary. For God's sake, what are we doing here?

She takes days off, hides in her room and sleeps, or walks by the pool. Her period doesn't come. She thinks she must be damaged inside because the pain's there, same as usual; maybe she's dammed up, somehow. She falls asleep and forgets it, floats to never-never land, wakes and gazes out of the window, lost in a reverie of being small and surrounded by treasures, rain drumming on a makeshift roof. She wishes she could turn back time. Time is a strange element, strange and passing strange . . . time is about her like a vault of stagnant air she can't get out of; but she knows that she's the one who's stopped, not the hands of the clock.

"What's up with you these days?" her mother asks.

"I think I've got cystitis," she says. "I keep wanting to pee all the time."

"Plenty of water," says her mother. "Drink plenty of water."

She waits by the church and catches the bus into town, goes into the library and looks up cystitis in the medical dictionary. Then, as if her hands are not ruled by her brain, they turn the pages until they reach a deadly, forbidden word: *pregnancy*. She sits at a wide polished table opposite an old man with a very bad cold, and reads patiently as if it were a school lesson till her mouth is dry with fear and goose flesh rises on her arms.

For a long time she sits gazing at the blue paint flaking off a radiator with the open book in front of her, then stands and returns the book to its correct place on the shelf, goes outside and walks through the crisp September streets. There is a building of shiny black glass and she sees herself in it, crossing the road. Criss-cross, criss-cross go her legs in patterned tights and high heels. She has a vision of how they used to be, thin with knobbly knees and ankle socks and scuffed red sandals. Where have they gone?

She stands at the bus stop and the wind blows leaves in eddies around her ankles. On the bus she keeps breathing on the window and making patterns with her finger on the mist. The streets are full of people with normal lives, people going here and there, sitting on walls, pushing prams, gossiping on corners, crossing roads, waiting at the lights. How funny, how innocent, how sweet they all seem. Only she is a tissue of dark secrets, a walled garden of thorns. She gets off the bus and goes to Mary's house where she never goes any more. It is familiar like an old soft armchair. Canned laughter fills the living-room, where Mary's dad polishes horse brasses by the fire and John and two of the younger children sit watching TV.

"Crikey, look who it is," says Mary's dad kindly.

"Hello, stranger," John says. The kids start babbling about the programme they're watching. They're pleased to see her. The realisation touches her and colours her face.

As if the whole world has not changed totally, she smiles and chats for a while, the greatest actress in the world, before running upstairs and going into a room for three that looks as if it's just been

45

raided and left in a heap. Mary's lying on a top bunk, wearing denim jeans and a shapeless shirt, eating toffee and listening to the radio and doing biology homework.

"My God!" she cries, closing her book and swinging her legs over the side. "I don't believe it! You're a rare species these days. What brings you out of your hole?"

Gloria laughs and climbs up. They sit cross-legged above the mess of the room. "I thought you were fed up with us all," Mary says.

"Of course not," says Gloria cheerfully, unable to drop this pretence. "Everyone needs to hibernate sometimes."

Mary leans back against a grimy candystriped pillow and lights a cigarette, blowing out a voluminous blue cloud and smiling. "I'm glad you've come," she says, "nice excuse for a break. Fancy going out somewhere? I know, the park, I feel like one of those lovely pink and green ice-creams they do . . ."

"In a bit," says Gloria. "Not yet."

Mary chucks her book on to the floor and gets comfortable. They talk for half an hour. Gloria is amazed at herself; frightened by the ease with which she converses, smiles, listens, laughs – false, false, utterly false – while another person entirely beats in panic at her brain, trapped: Let me out, let me out, please, let me out. Something's in there, some terrible parasite hooked into my inner flesh. She wonders if everyone is really two people, all the ordinary smiling faces spouting banal words really hiding gibbering wrecks. Mary says she's got a good book on astral projection she'd like Gloria to read. Gloria says she will. Mary thinks she'll fail maths. Gloria thinks she'll fail everything. Mary's still going out with Tony. He's OK, she says, bit obsessed with his bike but apart from that . . . Children come and go in the room below and Mary yells at them to shut up and close the door.

"At least you've got a room of your own, Gloria," she says. "Everyone should have a room of their own by law. You're dead lucky. Dead, dead lucky."

"I suppose I am," Gloria says, then laughs. "That's quite funny, that is. Quite funny."

Something must have given her away. Mary looks at her carefully. "What's the matter?" she asks.

"I'm pregnant."

Mary doesn't know what to say. Her face doesn't change. "You're not."

"I am."

"What?" says Mary, hushed and incredulous, her brow wrinkling. "How? I didn't think you'd ever . . ."

"I haven't."

They look at one another, baffled. "What are you talking about?" says Mary.

Gloria's face crumples up and she starts to cry in a slow, tired, shrill kind of way, leaning back into the corner and covering her face. One of the kids opens the door and starts scrambling about in the wreckage on the floor. "Go away, Piggy," says Mary, "and close the door. Can't you see Gloria's upset?"

Piggy, a little boy with huge ears, stands with a machine gun in his arms, pulling a hideous face at Mary. "You're always telling me to close doors," he rasps.

"Well, do as you're told then," she snaps. "Go away!"

They argue. More kids come to see what it's all about. "Get out! Get out!" screams Mary, leaping from the bunk and pushing them all out of the room. When they've gone she climbs back on the bunk and puts her arms round Gloria. "Now," she says, "tell me all about it."

"I'm pregnant," sobs Gloria. "I am, I am, I am."

"Oh, Gloria!" says Mary. "Oh, Gloria!"

After a while she says, "It wasn't our John, was it?"

"No," says Gloria, blowing her nose and wiping her eyes.

"Who was it?"

"I don't know."

"Well, who . . ."

Gloria stares straight ahead. "It was that night," she says, "at the poly, when you got off with Tony. When I left early. It was this . . ."

She stops short. She can't tell. She can't tell. She can't even think about it; it's a great pile of sludge that must never be disturbed, or it will roll down the slopes of Vesuvius destroying all in its path, clogging her breath, wiping her out. "Oh, Mary!" she says, covering her eyes. "Oh, Mary, Mary! What can I do?"

"Maybe you're wrong," says Mary hopefully. "Maybe you're just late. You know, worrying about it can make it late . . ."

47

"No," she says, "I know, I just know. I can *feel* it, I can't explain."

The door opens and two kids come frolicking in, giggling and shrieking.

"Ye Gods!" cries Mary. "I can't stand this place! Get out! Get out! Get out, both of you!"

"It's our room too," says a girl with adenoids.

Gloria blinks hard and smooths her hair back. "Let's go to the park," she says. "I'm all right. Honest. Come on, let's go to the park. You can get an ice-cream and we can talk."

So they walk to the park and sit at a table near the snack bar, the wind blowing their hair across their faces. Mary eats ice-cream and Gloria drinks Coke.

As she cannot tell the truth, she needs a story. "It was this boy," she says, "this boy I met that night. We went for a walk. We went in Fishmill Park and that's where it happened."

"Fishmill Park?" Mary looks bewildered. Behind her head, small birds hop and perch on a twisted branch in an aviary.

"We climbed the fence," says Gloria. The play unfolds. Hand in hand the two figures steal, drunk and giggling, from tree to tree. The boy is handsome, shadowy, gentle, kind. She tells Mary. "We talked," she says. "We talked for ages and then it just happened. It seemed the thing to do, you know? It was . . . you know . . . he was . . . *different* from everybody else, so it didn't seem to matter. We just kind of got carried away, I can't explain . . ."

"So, who is he?" asks Mary, perplexed, turning her face from side to side and frowning as she licks her ice-cream. "Good God, I mean, it must've happened really quick; I rang you as soon as I got in and . . ."

"Yes," says Gloria, "only it didn't seem that quick, you know; you kind of lose track of time."

"So who is he? What's his name?"

"John," she says, the first thing that comes into her head.

"And have you told him?"

Gloria panics, her mind races. "No."

"Well, you'll have to. You'll have to. He's responsible, Gloria, he's got to . . ."

"I can't!" she cries, clenching her fists. "I don't know where he is!" Then it unfolds rapidly before her.

48

He comes from up north, a long way, yes, Newcastle, but he lives in London now. He left home because he didn't get on with his family, and he was on his way back up there to pick up some of his things and just stopped off here for the night because he knew someone at the poly (no, I don't know who) and he was going to stop over here again on his way back and see me. He wanted me to go to London with him. He was in a group, played guitar (no, I don't know the name, he did say, but I've forgotten) and . . . and so . . .

He didn't come back.

"But this is ridiculous!" Mary cries. "You don't just take somebody's word for it, just like that. Some total stranger. And you didn't make sure he used something? Oh, Gloria, I can't believe you'd be so . . . Oh, the bastard, the bastard . . . Oh Gloria, don't worry, if there's anything I can do . . . Don't worry, don't worry, it'll be all right . . . Didn't you get his address or . . . Oh, Gloria, why not? Why not? I could shake you. I can't believe . . . why didn't you tell me?"

"I don't know."

"Why didn't you tell me? Why didn't you tell me? I'd've told *you* a thing like that."

Gloria starts to cry. "He's dead!" she cries. "He's dead, I'm sure of it. He *would* have come back, I know it. Supposing he crashed on the motorway. Supposing . . . anything could've happened. How would I know? He *would* have come back!"

Mary takes both her hands and holds them. "You don't have to keep it, you know. No one'd dream of trying to make you keep it. If you like, I'll come to the doctor's with you."

Gloria doesn't speak.

"You must tell your mum," says Mary briskly. "That's the next step. You must tell your mum. She'll know what to do."

"I won't have it," says Gloria, quietly and fiercely. "I won't have it."

"I know you're not telling me the truth. I *know* you," Gloria's mother says.

Gloria leans back against her pillow and stares her out. This is her story and she's sticking to it.

"Oh, well, I can't force the truth out of you." Her mother looks down at her hands, eyes heavy, mouth open. She is always thin and pale and tired these days. "Well," her mother says, wiping her upper lip wearily and pulling her nose out of shape, "it might not be. We'll have to make sure. Don't worry too much. We won't say anything to your dad yet; no point in bothering him if it all turns out to be a false alarm, is there?" She sighs deeply, looks at Gloria for a long time with sad, hooded eyes, then walks heavily to the door. No one will ever know what I suffer, her back says. No one will ever lift this burden from me. Gloria is full of guilt at the sight of her mother's back. She turns. "You're not on your own, you know," she says.

Gloria just looks at her. She can't stand this lifeless resignation. They stare at one another wordlessly for too long.

Suddenly her mother's face distorts. It could be anger. "Promise me you won't worry too much," she says fervently. "Promise me. Promise me."

But of course Gloria does, and of course this is no false alarm.

She sits staring into her mirror, her hands folded on her stomach. It's in there, this thing, this creature, this blob of jelly. It's impossible, like death, it only happens to someone else. Her face is still Gloria, you'd never guess to look at it. She mouths words at it, whispering, making faces. I'm still here, still here in spite of it all. Oh, no, it won't get me, won't get me – not as big as my thumbnail yet.

She makes her face up very carefully, making the eyes, the lips, more definite to prove she's still real. Then she sits back and smiles at herself for a while, still and mysterious, like Mona Lisa. When she hears her mother come upstairs and start sorting linen in the next room, she walks next door and sits down on her mother's bed.

"It's my decision," she says to her mother's back.

It starts again.

"Of course it's your decision," her mother says, "but you know my feelings on the subject."

"*My* life," Gloria says, "*my* life."

Her mother says it's a sin against life. You can't save your own by taking another. "Have it adopted, have it adopted, by all means, but abortion – no. No is final. Some things are just not open to question. Like this is one. Like it's murder, and murder's murder whatever name you call it by." She won't meet Gloria's eyes.

50

"I'd have to leave school," Gloria says, "right in the middle of A levels. You don't want me to do that."

"You can always go back after. Next September."

"I don't want to miss a year!"

"I've had my say, Gloria. I'm saying no more." Her lips and nostrils are tight.

"You're not the one that's got to have the bloody thing!" Gloria shouts.

"Shsh! Shsh!" her mother hisses furiously, looking at the door. "Do you want him to hear?"

"You're mad!" Gloria says. "Mad! I'm your daughter, for God's sake. I just don't believe you want me to go through with this. You care more about some stupid lump of jelly than you do about me."

"I care about life," her mother says wearily. She looks at Jesus and the cherub on the wall, her upturned eyes tragic. "I've already had one dead baby," she says. "God forbid we should have another in the family. They're all from God. All. All. Doesn't matter how they were conceived."

Gloria wants to scream, to jump from the bed and hit her mother. She closes her eyes. Tell her. Go on, tell her, tell her the truth. She's mad. Wouldn't make any difference. She's mad because she coos over a bloated little goblin she thinks is the son who died sixteen years ago, and she never even saw him. Because she thinks the dead are more important than the living, the dead who never even got born.

That was me, Gloria wants to say. That was me killed the little brat. Stuck my hands round his throat and squeezed, kicked him in the face. Me or him. Ha-ha-ha-ha. I was a murderer in the womb, what do you expect of me now? If I'm mad, I get it from you.

She sees her mother's face in the mirror and it looks as if it's dammed a million tears. She says nothing.

"I always wanted another baby," her mother says, "but I couldn't have one."

That night before she goes to bed, Gloria says to her mother, "I've decided. I'm getting rid of it. That's final." Her mother says nothing.

In the night she wakes and hears the sound of distant crying. She lies in the dark transfixed, cold with fear, sure that it's supernatural.

It sounds as if it comes from the room below, the old front parlour that's never used. It stops and starts, thin and drizzly, till she can stand it no more and gets out of bed and steals to the head of the stairs in the pale moonlight that slants in through the landing window. It's louder here. A terrible suspicion dawns and she tiptoes downstairs, just far enough to crouch breathlessly holding the bars with both hands and look through the gap of the parlour door to where her mother sits in her old winceyette nightie on the flounced, rose-patterned sofa, weeping incessantly as she looks down at a tiny blue pair of bootees that she holds in her hands. Her face is hidden by the thick, grey-flecked hair that falls in limp round coils on to her sagging shoulders; her bony feet are bare and pigeon-toed upon the carpet.

Gloria has never seen her mother cry. It is not possible. Watching, she is struck all at once with the full horror of nightmare; this faceless weeping figure with her mother's feet and hands and hair and nightie will turn its head, slow, remorseless, revealing the face of some ghoul, some dreadful spirit with hollow suffering eyes, fix her with its dead white eyes and send her mad. In the dark on the staircase in the middle of the night, she sees her hands tremble on the bars in front of her, unhasps them slowly, rises and silently goes back to bed and lies wide-eyed on her back listening to the sad ghost below for so long she wonders why morning doesn't intervene.

Somehow, she falls asleep in the end.

The next day is Sunday and she can't wake up. Finally her mother comes into her room and says, "Do you know what time it is? One o'clock."

Gloria gets up, eats three bananas and goes down to the pool. The bells ring out joyfully, endlessly falling down the scale. She walks round and round and round the pool and wants to drive a great wedge through her life, break it open and swim with the resulting flux. This place, her parents, school – dirty ropes tying her down.

She goes to see Mary and asks her if she'll leave, come to London with her, get a place together; Mary says she will but not yet, she wants to get her A levels first but then, yes, why not, she thinks she wants to be a nurse, she can go to London and do her training there. Oh, yes, yes, they get excited, side by side on the top bunk, thinking of their fortunes. Gloria almost forgets that she is pregnant.

She walks home, pauses on the wooden bridge and leans on the rail watching a few tentative drops of rain try out the surface of the pool. A lonely moorhen crosses the cold grey water. She wonders what they'll say when she tells them she's going. Her father won't care. Her mother will. She doesn't think they've ever considered the idea. It somehow seems presumed that she will one day get a job in town and catch the bus by the church every morning, maybe even the same one her father gets. The thought makes her desperate.

When she gets home her father's asleep in his chair, her mother's sewing a hem, a quiz show squawks on the TV and the rain falls steadily past the window. The house smells of food. Gloria sits down. Her mother does not look at her. Her face, bent over the hem, is stern and harrowed, brows drawn together in a painful knot between the eyes.

"What's the matter?" asks Gloria.

"Don't talk to me now," her mother says shortly. "I can't talk now." The needle flashes in and out, neatly stitching.

Gloria goes upstairs and lies on her bed, pulls her jeans down and looks at her stomach, touching it gingerly. She sighs. Poor creature. Little devil. Slug. She starts to doze, dreams fitfully while hearing still the rain on the window, tries to open her eyes but finds the lids have grown heavy like pieces of gold, panics, not sure if she's asleep or awake, struggles, falls and rises as if drowning, sees the light through slits, feels her ears pop, then hears inside her head a voice, clear as a bell, that says simply: *Why not?*

What? she asks, struggling. What?

Fool! the voice says, laughing listlessly.

"Gloria!" her mother calls from the foot of the stairs. "Gloria!"

She jerks upright, heart bursting. "What?' she yells.

"Here a minute."

Gloria goes down. Her mother stands in the hall looking yellow and sick and bent. "You'll have to serve up for your dad and you," she says. "I feel terrible. I don't want anything. I'm going upstairs." She climbs the stairs like a child, pulling at the banister.

"Do you want some tea or something?" Gloria asks.

"No!"

Gloria goes into the kitchen and dishes up food, eats in silence with her father then ventures into her parents' room. Her mother lies on her side on the bed, eyes open but dead.

"Can I get you anything?" Gloria asks.

Her mother doesn't speak at first. When she does her mouth is so dry that the lips have trouble parting. "I don't live," she says dully, "I just exist."

"What can I do?" says Gloria, terrified, "what can I do?"

"Nothing," her mother says. "Don't stand there."

Gloria runs away. Later her mother gets up and watches TV till bedtime. Next morning when she comes down, her mother tells her not to go to school today, she's needed here; she says she's not well, she's going back to bed and she'd like Gloria to do a bit of shopping and just pop up about eleven to see if she wants a cup of anything. Gloria makes breakfast for her dad, runs down to the shops and takes as long as she can, sheltering from the rain in a doorway with some old women who smile at her and chat. "In for the day!" they say cheerfully, nodding at the rain.

She comes back and tiptoes upstairs hoping her mother's asleep, but she's half lying, old and skeletal and frightening, propped up on the pillow with her eyes open, mouth slack, hands idle on the coverlet.

"What's wrong?" Gloria says, hovering anxiously. "Really, what's wrong?"

"Sit down, Gloria," her mother says.

Gloria sits uncomfortably on the edge of the bed. For a while her mother just looks at her, inscrutable.

"Oh, for heaven's sake!" says Gloria, jumpy. "What is this?"

"I want to talk to you, Gloria," her mother says, "very seriously." Then her face breaks up and she cries fiercely and silently, eyes lost in wrinkles, worse than when she laughs.

"Don't!" Gloria cries too. "Don't! Oh, don't! I'm sorry – Oh, I'm sorry, Mummy, I'm sorry."

Her mother opens her watery, bewildered eyes and shakes her head slowly from side to side as if something's stuck in her ears. "I want to talk to you, Gloria," she gasps. "I want to talk to you."

"Yes. Yes."

No one speaks for a long time. Then her mother says in a strong voice, "I want you to have this baby."

54

Gloria turns her face away and goes blank.

"If you don't want it," her mother says, her voice shaking, "I'll have it. You don't understand. You're very young: you could have this baby and be back at school, you've got all your life in front of you. You'd soon be right as rain, and you could do whatever you wanted – *I'll* take all the responsibility, *I'll* do everything. You wouldn't even have to stay in or anything, it'd just be like taking a year off for you, that's all, not even a year really, and you needn't worry about your dad, I'll talk to him, I promise he'll not be angry with you, I *promise* . . ."

Gloria walks out and goes into her own room, locks the door and lies down. The sound of her mother crying filters through the wall and continues, constant as the rain. I am hard, I am hard, says Gloria to herself, crawls under the covers, curls up and soon sleeps. She can always sleep these days.

She dreams of a foetus that unfurls itself in some deep black space, stands up straight on stick legs and unformed feet, shakes its puny fist at her, baring canine teeth in its great deformed head. When she wakes she hits herself in the stomach again and again till she can stand no more and lies gasping, thinking: Oh, my God, I killed it, I really did, I killed it. Her ears sing and she feels a little mad.

But then a deeper voice, one from down inside her body, one that knows, says surely: *Not dead, no, still there, still strong. Waiting.*

5

Early evenings in summer the yard is mellow with sunlight, casting a yellow glow into the seasonless, unchanging back room where they eat, as usual, separate and silent, with the TV on. Little furry creatures, half monkey, half dog, skitter across the screen.

Gloria has no appetite these days. She sits at the table by the window poking her knife into a pile of wet, overcooked mushrooms. Her mother sits on the settee and eats like a bird, her father chomps away solidly in his big chair. A narrator drones on. On the screen one of the little furry creatures sits on its haunches, spine erect.

"Isn't it funny?" her mother says brightly. "Isn't it funny, Gloria?"

"Yeah," Gloria says.

"Isn't it?" says her mother very quickly. "Isn't it, isn't it, isn't it, isn't it?" Then she puts down her knife and fork and launches into mute laughter, looking at Gloria and gesturing at the screen. She heaves and shakes till she's helpless, opens her mouth and closes her streaming eyes, screaming in horribly stretched silence.

She's mad, Gloria thinks. Completely mad. Her father fills his mouth full of bacon and cabbage and chews vigorously, seeing nothing but the screen. He doesn't know she's mad, thinks Gloria. He hasn't noticed.

She pushes her plate away and goes upstairs into her parents' bedroom and looks down at the big bald head of the sleeping baby, thinking she can see the pulse beating in the soft spot on top of its head. A long-nailed hand lies bunched beside it. She doesn't know what this ugly girl baby with fat cheeks and slimy little mouth has to do with her. Her parents spoil it something rotten. I'm sure they never spoiled me like that, she thinks, going into her own room and sitting down in front of the mirror where she ties her hair back and contemplates her face uncertainly. She's still overweight. She's let her hair grow wild and dyed it red, spent the pregnancy reading books on magic and religion and, when her father wasn't around to complain, learning to play a little ocarina made of terracotta. She picks it up now from where it lies next to her pot-pourri jar and blows a few plaintive fluty notes, remembers the baby, lays it down again and blows out her cheeks boredly, then starts coating her face with ghostly-pale make-up. The baby starts to cry. Gloria brushes away at her face with her fingertips and whistles through her teeth. The baby cries louder.

After a while she hears her mother come upstairs and go next door and croon. The crying stops and starts and changes tone; her mother's footsteps go up and down, up and down, then there is a long silence. Gloria unties and brushes out her hair bit by bit, watching it fly out electric round her face. Her mother comes in with the baby propped up on her shoulder and walks up and down smiling. Gloria gives herself a scarlet mouth.

"Oh! Pretty Kitty," her mother says again and again. "Pretty Kitty, pretty Kitty."

Two things Gloria has insisted upon: that the baby knows she's its mother and that she chooses the name. "*Kit?*" her mother had said. "Oh, I don't really like that, Gloria. It's a bit . . . I don't know . . . I like Hayley. I think that's a really pretty name."

In the mirror she watches her mother lay Kit down on the bed, poke gaily at her stomach and turn, lounging across the bed, to speak to the back of her head. "Mrs Eccles said you and Mary were walking about near that old factory," she says.

"So what?" says Gloria.

"So what? So what? Who do you think you're talking to? Watch your tone. You know it's not safe over there."

"Of course it's safe."

"What do you want to go there for?"

"I don't know." Gloria leans towards her matte white face, staring hard into its eyes. "It's private. We can talk without nosy old bags like Mrs Eccles flapping their great big fat earlobes around."

"Gloria!" her mother cries. "You're getting too cheeky by far, you are. I don't know what it is with you lately, you think you're special or something, you and that high and mighty tone, talking all nasty about nice people. Mrs Eccles got you that lovely Easter egg."

"I know," says Gloria. "She thinks I'm still eight years old."

Kit starts to cry. Gloria's mother picks the baby up and jogs her about efficiently, stands and walks up and down saying, "Pretty Kitty, pretty Kitty – oh, oh, oh, there, there, there."

"She's not pretty," says Gloria, "she's just another fat red baby."

"Oh, shut up," her mother says dismissively, sitting stony-faced on the edge of the bed and rubbing the baby's back. Its head is sideways on her shoulder, quiet now. Gloria applies deep blue shadow above her eyes, thick black lines Cleopatra-fashion all around them, watching her face become strangely beautiful and compelling, older, impersonal.

"Why are you putting all that on if you're not going out?" her mother asks.

"I don't know." She pushes her hair about with her fingers then starts pinning it high and rough on top of her head.

After a while her mother starts to play with Kit, picking her up and pretending to drop her, going, "Oh, woh, woh, woh, woh, woh, woh!" in a high voice. The baby screams with glee. Gloria's mother laughs and grabs Kit's arms, manipulating her as if she's a doll. "Clap handies!" she cries. "Clap handies!" Kit's pink porcelain hands go clap, clap. "Clap handies, clap handies, clap handies!"

Gloria gazes expressionlessly into the mirror.

"Naughty baby!" says her mother, poking Kit in the chest. "Naughty, naughty baby! Bad!" She taps Kit's hand. Kit's face crumples.

"Aw!" cries Gloria's mother. "Aw! Never mind, baba! Oh, poor baba!"

"Oh, mother, stop doing that to her!"

"What?" says her mother, irritated, turning towards her. "Stop doing what?"

"That!"

"You shut up," her mother says. "Who's a naughty, naughty baby? Eh? Who's been a naughty, naughty little girlywoo, then?"

Gloria sees herself in the mirror as in a film: all made-up and lovely, she leaps to her feet and sweeps the contents of her dressing table to the floor with both arms. The moment is glorious. Her mother jumps up, shocked. Kit whimpers. A door downstairs opens. "What's the racket?" her father calls up angrily.

Aghast, Gloria stands with clenched fists. Her mother runs past her on to the landing and leans over the banister. "Nothing, Pete," she says, "just something fell over."

For a moment Gloria hangs her head, but clicks to attention again immediately as if someone's given an order, runs out on to the landing after her mother and shouts, "Yes, there is! Yes, there is!" She feels exultant, intoxicated.

"You get in your room!" her mother rasps, gripping her arm, propelling her in there and slamming the door on her. The baby writhes and screams on the bed, outraged, and Gloria hears her mother run downstairs and speak pacifyingly to her father. Make-up debris litters the floor and the air is sharp with the smell of it. Suddenly deflated, she stands limp, then laughs, timidly defiant. Too much wrong in this house. Stupid people! she thinks.

She looks down at the baby. Ugly thing. Still, she can't help it. A watery sympathy stirs in her, but she feels shy and doesn't know what to say to the creature. After all, she's a stranger. "You great, stupid, ugly thing," she says, sitting down beside the baby. Kit cries, pokes a long, sharp-nailed finger right up her own nose and screams even louder. Gloria pulls it out. "That's a bit stupid," she says.

Her mother bursts in, furious, her face tight and long-suffering, grabs the baby and marches up and down. "There, there," she brays, "pretty Kitty."

"She isn't," says Gloria, "she's as ugly as sin."

"What's the matter with you?" her mother cries. "What's the matter with you? I just don't know what's got into you these days. Behaving like that! Look at the mess! Look at it! – there, there, there, there, there – who do you think you are? Your dad's sitting down there furious. *Furious*. And who do you think has to put up with the sulks?" She shakes Kit and the crying jags. "Not you! Oh, no, not you! Ha-ha-ha, oh, no! Muggins! Muggins here, that's who!"

"Oh, shut up," says Gloria, slouching by the wall. "You're stupid. I'm sick of hearing you moan."

Her mother is so amazed that she stops walking and looks at Gloria with a hurt, childish expression that tears at Gloria's heart and covers her with guilt. Then she finds her voice. "Don't you *dare* speak to me like that," she says, turns abruptly and walks out,

59

Kit lolling across her shoulder. Gloria hears her moving about next door, soothing the awful crying of the baby, which subsides after a while.

The house is quiet. What now? She thinks. What have I done? Again, she looks in the mirror. She looks beautiful and weird, hair wild, eyes big black bruises in a pale mask. She steals out on to the landing, glides downstairs and out of the house unseen, elation rising like fear. The evening is still and pretty, the privets fragrant. She walks right to the edge of the pool, stands in the squelchy ooze and feels cold moisture seep through her shoes, feels it distantly as if it's happening to someone else. Her jeans get wet. A strong beat throbs through the world, as if her own heart is beating outside her body.

The weather's on the turn, the pool grey and flat like satin, the sky above the houses the same. An empty bus passes along the other side of the pool where mist is gathering. A distant swan dips its beak in the water and the ripples it causes are vast and thin and slow. She walks along the edge of the pool amongst lush, wet growth, and gets wet to the knee, squats in the mud and looks at the little creatures that dart here and there on the water. An old Coke can lodges amongst the weeds and a sweet, wild childhood smell rises up from the trampled vegetation.

Gloria plays: she makes dams and creates a little bay. A dragonfly hovers as if interested and she smiles at it as she once would have done, without shame, and the years roll back like a great stone from the mouth of a tomb. Someone watches her from the bridge. People walking by in the road look at her curiously. I don't care, she thinks, and really doesn't. Strange she must appear, all mud-spattered and elaborately made up, but she likes the idea. She likes the way she is. I don't care, I don't care, she thinks, dazed, the freedom beat beating outside her, in the sky and close by her ears. Her eyes beat too, like pulse spots. She imagines them glowing red – throb, throb, throb . . . terrible things to turn on a person, gorgon's eyes.

She walks to the mushroom field, the first time in . . . oh, so long, she can't remember. She reclaims it. Someone has cut a swathe through it and there are tyre tracks near the gate. She sits down by the hedge in her favourite spot near the Africa tree and whistles through her teeth, sometimes singing softly in her deep voice, old songs and pop songs and nursery songs and TV jingles and songs she learnt at school. Twilight falls and the sky turns purple.

She starts to think about her green stick, how it used to rest by the gatepost waiting for her; she knows every knot and bend in it. "Green stick!" she calls softly, foolishly, smiling to herself, half expecting to see it rise up out of the shadows and walk towards her with spindly arms and legs like a thing in a story book. And then she gives a little start and opens her eyes wide, as if jerked from a light doze, and it's too dark to stay here, the mist is coming down, and she suddenly sees how small and scrubby and unremarkable a scrap of earth this is. She must go home. She sets off running but realises at once that home is not home and never has been, that there is no home anywhere. She is the Boll Weevil in the song she sang not long ago, looking for a home.

She stops and gazes into the dark mouth of the big hole at the edge of the pool where the water makes wonderful thunder, blanking the beat in her ears as it roars into the underworld. It becomes the sound of a million frantic, whispering voices. The orange street lamps all around the pool tremble uncertainly in a foggy haze, through which a bundle of light shimmers on the far side of the road. The pub. She crosses to it and stands outside, looking at it and thinking how strange, how strange the fog makes everything, pushes open a little door into the off-sales cubicle, where she sees a closed window and a bell and a Babycham poster. She rings the bell. A minute later the window opens and a yellow curtain billows out towards her followed by the enquiring thrust of a man's head, young and dark and savage-looking. It's so sudden and he looks so funny, like a tortoise sticking its head out from a shell, that she bursts out laughing. He frowns at her. "Yes?" he snaps. Fool of a giggling girl. It's very hard to remember what she wants, to speak, but she does, buys a big packet of peanuts and escapes, walks along laughing to herself and trying to breathe properly, her breath feels so funny, opens the bag and eats as she goes. The fog line marches on ahead.

Suddenly her ears pop and hiss. She swallows. Oh, dear God, dear God, dear God, she thinks, here it comes again, oh, my dear God, here it comes, here it comes. Strangeness falling like a season.

She starts to run but stops because she thinks she hears many voices in the distance, or close by but whispering, hidden by the sound of her footsteps and the beating that follows her feet, boom-boom, along the pavement, rising from the earth itself that lies beneath the cold stone. She stands still. It's like hearing voices in the wind when there is no wind. She walks again. Nothing. All quiet. Short of breath, heart racing. An ice-cream van comes out of the fog at the top of the road, its lights off, going home. She watches it as it trundles by, gets her breath, walks on.

The back door is open. The fridge vibrates. In the back room her parents will be sitting drinking tea and being bored with one another. She stands for a moment thinking: Yes, yes, I'm all right now, it's OK, it was nothing . . . Then she tiptoes upstairs wondering how she's lived this life for so long and how the break will be made, goes to bed and lies gazing at the ceiling with her hands behind her head. But after a while she becomes irritated by some quality in the dense, hypnotic, suburban silence pounding at the window like waves, coursing through the intricacies of her ears like babbling water. It becomes unbearable and she sits up, listening, perplexed.

She thinks someone's laughing somewhere.

She isn't sure, tries not to move or breathe, strains to hear. It's nothing. Or it's something very far away. She gets out of bed and stands at the window, pushes it open and leans out, breathing fog. Out there, on the remotest shore of hearing, somewhere in the flat grey-orange haze above the street lamps, someone laughs: silly, persistent, tireless, chugging on and on like a machine performing an endless chore.

She's cold. This is terrible, terrible, she tells herself, now I'm hearing laughter, and she stands and stands, listening to nothing at all.

It's worse than the slot-machine clowns at the seaside.

She closes the window and gets back into bed, closes her eyes and lies there scratching, turning, wriggling, anything to make noise so that she won't hear.

She does it again and again. Every night she makes up her face, creeps out of the house and walks about singing quietly to herself, whistling through her teeth and sometimes playing the ocarina when she's sure it won't give her away. In the early mornings the pool is surrounded by fog, a mystical, muffling halo of faintly moving vapours that fold her lovingly away from the rest of the world.

"Mrs Eccles saw you going down the street at four o'clock in the morning. She doesn't sleep. She says she's seen you twice now." It's Saturday, dinner's cooking. Gloria stands in the kitchen watching her mother's vague, incessant fingers scratch away at the skin of her arms, which is dry and yellow and much older than it should be. Her nails draw a multitude of fine wrinkles after them. "Drain that cabbage, could you," her mother says. "Keep the cabbage water."

"It's nice walking at night," says Gloria.

Her mother leans thoughtfully against the fridge. "I don't understand. What do you want to do it for? You're acting so peculiar lately. What is it? I keep thinking it's just a phase, but what is it, what is it, Gloria?"

"I like to walk at night," says Gloria. "I think."

"But what do you think it looks like? What am I supposed to say when someone comes up to me and says I saw your Gloria out last night at four o'clock? What am I supposed to say?"

"Oh, for God's sake, does it matter?" Gloria shakes food on to plates.

"Well, it matters to me," her mother says in a hurt voice, turning her back. After a short silence she says, low and distressed, "You've got me worried sick! Worried sick! You've got to come down to earth, girl. I mean it. I mean it." She clatters pans about, eyes downcast, frowning. "Think! You're seventeen. You're not a child any more. What about the future? Get your feet on the ground!"

Gloria sulks and carries the dinners into the back room. On the TV screen some astronauts are climbing out of a space capsule. An announcer stands holding a microphone as if it's a lollipop. "This is incredible," her father says, taking his plate without removing his eyes from the screen.

"Pete, will you have a quick word with her," her mother says awkwardly, coming in behind her. "Tell her she should stay in at nights."

"Of course she should," her father says absently.

Gloria stands in the middle of the room and begins to tremble.

Her eyes feel strange. Something like a trumpet blast explodes from the centre of her brain, and immediately after it a voice vibrates clearly inside her skull. *I hate you!* it says gleefully.

She stands terrified, shaking in the middle of the room.

"You're in my light," her mother says, sitting down with her dinner.

I hate you! the voice says again.

Gloria sways, then rocks round and round on the spot, holding on to her head with both hands.

"What's the matter?" cries her mother, afraid.

Her father jumps up and grips her shoulders and shakes her. "Gloria!" he yells into her face. "Gloria! Gloria!"

She thinks it's funny to see them both staring at her so. They look like outraged parrots. She starts to laugh, can't stop, goes on and on while their voices buzz at her like silly flies, till her father slaps her across the face. Her reaction is immediate and amazing and no one's ever taught her how to do it: she pulls out of his grip, steps back and lands a firm right hook on the end of his nose. Then she runs out of the house without waiting to see what she's done, giggles as she sprints down the road, passing Mrs Eccles at her gate without a glance, turning at the corner and looking back to see her mother and the old woman standing together watching her. Her mother lifts her hand and makes a tentative conciliatory gesture towards her. Everything's shaking, even her eyes.

Gloria runs away and hides in the shelter of the old factory, sitting very still with closed eyes against the big blank wall, as solid and reassuring as the Great Wall of China. Waiting for a voice. But nothing comes. Fear swoops about her head like birds. An hour passes.

She lifts her head in a dazed fashion and realises that nothing is solved. She rises and walks slowly back to the pool and sees her mother standing on the wooden bridge looking shabby in her old red coat, walks up to her and shrugs. For a moment they stand looking at each other, stony and wordless.

Her mother keeps sniffing, she's getting a cold and the tip of her nose is red and twitchy. "Gloria," she says solemnly, "you've made your father's nose bleed."

Gloria bursts out laughing, her old crude merry laugh, the first time she's made such a sound in ages.

"Stop it!" her mother hisses, looking around to see who's nearby. "Stop it!" She makes a funny, gauche movement as if she wants to slap Gloria's hand but changes her mind.

She's frightened of me, Gloria thinks. How stupid. She really is.

"I know where you've been," her mother says. "Don't bother lying as per usual. I know you've been hanging round that old factory again. Haven't you? You and Mary. I don't know, sometimes I think she's a bad influence on you. You follow her. If she wants to walk about in dangerous places that's her lookout; *you* don't have to. Use your sense. Some places you just shouldn't go. It's not safe for young girls."

"I'll walk where I like," says Gloria.

"Oh, don't be stupid!" Her mother paces to and fro, goes to the door then turns and tilts her head back airily. "Yes, I can just see it! She'll probably come to a bad end. She's just the type whose picture you see in the paper when it says things like girl strangled with pair of tights. She's got just that sort of face. They all sort of look like that, somehow."

Gloria springs from the bed and screams at her mother as loud as she can. "You stupid, stupid woman! You ignorant cow! You leave my friends alone, they're better than you! And him! And your horrible lives! Get out of my room! Get out! Get out!" She feels magnificent, as if her hair is on end, her eyes blazing, her veins throbbing. Her mother's face is startled and blank, beginning to register perplexity. "Get out!" screams Gloria, picking up the lamp that sits upon the bedside table and smashing it against the wall.

Her mother runs out on to the landing. "Pete!" she yells. "Pete!" But he's already coming up the stairs.

Gloria doesn't care. She's gone too far now, anyway, come what may, and it doesn't matter what she does. She stares down at the glittering fragments.

I will never be their creature again. Never. Gloria's changing, changing beyond recognition, thrusting in agony from her chrysalis skin. Metamorphosis.

She grabs the pair of long thin scissors that lie on the dressing table and runs about the upstairs of the house stabbing them into the walls repeatedly. She hears Mrs Eccles talking downstairs. Her father and mother call to her. Stab! for him, Stab! for her, Stab! for the nosy old cow. She stabs, stabs, here, there, stab on the bed, stab on the wardrobe, stab, stab on the chair, the door, the curtain. On the landing she stops, gasping for breath. They've gone, run away downstairs, run away from the mad girl. Unthinking, she starts down the stairs at a steady pace. They stand below, three faces looking up anxiously.

"Gloria . . ." her father says.

Half-way down, the voice speaks like a bell in her brain. *Down the wooden stairs*, it says sadly, making no sense. She drops the scissors and holds her head. "Go away," she says, "go away, go away."

The three faces just watch her. "There's a voice," she says, "in my head. I can hear it. Out there and in here. What is it? What is it?"

Her father starts up the stairs. She screams loudly, frightening everyone including herself, runs up to her room and locks herself in, then pushes and pushes and gets the dressing table across the door. Her father shouts, her mother coaxes, her father reasons.

It's all quite funny in a way. She smiles, sitting at her mirror in front of the barricaded door. I'm OK now. OK. They can all just go and jump. She yawns, stretches, painting her face like a canvas: snakes and vines and waves and stars till she can't see Gloria at all. She sings as she works.

Everything is quiet. There are hushed movements, hushed voices below. Her face is lush, vivid, not a face at all. Her eyes sparkle through it like jewels on a tapestry. She lies down on her back and laughs. Her father's on the phone.

Oh, what have I done? What have I done?

She pushes back the dressing table, unlocks the door and steps out. Gloria, unnoticed, smiling at how easy it is, glides downstairs and into the cold unused front room where the baby sleeps through it all, plucks Kit from her carry cot and walks out of the house and down the foggy road. Kit sleeps on.

I am taking the baby for a walk. And, after all, why not?

People passing look at her strangely and some little boys start to laugh. She walks on, talking to Kit. "They'll drive you up the wall," she says. "Honest. God knows how you'll end up." Poor thing! What did she do to deserve this? I should never have had her. Never. Better for her, better for me. What do I do with her

66

now? Leave her there? What will they tell her when she's old enough to ask? Your father, your father was . . . He died tragically. In a car crash. Or was it a motorcycle? A motorcycle's better. Oh, what a picture of him she'll have. How it will be part of her reality, a fantasy, a nothing, and so important. Gloria stands on the wooden bridge. Kit stirs, her face looks as if it's about to sneeze. When she wakes, she doesn't scream or cry but looks up calmly and glassily into Gloria's eyes.

"Once," says Gloria, sticking her finger in Kit's mouth, "a woman walked to her execution over this bridge."

Kit sucks, unblinking. Unnatural, the child's unnatural. She should be screaming for her bottle. What does she see? I wonder if she recognises me with all this paint on? I wonder what she thinks of me? I wonder if she knows I'm her mother? Looking up, Gloria sees a white swan glide across the long grey pool, glide and feed and glide and vanish into the fog line.

I'll walk on. I will walk into the fog line and vanish.

She hears the sound of car doors slamming nearby and looks towards it. A black car stands by the kerb. She sees her father and mother and, ridiculously, old Dr Ross, who stands looking uncertain, playing with his wattles. And there are people, vague in the fog, watching from the far side of the road. Her mother walks up to her, pale and drained, holding her arms out for the baby. Gloria just looks at her. Then her father's face appears, stiff and tense and laughably serious.

I've gone too far.

Her blood runs cold. Her father places a hand on her arm by the elbow and grips so hard she feels the blood checked. Her mother takes the baby.

"Come on, now," her father says, low and furtive. "Come on, now."

PART TWO

6

So I ended up here.

First there was the hospital, then the hostel, now I'm in this house. There's me and Tina and half a dozen others, and some cats.

I never *felt* mad, not in myself, only in the way I couldn't seem to live in the world very easily. They gave me all these drugs. The voices went away but my head felt funny. It was like wearing earplugs while someone battered on the doors and windows. Sometimes I used to hold my head very carefully because it felt as if a razor blade was stuck in the middle of my brain.

Dr Kite used to talk to me; sometimes he'd just sit and look at me as if he expected me to perform. I told him I was never going back. "Well," I'd say, and grin. "I did it, didn't I? Got away, didn't I?"

I told him my mother was mad. "How does this make you feel?" he asked. I didn't know what to say. They're always so deadpan, these doctors.

I wasn't lonely in hospital. I had Tina. She's a thin tiny cockney girl with a very still face and a fast voice, and she has this air of innocent confidence as if she doesn't give a damn about anything; like if you chuck something at her she doesn't duck, she just casually kind of raises one hand and plucks it out of the air as if she's expecting it: her expression doesn't even change. She's had ECT. When I asked her what it was like she just shrugged and said it gave her a headache.

I used to see her about the place, looking like a young boy with a small, pale, pointed face. Her voice was older than her face and it was a shock to hear it coming out of her mouth, as if a baby had suddenly spoken sense. Then they told me to go and clean the garden with her and I was nervous because she never smiled or spoke to me or anything, until it was time for a break and she said, "Let's get out of the sun, I hate the sun." We sat by the wall in the shade, sharing a cigarette that she'd rolled up out of dog-ends scavenged from the ashtrays in the common room.

"What are you in for?" she asked.

"I hit my dad on the nose and painted my face." I'd practised saying it.

She nodded. "Makes sense," she said.

Then I asked her about herself, and she told me this incredible story, which she swears is all true to this day.

First she lived with her mother. They lived, she said, here and there and all over the place, constantly moving on, always staying with people or looking after someone's house – she's vague about it. "So we're living with these people, yeah? My mum, she knew loads of people all over the show, my mum, she's a bit of a traveller, like; we was everywhere, we was down in Somerset, Kent – on the farms – over in Ireland, up in Scotland, up north, you name it. We was out in the country a lot of the time. And sometimes, like, I used to stay with some people we knew and she'd go off for a bit . . . So, anyway, where was I?" She seemed to forget what she'd been leading to, but then remembered with a little flicker of recognition but no emotion. "Oh, yeah. Of course. Well, my mum used to get these funny turns every once in a while. Used to get depressed and go a bit funny. Till one day a couple of years back she tries to strangle me, then goes out and ties a brick to each ankle and jumps in the Birmingham and Fazeley Canal and drowns."

"My God!" I said, horrified as much by the matter of fact tone as by the words. "Oh, my God!"

"Anyway," she went on, "so then I go up near Scarborough, see, up the Yorkshire coast, because I know these people up there from when I was with my mum, and I live with these people, and it's all right, I mean, I'm there for quite a long time and it's all right. There's loads of us, kids and all, and they have this big garden and people come and camp in it and there's always loads going on, we're all living in this big farm out of the town a bit, with all these fields out the back and then these great big cliffs going down to the beach. So when we're coming back from the pub we walk along the beach if there's a moon, and there's all these steps that go up the cliffs and we go up them and over the fields, and then over this little bridge to get to the house. Anyway . . . One night there's me and this girl coming back from the pub, Paula, her name was, she's just staying there for a bit, and me and her are coming back over the fields – I mean, these fields are *big*, really *big*, and we're right out in the middle of them, yeah? – and we meet the Grim Reaper."

"The Grim Reaper?"

"Yeah. You know. A skeleton on a horse with a scythe over his shoulder. You've seen him."

I didn't say anything.

"First of all we just hear him," she continued. "We hear this noise coming from a long way off over the fields and I says to her, 'What d'you think that is, then?' and she says, 'Yeah, I dunno, it sounds funny, don't it?' So we walk on, and it's just like a swishing noise, see, just like – swish, swish, swish, coming through the grass – the grass is very long, see – and it's coming along sort of parallel to us, keeping pace, and there's a moon so you can see everything, but we can't see anything, just this noise. So she says, 'Maybe it's some sort of animal,' and we stop and stand still and the noise stops too."

I went cold, watching the tips of the trees sway in the hospital grounds.

"And then when we start up, it starts up with us, like it's following us. So now we're scared but we just walk on and she says, 'Here, let's hang on to each other.' So we hold each other's arms and keep on and then suddenly it starts to head us off. And we nearly go mad, of course, and run like hell and when we get to the bridge it's got there before us and that's what it is – the Grim Reaper."

She stopped then and I coaxed her to go on.

"Well, that's it really," she said. "Nothing actually happened. I don't remember much about the horse. And him, well, he just looked like you see him on pictures – you know, with his arm up, like this, holding his scythe, only it's all just bone, and that's about all you can see, an arm and a leg because he's got some sort of clothes on, and his face – well, that was very clear, his face is horrible. He grins. Like this . . ."

She looked so funny and childish baring her big, crooked teeth, that I wanted to laugh. But she was dead serious.

"We flew," she said. "I don't remember how we got over the bridge or anything, I just remember me and her hammering like mad on the back door and them taking ages to let us in and not knowing if it was coming after us or not. And not liking to look.

And then, after all that, we get in and the silly bitch denies it all and says she hasn't seen a thing, says it was just me frightening her. Silly bitch." She went quiet, chewing the skin inside her mouth. "So," she said, "I went to bed after that because I kept thinking it meant I was going to die, and I didn't feel like I could get up any more. And in the end I came here."

We got really friendly after that, me and Tina. She talked a lot about the country, and she loved dogs and cats and was careful not to kill insects when we cleaned up in the garden. I thought she had a right to go barmy after the life she'd had; my own was so ordinary that there wasn't really much excuse for going off the rails. I felt like an imposter.

My mother came to see me. She'd been ill and Kit had had to go and stay with Auntie Norma because my father couldn't cope. She was much better now, she said, but I thought she looked dreadful, all thin and old and yellow, even the whites of her eyes were pale-yellow, and she kept scratching all the time in that light, awkward, irritating way.

"What is it?" I asked her.

"Oh, it's got some long name," she said with a dismissive little laugh. "You know me, I can't remember things. It's like a sort of a jaundice really. Dr Ross says I might just have to have a little operation. When I'm stronger."

Time ran under the bridge. I had cocoa and two biscuits every evening at the same time and I read a lot. I used to wonder what would become of me, look ahead in vain, seeing nothing. Mary wrote to me from London to say she was having a good time and the training was going well, and I dreamed of joining her but she was in a nurse's hostel so it didn't seem likely. Then Tina left. My God, I thought, will I be here for ever? What did I do that was so terrible? Maybe I should just go, just walk out, I'm not in prison, after all.

And then it was my turn. I didn't like the hostel. It had a great big staircase and a lounge with a TV, but there was no privacy. It was like being on a platform between destinations, waiting for your connection and reading books to pass the time. The social worker got me a job helping out in a vet's. I liked that. I liked writing out the little cards with the patients' names on: Sammy, Blackie, Tinker, Spot, Ginger. I took sandwiches every day and ate them in

74

the park. On Saturdays I went to see my parents, whose lives churned on as if nothing at all had happened, and sometimes I wheeled Kit out in her pram. I felt sorry for her. Living with my parents seemed such an awful fate to me.

Tina looked me up and said there was a room in this house, so I came here. I pay fifteen pounds a week. My room is half-way up the stairs near the pay phone and has two big windows overlooking the High Street. I can watch the buses and the people go by. I have flowers in a jug, a bamboo headboard for the bed and a nice red eiderdown with silky bits on. The house is noisy: I can play my ocarina and no one cares. I stopped taking the pills even though they said I shouldn't. I go out a lot. I'm OK. I see myself in shop windows and like the way I walk, head held high, swaggering slightly. Sometimes I just stop whatever I'm doing and think: My God, everything's OK and I'm going to be all right after all. Hallelujah.

I was eighteen yesterday.

I go to the ice rink on Friday nights with Maureen out of the house. She's no great shakes; she'd rather fool around and fall over than actually skate. So I don't really care that she's full of a cold and can't come tonight. Still, no one else is interested.

I sit around for a while watching rubbish on the TV before plucking up the nerve to go alone. I feel lonely and odd going in, getting my ticket, tying on my boots in the changing room with its dim yellow light. But I stand and shake my hair over my shoulders, brace myself, think: Who cares? and shrug and walk carefully out to the ice, stand holding the bar for a couple of minutes and watching the people glide and stagger and collide and fall and giggle in the glare. Pop music plays. Faces watch through the glass from the bar above.

I take off, skim across the ice with long, slow, regular movements, ignoring everyone, joining the stream of good skaters who circle the rink smoothly. Round and round I go, the blades making fine white powder. I start to feel that old soaring feeling – I love this, I love it – I forget everything else – on and on and on we go, together and apart; voices mingle, shriek, get lost in the music, and on and on we still go . . . I don't care that I'm alone, I could go on for ever.

At nine o'clock they clear the ice. People in fancy costumes and snow-white boots come on and dance. I go upstairs and buy a Coke and watch the dancers through the glass, leaning back and sipping through a straw.

Later I go back on the ice. A boy with a weird medieval face, hollow cheeks, tight jaw, catches my eye, skating alone like me, effortless, casual, arms by his sides as if he's just going for a walk. He wears an old black jacket and pale-blue jeans and looks young, slightly female, with a long graceful neck and straight brown hair that falls in his eyes. He looks miles away.

I don't really care about the rules any more. I move closer, skate in his sphere, not too close, not too obvious, just for the pleasure of having him in my sight. I feel graceful; so is he: round and round we go alongside each other like two swans. I don't look at him any more but he's always near, and it begins to seem that he knows I'm here and has somehow acknowledged me without words or looks. The music stops. I skate to the side and he does too. When I glance at him he stares at me wide-eyed and smiles a quick nervous smile that fades immediately, leaving him serious and awkward as he looks away. Oh, yes, I think. *This* one. I never yet saw one worthy of me, but this one makes me wonder. I sit down and fiddle with my boot.

"Which bus stop are you going to?" his voice says, soft but not shy.

I sense him standing on the step looking down at the top of my head, but I don't look up immediately. When I do, I notice things, his narrow nose and small mouth, a sensitive dent between the eyes. "The cathedral," I say.

"Is it OK if I walk down with you?" he asks, and I nod. "I'll see you out front," he says and clomps away on his blades, clumsy on solid ground.

In the clatter and chatter of the changing room I change into my shoes, get my coat on and look at myself in the mirror. I am not excited. It is not like going out there to meet a stranger: I don't wonder what I will say or how I should act; it will be all right whatever I do, I know it. I've suddenly clicked on course. I look jaundiced in the dingy light, like my mother, but then so does everybody else in here. The corners of my mouth twitch upwards. He's safe. I know it.

76

It's bitter cold outside and the pavement is crowded. I don't see him. I stand checking my bag and my purse, settling my scarf comfortably, looking at the posters peeling off the wall, and then he appears and we set off walking together without a word. The tips of his ears are red with cold and his shoulders hunch up as he puts his hands in his pockets. Our eyes are level, we match pace for pace. In the shadow of the cathedral we start to talk. His eyes are lazy and bright by turns. He's like his voice, quiet but not shy. He says his name is David and he's doing A levels, English, history, maths and geography. Geoggers, he calls it. He was seventeen yesterday. My God, my God, an omen. What else? Something in me quickens.

"It was *my* birthday yesterday," I say, "I was eighteen." We join hands and smile as we walk along, and it all seems really funny.

He looks sideways at me and we laugh. "Fated," he says softly, "obviously fated."

We walk fast through the freezing air to the bus stop. The pavement throngs with people. His palm moves against mine, the only warm thing in the world, and I can't help smiling. I tell him I work in a vet's and have a daughter who lives with my parents. Might as well get that one over with. He never bats an eyelid. My bus stands shivering in its bay.

"Can I see you?" he says. "Sometime this weekend?"

I stand on the platform looking down on him. "Yes," I say. He's not clear any more, the lights are getting in the way.

"When?"

"Sunday afternoon. Here. Two o'clock."

He smiles. The bus begins to move and he steps back and waves. I run upstairs and sit at the front and watch him walk away down the long, bright road full of cars and noise and people. He lopes easily along, straight-backed. When the bus passes him I look back and see that he's still smiling to himself, and I smile too, settling into my seat and looking at my face in the dark window.

It's funny how a face can change in your mind. I think I have it, but when I meet him on Sunday I see that I've remembered him all wrong. He's leaning on the rail with his hands in his pockets and his ankles crossed, and in the full light of day his face is harder, more hawkish, almost stylised, but his hair is softer and fluffier and this tones him down. He's probably just washed it. He straightens,

77

smiling, as I approach, and we stand together wondering what to say. I like his nervousness.

"What can you do on a Sunday afternoon?" he says. "Go for a walk? Would you like to do that?"

"There's the Sunday market," I say. "Let's go there." So we walk through the big gates into the cathedral gardens and wander through the maze of paths between dormant flower beds and benches full of old tramps and courting couples, out the other side and down a long dusty hill to an old, cobbled part of town where dim, exciting shops stay open all hours and old wooden barrows line the gutters. Here you can buy second-hand books, records, clothes, everything from telescopes to globes of the world. Old men with runny noses and mufflers stand guard.

The pavement outside the Gents' toilets is full of boxes of rabbits for sale; you see their round eyes and twitching noses as they press against each other in their prisons. "I hate that," I say. "I hate to see anything in a cage."

David smiles and puts his arm round me and we walk along in time-honoured fashion like two young lovers, very close. I feel his bony ribs. We stop at a stall full of old leather-bound volumes, turn our heads this way and that to read the spines. *Coral Island. The Ballad and the Source. A Tale of Two Cities.* He picks out a faded red book and smells it as if it were a bouquet. "When I'm rich," he says, "I'm going to have a library full of old books. Doesn't matter what they are. I'll get job lots. I won't read them. I'll just go in every now and then and smell them."

I laugh. "Oh, so you're going to be rich, are you?" I say.

"Of course," he replies with an arrogant movement of his shoulders. "I hate money. I'll have it so I don't have to think about it. When you don't have it you have to think about getting it all the time. Gets you by the balls." He shakes his head. "Not for me, all that. I'm just going to have it and then forget it. Give it away, that's what it's best for."

"And where are they coming from," I ask, "all these riches?"

He laughs. I notice what neat little ears he has. "Details, details," he says. "No, seriously, I have plans."

We go into a small brown shop full of old musical instruments and cardboard boxes filled with old 78s in ragged brown sleeves. David picks up a battered mandolin and plays it haltingly, pulling a face.

"Can you play?" I ask.

"God, no!" he says.

His fingers are long and slim, with three rings on his right hand – a big gold square, a thin silver band, a snake with its tail in its mouth. Like my lucky fish. This too is an omen. His hands are graceful, moving on the strings.

"I had something like that once," I say. "Not a ring. It was a little charm. A fish."

He smiles, saying nothing.

"I lost it," I say.

He nods, still smiling.

Suddenly I feel very sad. I walk outside and stand watching the big white clouds shift high above the tall buildings and the spire of the cathedral. After a moment he follows me out and takes my hand and we walk on down the hill to where the shops and stalls and people end and traffic hurtles by from one grey destination to another. It's so noisy we can't even talk, so we turn back and walk slowly up the other side of the hill, on past the market till we reach the cathedral once more. We sit down in the gardens on a bench out of the shade of the spire. Traffic hums distantly and fat pigeons strut on the flagstones and ancient graves.

He asks me about my daughter and I tell him the story of the boy who died so tragically, so young, riding his motorbike down the motorway on his way to see me. He's nearly real now, like Michael used to be real. Oh, what a good tale, no wonder they write so many songs about him. Every time I hear "Leader of the Pack" I feel sick. I watch the sheen on a pigeon's neck, purple and green. An old tramp hawks phlegm. David watches me. I tell him Kit lives with my parents because I can't take care of her. "I'm not very stable, you see," I say.

His interest grows, he leans towards me, never taking his eyes from my face as I grow reckless and tell everything: the voices, painting my face, punching my father, the hospital, everything. When I finish we just sit for a while. Then he moves towards me along the bench, opens his jacket as if he's lifting a wing and folds me away under it so that my head rests just under his chin. He smells clean and sweet. We put our arms right round each other and don't move for a long time.

After a while the gardens fill up with people and we feel awkward and move apart, glancing nervously at one another. I wonder why we haven't kissed and if there's something maybe I should do.

He takes my hand again. "Gloria," he says, "G-L-O-R-I-A."

I smile.

"I used to come in here," he says, "when I was a kid." His eyes stare straight ahead, deep-socketed, beautiful. His throat is nervous. "I used to feed the pigeons with my mum. Now, say what you will, pigeons are really brutal creatures. Nothing they enjoy more than putting the boot in where food's involved. Every pigeon for himself." He swallows, looks up at the sky. "Aeroplane," he says. I look up. "Nice to be up there, flying away somewhere nice. When I'm rich . . ." He stops with a sudden nervous laugh. I squeeze his hand, very gently, and he squeezes back. Now we don't know what to say again. It's very cold.

"Where do you live?" I ask him. "You've told me nothing at all about yourself."

He laughs. "Nothing much to tell," he says. "I can give you the whole story in a few words. Semi-detached house, suburb, one father, one brother, one sister, one cat, one dog. Mother deceased. That's about it."

I think how gentle his voice is. I stand, pulling him with me by the hand, and we walk, not talking. He pulls my hand into the pocket of his old black jacket. We find an open café, go in and sit down at a table by the window. The place is warm and gaudy, crowded with down-at-heel people sheltering from the cold. David goes up to the counter and buys two coffees and I watch the back of him as he stands there, and feel glad, foolishly so, as if everything that went before must somehow be all right because it was leading to this.

A small, black-haired boy of twelve or so gazes at me across the flap of the counter and I smile at him. David returns with the coffees, slopping some in the saucers. It tastes strong and good and we smile as we drink. He tells me that I mustn't laugh, this is serious, he writes poetry, honest, don't laugh. That's what he's going to do. Be a poet. "I'll show you some sometime, if you like," he says. "Only you have to be careful who you tell because some people – most people – think it's all just stupid and soppy. A poet! Ugh! There's hardly anyone I can talk to about it. I write stuff and have to hide it away. They all think it's ridiculous at home. My family, now, I don't know what you'd think of them. I don't like them; I know that sounds extreme but it's true, and I'm speaking quite objectively now. Sometimes I wonder what I'm doing there. I can't wait to be off. I'm going to university. They don't even think that's kosher, think it's all a bit uppity. They're completely unimpressed by everything I do. I'm the whizz kid at school. At home they just think I read too many books. I got ten O levels, did some early; I'm not boasting or anything, just telling you. What do I get from them? Not so much as a Well done. It's not that I expect people to fall down and bow and scrape but you'd think . . . oh, well, there you go . . ." He trails off, suddenly embarrassed.

We talk about books and poetry, get more coffee and hold hands across the table. An old man with cataracts and fingerless gloves clutches a steaming mug, nodding his head spasmodically and chuckling to himself. At a table near the door a sullen young girl with hollow eyes slouches alone, all dressed in yellow, bare legs purplish with cold. It grows dark outside.

"That little Italian kid keeps looking at you," David says.

I glance over at the counter. I see the dark boy look away.

"He fancies you," David says.

"No, he doesn't."

"He does. Because you're so gorgeous. You are. Really. You're beautiful."

I laugh stupidly, looking at all the distortions in the green fluted window.

It's time to go. He walks to the bus stop with me. In some strange perverse way I want to be home, out of his company, so that I can be alone and lie on my bed with my hands behind my head and gaze at the ceiling, savouring every moment of this extraordinary day. I want to imagine him in his boring suburban home thinking about me.

We kiss at the bus stop. He tastes sweet and his tongue is gentle.

"I like you," he says. "I do. I really, really like you."

7

And now it's all different. Of course, things are never what they appear to be.

He was very simple then, nervous and fresh like a highly-strung young horse. What is different now? He looks the same, his hair's not so short, that's all, but he's no longer nervous. He knows me so much better now.

We've been friends a little more than eighteen months. We've never made love; I tell him I don't feel ready and he never says But my God, you're nineteen, what's the matter with you? He kisses my fingertips, doesn't pry, says what we have is beyond the mere cravings of the flesh. I have a poem he wrote about it; it's terribly obscure. And, in fact, my flesh doesn't crave him at all, though it's nice to lie naked together in my bed and kiss and cuddle and get warm. He's bony and smooth and gentle and we fit together perfectly. We are very innocent, I suppose. Adam and Eve before the fall.

He's going away tomorrow. There's a little sick thrill in my chest. To see him no more apart from the occasional visit, letters, what have you. Oh, well. They get long holidays. Of course, he got his A levels, four grade A's, wouldn't you just know it? The university wanted him so much he'd already had an unconditional offer. He's a brainy sod. He's excited, longs to get away from here, break with the past, his family, boredom; but then he'll turn his face into my neck and say he doesn't want to leave me. "Come with me, why don't you, why don't you, Glory?"

Why don't I?

This is a mystery. I've turned it over and over all day, all week, months now. All I know is I get a sense of unease whenever I think about going with him for good. And yet he's so nice, so nice.

I've walked round and round my room all afternoon. He'll be here soon; we'll have – two, three hours? And then he'll go home ready for an early start tomorrow. After that – what will I do with weekends? Who to walk and talk with? Awful how you come to depend on one friend.

I pick up a writing book and a pen, lie across the bed and make two columns: FOR and AGAINST. In the FOR column I put all the things I'll miss. In the AGAINST column I put the things about him that get on my nerves and give me uneasy twinges when I think of going away with him. It reads like this:

FOR
1. He is lovely to look at.
Girls and women look at him wherever we go. They always look first at him, then at me, then back at him. He moves well. I think of him sitting in the kitchen eating cold macaroni cheese, gracefully dipping his long fingers in and out of the bowl.
2. He doesn't think I'm a fool when I say I think I may be psychic.
He's open-minded. We've tried to send messages to each other from a distance, but it never works.
3. He's read as much as me.
More. We spend hours in bookshops, separate, silent, heads stuck in books, but always together. We swap them around, talk about them, argue.
4. The way we just walk in all kinds of weather.
Arms around each other, talking and talking.
5. Sitting in our café.
Surrounded by dossers and drop-outs, looking at the patterns change in the glass, drinking coffee. They know us there now. The man calls him Tiger. If I go in alone he says, "Where's your Tiger?"
6. Holding hands in the pictures.
7. Meeting him from school.
This is over now, anyway. I wait on a bench in the little park in front of his school, and the boys in his class come and catch sly glances at me through the window. He says they think I'm really something.
8. His poetry.
I like the way he writes it, not agonising or theorising or trying

to make out it's something special. It's just something he does. He leaves poems in my room, and sometimes I get one in the post.

AGAINST
1. He's unreliable.
He hardly ever turns up on time and hates being pinned down. It's always just, "Oh, yeah, well, I'll see you," and then you never know whether to make your plans round him or not. Sometimes you've made plans to do something else and he turns up out of the blue and expects you to drop everything else. I almost think he makes a point of it.
2. He doesn't like animals.
It isn't that he's actually cruel to them, he just finds them irrelevant. The cats like him. They gather at his chair and try to get on his knee, but he brushes them aside disdainfully, scowling a little.
3. A certain arrogance in his manner.
I never noticed it at first, but now I think it gets worse as time goes by. However, this is also quite attractive in a funny kind of way.
4. Rampant hypochondria.
He's always listening to his heart or his breathing or thinking he's got meningitis or that thing beginning with strep, when really it's just a headache or a sore throat. He's convinced he'll die young.
5. He's always borrowing money off me.
Of course, I shouldn't really mind about this because I've got more than him. He gives it back but I usually have to ask for it first.
6. He won't give money to beggars.
He tells me I'm a pushover if I do. Once this poor old woman came up to us crying and holding out her hand and saying she was awful cold, and he just kind of made this banishing movement with his hand and walked on.
7. His poetry.
I can't make head or tail of it, and I'm not thick. I suppose it's very good, very clever, it sounds as if it should be. Anyway, it flows. I don't like to tell him I don't like it. It's getting hard to know what to say about it.

Eight for, seven against. Close.

And then there's Kit. She shouldn't make any difference to anything at all; she never was mine and I never wanted her. But some little part of me feels mean about running off and depriving her of those Saturday visits. She looks forward to them now. Sometimes I wish I'd never started. She's gone all soppy about me and calls me Mummy; waits at the gate when the weather's nice and they'll let her, holding the bars and watching me walk down the road. A poor thing in a cage.

I quite like her now, I suppose. She's two and a half. She's just a tough, round-faced, brown-haired little kid who runs about like a mechanical toy, pulls faces behind people's backs, talks to herself in gibberish and cries easily. When I take her out she yodels and yells and gives cheek, careers about the mushroom field screaming like a maniac with her mouth all clown-white from ice-cream, holding the cone aloft like an Olympic torch-bearer. She gets filthy. I let her. She brings me little fat handfuls of buttercups and clover and I stick a flower under her chin to see if she likes butter.

Sometimes she comes up and leans against me, takes my face between her stumpy hands, all dirty and stained with felt tip, and she looks me in the eyes as if she doesn't know what to make of me, her face all curious, half frowning, half smiling. I don't know what she sees. I see a plain child, nothing of me there, nothing of anybody else either, thank God.

She has spirit. I don't like how they laugh it away. I don't like how they make her look. Her hair's twenty years out of date. They put her in a pink tartan skirt and yellow cardy. I feel like we're two kids together in that house.

I bought her a red ribbon, silk, bright as poppies, two inches thick. She loves it. Treats it like a priceless jewel.

I hear David ring the bell, so I run down and open the door and see him standing there in the pouring rain, his collar up and his hair flattened to his skull. He comes in and dries his hair in the kitchen. Then we go up to my room and lie down on the bed, side by side, heads together. The house is quiet, they are all out. We talk of times we've had, laugh about some things, grow thoughtful, turn and hold each other. The rain thrums on the window. He has a particular smell that's just him, like a fingerprint, a clean, warm,

85

woody, tangy smell. I realise how familiar it has become, breathe it in and feel some little flutter start up, some instability in the chest, as if it's some kind of drug I'm sniffing. I think this must be what animals feel like when they pick up a scent.

Suddenly he breaks the silence. "I get this feeling sometimes," he says, drawing back his head to look at me, his eyes bright and staring, "like – like there's something fundamental about this thing between us, it isn't ordinary, like – like . . ." He stops with one hand clenched nervously in his hair, breathing loudly through his nostrils and staring glassily away into the distance. Then he says, "You're the one who'll be there when I'm on my death bed."

I can do without this intense expression of his. I hit him lightly on the head and tell him not to be so silly. "You're just neurotic," I say.

He grins and digs his fingers in my ribs. "All the best people are," he says. We hug and giggle and roll around, lick inside each other's ears, bring our open mouths together and dabble with our tongues, then get right under the red candlewick bedspread, pull it up over our heads and tuck ourselves in, pressed close, gleefully cosy against the dark rainy night. The light comes rosy through the thin coverlet; we see each other clearly. It's like being in a tent. "I feel as if I've always known you," he says. "I know you much better than I know my own sister and I've lived with her all my life. But that's different, I suppose."

"I had a brother once," I say, realising that I've never told him.

His face goes serious. "What brother? You never told me you had a brother." He sounds slightly jealous.

"Well, he doesn't really count," I say, "he died at birth. A twin. He came after me. They called him Michael." I see a fat cherub floating over pretty Jesus's head. Me kicking his dying face as I scramble eagerly out of the womb. Did he try to clutch my ankle, desperate for a lift? I frown. "He was very real, though, when I was little."

David is silent, biting his finger. Gradually a small smile dawns on his face. "God," he says in a wondering tone, "God. How funny." I hear him breathing close to my ear. "It's strange," he says, twisting his hair round his finger. "Yeah. Strange. God! It really is!"

"What?"

"Don't you see it? Don't you see it?" In the tent his eyes and teeth glitter, excited. "Didn't you feel it? Haven't I always said it was like there was some kind of recognition between us? Well? He died a year to the day before I was born. Me and you, the same birthdays – it makes sense. Don't you see?"

I laugh. "Why don't you go and knock on my mum and dad's door," I say, "and announce yourself as their long-lost son. I'd love to see their faces."

"You may scoff," he says, "but there's no such thing as coincidence."

"How original," I say.

"Huh," he says, "I thought *you* could have taken it seriously. You're the one that's supposed to be psychic."

"What's that got to do with it?"

He turns, smiling, and puts his arms around me. "My sister," he says. "My sister, my spouse."

Then we stay quiet and still for a long time, realising that tomorrow everything changes. I feel very sleepy. Tomorrow, I think, will be full of the knowledge that he's gone. I must do something with the day. Go somewhere. Suddenly, I think I'll go to the coast, catch a train to that place I remember where I walked on the cliffs, where the salt marsh had such a tang. I can be there in an hour or so. I'll take Kit. The rain pours down. The idea is ridiculous: a day off work, the weather awful, and God knows where the notion of taking Kit sprang from. But somehow I know I'm going to do it.

"Let's play a game," David says.

"What?"

"Let's play we're in a womb."

"Oh, don't be stupid!" I fling back the stifling cover, sit up and blink, looking round as if surprised the room is still there. "Have I been asleep?" I ask, disoriented.

He sits up too. "My God, look at the time!" he says. "Oh, no."

It is ten o'clock, just turned.

We look at one another, our hair awry, our clothes rumpled.

"I have to go in a minute," he says. "I have to get up at six in the morning."

I hate goodbyes. I want to be distant, uninvolved.

"Oh, shit," he says. "I'm really nervous."

"Oh, you'll be all right."

He groans, then gets up and jitters about the room for a while. "Now I wish I wasn't going," he says. I go to him and put my arms round him and tell him everything's going to be fine. "Write to me," he says. We kiss, stand awkwardly, oddly, as if we're watching two other people we don't know very well saying goodbye.

We go downstairs and open the front door. The rain pours down.

"Cold," he says.

"Freezing," I say.

We kiss briefly, brother and sister.

Then he goes off in the rain and I close the door and shiver in the hall. I make myself a mug of drinking chocolate and go to bed and sit up sipping it, hands curled around the mug, listening to the rain, feeling empty. I hear people come in and make noise below, run humming up to the bathroom, turn on the TV, make late-night snacks in the kitchen. I write a long letter to Mary in London. I play my ocarina under the bedclothes. At one o'clock the house is quiet. At two the rain stops. I open the door and let some cats in for company, fall asleep to the sound of their purring.

I'm out of the house and walking through the crisp cold air before six and by seven I'm letting myself in the back door of my parents' house with my old key. The first thing I see is my mother sitting at the kitchen table, a glass of flat, cloudy liquid in front of her. She looks awful. Her face is falling in upon itself, the skin round her eyes and mouth and neck sagging down as if dragged by gravity. She wears an old pink dressing gown that somehow looks grey, with old pink slippers and thick white socks on her feet.

"What are you doing here at this time?" she asks wearily.

"What's that?" I point to the liquid.

"My tablets," she says.

"Where's Kit? Not up yet?"

"She's never up this early. She sleeps late."

The house is grey too. No wonder she isn't up and running around like any normal two year old. Dreams are far more fun than this house.

"She's too much for you," I say. "You look a wreck."

My mother's face makes a tired attempt at a grimace. "Don't start," she says. "Just don't."

"Well, anyway," I say brightly, "you can have a rest today. I'm taking her out for the day."

She sighs and sags and twists her mouth, as if it's all an incredible nuisance. "Oh, Gloria! I wish you'd take the trouble to let people know these things. What do you mean, taking her out? Where? She's not prepared."

"She doesn't need preparing. For God's sake, I'm not taking her on a world cruise, it's only a piddling little day out."

"Well, where? It's not a very nice day."

"It's fine," I say. "Going to be sunny all day; I heard the weather forecast. I'll wrap her up well."

I leave my mother sitting there looking worried, go upstairs, past my parents' bedroom where my father snores softly, into my old room. Kit's asleep in my bed, both arms flung up over her head as if she's surrendering. Her hands are broad and pink and stubby, her hair fine and fluffy and hopelessly tangled. She has wide flushed cheeks and a bright-red mouth, a yellow collar that looks too tight. She's so vulnerable. There are fine blue veins on her eyelids.

"Kit," I say, "wake up, Kit."

She sleeps on.

"Kit!" Her lashes flicker, the white beneath them rolls into view and vanishes again, slick and shiny like the underbelly of some creature. Then she opens her eyes fully and looks blankly at me, still asleep, dull and disconcertingly old. I feel afraid.

Oh, God, I don't know what to do with her, what am I doing? How did I ever get into this? She isn't mine, nothing to do with me, nothing at all . . . Oh, my God, she's real. She is.

I feel so terribly sorry for her, doomed to be a second me, in this bed, this room, this house. I have to give her a day out.

She sits up, making sticky noises with her throat. "Is it Saturday?" she whispers.

"No," I say. "We're going for a little trip. A day out. Would you like that?"

"It's very cold, Gloria," my mother whispers in the doorway. "Where are you going, anyway?"

I tell her.

89

"Don't be daft! It'll be bitter there. The wind in off the sea . . ."

Kit is scrambling from the bed all eager. I rummage in her clothes drawer. "It'll be all right," I say. "Look . . ." I gesture towards the sun coming brightly in through the curtains. "I told you. It's going to be a lovely day. Honest. I used to like it there. I haven't been there for years."

My mother stands with folded arms and anxious face. "I do wish you'd let me know," she says. "I'd have got her some sandwiches."

"We'll have something out."

"Oh, don't let her wear that! That horrible old thing. Oh, let me see to her." She falls to one knee and fusses. When Kit is dressed in three layers of clothing, I take her hand to lead her out on to the landing. "Her hair!" my mother says.

"Oh, it's all right," I say, straightening it quickly with my hands.

"It is not!" She makes Kit sit on the bed while she pulls and tugs at the impossible tangles. Kit smiles at me and I smile back. Yes, we tell each other wordlessly, she does fuss, doesn't she?

"I want my ribbon," Kit says.

"Where is it?" I ask.

"Here." She plucks it from some hidy-hole at the end of the bed.

"Keep still!" my mother says. The red ribbon shines in Kit's hands. She had it there to hand, just the way I used to have my lucky fish. I watch my mother tie the ribbon into her hair and let her go.

"Where we going?" Kit asks. She's learnt to whisper, we are all whispering.

"To the seaside," I say.

"A-a-aw! The seaside!" she whispers.

We go downstairs and I ring work to tell them I'm sick while Kit has her breakfast.

Then it's time to go and we set off down the road, pass Mrs Eccles at her window, turn to wave to my mother's lonely figure standing at the gate. I think I see her wipe a tear from her face but I can't be sure. Once we're round the corner, we look at each other and laugh conspiratorially. We walk on briskly as the sun begins to warm the pavements, catch a bus and then a train. Kit sits staring out of the window, fascinated, clenching her fists and bouncing a little with excitement. She carries a toy rabbit by the nose, never

taking any notice of it, as if it was a bag or something she just had to
carry around. And, when we reach the place, off-season and dingy
as it all is, the sight of seagulls, candystriped railings, closed
shellfish stalls, a silent fairground with its bright colours glowing
under wraps, all these things render her open-mouthed and
awestruck as if I've brought her to a land of minarets and flying
carpets.

We walk along the prom, look in all the shops, buy rock and a
funny hat and a postcard of a donkey, eat in a café then go walking
along the flat, empty beach, damp and patterned with worm casts
and the footprints of birds. Kit screams and whoops at the vast
expanse, running out into it and scattering a cluster of seagulls that
sit breast-deep in the sand watching the horizon. Some old men are
putting out to sea in a rowing boat from a distant jetty. Everything
is atonal, hugely silent, with a hissing on the edge of consciousness
– listless waves breaking on the rocks that frame the bay.

It's a long way to the water's edge but we walk there and follow
the dark line that the waves leave, rolling in and rolling out. We go
on and on till we reach the track that winds its way to the top of the
cliff, climb up it and carry on along the cliff-walk above the salt
marsh. And now it is so strange, so familiar, how I walked here so
long ago with my father. Nothing has changed. A breeze shakes the
stiff grasses. We walk on, much, much farther than I ever went
before. She is tireless, demands songs, and we sing all this corny old
stuff that she likes. She knows all the words to "Old Shep".

In late afternoon we sit down and eat some chocolate and watch the
shining line of the sea. Clouds gather over it. We find a track that
winds towards the plain, make our way down and wander across the
soggy flats of salt marsh back in the direction of the bay, skirting
pools of slimy yellow vegetation. The smell here is sharp and rank
and tangy and gets in your mouth like a taste. Strange birds with
long beaks stalk the marsh, crying out with harsh, weeping voices.
"What's that?" Kit asks.

"Er – curlews," I say uncertainly.

We walk and walk, hand in hand, towards a great outcrop of
many-coloured rock that marks the boundary of the bay. The sea
twinkles. From time to time we find our way blocked by a long arm
of slimy water, too wide to jump, reflecting the sky between

floating mats of weed. We have to keep backtracking. The rock is far and near, far and near.

I stop, look around. Suddenly I'm unsure. What looks like passable ground has turned out too many times to be booby-trapped, wobbling like jelly as soon as you set foot on it. I look back and look forward, but it's all an invisible maze whatever I do; so we just carry on, advancing and retreating, taking detours, squelching through streams that appear as if by magic in front of our feet. We are forced further out towards the sea to avoid a small lake that I could swear was not there when we set off. I shiver as the breeze grows sharper, more playful, pushing bossily at our backs. I think I'll have to put her on my shoulders at this rate, get my legs wet before I'm out of this.

"Mummy," she says, stopping and pulling on my hand, "do my ribbon."

I stand silent for a moment, looking at the great rock turn pink in the early evening light. A thin silver line joins it to the horizon. It's true. The tide's coming in. Too fast.

"Do my ribbon!"

"OK, OK!"

I squat down and yank Kit's red ribbon from where it dangles loosely from her spilled hair. "Keep your head still," I tell her.

"My ribbon, Mummy," she says.

We can't get round the rock. We have to go back. We have to go back. I'm tired. Or maybe we can find a way up and over the rock. I could do it on my own but not with her. The ribbon knots, my fingers pick at it. It sticks, the damn stupid fucking thing; I can't get a hold, can't get a hold at all. A curlew, or whatever the hell it is, cries plaintively. I look up. The sea comes in like a great shining armchair, to the right and to the left of us.

"We have to go back," I say to Kit.

"My ribbon!" she cries, shaking her rabbit by its nose.

I swear and tie the damn thing all rough and knotted into her hair, any old way. Someone'll have hell getting it out again. Oh, God, I think, here we're going to drown and she's worried about a stupid ribbon. Standing, I see a clear path back towards the foot of the cliff where the track we came down emerges amongst pools and scattered rocks. I crouch down again. "We have to hurry," I say. "Get on my back." She scrambles on board gleefully, giggling with

92

delight. I stagger to my feet, amazed at the weight of her, and set off as fast as I can go. She weighs a ton. "Oh, you lump," I say, and she laughs and clasps her hands over my forehead. My feet go squelch; my shoes leak water at every step. I trudge bravely, eyes fixed firmly on my destination, skirting pools of winking water, hoisting Kit's weight, singing "Old Shep" to keep her amused and take my mind off things. It's OK. We're getting there . . .

After a time I look back. The silver arms have widened and thickened and developed rippling edges of foam that suck the land. I keep on and on. "Sing 'Old Shep' again," she says; so I do, enjoying every minute of it. She sings along tunelessly with me. My eyes are very tired, everything is sparkly. It takes a while for me to realise why everything is changing colour. When I do, I stand still, calm for a moment, accepting the fact, very simple, that I am on a marsh island in a world devoid of people, cut off from the foot of the cliff, from the great rock, from everything but a few pools of yellowish vomit-like stuff.

My first thought is: This is getting silly.

I prod some of the yellow stuff with my toe and it shivers and shifts as if alive. Bits flake off at the edges and float out into the dark water. How horrible. I don't want to go down choking in *that*. My feet are freezing. I circle about slowly as if inspecting the terrain for a secret passage back to the shore. I laugh quietly. This is ridiculous, really ridiculous. Kit, from her elevation, must be able to see the situation, but she sits there in perfect calm and confidence, waiting for the grown-up to sort it all out as grown-ups do. But I'm not a grown-up, I'm just me.

I could have got out of this if it wasn't for her.

"Get down now," I say. "You're too heavy."

She gets down and holds my hand. "Home now?" she says.

God, I think. My mum'll be upset.

We walk about for a while, pretty aimlessly. I don't know what to do. I've got three squares of chocolate left in my pocket so I get them out, eat one and give her two. "Go home now," she says.

And then I get this feeling in my belly, not quite fear, more like anger: It's not fair! It's not fair! This is just too much, too ridiculous; it isn't happening – it isn't, it isn't, it isn't! And I feel like throwing myself down on the cold wet ground and drumming my heels and beating with my fists and screaming at God: Come on, now, God, what are you playing at? You know you can't do this, you just can't get away with this. This is *me, me,* not just anyone, for Christ's sake – do something, do something, do something *at once*!

And God does.

God sends a rowing boat, appearing like a miraculous black two-humped creature on the silvery expanse. I jump up and down and wave and shout. Kit does, too, giggling and cackling. "I can shout louder than you!" she crows, and does, and screams and yodels and whoops like a Red Indian.

The boat comes nearer. I take her hand and we walk to meet it, sinking beneath our ankles in the mire. The black humps shift about and turn into two old men, who hail me angrily and call me a fool.

The boat is tiny and wobbles about as I hand Kit in. Then I climb in and sit there shivering and we push off and speed thrillingly out into the waves. The prow goes rising and falling like the beak of an animal. The bottom of the boat is covered with dead fish, and one or two not quite dead that flop lethargically now and then, hopeless. Kit is struck dumb. It's the first time she's been in a boat. She hugs her rabbit and looks open-mouthed at the sea and sky, the ribbon blowing out at the back of her head. Then she looks at the dead and dying fish for a long time.

After they've scolded, the old men become jovial and speak volubly, winking kindly at Kit and telling me stories about all the people who've died on these marshes. If the tides don't get them, the quicksands do. They laugh heartily as if it's a great joke. I laugh too, but my cheeks are stiff and funny and I can't speak, and, when I look back and see where Kit and I have been, my teeth begin to chatter and I wonder if it's really true that I'm here now riding back to safety. Or am I still there? Is the water lapping at my feet already? Am I sinking, going under, dying under this bland indifferent sky? The waves go slap, slap, the oars grind. The seamed old faces are mythical. Am I dreaming?

8

Sometimes, I think I should break it off with David; I don't know why.

I go and see him at the university, and he comes here. We're such a pretty couple, so familiar, such a habit. We sleep in his single bed in his room on campus, under the bookshelves so heavily laden with his books they'd probably kill us if they ever collapsed. We sit up late reading, side by side, propped up against the pillows. Then we lie down and smile and kiss and fondle, arms and legs entwined, feel every inch of each other but still we don't make love; and now we never even talk about it and I don't know if he ever thinks about it. I do. I think I want to know what it's like to want someone and wonder if I ever will; sometimes I lie and imagine it and put my hand down between my legs and rub myself until I come. He's never there in my fantasy. Never.

I just don't feel that way about him.

He's a selfish sleeper. I always wake cramped and cold on the edge of the bed in the morning, an ashy smell in my nostrils from the bedside table, which comes swimming up through my dreams covered in its mess of books and papers, tobacco, chewing gum, keys, David's Zippo lighter. Sometimes I just lie there looking at our clothes that litter the floor, the careless clutter he collects, the lights coming through the wavering curtains with their standard geometric pattern that matches the bedspread. Sometimes I turn over and look at him as he lies there, his face pale and smooth and innocent in sleep. I'm desperately fond of him.

He's different from the boy I used to walk with. Is he? Or is it me? Have I changed?

He's in his second year now, something of a celebrity. He's quite brilliant. By the end of the first year he was a known name, sailing through a sea of A's without appearing to work at all, filling the drawers in his desk to overflowing with poetry, contributing regularly to the university poetry magazine. All this with an air of disdain for the institution, staying up all night with the drinkers and smokers, playing guitar, looking sexy, wearing a black leather jacket and very tight jeans that show every movement of the muscles in his bum, lounging in corners looking appealingly androgynous, getting his name on nearly every page of the trendiest student newspaper. The hub of the in-crowd. When I visit I'm treated with a certain respect, not because I'm me but because of him. The great man's beloved.

Oh, I have a good time, I can't complain.

I remember sitting in the dim little room where they have the poetry readings. God, I hate these things, so does he, or so he says. But sometimes they prevail upon him to read.

He was nervous, sat there wide-eyed, gulping, waiting for it to be his turn. On my other side was this woman called Phyllis who I'd just been introduced to, the editor of the poetry magazine. "He's one of our mainstays," she'd said in a very plummy voice, and then the reading started. The audience sat on three sides of an open space where the people stood to read their stuff, all so serious and worthy, all in one voice, and I listened and looked, embarrassed, waiting for it to be over. I hate poetry readings. Clap, clap, clap, we went at the end of each turn, and it dragged on for ages.

Then it was David's turn. He went up like a doomed man, eyes bright and glazed, and just stood there for a while with the piece of paper in his hand. There was no sound. It was agony. My throat tickled and I wanted to cough. There he stood like some artwork on display, dead still: serious mouth, set face, ivory shadowed skin, neat nostrils, little pouches of skin in front of his ears, the back of his neck straight, his head sculpted, the hair on it glossy. Suddenly, I thought: That's not nerves, that's a show. He knows exactly what he's doing. And I liked him less. He read one six-line poem in a low-voiced, shambling kind of way, and walked out immediately afterwards. There was a moment of awed silence and then everyone applauded the empty space where he'd stood. They gave him more than anyone else. I hadn't got a clue what the poem was about, but it had a biting, vicious ring to it that lingered in the air. I squirmed. I wanted to leave but was too nervous to get up and shift all those people between me and the door. A man with a beard got up and read something about space travel, his face tortured with sincerity.

He couldn't follow David. Bastard, I thought. He'll be in the bar now.

"Immaculate timing," whispered Phyllis. I turned to look at her and saw that her face was faintly sarcastic.

"Who?"

"Who do you think?" she said.

Later, I went to the bar with her. David was nowhere to be seen. It was hot and smoky and oppressive, the walls painted blue and purple, and I started getting drunk because I felt angry and didn't know why. Phyllis had round shoulders and round cheeks. Her clothes were expensive and unfashionable, her shoes sensible. Obviously rich, she spoke and moved in a manner both relaxed and rather haughty, her voice more elegant than her appearance. She smoked constantly and told me that creative people were always totally impossible. One had to make allowances.

"Good God," I said.

David appeared and sat between us without a word or a glance, placing a brimming pint on the table.

"How very dramatic your exit was," said Phyllis coolly.

"Piss off," he said, lounging broodily, his eyes on the people massed four-deep at the bar.

Phyllis picked up his drink and emptied it over his head. "One can't make too many allowances," she said to me, rising and going to the bar with the empty glass to buy him another.

David sat there dripping, nonchalant. No one seemed to be taking any notice. "Bitch," he said listlessly. A little pool gathered at his feet and the seat was wet. "Give me a dry cigarette!" he called to the people at the next table, and someone came over and placed one in his mouth and lit it for him, throwing the match into the ashtray that sat like the hub of a wheel in the centre of the table.

His hair hung becomingly into his eyes.

"You flash bastard," I said.

He grinned suddenly and leaned towards me. "That's what I love about you," he said.

"What?"

He laughed. "If you don't know, I'm not telling you." He kissed me on the lips and his wet hair dripped beer down my face.

When Phyllis returned with another pint they sat and talked as if nothing had happened. She said she was fed up with editing the poetry magazine; she wanted more time to get into photography, and anyway there was so little real talent around. Present company excepted, of course.

"I hope you don't include yourself in that," said David.

"Thank God, I don't," she replied. "The artistic temperament is a boor and a sham. I'm very glad it's not mine."

He turned to me with an evil smile. " 'Tis pity she's a bore," he said.

Phyllis lit another cigarette and enveloped the table in a blue cloud. "Don't worry, Gloria," she said, smiling. "We understand each other very well. It's always like this."

Then they discussed the sonnets of John Donne very knowledge-ably till I felt like knocking their heads together. Our table filled up with people and I shared a carafe of wine with someone I didn't know.

Later, a babble of people went back to Phyllis's for food and more drink. She had a big room full of lush potted plants and expensive Japanese prints, shelves full of sociology books, subtle lighting artfully displayed. Music played. People sat or sprawled, lay back against fat silver cushions, laughing and passing a bottle of vodka. A very beautiful girl with long black hair sat on the desk swinging her long, graceful legs. "I don't care," she said, "I'll tell him right where he can stuff his thesis." And she raised her arms horizontally, moving to the music, long snaky movements passing like shudders along the line of her arms and shoulders. It oc-curred to me that he was here all week with girls like this, without me.

A huge pot of Indonesian stew appeared on the floor in the middle of the room and everyone helped themselves. "I get my tamarind sent up from London," Phyllis said, "and the shrimp paste." I had never tasted such food outside a restaurant before and was amazed. It was so delicious I wanted more, but there was no more. "I love cooking," Phyllis's homely face smiled. "I love cooking and I love food." David fell asleep with his head on my lap. Someone played a flute.

"Oh, Gloria," Phyllis said, as we were leaving, "do keep in touch, won't you?"

Outside, we started to giggle. It was three o'clock in the morning; navy-blue clouds scudded across a bright, glowing moon.

We walked quickly across the sleeping campus to David's block, leaning together and staggering from time to time.

"Stop a minute," he said, and we did. He put a finger to his lips. "Shsh. Listen. Listen. Just stand still." We stood a while. A long lawn sloped away from us. "All this brainwork," he said. "All this study concentrated into such a small area – it's as if the atmosphere's charged and at night you can hear it. Listen."

It was true, you could hear a faint Om-like buzzing in the air, a distant hissing like blood in your ear. "It's the motorway," I said.

He laughed and pushed me and grabbed my head and kissed it. "I love you," he said. "I love you so much."

We climbed the stairs to his room. He couldn't find his key and I scolded him, searching his pockets efficiently while he stood with his arms out like a prisoner being frisked.

"You're the only person in the world who understands me," he said.

I found the key and let us in. "Poetry readings!" he spat, pulling his clothes off and flinging them into the wreckage of his room. His back was narrow and knobbly and the cords in the sides of his neck stuck out. "What a load of bollocks! I'm never going to one again, I hate all that bullshit." He got into bed and held back the covers for me while I undressed. "They're just a bunch of pseuds. All except me. Did you hear that soppy one about some fool wanting to be a tree? I ask you!"

He kissed me as I climbed in beside him. "I don't know what I'd do without you," he said. I turned off the light. We were too drunk to embrace. There was a silence. Then he said, "To lie beside you is the great purpose of my life."

"Shsh," I said. "You're drunk."

He's changed.

His poetry now appears in highly respected quarterly literary magazines. He's been lavishly praised in several reviews and included in an anthology.

He's the centre of a club with no name, a tight little core of desperately fashionable people, male and female, playing their games. He's cynical and cutting in speech, cruelly truthful to everyone, whether or not they can take it, whether or not the world's listening. And still people want to be near him.

It's very tiring.

Now here I am getting carefully ready, applying lipstick to my mouth: Look at me, look at me, Momma, I'm beautiful. Friday night. I hear Tina talking to the cats downstairs as she feeds them. I'm off to the university to see this fine handsome clever boyfriend I haven't seen in ages. I had to look after Kit and my father while my mother was in hospital having her splenectomy. It's a preventive measure, she says, though she doesn't seem sure of what. But now she's home and rested and I'm free again, at least for now.

I take a train and he meets me at the station and throws his arms round me, kisses me extravagantly, squeezing the breath out of me. We catch a bus to the campus, go to his room and lie down on the bed and talk and talk till it's time to undress and get in, cuddle up in warmth, so sweet and familiar. In the morning before he wakes he turns and wriggles into my arms, his eyelids shiny and heavy, a sigh catching in his throat. Sounds begin. Someone starts playing records in another room, voices and footsteps pass along the little path that runs beneath the window. We get up and dressed, drink coffee with Marvel floating on top, go in search of breakfast. Once out of his room he seizes my hand possessively, swaggers down the road with long-legged strides, a look of slit-eyed menace on his face, a liquorice paper roll-up clamped between his lips. In the refectory he sits with one shoulder higher than the other, wolfing his food down greedily.

We go to someone's room. It's full of people. Someone plays a guitar and everyone talks. In a corner someone starts to laugh and the laugh spreads, they're all laughing, someone amongst them high and hysterical. What are they laughing at? A girl with fair hair and turned up nose lies with her bare legs along the back of a chair. "Let's have a truth game," she says. "You can ask me any bloody question you want to, I don't care." Someone turns the volume up on the stereo. Lou Reed sings "Waiting For The Man". "Uninvited guests," the fair girl says, stretching her legs, toes curled against the rim of the radiator, "fucking straights, Jesus, so bloody shallow," and she puts her hands over her face and yawns. The sun shines on the winking leaves of trees outside the window. The room is hot and full of smoke. David's dressed all in black. He is aloof while they play their game. Someone asks the one playing the guitar why he's such a nice guy. Everyone sniggers. "Nice guy" is an insult.

Someone asks the fair girl how many people she's slept with. She counts them slowly on her fingers. "Eight," she says eventually. I think I'll go for a walk and get up to leave.

"Can't you take it?" someone asks.

"Getting nervous?" says another.

"Fuck off," says David, standing to follow me.

"Not nervous," I say, "bored."

I hear a loud burst of laughter in the room as I walk down the corridor. David catches up with me by a big lump of modern sculpture on a concrete plinth. He takes my hand and we walk for a while, then go up to the snack bar in the Union and buy a coffee. Pretty soon we are surrounded by a crowd. Ping-ping goes the pinball. A tall shaggy-haired boy stands over it, around him a little band of spectators. "Wor-r!" they cry from time to time. Another crowd surrounds the table-football players, whose wrists revolve rapidly as they crouch over the game, playing intently and with great excitement. Figures drift in and out of the door. Our table fills up with people David knows and I vaguely know. A small, nervous girl called Faye sits opposite us. She's had poems in the magazine.

"Do you think it's important to actually, you know, count the stresses in each line?" she asks David, over-stirring her coffee. "Cos someone was saying to me, you know, like how you're supposed to count the stresses in each line really, so that . . . and I never do. Well, not all the time. Do you think those kind of things are important?"

"I wouldn't know," David says, smiling faintly.

"I mean, I've written poetry on acid. I mean, who stops to count stresses at a time like . . . Do you think poetry written on acid is valid?"

"I don't know," he says.

Faye lights a cigarette, pushes the brown hair back from her small, enquiring face, leans heavily on her elbows and says, "What do you actually think of my poetry?"

"It's like your face," he says, "nice enough, but no character."

Silence falls. Faye's face doesn't know what to do. It goes red and the muscles round her mouth twitch. David leans back, casually flicking his Zippo lighter with a double-jointed thumb. The flame licks all over his thumb but he doesn't seem to notice. I walk out, go back to his room and sit there, fuming.

"What's the matter with you?" I cry as soon as he appears. "What's the *matter* with you? What a horrible thing to say to that poor girl."

"Faye?" He takes his shoes off and stretches out on the bed. "She shouldn't ask such stupid questions. Anyway, she fancies me."

"You pig!" I yell. "You pig!" I want to smash my fist into his smug face, but instead I go and stand at the window looking down at the lads playing football on the lawn. They roar and leap. The big black and white ball flies through the air. "The trouble with you, David," I say finally, turning from the window and standing over him, "is that you're too easily influenced. You so desperately need to be like the rest. The ultimate conformist. All the little trendies sitting round cutting each other up and thinking they're all so cool, so clever. And you know what? You know what happens? You just turn into a nasty person. I don't know why you think it's so clever to be hard. Nice is a dirty word with your lot. Just to be nice. Just simply to be a nice person. I think it's pathetic. Pathetic little kids seeing who can shock the most."

David blows smoke at the ceiling. "The world's full of nice people," he says calmly. "Bland multitudes of them clogging up the drains. Having coffee mornings. Going out to work. Dying of boredom."

"Brilliant," I say. "Terribly original." I look across at him and see amusement in his new, hard eyes. "This isn't you," I say. "I know you. You're not hard. It's an act."

He jumps up and stares at himself in the mirror. "I *am* hard," he says defiantly. "I *am*. No illusions, Gloria. I am hard. I feel it inside me. Oh, Christ!" He turns aside with a dramatic gesture, hand to brow. I laugh.

He runs out of the room, leaving the door open, and I run to yell after him, "Grow up, you stupid little prat!"

An hour later he comes back, a little drunk, and lays his head on my knee. "Whatever I do," he says, "I never intend to hurt you."

"You don't hurt me," I say, "but you'll end up hurting yourself." I'm not quite sure what I mean by this, but it sounds wise.

"Do my back," he says. "Go on, Glory."

He lies face-down on the bed and pulls his shirt up. Sighing, I sit beside him, rub his neck and shoulders and the knobs along his spine, digging my fingers between his ribs and making him squirm.

He lifts his arms and lays his face on them. After a while he sleeps, and I sit on for a time in the darkening room, drawing my fingernails idly up and down his spine. Then I pull down his shirt, yawn and stand up briskly and leave the room, wander aimlessly towards the Students' Union, watching the sun go down over the science buildings. Shadowy figures pass here and there down the paths and over the lawns.

"Hello, Gloria," someone says. Turning, I see Phyllis with a French loaf lying against her shoulder like a cricket bat. "Wandering like a lost soul. Are you all right? You look half asleep."

"No, actually. Right at this moment I feel like kicking someone's head."

"David's, of course." She falls into step beside me. I haven't seen Phyllis for a while though I got to know her quite well during last term. Her sensible feet turn out briskly. "Well. It's no surprise. If you will pick these tortured souls." She stops by a silver car parked outside the library and jangles a bunch of keys. "Want to come and have a coffee with me? I left some on the go. Should be just right by now."

"OK." I smile. "Why not?" I get in and lean back against the headrest. It's a roomy, comfortable car. "Nice car," I say.

"My birthday present." She lights a cigarette and holds it in her mouth as she drives smoothly away. "I absolutely cannot live without a car. Where is the great man?"

"Who? The spoiled brat, you mean? Sleeping." I hesitate for a second then tell her all about the incident in the snack bar with Faye. My nails are digging into my palm by the time I've finished. Why? I think. Why am I so angry?

She doesn't seem surprised. "Well," she says, not even raising her eyebrows, her hands on the wheel sure and steady, "there you go. Unfortunately, Davids will always be Davids. And unfortunately they will go on getting away with it because of things like fine bone structure and a pretty turn of phrase. Of course, Faye was as much to blame. She walked right into that one."

"That's not the point."

"Of course not. But she knows what he's like." She slows down and parks expertly outside a tower block that stands incongruously on a little green hill. We've been in the car less than two minutes.

"I bet you don't get to walk much, do you?" I say.

"I'm a lazy pig," she says, opening the door, speaking round the cigarette. "I could quite easily walk anywhere on this campus but I adore driving. No doubt I'll be gross by the time I'm forty." We push our way through double doors into a cool entrance hall. "However," she says, "there are five flights of stairs to walk up." Her room is right at the top with a fine view of the campus. It's dark now. I look out on a deep-blue scene with rows of yellow lights and a pretty crescent moon that hangs above it all like a silver earring. "Yes," she says, as if I've spoken, "I was lucky to get this room. It's the one I would have chosen. I love living in the sky." It's low-lit and smells of coffee, a replica of her other room. I wander about looking at the Japanese prints and the plants and the rows and rows of books, then sit down on a big floor cushion, one of several scattered here and there.

"Cream?" She stands at the desk with a coffee pot in her fist.

"Please."

She pours coffee, then cream. "I can't drink it without cream," she says. "I know it's a desperate extravagance, but I simply don't enjoy it without." My nostrils curl at the bitter steam as she hands me a cup. Real coffee, very strong.

Phyllis sits cross-legged on the floor and talks, face calmly smiling, stomach bulging in pink cords. She has a brown jumper and thin brown hair that she keeps pushing behind her ears. She has another year to do, she says, after this one. Then it's off to London. She's thought about being a social worker but in all honesty doesn't know if she could stand it – there's so much to do and one feels so useless, like pushing back the tide – and then one just gets angry and that helps no one. "If nothing else," she says, "I hope I am realistic. I know my limitations." I keep thinking about David's face as he flicked his Zippo lighter and Faye crumbled. Phyllis lights another cigarette. She'll live in father's flat in Pimlico. Father lives in Philadelphia. Mother's in Reigate and hardly ever comes up to town.

"I've got a friend in London," I say.

"You'll have two," she says quickly, smiling.

"She's a nurse. She lives in Lewisham. I went to see her a few times but it's not so easy now, she works a lot of weekends. I was going to go down there myself to live once. We were going to get a flat together . . ." I shrug.

104

"But instead," says Phyllis, "you met David."

"I met David."

She goes away into a dim leafy part of the room and returns with a scruffy file which she hands me with a slight air of embarrassment. "My photographs," she says. She pours more coffee while I look through them. They are very good, glossy black and white blow-ups of littered streets, rain, doorways, hostile cats and snotty-faced children. I express surprise and admiration.

"All local," she says. "All just about visible from this window." She spreads them out on the floor. "I thought I'd be a photographer once, but it's really just a hobby now. *That* one, that little boy – he was so – oh, such a charmer. Such – such *fun*!" The little boy mugs at the camera, a backdrop of bleakness behind him.

"The deprivation is appalling," she says, returning to her former position and stirring her coffee slowly. Poor little bugger, I think, looking at the boy. Wonder what they thought of her, those kids. Posh lady with a camera.

"What about your own child?" she asks me. "How does she get on with David?"

"Oh, all right," I say, gathering up the pictures and putting them away, "he's only met her twice. Very briefly. You know she lives with my parents?"

She nods, looking thoughtful. "How dreadful it must have been for you."

"What?"

"Her father dying so tragically. So young."

"Oh. Yes." I look away, draining my coffee. "Well, I'm over it now," I say inanely.

"Will you ever have her to live with you?"

"I don't know. She's happy where she is. I'm going to see her tomorrow."

"Mmm," she says, frowning slightly. "Only it had occurred to me, I mean, that if you *did* decide . . . after all, blood's thick and circumstances change. How do you think he'd react?"

I gesture, put down my cup and saucer on the floor.

"He doesn't strike me as the ideal daddy," she says.

"I'm not sure he's the ideal anything," I say, standing up and browsing round her room. She has some little glass animals on a shelf and I pick them up and inspect them, one at a time.

"What I mean," she says, "is that your child is more important than a pretty poet with an outsized ego."

I wonder what business she thinks it is of hers. I say nothing. Slick turn of phrase she has. As bad as him. Who does she think she is?

She sighs. "I find this incredibly difficult," she says, "and I realise how bitchy it's going to sound. But someone has to tell you." I turn and look at her and she looks me straight in the eye. I think in some funny way she's enjoying this, her righteousness. "He screws around," she says. "He's even tried it on with me."

I don't feel anything. I don't say anything. I just look down at Phyllis sitting on the floor with her third cup of coffee and cream.

"Of course, I told him to fuck off," she says. "But it's all one to him. I don't know how many. About eight or nine, to the best of my knowledge. Faye's one. I really don't think it means an awful lot to him, but for what it's worth I think you should know."

"Oh," I say. "Oh. Thanks for the coffee."

I leave and walk down the five flights of stairs and out into the cool dark night, across the campus, past the Union building where little stick figures move about in the warm glow of the snack bar windows. I feel alone, disoriented, slightly queasy from all that rich, creamy coffee. Sex. That's all it is. He should have told me. Let's have a truth game. How many people have *you* slept with? Oh, let me see . . . Eight? Nine? Gloria, how about you?

Everyone knows.

I get a bar of chocolate from the machine at the back of the Union and eat it slowly, sitting on the library steps and looking up at the flat, black, starry sky. The stars form constellations like question marks all over the sky. I've noticed that before, on those long mad nights when I used to walk till dawn. How neat. How symbolic. Life is really like that sometimes. A small thread of fear coils finely in my chest, poised like a snake. Because, of course, everything changes.

He should have told me.

When I get back he's sitting up in bed watching TV in the dark, his pale hairless chest reflecting the flickering light.

"What are you doing in bed?" I ask. "It's only eight o'clock."

"Tired," he says, holding out his hand to me. "I've had this funny feeling in my chest. I've had it before, I don't know what it is. Seem to be breathing wrong. Anyway, this is the most comfortable place to be."

I ignore his hand and stand looking at the dark outline of myself in the mirror by the inconstant light, fiddling with my hair. I'm not worried. He always thinks there's something wrong with him. "I met Phyllis," I say.

"Uh-huh. Incredible," he says, gesturing towards the screen. "These kids."

I go and sit beside him on the bed. Shoulder to shoulder, we watch the flickering pictures. The street children of South America put on a show for our entertainment. Barefoot, they pound the dusty pavements; babylike, sleep in heaps on gratings. They have huge dark eyes that stare into mine. "Have you seen Phyllis's pictures?" I ask.

"No." He leans against me, dreamy and distant.

I watch the screen, mesmerised. Such eyes. You'd wonder how such power can get into someone's eyes after only – what – five, six years or so? "Yes," I say, "they do make very good photographs."

"What?" he says. "I'm sure I've been bitten by a flea. I bet you brought it with you from that menagerie of yours." He scratches, his face pained. "I'm sure it's a health hazard."

"Supposing I brought Kit to live with me?" I say. God knows, I don't actually mean it.

He looks surprised in a casual kind of way. "Up to you," he says.

We sit then without speaking until the programme ends. A woman comes on and announces where you can send money if you want to help the street children. I reach for a pen.

"Don't be daft," he says.

The pen doesn't write. "Damn," I say. The address fades from the screen. "And after the break," the woman says with a brisk smile, "a look at the great gardens of England."

"What do you mean?" I say, irritated. "Don't be daft, indeed. What are you talking about?"

He rolls his eyes to heaven. "Gloria and her bleeding heart. It won't do a blind bit of good. Probably wouldn't even get there. All it does is make *you* feel better but it doesn't do a thing for them. They'll still be there tomorrow and the day after and the day after

107

that. What are you going to do? Solve all the world's problems? If it's not them, it's someone else. What's the point? Day after, someone comes along and tells you about something else happening on the other side of the world, and it's all desperate, desperate, of course it is. The world's bloody desperate. To be quite honest, it doesn't mean a thing to me. Well, of course it does abstractly, but I live in the real world . . ."

"Oh, you do, do you?"

". . . I suppose I might feel different if it was happening down my road, but it isn't. It's got nothing to do with me. This is my life here and that's that."

I fold my arms and just sit there. Suddenly I'm very tired.

"It's like all those bloody cats. There's still about ten million more out there. All you're doing really is making yourself feel good. Dropping a penny in the poor box." He rolls himself a cigarette with languid movements. "You're too soft for your own good." He sticks it in his mouth and reaches for his lighter. "No one really gives a fuck. Not really. Not if they were honest."

I feel all achy inside. "Are you so honest?" I say.

He blows out smoke. "More than most."

"I thought you had a bad chest."

He says nothing, looks at the end of the cigarette with affectionate eyes.

"All this toughness," I say. "I know what it is. You're just scared of feeling."

"Ooh," he says, maddeningly humorous, "Gloria's getting deep."

I stand up and go to sit at the desk with my hands clasped between my knees. "You're screwing around," I say, not looking at him.

I hear him stir in the bed and feel his eyes. "Gloria," he says softly after a moment. I don't answer. "Gloria, please look at me."

I look at the great gardens of England instead, vast banks of azaleas in black and white. "I don't care," I say. "It doesn't matter what you do. But where's the honesty, David? Just tell me, where's the honesty?"

We are awkward, as if we've only just met. The camera pans over ornamental ponds, closes in on a cluster of lily pads.

"Oh, Gloria," he says, "Oh, Gloria."

I laugh. "Oh, it's very nice to be told by someone else," I say. "With pity."

"Who does she think she is?" he cries, and I turn my head to look at him. He looks wronged, puzzled. "Wait till I see her! Some fucking friend! Jesus!" He holds his head in his hands and breathes loudly through his mouth, then looks up at me with anguished eyes. "This makes no difference to *us*. Not to *us*, Glory. It's not like that with us. It means nothing. Nothing! It's only sex!"

"It's not so much where you stick your prick," I say coldly, and begin to feel sorry for him. After all, I never wanted it with him anyway. What I can't stand is his pretence of innocence, all this time. "It's where's the honesty. And everyone but me knowing. How does that make me look? An idiot. Oh, poor girl! Poor Gloria! Her boyfriend's screwing everything that moves. Everyone knowing!" I get angry. "Phyllis! You tried it on with Phyllis, for Christ's sake! And Faye! My God, she must be a bloody fool. You sleep with her and then you treat her like that. What's wrong with you? What's wrong with you? Are you going mad, or what? You just don't treat people like that!"

"Don't shout," he says. "I can't stand it when you shout."

I burst out laughing, walk round the room holding my elbows, searching for the next words.

"Anyway," he says, making his face blank and staring at the screen, "she likes it. Faye. She likes to have the arse shagged off her and then be treated like shit. That's the way she is."

A rage comes, terrifying me, shaking me dry, burning my eyes, an invisible destroying force that flies out from me and strafes the room, ripping all that can be ripped to shreds, smashing all that can be smashed, tearing off his face and grinding it into the floor. But it doesn't really happen. Instead I sit at the desk and tighten like a rack, trembling imperceptibly.

I could kill.

"You don't count any more," I say. "You just don't count."

"How can you say that? How can you say that?" He jumps up and starts pulling on his clothes, as if for protection.

"And another thing," I say. "Who gave you the right to talk about me? Phyllis seems to know all about me, about Kit's father . . ."

"I talk about you," he says loftily, "because I love and admire you."

I laugh, as loud and harsh as I can. "Oh, so grand!" I cry, jumping up and tipping him off balance while he tries to get his jeans on. He staggers, cursing. "Oh, so grand and noble! Such a gentleman! Does Faye think so?"

"Don't ask me to explain," he says, fully clothed now and sitting on the edge of the bed. "Don't ever ask me to explain anything because I can't." His eyes fill with tears.

"I have no sympathy," I say, stalking up and down and mocking him. "I'm hard. Yes, I am, I'm hard, I'm hard, I *am* hard. Oh, yes. It's the only way to be."

"Don't!" he yells, covering his face.

"You're too soft for your own good," I say and walk out of the room, down the corridor and into the big empty communal kitchen. I stand for a while gripping the sink and gazing out of the open window at the opposite block. Voices talk somewhere below, carrying clearly on the still night air. I watch my hands vibrate finely, the veins blue, the skin tight-stretched on the knuckles. "I'm supposed to have it in by Monday," somebody says. "Oh, balls!" says somebody else. "Just tell 'em you've been having some awful trauma over the weekend." The strip light flickers annoyingly. A vague sickly smell pervades the air and the table is covered in slops. Gradually my hands relax, grow still. Two little figures cross the quadrangle. Laughter rises from them. Now I am calm. I turn and walk back down the corridor, into the room where David still sits exactly as I left him. Happy jingles squawk from the TV screen. I sit down beside him but not too close. His chest is wheezy.

"I'm going home," I say. "There's a train about half-past ten."

"Why?" he says.

"Why?" I repeat. "Why? It's all changed. *You've* changed. I don't think I want to say any more."

"Oh," he says tonelessly, "thank you very much." He re-lights his cigarette that was lying discarded in the ashtray. "Well, you'd better be going, I suppose. I don't want to keep you."

But as I am lifting my coat down from the back of the door he catches me by the wrists and puts his arms round me and wheezes into my hair, asking me please just to stay with him till morning, he thinks he might be going to die during the night – really. "I've got this tightness in my chest. Can't seem to get my breath. Gloria, one last time, one last time for me, please."

110

God knows why, but I stay. It's such a long, boring way to the station. He's such a fool. Such a pathetic infant. I'll get the early morning train and that will be it. Never again. So I sit in the chair and keep him company this last night, like a death watch for everything we had. He's up all night thinking his heart's giving out, making potions out of stewed potato peelings because he's heard somewhere that it helps. In the early hours he falls asleep. I am so tired. I sleep beside him on top of the covers for an hour, waking with his body pushed up close against me. The light filters in through the curtains.

"You can't leave me," he says. "You can't. I can't possibly live any kind of life without you." He starts to cry and I hold him, aching with weariness, till he falls asleep again. Then I get up and get ready to leave, making no sound. He sleeps peacefully, evenly breathing. A mug stained with the scum from potato peelings stands on the bedside table.

As I walk along the little path that runs beneath his room I hear a window scrape upwards. "Gloria!" he calls, leaning out, pale skin and wild hair.

I stop. "What?"

He smiles at me. "It's not as simple as you think," he says. Then he withdraws, pulling down the window, and I walk on, shivering a little in the early morning chill.

9

My mother calls me up one evening. "All right, love?" Her voice sounds many miles away. "How are you?"

"I'm fine," I say. "How are you?"

"Oh," she says, wan but resigned. "I'm not wonderful. Actually, that's what I'm calling you about. You couldn't have Kitty for a few days, could you? I know it's awkward with your new job and everything, but it's getting a bit chaotic here. I'm down with my stupid blood again and you know what your dad's like, he's useless with Kit; I mean, he loves her and everything, thinks the world of her but . . ."

"What's wrong?" My brain spins: get time off work, lose money, leave her with Tina some of the time – anyway, what's wrong with her? She's supposed to be OK now; what was the point of the operation?

I see a new moon through the bathroom window as I clean my teeth. I remember the books on magic I used to read when I was pregnant. New Moon – now is the time for good magic, while the moon waxes. How pretty it would be to work a spell, to make everything all right – but I can't remember the details. I feel heavy, as if there's a stone inside I can't dislodge. It's there when I go to bed and when I get up and ring work, when I leave the house, catch the bus, get off a stop too soon in order to walk past some of my old haunts. It's clear they're levelling the mushroom field. Gone are the trees like lopped torsos. I wander round the perimeter, past the Africa tree, along the length of new barbed wire that separates the field from the new building development going up where the scraggy copse used to be. Then I wander out into the middle and gather flowers, clover and tall, branching buttercups; by the gate I stand on tiptoe to take some elder flowers from the old tree, whose old joints creak as I gently loose the branch. I carry a nodding, lanky spray of flowers as I walk down the road towards my parents' house, ignoring as always the nosy face of Mrs Eccles at a downstairs window.

Kit's waiting at the gate. She stands watching me till I'm nearly there then steps out on to the pavement and blocks my way solidly, feet apart, grinning. "Granny's in bed," she says. Her hair sticks out in a big clump at the back.

"I know," I say. "She's not very well, is she?"

"Am I going with you?"

"Yes."

She grows coy, takes my hand in both of hers and swings it to and fro coquettishly. "Am I going to stay at your house?"

"Yes. Will you like that?"

She giggles. We go round the side of the house and through the back door into the kitchen, where my father is spreading butter on a slice of toast. "Oh, hello," he says. "They didn't give you any trouble at work, then?"

"No."

"How's it going, the new job?"

"Oh, fine. I'm really enjoying it."

"What is it? Like where they board them out when people go away?"

"No," I say. "It's for stray cats. We try and get homes for them. Get them their jabs and all that."

"Oh." He's round with all his weight about the middle, like a spinning top. "Your mother's not well," he says wearily.

"I know. How bad is it?"

"Well, she's in bed," he says, as if that explains it. "Are those flowers for her? Why don't you take them up? Cheer her up; it's a bit miserable up there, wants decorating, really."

I find a jug for the flowers and run water into it from the tap, getting a sense of *déjà vu* as I stand over the sink. The smell of the place, the view from the window, the splashes on the tiles. "I can't get this pilot light to work," my father says. "I keep having to use matches." I've heard it before, seen my fingers flouncing the flowers out in the jug, just so.

The feeling only leaves me as I'm running upstairs with the handle of the jug clutched in my fist. My mother looks awful. She's sitting up against a very clean candystriped pillow, and her face looks dirty against it. Her teeth are out, her cheeks have collapsed morbidly. I'm shocked but don't show it, a little relieved to hear her voice emerge and not some demon's. "Oh, I don't like your hair like that," she says. "It looks like straw." Then she looks at the flowers and smiles. "You shouldn't bring Motherdie into the house."

"What?" I say weakly. The room depresses me with its old, stale smell, thick as gravy, a smell I've known from childhood. I never smell it anywhere else and I don't know what makes it. The walls are covered in rows of faded blurs that once were gilt flowers, and a great, blank, brown sideboard stands naked of anything but a tin of Nivea and a clotted hairbrush.

"Those white flowers," she says as if it means nothing at all. "Supposed to be bad luck if you bring them into the house."

How could I forget? I knew it once as surely as I've ever known anything. "Oh, God," I say, setting the jug down on the dusty sideboard next to a burned-out match and a dead moth. A dying fly kicks a leg hopelessly on the windowsill. How yellow and dingy are the old lace curtains, like my mother's face. Jesus and Michael watch from the wall.

"Or so your old Granny Jukes used to say," she says, watching me. "Oh, you don't have to take them out, Gloria, don't be silly. I didn't mean anything. Oh, I wish I'd kept my mouth shut, now."

I pluck the elder flowers from the jug, one by one. The buttercups and clover look weedy without their pale froth. "There!" I say, going to the window and throwing them out. "Take no chances." I put the fly out of its misery.

"Oh, what a shame! They were quite pretty. Of course, they'll be all down the side of the house now." She sags back against the pillow. One hand, very wrinkled and much too old, rests on a thick, dog-eared paperback with something lurid on the cover. Suddenly I'm very angry with her.

"What have you been doing?" I scold. "Why do you insist on carrying on past your strength? She's too much for you. This is ridiculous. When will you admit it?"

"Don't shout at me, Gloria." She's weak and weepy, full of the victim, and this makes me angrier.

"You've just got to be sensible," I say. "You're supposed to be taking things easy. What did the doctor say?"

She sulks and ignores me and I feel bad for upsetting her. This

114

smell, this smell from childhood, now in another child's nostrils. It's stifling.

"Don't worry about Kit," I say. "I'll take care of her." I kiss her awkwardly and leave the room, get Kit's bag and go downstairs. No child deserves this, I think. Kit's sitting at the table in the back room, eating cake and drinking tea. My father watches TV. They don't communicate.

"When are we going?" she asks.

"When you've finished your tea. Run upstairs when you've had enough and say goodbye to Granny."

She drinks her tea obligingly, holding the cup with both hands and breathing loudly as she gulps. Then she picks up a slice of cake, plain madeira by the look of it, and starts packing it into her mouth like a plug.

"You'll choke yourself," I say. "That's too much."

She looks surprised when she realises the truth of it, tries to chew and finds it impossible. Then she gets the giggles, shakes with suppressed laughter, a little hamster of a girl. She looks at me with merry eyes, her mouth tightly closed around the enormous mass because she's been taught it's wrong to eat with your mouth open. I start to laugh too. Kit chews and shakes and struggles. God knows how, but she's getting it down. She holds my eyes. We laugh together, never making a sound, behind the sparse grey head silhouetted against a screen.

It's like a holiday. I got four days off work and we've been all over the place: the zoo, the museum, the market, the park to see the little yellow birds in the aviary, the carp in the pool, the fountain. I bought her a pair of plastic sunglasses with pink, glittery frames and she wears them all the time, looking at herself in mirrors at every possible opportunity. She sleeps on a truckle bed across the room. At nights she's afraid of the ghost of the turkey, an image from some old song. She wakes me at six each morning by jabbing me in the shoulder. "Wake up," she orders. "You've got to take me to the toilet." She's scared to go out on to the landing by herself.

She has her own reality and gets quite impatient with anyone who can't tune into it. She calls herself the Great Baba and is some kind of guru to an invisible tribe of little people who follow her everywhere in a cart pulled by a horse about six inches long.

Whenever she has to get on a bus or anything, they take off up a bridge made of pineapple chunks that vanishes into some other dimension and reappears exactly at the point where she emerges. She gives everything names, not just the rabbit she carries by the nose, but her shoes, her purse, even her individual fingernails. They aren't exotic names. The purse is called Brian. I watch all this like Alice in Wonderland, on my knees in front of a door so small I could never get through.

The other night, the first time in ages, I played my old game, closed my eyes and lay down in the moose's antlers. I swear I could feel them sway. I never used to have to think about it: they just came, just carried me off to sleep. I'm getting rusty. Maybe if I do it more often they'll start to come more easily. Anyway, I'm sure I got a better rest.

Today I feel fine. It's her last day. Tomorrow I take her home. We go for a walk past the local school playground at break-time and hear the shrill voices of the children, hidden by a high brick wall. Further on there's a tall black gate through which we look and see a corner of the yard, with a group of children standing round a bent metal structure.

"Wouldn't it be nice to go to school?" I say. "Wouldn't you like that? Meeting all the other children?"

Her face crumbles instantly. "No!" she cries in horror. "No!"

"Oh, dear," I say, half laughing. "It's not that bad."

"I'm not going! I don't have to! Granny said!" She covers her face with both hands. "I hate school!"

I fall to one knee. "How do you know? You've never been."

"I know! I know!"

Someone starts bawling in the playground. Perfect timing. I stand up and take her hand, but she screams and clings to the gate as if I'm about to haul her forcibly into the school there and then. "Don't make me!" she sobs. "Don't make me, don't make me, please, please, don't make me."

Oh, God, I think, what do I do with her? Some people on the other side of the road are looking. "Kit," I say firmly, "no one's making you do anything. Look, we're going now. See? Shut up, for God's sake." But she goes on crying, makes a big show of it, even after she's agreed to take my hand and be led down the road. When I try to speak to her she cries harder. "Oh, shut up," I say. We walk on. At the bus stop we sit on a wall to wait. Her nose streams and she's running out of steam. I sit her on my knee, wiping her face. "There," I say. "See? Everything's all right now. You know what we're going to do? We're going to go home and see Tina and help her with the kittens."

"I don't want to go to school."

"Why not? Wouldn't you like to play with some other children?"

"No."

"Why not?"

"Because they won't like me," she says.

I could cry. "Of course they'll like you. They're bound to. You're so nice."

"No one likes me," she says.

"They do. I like you. Granny and Grandad like you."

"No," she says, "no, no one."

At home she cheers up and plays quite happily with the latest two kittens. Tina says they have to have their shots this afternoon, so later we call a cab and go to the PDSA with the kittens in a basket; Kit talks to them all the way. Their anxious grey-eyed faces peer through the bars and they cry pitifully.

It's dingy and hot in the waiting room. People and pets crowd the benches. Daylight comes through a narrow strip of window somewhere up near the ceiling. A girl of about fifteen in a pink blazer sits down next to us with a dog on a lead and a pup in her lap. The dog is a big brown mongrel bitch with great fat belly and swollen udders, sitting as solid as an old armchair and gazing calmly at the room with narrow, rheumy old eyes. She pants as if life itself is an exertion, her heavy brows twitching from time to time. The pup is a manic brown streak with a face full of hilarity, constantly trying to run up on to the girl's shoulder.

"What's up with her?" Tina asks.

"She's got a growth," the girl says. "She's got to be put down."

"Is that her pup?"

"Yeah. That's got to be put down, too." She shows no emotion, hauling it wearily off her shoulder for the umpteenth time. "My mum said."

"Why?" I ask. "It looks healthy."

"I don't know," she says. "My mum says."

117

"They won't put it down just like that, you know. Not if it's healthy."

"You ought to take it to the dog's home instead," says Tina.

The girl looks away. We sit and wait. Everyone waits. The place is too hot. The kittens stride about their basket, mewing tetchily. The pup makes a mad breathy sound, turns its head and looks straight at me. Its eyes are bright black, its mouth square and whiskery, its brow furrowed. It has two black blobs like eyebrows, one over each eye, and little snow-white milk teeth. You'd swear it was laughing.

"I'll have the pup," I say.

Oh, my God, what have I done?

Now I am holding it, it breathes mildly onion-flavoured breath into my face then ducks its head bashfully, trying to get into my armpit. Its feet are enormous. Kit, struck dumb with delight, puts out a hand and gingerly touches the fluffy fur. "Snatched from the jaws of death," Tina says in her deadpan voice. The pup's mother turns her head and watches, a limp smelly tongue hanging from the side of her mouth. She looks fond and tired.

I didn't want a dog.

In the cab on the way home I say to Kit, "What shall we call him?"

"Shep," she says immediately, poking him. He's gone all shy and sits shivering on my knee, refusing to make eye contact with anyone.

"Don't poke him, he's scared. Shep's a sheepdog's name. He's nothing like a sheepdog."

"How do you know?" she says.

"Because he doesn't look anything like one. More like a terrier. Think of something else."

"Bonzo," says Tina. "Fido. Rover."

"Shep," Kit says determinedly. "That's his name."

"Shep's really corny," I say, but it ends up sticking.

I get Kit to bed as early as possible, take the pup out and watch him shit in the garden, sit watching TV downstairs for the rest of the night while the pup gnaws my knuckles. He has to sleep in my room because of the cats. I wake about six, smelling shit. The pup goes pad-pad-pad, pad-pad-pad, whimpering. There are three pools of runny diarrhoea, one by the window very big, none of them on the newspaper. Little diarrhoea footprints are everywhere. I get up, groaning. The pup stands still and puts down his head and vomits something solid and pink that steams in a little yellow pool, then totters away, his big white knees knocking.

Kit wakes up. "Poo!" she says. "What's that horrible smell?"

"Watch where you put your feet!"

It's a terrible morning. I spend ages clearing up shit and yelling at Kit to watch what she's doing. The pup is quite obviously ill. He trembles in a corner in a strange half crouch, his face suffering. We take him to the PDSA and get some pills down his throat, take him home and make him warm and let him sleep. I'm sure he's going to die. I tell Tina to keep an eye on him and dash off to my parents' place with Kit, leaving her very casually with a kiss. I hate goodbyes. My mother looks better and says she's fine. I leave her very casually too.

"I want you to give my ribbon to Shep," Kit says, running after me down the path.

"He'll chew it to pieces," I say, then think: What the hell, he's going to die anyway. "OK," I say, taking it, "I'll give it to him. I'm sure he'll love it." I put it in my pocket and forget about it, go home with air fresheners and disinfectant and find him lying as I left him, breathing lightly, too ill, too still. "He hasn't moved," Tina says.

At midnight there is still no life there. I go to bed and fall asleep, wake in the small hours and watch the night light flickering on his prone body. The breath comes and goes, scarcely visible. Poor thing! Poor thing! How stupid for this poor thing to be born and run about for six weeks or so and come to die in my room, for my eyes. Why? I start crying, quietly at first because the night is so quiet, then louder as some relentless sadness settles into me.

I feel so lonely, so terribly, terribly lonely.

The pup lifts his head at the sound, opens his eyes and looks at me. I can hardly believe my eyes. I stop crying and get out of bed and go to pet him gently. "It's OK," I tell him. "Poor old Shep. It's OK." He puts his head down again and sleeps and I go back to bed.

In the morning he gets up groggily and shits out a mass of dead white worms, long and tangled like segmented spaghetti. Then he begins to pad again.

Tina calls me to the phone at tea time. It's my father; that's very

119

unusual. His voice is slow and placid. "It's Dad, Gloria," he says. "Can you come? Your mother's very ill. They've taken her in. Norma's here. She's useless."

"What is it? How bad?"

"Well, who's to say?" He stops. Then he says, "She looks terrible. She looks terrible, Gloria. Terrible." An edge of panic touches his voice. I've never heard anything like it there before.

"I'll come," I say. "Right now. Shall I? Shall I come? Shall I come?"

10

It's three years since she died, my tall, weary mother. I brought Motherdie into the house and it worked. I missed her. I resented her. I couldn't bear to think of her thin bare legs as she stood at the kitchen sink, her dreadful laughter, her old red coat. I felt all those things like guilt and anger that go to make up grief.

One day, going through some things of hers, I came upon an old charm bracelet, and there, unbelievably, was my fish: big round eye, silver scales, tail in mouth. My heart gave a little flop like a fish turning over, something painful and sweet. I took it and turned it all day with my fingers in my pocket, and felt unreal yet more real than ever, as if my legs were once more thin and knobbly-kneed, my feet in scuffed red sandals, the straps gone thick and hairy and curling up with age. My heart felt loose, as if it might fly away, nudged awry by that old misery, childhood, gone never to return yet returning now like a wan ghost at some window: *Let me in, let me in, don't you know I never left you?*

My father went to live with Auntie Norma and Kit came to me. I suppose I should have realised she would in the end. He gave me five hundred pounds for her, like a dowry. That, and the picture of Jesus and Michael, which I hated and she loved, or wanted, anyway.

I did a deal with someone for a bigger room in the house, hung a curtain across to cut it in two and let her make her own little place in there, which she did with colouring books and toys and the awful picture on the wall.

Sometimes she cried for her granny. Sometimes she'd say, "I want to go to my house," and I had to make her understand that she couldn't, that someone else lived there now, that it was gone for ever.

She ate like a horse and grew almost visibly. Worry ticked in my brain like a clock: how much are children's shoes, a dress, a new

121

coat? Winter's coming. She ran around, up and down the house, in and out of rooms; Shep flopped along after her.

They let me take her into work with me till it was time for her to start school. She learnt to be good with animals. Twice a week I pulled pints in a pub. I went out with a couple of blokes, nothing serious. Life was fine. There was always someone around to babysit.

In September I put her in school. She's never shy with adults but she screamed with horror at the prospect of a class full of infants, said she hated it when I showed her round the school and introduced her to the teacher, said she didn't ever want to play with other children or read and write and paint pictures and make things and play on the apparatus in the playground; and she scowled and jerked away when the teacher tried to put an arm round her. I took her home and talked to her for a long time, trying to win her round with a little satchel and a lunchbox with balloons and clowns on the lid. She sulked and turned her back, went and sat on her bed with her arms wrapped tightly round Shep, who squirmed and stared into her face avidly and licked the tears as they gathered on the end of her chin.

She's used to it now. She got tough and settled down, but started wetting the bed. She had night fears. She had to make sure all the books were closed before she'd go to sleep because she thought the people would come out of the pages and get her. Then she had nightmares about Michael, that awful little supernatural pig of a baby, coming out of the picture to carry her away. So I took the picture to a jumble sale on my way back from work one day and left it on a stall. The woman seemed very pleased and hung it on the wall. Jesus's eyes, reproachful, followed me as I wandered about the room, saying: How can you abandon me? How can you give your childhood away? How can you deny your brother? How can you trample your dead mother's feelings?

When Kit discovered the picture was gone she started sobbing.

"But you were frightened of it," I said. She just cried like a running tap. I thought: I can't win, I can't win.

She was with me everywhere when she wasn't at school. Me and Kit and Shep, in the street, in the park, in the house. Life wound on, unfolding. The days were crowded. And at nights I'd leave her small and still under the covers behind the curtain, call Shep and go downstairs and turn on the radio in the kitchen, falling into an easy chair. I'd call Shep to me for the comfort of his soft fur and his affection. He never failed me. My God! I'd think. What's happening? I've got this child. This dog. I didn't ask for them, they just came. And I'd gaze into my dog's guileless eyes as if some answer was there, stroking the head which rested on my knee.

He thinks I've got all the answers. He thinks I'm wonderful.

There came a tapping one night in spring, a tapping at my door unheralded by footsteps on the stairs. I started. It came again with a shifting of footsteps and I opened the door boldly, only to fall back in amazement. It was David. He could have been a ghost. He was dead pale, serious-mouthed, gaunt and eccentric, dressed all in black with a wide-brimmed hat that shaded his eyes. For a moment no one spoke and I was cold. I thought: My God, he's dying somewhere distant and appearing to me as an apparition. Then I saw the muscles in his cheek move.

"Who let you in?" I asked.

"Some woman downstairs."

I just looked at him.

"Aren't you going to ask me in?" he said, and tipped the hat back on his head so I saw his eyes. They were clear and steady and very beautiful.

"Wait," I said, "Kit's asleep." I stole back and checked on her then came out and closed the door softly. "We can't talk there. We'll go in Tina's room." Tina was up in Scarborough visiting old friends.

I led him along the landing and up another flight, explaining as we went that my mother had died and Kit lived with me now. We were very formal. "Oh," he said, "I'm sorry about your mother."

In Tina's room he sat on the bed and I sat in a chair. I felt as if I was interviewing him. Tina's room was cold. She had an old rag rug on the floor, clothes hanging from nails stuck in the wall, wildlife wallcharts and a Beautiful Ireland calendar.

"So what brings you around?" I asked him pleasantly enough, hands folded in my lap.

"I thought it was time I came to see you," he said, smiling

123

quickly and childishly, glancing away and swallowing. I saw his Adam's apple move up and down. "I wanted to apologise," he said. "I wanted to say all kinds of things." He looked down at his hands and neither of us spoke. I tried to think of something to say but couldn't. I felt strange, unsure, moved by his familiarity. We had been such close friends. We had talked many nights away. We had spent days on end together and sometimes we had not needed to talk. I used to think there was an invisible string between our minds.

He started to talk suddenly and nervously, not looking at me but all over the room with self-conscious, staring eyes. His nostrils were tight. He said he'd missed me. Missed me terribly. He said he spent hours lying on his back staring at the ceiling thinking about me. He gave a nervous little laugh. "Sometimes," he said, "that gets boring so I turn over and stare at the wall and think about you."

Then he looked straight at me. I'd forgotten quite how he looked, quite how well I knew him. It was like looking at an old picture of myself and thinking: Yes, this is how it was, these were the feelings, nothing ever goes away, it's all still there.

"I don't deserve to be believed," he said, "but I swear it's different now. I live like a monk. I don't want anyone." He took his hat off and his hair stuck up. "I'm sorry. I'm sorry for everything."

He's the kind you'd notice in the street. You'd turn your head, watch him out of sight, wonder who he was and what he did. I can have him if I want him.

I looked at my watch. "It's late," I said. "Why have you come so late?"

"What?" he said, incredulous, getting up and stalking about, pushing his hands through his hair. "What's time got to do with anything? I'll go away again if you want me to. Do you want me to?"

I wanted him to go away. I felt a little sick. But if he walked out now I'd never see him again. I'd always wonder what would have happened, what my life would have been like. He was hopeless, I saw that quite clearly. He was a child, a very clever fool. But he took more notice of me than anyone else ever had, showed me his soft underbelly. I'd let instinct decide. "Come here," I said. "Stop marching up and down looking dramatic and come here."

He came and knelt before me and I felt a surge of power. My

humble servant. He'd never speak to me like he spoke to Faye. Rather, I could say anything I wanted to him. I leaned towards him and smelt his hair and it was woody and fresh like it always was, the smell of my teenage years, of cold Sunday walks and seedy cafés, liberation from my old life. Me and him under the covers, safe in a cocoon. This funny little flutter started in my chest and I thought: That's desire. "Oh, you fool," I said and put my arms round his neck. He buried his face in me and cried.

After a while we lay down on Tina's bed. It was so cold we got under the covers, then we got undressed and curled up. We kept kissing furtively, like school kids stealing time in this strange, cold place.

"Can we? Can we, can we, Gloria?" he asked.

"Shsh," I said. His mouth was hot, slightly sweet and slightly stale. I didn't want to talk. Let instinct decide.

The small of his back was warm. He came inside me little by little till it was really happening, and it was hectic and perplexing and disappointing but there was some comfort in the way he lost control, shuddered with raw want, all his pride and arrogance gone out of him into me. His hips were so bony they hurt. Later he slid out of me and the sheets got wet. He lay with his legs drawn up, his lips apart, his lashes wet. And when he opened his eyes he smiled and looked very happy.

We lay and talked. He had Finals soon. If all went well he'd start a postgrad. course in London in October, but only because he couldn't think of anything else to do. It would give him time for his poems.

He wanted me to come with him. "It'll work out," he said, "me and you in London."

"And Kit," I said.

"Well, of course. That goes without saying. I can't go without you. If you don't come I'll have to throw it all up and stay here and become a layabout."

"I'll think about it," I said.

I went to see him at the end of term. I left Kit and Shep with Tina and took the train. He was waiting on the platform. "I got a Double First," he said casually after he'd kissed me, "with Honours."

"Thought you would," I said.

"I hope you're not impressed."

I smiled. "You should know me better than that."

He had a room in a house off campus. We rode a bus down a hill, past a church where big red evangelical letters screamed through the sunshine God is Love. He smiled all the time, his thigh against mine, raising my hand to his lips frequently, kissing the side of my face, saying how wonderful it was to see me. He was writing an epic poem, he said, the best thing he'd ever done. He knew in his bones that it was great. He got very excited, talked about it all the way from the bus stop to the old terraced house at the dead end of a cul-de-sac where he lived.

His room was terrible. There was a candle in an empty tomato can, dirty windows, a stale, narrow bed, an ashy grate, a teaspoon and a broken cup, two scratched records. One was the Doors. It kept getting stuck, playing over and over again. "This is the end, beautiful friend, the end, this is the end . . ." I thought how sad it was that he should have to live like this, how lonely the room, how cheerless. It must be because he was all alone. With me, things would be different.

We didn't bother going back to campus in the evening for the drunken revelries. We bought some wine and got drunk together by candlelight on his bed. There was something fundamental and impressive about his appearance, and I wanted that. The angle of his head on his shoulders, the lock of hair hanging over his forehead, the parted lips, the curve of his jaw, the black symmetry of his eyebrows, the deep eyes. I didn't care what happened, whether it was wise or foolish. I just wanted that, all of it.

We planned. He had his course and he would write. Success would come. How could it not for someone like him? I would take my time, think, look around. I could catch up on the education I'd missed through having Kit. I was the best in school once.

"We're not taking the dog," he said.

I said I wasn't going without Shep.

"Oh, yes?" he said. "And how do you think we're going to find a place to live with a scruffy mongrel trailing after us? Who's going to take it out for walks all the time?"

"I am, of course. I do now. It's got nothing to do with you." I felt very happy. I knew I'd win. I leaned back against the wall with my

126

glass of wine, watching the way his hands moved as he flicked his Zippo and lit a cigarette. He'd learn to like Shep. How could he not? Shep liked everyone and harmed no one.

It grew chilly. We lit a fire and blew out the candles and sat there looking down dreamily into the flames as they hissed and popped.

"I wonder what our lives'll be like," he said, "I mean, really."

I was half asleep. "Good," I said. "It's up to us. We'll make it good." I shuddered with excitement at the changes that were coming.

"I know one thing," he said with an edge of tension in his voice, "I don't want it to be *ordinary*. Boring. Mediocre. Predictable. I'd rather *die* . . ."

"What a baby you are," I said. He looked towards me with the firelight flickering on the tight-stretched skin of his face, his eyes completely black. Then he moved into the light and for no more than a fraction of a second, subliminal, I saw a strange look in his eyes, something like feigned madness.

Then he came and leaned against me. The fire made a sound like the slow flapping of a sail. We crawled into his bed, made love, lay close, pressed in its narrow confines. He fell asleep with his open mouth dribbling into my hair. I couldn't sleep. My womb began to throb softly and weariness ran through my limbs like a thrill. The fire was a violent orange cradle in the dark. I moved him away gently and lay for a long time with open eyes, conscious of the fireglow as a faint, hypnotic undulation on the edge of vision, soft as shallow breathing. The coals settled with a sound like the chimney slowly clearing its throat.

In the morning I woke to a hot, clawing pain, lay with it for a while then got up and reeled to the bathroom, half asleep. The room was poky and grey with paint flaking off the walls. A bright thin stream of blood stained my fingers as I fumbled in the dawn light that trickled in at the lumpy window. Red blood, white fingers. Beautiful. I looked at it in fascination. The world was very, very quiet and the sound of birds' feet on a roof was loud. I moved but I was in a dream. Something from an old book came into my head, and I smiled. I saw myself, a young girl, lying pregnant on my bed, reading a book on magic. Aha. Yes, I thought. I'll bind him. How easy.

I woke him with a cup of coffee that contained a few drops of my menstrual blood. I watched him drink it, every drop.

I liked London. We had two basement rooms with access to a garden where Kit could play. I took in typing and worked in a bookshop, went to visit Mary, who lived a bus ride away. She would read my tarot cards, do my hair, tell me all about her patients. She'd turned into a tall, stately woman with a magnificent throat and wild red hair, who knew hundreds of people and bullied her boyfriend, a plump, heavy-browed Nigerian man with wounded eyes, whose name was Jim. She'd changed. She seemed to me to have grown worldly and sure, to have walked right out of our childhood without a backward look, discarding all inhibitions on the way.

I took her with me when I visited Phyllis, who'd got in touch to say she was married now and staying in her father's flat in Pimlico, and I must come over. She'd changed too. She looked as if she'd decided on middle age as the most desirable state and was living her life accordingly. She was all quick smiles and chins that appeared and disappeared, and she was bigger all over, but then I put that down to the fact that she was pregnant. She lay on a couch under the window in a wide room full of leather furniture, potted plants, framed pictures of prize greyhounds and horses, and some more incongruous ones – lurid colour photographs in ornate frames of an Indian guru sitting on an opulent throne with flowers round his neck and at his feet. I wondered which were hers and which her father's.

Roy, her husband, shook our hands very firmly when we came in, then sat down boyishly on the floor. He was a thin, polite, eager sort of man in a loud jumper, who had a job in merchant banking and played the guitar. Phyllis said she'd barely started her job when she'd got pregnant, and now she felt tired all the time so she'd had to pack it in and take things easy. She leaned over and stubbed out her cigarette in one of several heavy gold ashtrays smeared with ash. "Make us some more coffee, darling," she said. "There's a pet."

Roy got up and went into the kitchen and clattered about, whistling cheerfully. The smell of strong, expensive coffee soon came wafting out.

128

"It's not good for the baby, you know," Mary told her. We were sitting stuffing ourselves with pistachio nuts on a big brown sofa that squeaked when we moved. "It's the caffeine. You really ought to cut down."

"Listen," said Phyllis firmly, rolling about and getting comfortable, "I've already cut the fags down to ten a day. That's heroic. Coffee, no way. I am an addict, I don't mind saying. Deprive me of my coffee and you deprive me of my sanity." She leaned back and sighed, patting her belly. "This baby would prefer a sane mother to a pure one."

She said they were skint. God knows what they'd do without dear old father. This place was all right for now but they'd certainly need something bigger when the baby arrived.

"Yes," I said, "we're a bit overcrowded, too, where we are."

"And how *is* the great man?" she asked.

I said the great man was dissatisfied.

"Goodness me," she said. "How unusual. How's his course going?"

"He gave it up just after Christmas. He's teaching now. English. School in Hackney. He's not keen on that, either."

"Amaze me," she said. "What *is* he keen on?"

I grew quietly angry sitting there on her plush sofa licking salt from my fingertips, watching the reflections in the dusky polished glass of the low table where a Chinese bowl, genuine Ming, for all I knew, sat smugly next to a small antique lamp. Roy brought in the coffee, all smiles. Who's she, I thought, with her big fat legs and boring husband and money, who's she to raise her eyebrows and sigh and laugh dryly over what I've got? I was glad I had Mary, who sat there swinging her foot and looking through a book of cartoons, who burst out laughing as soon as we got outside. "Skint!" she said. "Skint, my arse." We slagged Phyllis off jealously all the way to the bus stop, where we parted.

But when I was on the bus swaying along watching the patterns of the leaves on the windows, I thought: She's right, she's right, he's never going to be happy. What would make him happy? Acclaim. Fame. Absolute freedom to do what he wants. No responsibility. Ever since I've known him he's thrown scorn on the occupations life demands of him. He just wants to be a poet. Who can make a living out of that? He grows more and more bitter because the world doesn't understand, because the occasional praise, the occasional poem on the printed page doesn't make him rich and happy and respected. Because talent isn't enough. I could cry looking at him sometimes. I want the world to recognise him. I tell him Yes, you are talented, you are important. He needs me to tell him that.

Out of the window I saw the people queuing up to go home, women with shopping bags, schoolkids in uniform jostling and jeering in spotty, raucous knots. David taught fifteen year olds. He said he couldn't feel like a teacher, he felt more like one of the kids. What good was Chaucer to some poor bastard from a shitty estate? I could see him in my mind's eye, twisting his three rings on his fingers, his eyes intense. "It's terrible," he said. "You know what we're teaching them? To keep to a timetable. To know their place. To expect nothing. To be mediocre. I'm a collaborator with the enemy."

He wore a long coat and scruffy boots and took pride in not looking like the other teachers, who, he said, were all boring middle-class nerds. He took days off, wrote frantically in the little room that doubled as his study and Kit's bedroom. Sometimes he refused to come out for anything.

Kit complained. "I went in to get my paints and he told me off for making a noise. It's my room too. Isn't it? Isn't it? Tell him." The little room was a mess, the floor littered with toys, books, crayons, crumpled paper full of failed bits of poems, fluff and dust and bits of nothing. Kit and David argued all the time like two children, mostly about whether or not Shep could come in the room.

She didn't like him. "He's stupid," she said. "What's he living with us for, anyway? I'm not eating *that*. *He* made it."

David didn't know what to do. He either talked to her like he'd talk to an adult or ignored her altogether. Now and again he made a big effort and took her out to a funfair or a park, and she'd come home and go out in the garden and swing in an old tyre he'd hung in a tree for her, sucking her thumb and watching Shep as he roamed in the long grass, grazing like a sheep. She wouldn't talk about it.

"She had a good time," he'd say, exasperated. "She bloody well did. She just won't admit it. Honestly, I don't know what's the matter with her; she was laughing and chattering away and holding my hand – she just stops as soon as we get back here. She just cuts off dead. She'd rather die than admit she had a good time."

"She'll come round," I said. "Wait till she starts school again. She needs kids her own age."

She said she wouldn't go unless we got her a kitten.

"That's blackmail," David said. "The last thing we need around here is another animal. Anyway, Shep would eat it."

"Wouldn't," she said. "He likes cats."

But she went anyway, and this time seemed to settle in without a fuss. She learned fast. Then she took to appearing by the bed in the middle of the nights like a small, bad-tempered ghost.

"I can't sleep," she said. "I'm hot.

"I'm hungry.

"My window's making funny noises.

"Look at him. He's got his mouth open. Ugh! Doesn't he make you feel sick?

"I don't like that room. It's haunted. All his stupid things are in there. Why can't he sleep in there and I can sleep with you?

"He smells.

"I want to go home.

"I want . . ."

"Kit!" I shouted, rising from the bed in fury one night, drunk with sleep, waking David from a sleep so deep that he cried out in sudden fear. "Enough! I've had enough of you! Get back to bed! Go on! Go on!" I advanced with pointing finger, hair disarrayed, eyes staring, feeling mad. Kit burst into tears and ran into her room, slamming the door.

"Jesus Christ!" said David. "My heart's going like mad."

I walked backwards and forwards in the dark. "What's wrong with her?" I asked. "What can I do?"

"Oh, it's all right," he yawned. "We're all adjusting. It takes time."

We heard the sound of Kit whimpering next door. I couldn't stand it. I yawned till shivers ran through me then went and sat on Kit's bed and placed a hand on her heaving shoulder. Her head was a tangled clump on the paler pillow. "I'm sorry," I said. "I'm really sorry, Kit. I didn't mean to frighten you. I'm sorry, I'm sorry." I sat there for so long that my eyes closed and my teeth chattered and she was still. Then I crept back to bed.

131

David put his arms round me. "The poor little sod," he murmured. "I mean, when you think about it – all these changes – all gone, her granny, her home, everything she knew. It can't be easy. Poor little devil!"

The next day he went out in the afternoon, came back while Kit was having her tea and stood around smiling oddly, hands in his pockets. "How was school?" he asked her, walking about with Shep trailing after him snorting eagerly at one of his pockets and wagging his tail.

"OK," she said, stuffing a piece of bread into her mouth.

"What did you do?"

"Nothing."

"I've got something for you," he said, sitting down beside her at the table. "Piss off, Shep."

"What?" She turned and gave him all her attention, coldly, obviously.

He pulled a scrawny black and white kitten by the scruff of its neck from his pocket and dumped it in her lap. It mewed hoarsely. She seized it with both hands, clutched it to her and ran to the settee. David sat there looking pleased and self-conscious.

"Let's see," I said, "let's see. Aw, the poor little thing!" It scratched her and jumped down, arching its bony back. Shep bounced at it, stupid, delighted. "Shep! Shep!" I said. "Leave it!"

"Is it a boy or a girl?" Kit asked.

"A girl," said David.

The kitten skittered under the table and Kit crawled after it.

"Aren't you going to say thank you to David?" I asked.

"Thank you," she said. It meant nothing. The kitten ran out into the middle of the floor to get away from her. Shep blocked its path and it bashed him on the nose, scarcely breaking its stride. He gave a curious little whine and ran to me.

"What are you going to call it?" David asked.

She ignored him, crawling on hands and knees after the kitten. It had an unbearably sweet face and seemed so frail you'd think you could crush its bones in one lazy fist.

"Call it Cat," said David.

"Stupid!" she said scornfully.

"Don't you dare be so rude!" I told her. "Have some gratitude for once."

She grabbed the kitten and forcibly hugged it for a moment before it squirmed free and ran behind the settee.

"Esmeralda," I said. I'd watched *The Hunchback of Notre-Dame* on TV the night before.

"You're joking!" said David. "That's a terrible name."

"Yes!" she cried. "Esmeralda. Esmeralda! Esmeralda!"

"I see," said David dryly, "I see."

"Shut up, you," she said.

"Kit! I'm warning you!" But she ran out into the garden before I could say more.

"She needs her coat," said David. "It's freezing out there." He went into the next room and closed the door.

It was quiet. I felt tired. I sat down and closed my eyes for a moment, opened them when I felt Shep come jealously bundling on to my lap, anxiously butting my chin with his head. "Good boy, good boy," I told him over and over, fussing him till he rolled on to his back in a ridiculous leggy mess, one white knee bent, tapping on my chest. "Poor Shep," I said, stroking his lolling head. "Poor old Shep."

The kitten appeared in the middle of the floor, watching with huge, outraged eyes.

"Poor puss," I said. "Poor puss."

One day David came in all excited and said he'd been talking to someone he knew from university who knew about this place in the Lake District, a cottage that wanted caretaking. The people were going to Australia for a year and wanted someone to look after it till they got back. His eyes shone. He wrecked the bookshelf searching for the atlas, which had been put away back to front, and pored gleefully over it, tracing roads and rivers with his fingers.

"Think," he said, "think about it, Glory. Think of how we're living. Enough of this chasing our tails. This is no good, no good, it leads nowhere. Where are we going? Really, where are we going?"

Where? Where?

Such a picture he painted.

Freedom, beauty, lakes and fells, mountains – think of Kit, these poor animals; think of the city, rapes, muggings, crap in your lungs – he could work again there, really work, he knew he could.

Money? Who cared about money? We could sign on for a bit. You couldn't let money rule your life.

It seemed there had always been a home somewhere I was travelling towards. Maybe this was it. I saw Kit happy at last in a little village school. I saw wild red roses tumbling down a grey stone wall. I saw me and Shep roaming the fells. I saw myself learning to paint, making things, having the time. I saw the sky, a vast starry dome at night. I saw foxgloves and hollyhocks. I saw the kitten sunning herself on a garden path, bees humming lazily in a bed of wild flowers. I saw David working, working, in a room with whitewashed walls. I saw him happy, cheques arriving in the post.

He began to sort out all his old poems, sitting on the floor surrounded by Kit's toys.

"How would you like to live in the country?" I asked her next day, taking her to school with Shep trotting at my heels.

"Yes," she said simply.

11

It was like freefalling. Nothing lasted. There was never a time when I could look forward and say Yes, one year from now I will be . . . because I never knew.

We lived in London, Cumberland, Scarborough, Hull, Shepton Mallet, London.

Kit loved the country. She relaxed there, grew brown and wild and sturdy, led the way, got in with the locals, found all the short-cuts. She went to school walking along the tops of the walls and came home whistling, striding in through the rickety old gate in her rainbow-coloured wellies. In her bag there were eggs from the farm, sweets, a loaf, a lettuce. People gave her things.

In Cumberland I painted boring little watercolours of local beauty spots and sold a couple in a gallery. But we were poor. The money from the teaching soon ran out. David wrote a lot but nothing got published. He went fishing but nothing got caught.

Near Scarborough I spent a lot of time walking with Shep by the sea, along the clifftops, down the lanes. In the moonlight I was drawn again and again to the fields above the beach, searching defiantly for a mounted black-robed figure of bone. You don't frighten me, I told it. Just you bloody try. I sat with my back to the land, playing my ocarina in the wind so no one could hear. I would become charmed by the silver crescents winking on and off over the sea, float into a daze, return sure of something at my shoulder, turn and find nothing, only my dog grazing in the dim light. And when I found nothing I was almost disappointed.

Then I found myself remembering more and more the time when I was mad, the strangeness that used to descend like a mist, my voices, night laughter – all remembered with a sense of wonder. All gone now, a dream I once had. Sometimes the memory would be so real, like a blow in the chest. It was real. It *was* real. It *was*, it *was*.

Then I was real. What was I now? I could say I missed it.

I'd walk back across the meadow, pausing now and then to listen for the sombre swishing of a scythe. But I heard nothing. So I'd arrive safely at the house where David was, slip in at the back door and find him staring into his own eyes in the mirror. He did this for hours. He was turning into something else and I was watching him, wondering what to do, wondering why, wondering if it was all in my imagination. I was watching him create himself again – after the gentle, friendly boy who loved the smell of old books, after the moody student, what would the next one be? He got bored with himself so easily. He drank but never got drunk. He was working on a body of poems to be published as a collection. His work, which once had flowed so casually, now came in hard, bitter lumps that he gave birth to in silent anguish.

And there was here, and there, and somewhere else and back again, till we ended up here in London again. We found a place through Lisa, a friend of a friend of Tina's, on the top floor of an ancient, creaky house where chaos piles up in corners and people come and go at all hours. We've lasted all of eight months, going on nine. It's OK. David works in a library and I've got a job in a flower shop. I can make bouquets.

Kit's grown in every way, not just in inches but in the way she walks and talks and conducts herself. She's got sense. She treats David indulgently, almost fondly, as if she's the adult and he's the child. She takes new schools, new places in her stride. And sometimes she acts like a baby, hauls Shep up on to her knee, dresses the big patient thing up in bonnet and shawl and rocks him gently, crooning into his ear. He looks like the wolf dressed as Granny in Little Red Riding Hood.

I think Lisa's fallen for David. She's a tall, emaciated woman of about forty who lives downstairs in a room that looks like one of those very cluttered downmarket junk shops you find in the back streets of poorer areas, with overflowing tables of all shapes and sizes, dust-covered stacks of books advancing from the walls, an unmade bed scattered with fake flowers, loose change, keys, clocks, shoes. A rusty xylophone wedges the door open to let in some air, and the tiny fireplace erupts dead ash, apple cores, an exploded population of cigarette butts and used matches.

Lisa's friendly, lethargic in voice and movement. She puts her hand on your arm when she talks to you and looks hard into your eyes; her hand is thin and claw-like, very pale, the knuckles very large. She was once very beautiful, her facial bones tell you, and might be still if she were not so faded and dirty. She has a lofty elegance that contrasts strangely with the appalling mess she leaves wherever she goes: the scum in the bath, the bits of crud from her teeth in the washbasin, the food splashes all over the kitchen.

Lisa trims my hair when it needs doing, teaches Kit about the religions of the world, listens seriously to David's poetry when he goes down and reads to her, standing on the flattened rug in front of the bloated fireplace.

"Your man," she says to me, "is the most beautiful thing I've ever seen."

"She thinks I'm a genius," he says smugly. "I am, of course."

"Do you know how many kids I've got?" she says to me one day, standing at the kitchen sink we all share, leaning heavily on one hip. "Five at the last count. Two in Scotland, one in Leeds, and I'm not sure where the other two are at the moment. Eldest's twenty-three, youngest's six. I believe in giving kids their freedom. You bring them into the world and then they do their own thing: they're people in their own right. I hate to see parents *mould* their kids. Put them in straitjackets, more like. All this mother-and-child-sacredness stuff's just a pile of dog turds." And then she begins to sing unselfconsciously and very well, turning on the tap to spray water into the sink. She has long dark hair with grey at the roots, tiny breasts with huge nipples that show through her dirty yellow T-shirt, a lopsided bum in pale skintight jeans.

Lisa gives him the idea about Scotland.

"There's this big house," he says, "in Scotland. It used to be a school. It has ivy growing all over the outside and a rookery at the back. It's half-way up a hillside, overlooking a loch. Lisa's ex-old man lives there with two of her kids and it's so big they're just rattling around like peas in a pod. He bought it for five hundred pounds years ago and did it up. There were some other people living there but they've gone to Spain and now he's looking for someone else to move in. There's so much space. We could have a room each, no more breathing down each other's necks. Just think how Kit'd love a room of her own, now that she's getting bigger, and you could have a studio if you wanted. They've got a pony, she could learn to ride. And it's really beautiful, really beautiful; there's this big mountain and some old earthworks and you see eagles and deer. Lisa says in summer it's like heaven on earth. She says you can look out the back of the house and see . . ."

"No," I say, "I'm not taking Kit out of school again."

He gets depressed. He can't write. He says the city's killing him slowly. "It's dangerous," he says. "Every time you go out I'm worried sick about you, you hear such desperate things. Anything could happen. I'd go mad if anything happened to you, Gloria."

He becomes ill, lies wheezing loudly on the settee, one hand on his chest as if to feel the life within. His eyes water. His nose runs. He says it's the fumes – God knows what they're doing to us all.

Looks like we're moving again. Maybe this time we'll stay.

At times I think the beauty of the place is enough, I think: Yes, this is it, I'm happy here, nothing could ever be better. Cattle pass the gate morning and evening. Two round hills like breasts are ringed with cloud in the distance. The lane is narrow and steep, twisting and turning high above the grey, glittering loch, growing muddy and rutted and full of cow dung where the land falls sharply away to the left. Finally an offshoot of it struggles in through the tall wooden gate that is never closed, and cannot be closed because of the way the surrounding earth has swallowed it, into our yard where the chickens strut outside the half door of the grey gabled house. At the back a wide meadow slopes up to the ridge where three ancient burial mounds rest in the shadow of a flat grey rockface like a giant door in the side of the mountain. The mountain changes colour, blue-glazed in the morning, acid pink at night, purple when the heather's out, rusty in winter. On its side there are swelling fields of a million grasses and wild flowers. We live in a lush earth bowl; after the rain it sweats its scent like something on heat. In summer there are banks of bluebells, so profuse, so graceful, you expect them to form lines and start dancing a stately pavane. And there are times, when the valley is full of mist, when this place seems like Avalon – certain blurrings of afternoon and evening, of pearl-grey sky and silence and thick white fog lying low round islands of rock. Everything is dewy and fragrant, breathing palpably.

We never lived anywhere so wild.

The house is delapidated, with large flagstones at its roots. It has green doors and yellow windows, a massive flagstoned kitchen with wormy oak beams, rush matting, a black iron range, a cavernous fireplace with ladles and pots and great hooks hanging in interior darkness; a spiral staircase with a stained glass window half-way up depicting Joseph and his brethren. There are outhouses full of bits of cars and piles of rope, harness, boxes, wild cats with haunted eyes; there is a vegetable garden, a fat red pony called Sally, a grey goat called Babe.

The kitchen is the centre of the house where everyone gathers: me and David and Kit and Alastair and Tim and Sylvia. Alastair's a painter but I've never seen him paint. He's fifty years old, dreamy and quiet, with money coming in from somewhere and a deep fear of the world outside. He spends all his time making wine, messing about in the outhouses and walking on the mountain with his three great leggy dogs. He calls everyone honey. Sometimes when he's drunk he gets sentimental and embarrassing; sometimes he's struck silent for days on end, vanishing into the mist, appearing at the end of a corridor like a ghost, smiling all the time.

Tim and Sylvia are his by Lisa. Tim's twelve and Sylvia's eight. Both of them are beautiful, with lustrous brown hair and sultry mouths and wide dark eyes. Both of them have an untamed, unchildish air. Neither can read nor write though the house is full of books; but they can dig ditches, put a roof on a shed, ride bareback, milk a goat, skin and clean a rabbit, shoot a trespassing crow.

I remember my second night here, Alastair's room under the eaves, a place like a ship at sea with the storm howling at the window. I sat on an upturned box drinking cocoa, he sat on the bed, a spartan regimented bunk without a wrinkle. A print of Picasso's *Weeping Woman* was on the wall. A huge dog lolled against his legs.

"Thank God you've come," he said, "it can be awful in winter. Summer, the place is full. Winter, everyone buggers off. Might as well be on the moon. Thank God for human company." His face was worn and lean and pleasant, mild-eyed, his dark hair matted, overalls so old and filthy they were fascinating.

"You've got the kids," I said.

"They're not human. The dogs are maybe. But not the kids." He smiled to let me know he wasn't serious, put a gnarled brown hand on the head of the dog and looked at the window, his profile stark and long and dramatic. "Look at it. Black night, hailstones, wind screaming like a devil, ghosties and ghoulies and long-leggedy beasties. This is what it's like. Twelve years I've been here. The magic soon wears thin."

"Why do you stay?" I asked.

He lay on his back and blew smoke at the nicotine-stained ceiling, still smiling. "That's something I'm still trying to figure out," he said. Then he turned and looked at me, his eyes bland and innocent. "You're nice, aren't you?" he said. "I'm glad you've come. I like nice people. You can be my friend."

At first when he spoke like this I was taken aback. I thought he was just a silly old poser, playing some game. But I got used to Alastair. We all did. He's just a fifty-year-old child that wants nice friends.

God knows I can't see him with Lisa, but then I can't see him with anyone. He told me things about her: she used to work in a bank, she's hard as nails, got a record as long as your arm, been in Holloway twice, used to be a female mud wrestler, once did a dope run from Turkey, served time for causing actual bodily harm in 1976, comes from quite a posh family, carries a knife and knows how to use it, once had a job castrating pigs. He showed me a picture of her when she was about twenty-five. She sits on an upturned barrel like Marlene Dietrich in *The Blue Angel*: long legs, high heels, black suspenders, small breasts bare, head thrown back, party streamers threaded into the thick wavy hair that tumbles down beyond her waist. Her face is exquisitely smooth, lips and eyes dramatically black. Her expression is wry, one eyebrow cocked.

David came and looked over my shoulder. "Wow!" he said, then took it from me for a closer look. "Wow!"

"That's when she was a topless go-go dancer," Alastair said.

Kit loves it here: runs with the dogs, rides the pony, milks the goat, cooks incredible stews, goes to school in the valley, reads *The Borrowers* in instalments to Sylvia. Sometimes Tim listens too. I watch her sweep the snow from the front of the house with a witch's broom. The wind tugs at her skirt, a headscarf covers her hair, her legs are thin above the big wellies she wears. My God, I think, she'll be up to my shoulder soon. She's hardly a child any more. Her voice is confident and she speaks well. Her face is gentle and plain and round, the skin pale and freckled; her eyes are hazel, her nose snub, her mouth very pale pink. She smiles a lot.

David comes into the kitchen, rubbing his eyes and sighing, hair standing on end. "Ah," he mumbles, "some of that soup," gets a bowl from the dresser and ladles himself a good portion. He sits at the table breaking bread and dropping chunks of it into the soup then mashing it about with his spoon. Esmeralda rubs against his leg in passing and he jerks with annoyance. He's been edgy ever since he finished his poetry collection. He sent it away before Christmas, got one rejection three weeks ago, cursed for a day then sent it sent it somewhere else. We keep telling him it's too soon to hear, but still he watches for the post van struggling up the track; still he wilts with dejection when there's nothing for him.

"Tomorrow," he says, looking at the dark wet window, "if this clears up a bit, I'll take the dog and catch us a rabbit or something."

"Who? Shep?"

Shep hears his name and watches us closely, switching his eyes from one to the other.

"Who else?" says David. "Stupid, lazy animal. Let him earn his keep. He's just a passenger. At least the cat catches a mouse now and then. What does he do? Never know, might even catch a deer, there's enough tracks around."

"Oh, I couldn't fancy that," I say. I have this vision of David returning dark against the snow, a young doe slung around his neck, blood dripping from the end of her velvet nose.

"Ian's dad got a deer," says Sylvia. "He put it in the freezer. He gave us some, didn't he? Remember, Tim?"

"Shep might catch a bunny," says Tim wisely. "He'll never catch a deer." He laughs at the idea.

"Well, of course not," David says, "I know that. I mean *I* might catch a deer if I take the gun."

The gun is an old air rifle that Alastair uses for shooting crows.

"You just want to play at Man the Hunter," I say. "We've got plenty to eat as it is. What's the point?"

"The point is," David says, "that there's free food all around us and a stupid great dog snoring by the fire."

Shep wags his tail foolishly as if he's being praised.

"Take one of the others," Alastair says. "You'll stand more chance."

But David insists. Shep must earn his keep.

Next morning is crisp and bright. The snow lies hard-packed beyond the yard, criss-crossed with the prints of people and dogs. Alastair and the kids are out somewhere. The back door stands open. I get a cup of coffee and stand warming my hands round it, looking out and listening to the dripping from the eaves. I hear a shout. Shep appears from the side of the house, greets me wetly and runs into the kitchen to roll on the floor kicking his legs, staring at me with bright eyes. He's all damp and spiky. Then David appears, hesitates when he sees me and looks back over his shoulder towards one of the sheds, seeming to consider for a moment. He doesn't smile. "Keep the dog in," he says. "Keep the door closed for a bit." He turns to go.

"Why?" I ask.

"I'm busy," he says, "tell you later."

I finish my coffee, pull on my wellies and step out into the cold, closing the door to softly. At the shed door I stop and listen, hear nothing, so go inside. It's gloomy in here and for a moment I don't see anything, just smell straw and hear David say, "I *told* you I was busy. Now you'll go getting all upset." Then I can see. One of the dogs, Janey, lies on her side in the straw, licking and licking a blind squirming pup with shiny black fur. It looks like a mole. Over by the wall David squats by a bucket with a piece of old lino over the top held down by a brick.

"Why?" I say. "What are you doing?" I take a step towards Janey and she flops her tail about, rolling one eye at me but never pausing in her task, slurping noisily at the black fur, pushing it about with her nose. It squeaks like a mouse, then somehow moves on its belly to one of her massive overfilled teats and starts to suck. Its feet splay outwards, pink-nailed, its tail is a pointed stump.

I walk over to David and squat beside him. "You're not," I say. "You're not really drowning them, are you? I can take them into town and find homes for them."

"It's done," he says.

I pick up the brick and the lino. "Don't," he says. I have to see. "Don't," he says.

142

Three of them lie dead at the bottom. The fourth is still alive, I see it move. I plunge my hand into the lukewarm water and grab it.

"Don't," he says.

It's fat and warm and squirms weakly in my hand. As I pull it into the air, its face turns towards me, black with a patch of white about the small pink nose. The whiskers are drenched. Of course it's blind but it seems to me that it's clenching its eyes in fear. What are they doing, these monsters, these monsters? What is this torture, what is existence but an outrage? And then it opens its mouth and screams without a sound, right into my face, and I start to cry, the tears blind me. I hold it all wet against my breast and cry.

"There," says David, "I told you not to. Gloria! Gloria! Don't, please! Do you think I like doing this?"

It pants against me, soft and wet. I see nothing. Then it dies. Water drips from its paws, from the sharp pink nails. I open my eyes and look at its face, the open mouth, the broad bony cheeks and tiny ears. David takes it from me gently and puts it back into the water.

I sit back on my heels. Janey licks, snorts, slurps. Her pup feeds. "She's OK," he says. "I left her one." He groans. "Oh, shit, I wish you hadn't seen this. I really do. Forget it now. Just forget it. It didn't happen. Right?"

"Why, though? Why? She's not even your dog."

"Oh, Gloria!" he says indulgently. "What does it matter whose dog she is? Better to do it straight away than when they've had time to run around. If Alastair had been here he'd have done it, you know that. Or Tim. Or even Sylvia, I bet. It just happened to be me." He takes my hand and kisses it. "It has to be done. They don't feel a thing. Honest, Glory, it's better this way. There are just too many dogs in the world and no homes for them. Doesn't hurt them – straight out and straight in again."

"You didn't have to do it in front of her."

He sighs and looks away, gestures helplessly. "She's a dog! It's not the same. Please, don't make me out to be some sadist. I was just helping out, that's all."

I see the pup's face scream at me, I look into the complex cave of its bright new mouth, shiny and pink. "Don't you tell me they don't feel," I say. I get up and walk out. I sit in the kitchen drinking coffee. He comes a short time later and sits near me, talking miserably, justifying, wanting me to tell him it's OK. He talks and talks and then sits sighing with his head in his hands. I make some more coffee.

"Oh, for heaven's sake!" he bursts out. "This is the country! This is what it's like! My God, do you think the farmers weep and agonise every time they have to do a thing like that? They'd probably laugh if they could see how you're reacting. It's just how things are. Come on, Gloria!"

"All right, all right," I snap. "It's done. I'm saying nothing. Just don't expect me to like it."

He puts on his battered black hat and an old coat, slings a sack across his shoulder and heads for the door. "Come on, Shep! Shep!"

Shep scrambles eagerly to his feet and runs to the door.

"You and me'll catch a rabbit," David says.

I watch them meander across the foot of the white mountain, David walking solid and steady, Shep bounding ahead, running back, prancing, shaking himself. After a while I go and see Janey with food and milk. The bucket is gone. Janey's pup feeds.

I bring Babe from her pen, take her into another shed where plastic pails hang from pegs on the wall, and milk her. Chewing hay, she leans against me, turning her head sometimes to look at me with her mild, sweet face with the silky beard, the mouth that always smiles, the weird yellow eyes with their slitted burgundy pupils. I talk to her as I milk, nonsense mostly. She is hot and smelly and she looks very wise. Her milk spurts out in rhythm, warm and bubbly, frothing in the pail. "Oh, Babe," I say and start to cry again, wetting her flank. She watches me calmly, chewing and smiling. "Oh, Babe," I say. When my eyes clear, I look at the picture framed by the door, the snowy mountain rearing its great head against the sky. How often I have sat just here, the goat leaning against me, the new milk rising in the pail. My fingers are sure. The scene in the doorway changes, passes through fair and foul weather, sun, rain, snow, mist. I've always loved this task. Soon I grow calm again.

12

Spring comes slowly, quiet and full of mist. David labours on a nearby farm, grows lean and weathered. I learn to drive Alastair's old red Escort van and rattle up and down the steep tortuous lanes with Shep in the back. At certain spots we stop and go walking, miles and miles in the swirling mist. He runs like a mad thing, possessed, long feet striking silver spray from the spongy ground as he bounds ahead into the fog line, out of the fog line, which goes on before like a moving wall. At walls and ditches he soars. His nose shimmers. At home he likes to lie in the yard in his favourite spot, under the branches of a huge olearia that droops over the wall. David still takes him rabbiting but he never catches anything. He's come to dread those trips, poor dog, looks at me for help as he goes unwillingly to the door with his tail between his legs. "Oh, leave him," I say, but David insists.

"He'll learn," he says, "I'll make a real dog of him yet," and off they go. I should put my foot down, get him off the hook, but it's such a pain to have David sulking about the place. He's always moody these days. I wish to God his manuscript would come back.

Morning and evening, ghostly in the mist, tiny bullocks pass the gate, doe-eyed, wet-nosed, knobbly-kneed creatures who turn their lovely doomed heads and look in with passive interest, dew beading their foreheads. There's a little brown one that blundered in one day, panicked and clattered about the yard for half an hour before I could get him out; now he comes in whenever he can. I blocked the gate with bits of wood but still he gets in. He seems to like it here. He's curious, never lets me get too close but comes and stands and stares me out and seems to listen when I speak. He's scarcely higher than my knee. The hair on his forehead is snowy, soft and whorled on his chest. The pink rims of his eyes are clean and smooth. These cattle grow into lean filthy creatures, splattered with mud and dung, standing close-packed in the byre looking out through the

145

bars, their raw voices bellowing over miles. Most of the males get killed, I suppose. I keep throwing this bullock out and blocking the gate. Still he appears in the yard, fixing me with his glazed brown eyes and watching me patiently, as if waiting for something.

The mist stays for weeks, shrinking boundaries and muffling sound. Then one day it's gone and the world's come back, full of flowers and birds and great arching blue skies. Hawks swoop across the meadow at the back of the house. Hares go mad on the mounds. Babe grazes the lower slopes of the mountain with two white kids, strange fairylike things with wise thin faces and gentle eyes. They stand in silhouette, the three of them, high on a rock with the sky turning purple behind. And when I call, they come.

In summer people come and go, some stay a week, some a month, some longer. The house is full of children, a little lost core of whom seem to belong to no one. I never quite work this out. Alastair tries to explain. "That one over there's one of Lisa's but she lives in Leeds now with Annie and Jo. They're in America. Wendy and Tom are Annie's from when she was with Paul. See those three piddling about on the mound? One used to live with Jo's ex-old man, the others are just over from Ireland, their mum's sick. That big one over there I'm not sure about, I think she just kind of moves around. Reckon she's about fourteen. Sandy's mum lives in Peckham and likes to get rid of her a bit. She's on her own so she needs a break. And the one that's always picking his nose is Paul's by some woman in Cornwall."

They range from three to five foot. They are everywhere. Kit loves it. She runs around wiping noses and mouths, shouting and instructing, picking up and dusting down. The elder ones she plays Monopoly with and takes down to the farm and into her room. Sometimes they flock around me, little shy ones and big bossy ones, wanting food and money and attention. I'll never have more, I think, I have my share of other people's, brushing out the silky hair of a quiet little girl who says she wants plaits, that's how her mummy used to do it.

There is news from the world outside. Mary is pregnant. She wants to leave Jim. Phyllis writes on fancy multicoloured notepaper with a peacock in the margin: she's pregnant too; she's just had a wonderful time in Tunisia; she went to see the guru in America. "Stay centred in the bliss," she closes.

Tina comes to stay. She brings an old mandolin and sits outside all day teaching herself to play out of a book of "old-tyme" favourites. She thinks she'll go to London to earn some money then retire to the country for the rest of her life. She says the cities are shitty.

I find a book on wild flowers in a box in Alastair's room and spend hours with it on the mountain and the mounds. One quiet day I find Kit kicking a stone around the yard. Sylvia straddles the wall, Tim rides Sally, the fat pony, round and round the meadow.

"Where's everyone?" I ask.

"Gone to town," says Sylvia, swinging her leg and swatting flies from round her head. "Alastair took some, that mandolin woman took the rest."

"There wasn't room for us," says Kit. "Alastair said we'd been plenty of times before so we had to stay here."

It's a beautiful day, clear and peaceful, with just the right amount of warm breeze. We don't make plans, just end up walking, out through the back yard, over the stile into the meadow, which has become a fabulous chaos of wild grasses and flowers, pink, white, blue, yellow, garnished with butterflies and fat furry bees. It comes half-way up Kit's chest and covers Shep, trotting ahead with his tail aloft. The world hums and buzzes and the grey rock shines like polished pewter. We walk up to the ridge and lie down on our stomachs on the middle of the three mounds. These are riotous too, long-haired and fragrant. Tim leaves Sally grazing below and joins us.

"Think," I say. "Lots of people in the cities don't even have a garden and we've got all this. Aren't we lucky? It makes it all seem worthwhile somehow."

"Makes all what seem worthwhile?" asks Kit.

"I don't know. Everything." All the times I hated the cruelty of this place. This is the country. This is how things are.

"Alastair says there's dead people under here," says Sylvia.

"That's right. This is where they buried people."

"Would you come up here at night?" asks Kit.

"I have," says Tim, "many a time. They don't bother me. Only a bunch of old corpses. When you're dead, you're dead."

Kit gets down close to the earth and cries out. "Get down! Look at it from down here! Look! It all looks funny." We all get down and see a dense, high, jungly landscape full of alien creatures of every shade, shiny and matte, that cling to leaves and blades, scurry in the dirt, wave legs and antennae, flex wings, look back into our gross, globular, red-veined eyes with their own invisible, inscrutable ones. Suddenly I see on one slim blade of grass, motionless, a winged black fleck with legs and eyes and the glyph of Neptune in silver on its back. I watch it till Kit makes a move and it flies away. We catch each other's eyes through the jungle grasses and start to laugh, then sit up one by one, colossi rising from the earth. Sylvia rolls down the mound, runs up, rolls down, runs up. Shep pants noisily, spraying saliva when he flicks his tongue. Cattle call distantly.

This is it, I think. This is it. I'm happy now. Everything's all right. Everything always was and always will be.

When I get home the house is full of children. Tina sits by the back door playing "You Are My Honeysuckle" laboriously on the mandolin. She always sits in the shade, her skin is very white. "I think you should go and see David," she says at the end of a phrase. "He's up in your room. The postman came and gave him a package." She plays on.

My heart sinks. "How did he seem?"

She shakes her head then says, "Serious."

I sit beside her for a while, watching Kit and the others cross the meadow, listening to the babble in the kitchen. "What happened to the whizz kid?" she asks, playing the same four notes again and again. "How come he was always in print and now nothing? What changed?"

I think for a while. "He won't compromise. He says everything he wrote then was crap, none of it counts. The stuff he's doing now is his real work. Only no one wants to read it. He's the only one in step, the rest of them are idiots."

"What do you think? Is it good?"

"I don't know." I'm sick of it all. "I can't make head nor tail of it."

I go upstairs. The house blinds me with shadows. David lies on the bed with his face in the pillow, one arm trailing down to the floor which is covered with torn fragments of paper curling gracefully up on themselves, words, bits of words, bootmarks. All his poems. He senses me in the doorway and turns his flushed face

148

towards me. "They turned them down," he says. "Fools. That's it now, then. That's it. The finish."

I dread this scene. I want it to be over. I go and sit beside him on the bed like a mother with a sick child. "It seems worse than it is," I say. "You'll get more perspective on it in a day or two. Now I know you've got copies of all these. What you're going to do is try again. Two rejections is nothing. Six is nothing. Even ten. You have to be able to take that."

He jerks his head away. "Don't say anything! I mean it. Not a word. How could you understand? It's *my* life. That's it now. I mean it. No more. No more. Get it through your head and don't say another word." He breathes loudly into the pillow.

I feel suddenly like hitting him, shaking him till he rattles, slapping his face, crying Think you're special because you write poems? Who cares? We've all got problems, not just you, the great man, the great man! What about me? But instead I stand and walk to the door.

"Gloria!" he cries.

I hesitate. I think he's crying. I go to him, see his face shiny and creased, his lips dry, dirt in the corners of his eyes. "Gloria," he says, wiping his nose and wet upper lip. I lie down beside him, put my arms round him and comfort him. His head in the hollow of my neck brings me no comfort. His breath is sour: that, and his shiny red skin, make me feel a little sick.

Alastair makes wine. He and David get drunk every night.

David slouches through the summer, slouches on the mountain, slouches about the house, kicks stones in the yard, gazes into the fire, gazes into the mirror. Sometimes he stays in bed till three. He doesn't comb his hair, his clothes stink, his jeans droop baggy round his bum and at his knees. His mouth sneers. I talk to him, ignore him, scold, reason, spoil, jolly him along.

"Leave me alone," he says.

He farts at the dinner table, terrorises the animals, laughs raucously and stupidly at boring comedy programmes on the radio. His eyes develop a shocked look at times. At night he lies awake beside me, twisting his hair round his finger. We don't touch.

"You won't ever leave me, will you?" he says. "You wouldn't, would you? I couldn't survive. You know that, don't you?"

"I won't," I say. "Don't worry."

How can I leave him like this?

The rain comes. It starts in early September and goes on like an endless fugue, drifting, whispering, babbling, day and night.

One day Shep goes out with David and never comes back. A storm rages over the house. David eats soup by the fire. "Dog's gone, the *bastard*. Ran off after a hare or something and wouldn't come back."

We go up the mountain under a mad, boiling sky, Kit and I, calling uselessly, soaked, blind, deaf and dumb.

"It's no good," I shout into her ear. "We have to go back." Her face collapses like the ugly baby she once was. We put our arms about each other and weep for Shep, lost somewhere in all this.

I cry for my green stick, my lucky fish, my mother, my dog. I am Picasso's Weeping Woman.

"There's other dogs," David says. "Don't take it like this, please don't. I feel terrible when you cry. Honest, there was nothing I could do." Then he rakes his fingers through his hair and looks around with that slightly wild look he has these days. "My God, you can't move for dogs round here."

"I hate him," Kit says. "It's his fault. He lost Shep."

"It's no one's fault," I say. It's mine as much as anyone's. I could have put my foot down ages ago, said leave the poor beast alone and stuck to it.

"I hate him," she says, newly hard.

"No, you don't."

"I do. I do really. You don't know how I can hate. You keep telling me I don't, but I do. You don't know anything about me." I look at her – feel wordless, weary, overwhelmed by her reality. I don't know this serious, angry child who speaks so compellingly. She frightens me. She's right. I can't tell her how she feels. She has a right to hate if she wants to. Anyway, what can I do about it? Sometimes she acts as if David doesn't exist, sometimes she insults him to his face, sometimes they are sparring partners: they play silly, sneering games like two spiteful children each trying to do the other down. Who can outstare the other? Who can spit the furthest? Who can take the biggest bite out of an apple? He always wins, of course, that's the way of it. Then he goes and lounges

150

somewhere and looks poetic and doomed and beautiful and all that tosh he still does so well, while she just sits there and burns, a plain little girl who's lost again.

"Don't be so stupid," I tell him. "You think that's a great victory? Competing with a child? You know damn well you'll win. Leave her alone."

"She starts it," he says.

Sometimes she comes and hangs around me as if she wants to say something but can't find the words. One day she comes into the shed while I'm stirring mash for the chickens and says something in a low voice I can't catch. I'm preoccupied, thinking of an old red dress of mine I used to wear, how it made me look, how sick I am of these old country clothes, how I want to dress up and go to town. I see the dress hanging in my wardrobe, neglected.

"What?" I say.

She mumbles again.

"What?"

"You don't want me, do you?"

"What!"

"You don't want me."

"Of course I do." I stop what I'm doing and look at her bland face, her hands twisting a length of twine. "What a terrible thing to say."

"You know what I did yesterday?" She smiles, looking down.

"What?"

She giggles. "When I took his dinner up to him, I spat in it. I spat in it and I put a dead worm in it. I chopped it up really small so he couldn't tell. Serves him right. I hate him."

"Kit! Are you mad? I don't believe you." But I do, I do. What's happening here? My blood runs cold.

"I did, I did."

I don't know what to do, I don't know what to say. For a moment I hate them both, want to knock their heads together till the skulls break.

"Don't you ever *dare* do a thing like that again. I don't believe this. That's a horrible thing to do . . ."

"You don't want me, do you?"

"Oh, don't be ridiculous!"

"But you don't really, do you? I know because you said

151

something the other day, I'm not telling you what it was but that proved it."

"I said something? What did I say?"

"I'm not telling you."

"Oh, I'm sick of this. I just don't know what you want me to say."

"It's not what you say, it's what you do!"

"All right then, I don't know what you want me to do."

"I think it's terrible that you don't want me."

"I *do* want you."

"You said something the other day."

"What?"

"I'm not telling you."

I start to cry. She leans forward and observes me closely and dispassionately. This is what she wanted. "You're all right," she says coldly, and walks out. I weep into the bowl of mash and think of my old red dress.

I feed the chickens then go walking in the misty rain on the lower slopes of the mountain. I walk for a long time, wade through little streams, climb into and out of gullies, over fences, step from tussock to tussock, skirt boggy bits. The mist swirls round me, wetting my face, stringing the gorse bushes with lacy cobwebs, toning everything to a pastel piece. Cattle graze here and there, lifting their heads to look at me as I pass. The rocks glisten.

At last, in a bowl-like depression bordered by a drainage ditch and a fence, I see from afar something like an old brown rug that's been left out in the rain too long. Yes, I think, walking towards it, I knew I'd have to see this one day. I come close and stand looking down at the rotten body: eyeless, eaten, dirty white ribs protruding. It lies on the wet stones of the ditch, the head stuck through the fence, the collar caught on the barbed wire. He died here trapped, if not killed, by the storm's fury, then slowly – starving and exposed. He used to run ahead of me, look back to check, lean against me at the top of a climb. I kneel down and stroke the meagre matted remains of his coat, in spite of the stink and wet that sticks to my hand. I remember that terrible night, imagine how he closed his eyes against the rain that must have drummed relentlessly on his whiskery brow.

152

After a while I unhook the collar and take it with me, home. I'll never tell anyone. I'll never walk this way again.

Winter deepens. I'll dig out my old red dress, I think one day, driving home from the village. So what if there's nowhere to wear it? I'll wear it for me, in my room. Then I think: I don't want another winter here. I'm surprised by the suddenness of this conviction. I yawn, gripping the wheel with cold hands, dog tired, tired of David, Kit, this place, no money, mist, rain, myself. At home, the kitchen is warm and cosy, Tim warms his feet by the fire, Alastair stirs something in a pot, Sylvia feeds the dogs. David is nowhere to be seen.

"Oh good, you're back," says Alastair. "Could you put the sticks over the gate, honey?"

I go and fix the elaborate mesh of sticks over our gate as the cattle go patiently by in the lane, dim heavy beasts breathing smoke, smelling of dung and rain and the fields in winter. Everything drips. The little bull steps out of the herd and stands looking at me through the bit where the slat's missing, his eyes mild and tired, a crease in his soft pink nose brand new, like a pleat someone's just put there. Some olearia clippings lie round the gate, pale belly-up, glimmering, strewn from the spot by the wall where Shep used to lie. It's getting dark.

"You can't come in here," I say.

He lowers his head and works his jaw, snorting gently.

"It's all right," I say to him foolishly.

He lets me tickle his rock-hard brow for a moment or two, then takes fright and clatters aside but returns again immediately, waiting patiently to come in, watching me with his inscrutable eyes.

"I can't," I say. "I can't let you in."

His tongue flicks out, long and blue. He is so lovely I could cry. It's night in the lane now. I send him away into it. I put up the barricades, walk through the darkened yard and into the desolate vegetable garden where a few damp T-shirts and a pair of blue tights hang limply on the line, unpeg them and stand dreaming for a while with the pegs in my hand, leaning a little on the line. A terrible sadness falls through me, as if a light that's been flickering all evening has suddenly died, leaving nothing but the dark. I start and hurry towards the lights of the house. I can't stay here. I can't.

153

Where will I go? Oh, Lord, more change, more change. Courage, my heart. Don't let me down this time.

I'll dig out my old red dress, that's what I'll do. I go into the warm house, through the kitchen and up to my room, draw the curtains against the night, delve in the wardrobe.

The moths have eaten holes in my old red dress.

So what?

I go to bed early, lie in the dark and listen to the steady drip, drip, drip of moisture outside, hear the muffled talk of the radio and the people in the kitchen. I close my eyes. Ever trivial, guilty, I say a quick prayer for jeans that fit, a coat that I could wear to town, soft ankle boots, a scarlet sash, socks without holes. Distant as the dunes of Araby, they fade. I dream. I'm walking downstairs. Everyone else is asleep. I come into the low, pretty kitchen. The light is on but the fire's out. I stand in the dead centre of the room in the dead centre of the night and say: I really love this house. Why don't I stay here? And notice as I speak a very small sound like birds singing – maybe it's coming from the chimney or the gable wall – then see them, three small fluffy blue birds sitting in a row on a ledge above the fireplace, little toys with sweet anxious faces. They seem tame, so I walk towards them slowly and hold out my hand, thinking I'll get one to step on my finger. But they fly up in rage, all three, screeching and deadly, attacking my face and the hands I throw up before my eyes for fear they'll peck them out, and I fall back and fall and fall and fall.

I just keep falling. I don't even wake. I don't know where this will end.

13

We came back to London, but Kit refused to move.

At first she rang me every day, reversing the charges. I couldn't believe in her voice coming from that long-lost house at the foot of the mountain, as dim and romantic as an old sepia postcard. She might have been in a time capsule, or spinning through the universe in a flying saucer. And then finally she called me and said she'd made her mind up, she wasn't coming back, it was all right, Alastair said she could stay if it was all right with me, and it was, wasn't it? It was, really, Mummy. Something turned over inside me. This is my daughter, not yet thirteen.

She wants to leave me.

I said no.

"But that's stupid!" she cried. "I hate it down there. What's the point? You know I hate it. All my friends are here." She started to cry. "This is my home. *Home*. Don't be so horrible and cruel to me."

"You're only twelve," I said. My voice didn't sound like mine.

"I'll go to school," she said, "I promise. I *like* school here. I'll be good, honest, I promise I'll be good." Then she said, "You come up. You leave him and come up here. He's such a stupid fool, anyway."

"No. Don't you tell me what to do, Kit."

"I hate you, Mummy," she said, and put the phone down.

We called back and forth, arguing, for nearly a week. Alastair came on the line. "She's fine," he said. "She's not running wild or anything. I'll make sure she goes to school, if that's what's worrying you. I don't think anyone can force her now to do anything she doesn't want to do. Very sensible for her age . . ."

Is she?

I didn't believe in the place any more. Reality was the sound of a bus starting up in the street, my washing dripping on the balcony. Talking to Alastair was like talking to some fictional character. Kit

155

was fading into the pages of a book. She came by chance, she goes by chance. Of course. I just carried her part of the way.

It's as if a little cloud forms around everything as soon as it's lived. Sometimes it swells into the present, falls around me as I walk through the streets, sit on a bus, shooting like an arrow from a bow from the misty past into the lights of London.

One afternoon as I'm walking home from work I see David and Lisa looking at some shiny new motorbikes in a showroom window. She's painted herself in. She swans down the street in a leather jacket and torn jeans, smoking a fag between her lips, ageing hoodlum, vampiress, white skin and black hair and blood-red nails. Style.

I stand for a while unseen on the other side of the road, watching them. I know. I just know. They don't touch or anything; it's not as simple as that. They don't have to speak or look at one another – they don't have to do anything; it's how they stand and walk, together, easy, matched pace for pace, long leg by long leg, she in her tight black leather trousers, he in his old black hat. How he loves to hang on to things. Old black hat. Zippo lighter. Me. At the kerb they stop. She touches his elbow. He touches her shoulder. They cross. Where are we going? Where? Away from my home, away from hers. What mysterious journey are we on?

I go home and lie down on the bed, draw my knees up and caress my stomach. It grows dark in the room, dark outside, the neon flashes on, off, on, off, on, off. The clock ticks. I don't care, I really don't. Unruly kids brawl in the street below.

Once there was a little girl who lived in a vast primeval forest and rode a gentle moose with giant antlers lined with moss. Once there was a little girl called Gloria who played in the mushroom field. She grew up and had a daughter and a man. Then they were gone. Now she has flashing neon and a balcony and a little cloud.

I get up too quickly and stagger dizzy to the kitchen, grab some food and curl up on the settee with Esmeralda, a big cantankerous creature now with several chins. I'm sick of being poor. I'm scared that what little I have left will be taken from me. I'm scared for the shoes on my feet and the warmth in my bones and the food in my mouth. Living on the edge, always on the edge, oh, how it tires the soul.

156

I wish Kit was here. She'd have come home from school and flopped down and kicked her shoes away; I'd have put the kettle on and given her something to eat. How was it? I'd have said and she'd have pulled a face. Now she'd be listening to records or watching the TV in bed, her knees up and Esmeralda on the coverlet, flicking her stray straight hair back and calling Mummy, guess what? Guess what I read today?

But she's not here, she's there. I can't stay here; I don't want to go there.

David comes in an hour later and says, "Got the miseries? My poor Glory. Shall I make you a cup of tea?" He goes into the kitchen and clatters about, returns with two mugs, then turns on the TV and watches a comedy show. Detached, analytical, I watch him watching, his face laughing in profile, bathed in the light from the screen. He looks older than twenty-eight: the wrinkles at the corner of his eye curl round in a layered semi-circle into his cheek, which is hollowed out as if by a scoop. He has a tooth missing at the side. His hair's dirty, his collar's dirty. I've known him for ever. Somewhere in him is the way he used to be. I never see that any more. It's like a death – no, like a coma; like he's gone into a coma and they've put him in this coffin, his own new self. I don't mind losing the new one, but when that's gone so is the old. Finally gone for ever.

And then I'll be all alone.

I need to meet new people.

Something must be done. I work hard and there's never enough money and his new book's never going to be finished, and, when it is, so what? No surrender! He will be what he is and the world can go to hell. He expects nothing. They'll never recognise his genius. Fuck them all. The fools.

He sits in a corner writing violently. I want him out of my sight.

Sometimes he comes and leans against me. His eyes are wild, his lips cracked and dry. He gets sulphate from Lisa. He says it's good for his work. His breath always smells a little these days. Why does he lean on me so much? Am I wrong about Lisa? His head is a sweaty balloon under my chin. "Oh, God! Oh, God, Gloria! Hold me. I can't write any more! Why should I? Why should I? What else can I do? What else *can* I do?"

In bed he pushes up against me in his sleep, slings a heavy arm

157

across me, breathes in my face, pulls my hair, sweats and writhes and tosses.

"Give me more room," I say.

In sleep he scowls and turns away, offended. Half an hour later it begins again.

"Give me room," I say a thousand times, and give up and sleep on the edge of the bed.

I have to do something. I'm in a cloud. Half asleep. Out of the cloud come flashes of intense clarity, moments, random.

I stand on the balcony, hanging out my clothes. Down below is a long yard and a gate and some weeds, the back of a row of houses. How funny to hang out my clothes like this, the limp, dripping, second-hand crap for all the world to see: This is me. This is what I wear. Look, look at the bits I choose to put on. Puddles form on the balcony. My breath makes clouds.

I go back inside and sit down at the table and wonder what to do. It's Saturday. I am strange: here it descends, the old strangeness, again, like a reverie. I look down at my nails and think they are like eyes on the ends of my fingers. Something in me gets comfortable, slots into place, comes home. My heart beats very fast. It's *mine*, *mine*, I don't want to be cured. The dear, familiar strange; the strange and the passing strange; I put it on like an old glove, it fits perfectly. I flex my hand. How it clings, how it stretches, a second skin. I will just sit here now and reminisce about the time I was mad, like old people gazing fondly on the good old days of the war. Ah, but we had spirit then! Isn't that true? I must go and talk to Tina. Where is she? Yorkshire. What good is that to me? How dare she be in Yorkshire. Remember punching the old bastard on the nose? Oh, joy! Oh, power!

Someone raps on the door. I jump. I'm not expecting anyone. There it goes again, officious, rap, rap, rap. I get up and go to the door. An unaccountable eagerness rises in me. It will be an old friend, I know – the Grim Reaper, standing there on my homely balcony in the middle of town, his great eyeless smile fixed upon me, the scythe gleaming on his shoulder. All this way he's come to see me. But when I look out there's just this scruffy man with a woolly hat and very thick glasses, standing there amongst my dripping clothes. Perhaps it's a disguise. His thick knobbled hand clutches a knife, the pointed blade towards me. This, too, is part of the strangeness. I'm not afraid. I can't see his eyes, the glasses are too thick.

"I'm looking for Dave," he says aggressively.

"Well, he's out," I say, and I'm so unafraid that he peers at me curiously before speaking again. I should try, I really should, to be afraid.

"Well," he says, "you just tell him I was – no, on second thoughts, I'll just come in and wait for him." He makes a move.

"Oh, fuck off," I say, and close the door. I lean against it, giggling. Hah! That showed him.

He rattles at the letterbox. "Aw, darling," he calls through it, "I didn't mean to frighten you."

"Fuck off!" I shout gleefully.

I hear him stomp about, breathing heavily and muttering to himself.

"I'm calling the police!" I call through the letterbox. Do you like my knickers, hey? The tights with the holes in? The T-shirt that's lost its shape? Oh, piss off!

"Darling," he calls, "it's your old man I want to see. You tell him Larry was here. He'll know. You just tell him to pay his debts, all right? Pay his debts and there'll be no trouble. Right?"

Then he goes away.

At midnight when David comes home I'm sitting eating corn chips from a bowl. He hulks by the fire with his big coat and hat, his eyes in shadow, his lips parted and pouting.

"There was a man with a knife looking for you," I say, as if it's nothing. "Larry. Said pay your debts, or else."

His head jerks up, his eyes are startled. He falls to his knees before me and grips my shoulders. "Did he threaten you?" he asks. His face is all cold from the walk home.

"No." I shrug him off with annoyance. "*I* don't owe him any money." I laugh. "Called me darling and apologised for scaring me. But I wasn't scared. Huh! Not much of a hit man, really."

He looks at me closely for a long moment, uncertain. "Gloria," he says, "there's something strange about you . . ."

I laugh and grab his cheeks and squeeze them viciously, shaking his face, seized with a sudden urge to rip his flesh with my nails. He pulls away, frightened of me, then takes my hands and holds them tightly where they can do no harm. I hate his strength.

159

"*Let go of my hands!*" I cry in a terrible voice.

He drops them and backs away quickly, walks over to the other side of the room. "I'm sorry," he says, "I'm sorry, I'm sorry you were frightened . . ."

"I wasn't," I say.

"That *bastard*, coming round here. I'll *kill* him when I see him . . ."

"He's the one with the knife," I say, jumping up and seeing with satisfaction how he tenses at my movement. Of course, I think, this is new to him. He never saw me the first time round. "What is this, David? What have you been doing? Who've you got involved with? Men with knives coming to the door, indeed! How much do you owe him?"

He shrugs sheepishly. "Oh, not much, he's just being dramatic. Stupid sod."

"How much?"

"About sixty quid."

"Oh, God, David," I groan. "Where do you think we're supposed to get sixty quid from? You can't afford to go running up debts . . ."

"I'll get it," he says snappishly, "I'll get it. It's not your problem. You don't even have to think about it."

"Anyway, who the hell is he? Why do you owe him money?"

"That's not for you to know," he says.

Then I really lose my temper. I yell and scream at him, shake with rage, throw the teapot against the wall so that its tepid contents leave a great splashy brown stain, tell him he's a stupid, hateful, arrogant, selfish, pretentious, weak, weedy, pathetic, talentless little prick and I'm sick of him, sick of him, sick to death of looking at his stupid ugly face. He stands stiff, white, ready for any unexpected move. I go into the bedroom, slamming the door, get into bed and lie shivering and listening to my heart beat. The neon flashes on the wall. I hear music.

Pathetic, I think. I could've done better than that in my heyday. Give me time. Give me time.

Half an hour later he comes in and turns on the light and sits on the edge of the bed. We look at one another. He tries a faint smile but I don't return it, so he lets it go. "Hello," he says sarcastically, "my sister, my spouse." I look away. After a while he gets on to the bed and lies beside me staring at the ceiling. "I'm sorry," he says softly. "I really am. I'm sorry, Gloria. I'm stupid, you're right. I don't know why you put up with me." Then he turns and rolls against me and stares into my face. "Gloria!" he says urgently. "Please! Don't carry this on. I'll crack up."

Suddenly, I'm so tired, I just don't care. I sigh. "Oh, let's go to sleep," I say, closing my eyes.

He doesn't speak. When I open them again he's closed his. The long, lovely lashes are wet. "I need comfort," he says. He undresses slowly and lies naked on top of the covers, pressing against me and caressing my shoulder.

"No," I say.

"Gloria," he says.

"No," I say.

He's just a piece of flesh, going off slightly.

He seems not to hear, moving the covers away from my breasts gently. I pull them up again, then reach out a hand towards his hard prick. "If you think I'm letting you put that thing inside me after it's been in Lisa," I say, "you've got another thing coming." I flick it hard with my fingernail and watch it wither. As soon as I look at his eyes I know that it's true.

"What?" he whispers, incredulous, the worst liar in the world. "*Lisa?* What? Is that what you think?"

I turn over. "I'm going to sleep," I say.

When he doesn't pursue the matter, just lies blinking and gulping and staring stupidly at the ceiling, I know it even more. I close my eyes. Sleep, Gloria. Stay in the cloud. Sleep. Soon you'll know what to do. He lies still for a long time, then turns off the light and climbs carefully into bed as if I'm an unexploded bomb. I think he's crying.

I thought I could sleep but I can't. It's too sad, too sad, it'll break the world in half. He used to be so lovely. I could've looked at him for hours. Now he is this. Was it me that ruined David? If it was, I didn't mean to. But I've been with him so long, I must have had something to do with it. I'm sorry. I'm sorry. Don't cry.

I try for the moose's antlers. They don't come. They never do these days.

★   ★   ★

May.

I throw out all my old clothes, leave a note under the clock: Gone to Scotland. I take only my ocarina and my lucky fish. I take an overnight bus to Scotland for Kit's thirteenth birthday. I pass through the misty lowlands as dawn rises, change at Glasgow, go into the toilet at the bus station and see in the mirror that my eyes look bruised from lack of sleep, staring and fixed. I go and make a phone call.

"Yeah?" says a sleepy voice.

"It's me," I say, "Gloria. I'm in Glasgow. Can you meet me off the bus? Gets in at midday . . ."

"Gloria. Gloria!" Alastair wakes up. "Oh, Gloria! Oh, this is fantastic! Is David with you?"

"No. Just me."

"Fine. Gloria alone. Sounds like the title of a book, doesn't it?" He sounds as if he's smiling. "Well, I'm knocked out. Really, really pleased. You're our first visitor, and the best. Oh, this is cause for celebration all right! Obviously time to kill the fatted demijohn. You've been away too long, you know that?"

"Tell Kit," I say. "I have to go now. See you soon."

"We've missed you, Gloria," he says.

His voice has made me melancholy. I play my ocarina sadly while I wait for the bus. People look at me strangely. I look back at them. So what, you silly sods. I don't care. The bus comes and I get on board. The sleeping streets glide by under my mesmerised stare. I see an old man in a long coat throwing some bread to a flock of pigeons. Then I see lanes and trees, then a river, thawing fields, mountains, some with snow on their caps and in pockets here and there. I see rabbits in a field. I see people walking about in little villages. I fall into a trance. I see cattle, heavy-horned Highland cows with their growing young. I see a dog shaking itself. I see people in walking gear. My God, I think, I'm in Scotland. What am I doing here? And finally I see our old red Escort van and Alastair and Kit and Sylvia and Tim.

They hug and kiss me in the sudden bright sunshine that gets in my eyes. What they don't know is that I'm in my cloud. It's all woolly around me, gets in my ears sometimes so I can't hear properly, gets in my throat so I can't breathe. I think people must be able to see this ghostly aura that moves with me everywhere, but no, they reach through it to touch me, unaware, laughing and merry. It doesn't leave dew on their hands. "Where's your bag?" asks Alastair. I haven't got one. They seem surprised.

I go with them, find myself in the passenger seat with the kids in the back and Alastair at the wheel, everyone talking at once. The kids, of course, are huge. Alastair's hair grows in a long, matted clump down his back. He's old, so old, grizzled and grey. Kit's nearly as tall as me; she's lost weight from the body but not the face, which is just the same but now freckly. Her hair flops in her eyes. She leans over my shoulder as the van winds its way up to the house, and she points things out like a guide, as if I've never been here before, don't know every bend in the road. Her hands are bigger than mine.

It's agony. Here I would stop to rest, looking down over the loch, my hand on Shep's head. His ears would twitch at a distant sound, his brows at a distant sight. Here's where the celandine grows. There's where I hurt my ankle climbing over the wall. Nothing's changed. We turn into the yard. How strange that I thought this was all a dream, when all the time it was real and I was the dream, I was the one in the cloud. Chickens flutter in the yard. The paintwork peels. Oh, God, there's Babe grazing with her new kids on the side of the mountain. I can't stand it.

"Come on, Mummy," Kit says, grabbing my hand and pulling me into the house. There's where David drowned puppies in a bucket. I hate him. The dogs bounce up to greet me with their sloppy great tongues and bright eyes. She leads me by the hand through this house that twists my heart like an instrument of torture, showing me around proudly like a new owner. Joseph and his twelve brethren look down over the staircase. Sunbeams swirl in the hall. Something's cooking and the smell has drifted upstairs. An electric kettle sits on the landing, its flex still stuck in the wall.

This will kill me. I never wanted to come here; why have I come here? I was looking for a home, again, again, again; but it's not here either. God help me, I have no home.

"These are my pictures, Mummy. Look." Plastered all over the walls in her girlish room, silver and black abstracts, pop stars, star charts. And photographs. Me. Her granny and grandad. She sees me looking at them. "When I was little," she says, "I thought everyone lived with their granny and grandad and had a mother

163

who visited. I just thought that was how things were done. I can remember being really surprised when I found out other people were different. But look . . ."

We cross the landing.

". . . some of your things are still here. You can have your old room back if you like."

The room where David and I slept. A mausoleum. No one, it seems, has crossed this sacred threshold this many a year. Dust coats everything. Cobwebs grow black on the beams. Skeletons surely raise their dreadful heads in cupboards.

She stands smiling in the doorway. "So how's the pain-in-the-arse poet?" she asks.

"Still a pain," I say.

She giggles. "I don't really hate him," she says magnanimously, "I just think he's stupid. I feel sorry for him, really. I mean, when I don't have to live with him I'm even quite fond of him in a way."

She's better, mellower. She was right to stay here. She's got a home. At least she's got that. I can stop worrying about her now.

I pull open a drawer. Ancient memories stab me. Kit's old red ribbon, faded. The day we nearly died on the salt marsh. What's this at the back? A dirty old brown thing, the silver bits rusty. Shep's collar. A lump rises in my throat.

"I've got some really nice friends down below," says Kit. "From school. Come into town with me on Monday. How long are you staying?"

"I'm not sure." I pick up the ribbon. So pretty. It lies over my fingers. I pick up the collar, then sit down on my old bed, holding them both to this ache inside which threatens to shake me out of myself.

I start crying very suddenly, frightening myself. Kit runs to me and hugs me fiercely. "It's all right, Mummy," she says, "it's all right, it's all right, honest it is, it's all right." I can't stop. "You're not well," she says. "Come and lie down in my room. Come on, please."

"I'm in a cloud," I say through my tears. "I'm in a cloud, Kit. I'm in a cloud."

She leads me from the room, into her own, makes me lie down on the bed. "There," she says, covering me with a quilt. "I'll bring you a nice cup of hot chocolate and then you can go to sleep. A lovely long sleep. Don't cry, Mummy. Everything's all right." And she runs down the stairs.

I curl up and cry, the ribbon and the collar to my face. They smell of ancient days. They catch my tears.

The cloud lifts in time. It's all right here where the real world doesn't intrude: I can forget where I'm going, I can drift, I can walk in the meadow, lie on the mounds, sit in the doorway watching the shadows of the clouds scudding across the mountain. No one thinks I'm mad.

David calls me every day at first. He cries and lies and rambles. "I need a break," I say.

A total break. Tell him. Tell him, go on.

"I hate it," he says. "I can't seem to get anything together when you're not here." The line crackles. "I haven't worked at all."

"I need a break. You'll be OK." Ask about Kit. Go on. Just ask. Talk about anyone, anything but yourself.

"What are you *doing* to me?" he cries, exasperated. A little voice from another planet.

Two weeks later he calls again. "This is crazy," he says. "I don't know what game you're playing. When are you coming back?"

Tell him. Go on. What point? The longer the separation, the easier the break. "Not for a while," I say. "I'm staying for the summer at least."

"You're crazy!" he cries.

The June flowers come. I milk Babe, she leans against me, we breathe together. I climb very high and see deer, far away. I get drunk most nights with Alastair. His wine tastes like nectar. Sometimes it rains, long, peaceful, steady strands that hiss when they hit the flagstones in the yard.

The July flowers come. I sit in the back doorway. Alastair brushes my hair gently, letting his fingers graze my cheek a little too often. Sometimes, late at night, drunk, we cry together by the fire. It's all right. He's mad too.

"Sometimes I get so lonely," he says.

"Me, too," I say, wiping his face for him. The tears catch in the deep seams under his eyes.

"You're a beautiful woman," he says.

165

"Alastair," I say, "it can never happen." My head swirls, the fire sighs.

"I know," he says, smiling. "I know all about that. Don't worry."

We lean together, laughing soddenly. We hold hands and watch the flames. The cloud envelops both of us. "This is nice, isn't it?" he says. "Life should always be so nice."

"Alastair," I say, "you should have gone away from here long ago. You're wasted. Why didn't you?"

He smiles. "That," he says, "is something I'm still trying to figure out."

And I think: It could be me, growing old alone on a mountain with my dogs and my wine, weeping into the fire at night.

The August flowers come.

I sit on the middle mound with Babe and her kids. The sounds are familiar, the faraway barking of a dog, the humming of insects, the cropping of the grass and the faint swishing as the goats roam through it, catching seeds in their long coats. My own breathing. Into this another, harder sound gradually intrudes, whining, labouring, growing louder, the sound of a noisy sputtering car. Then I see it, blue with mud splattered all over the undercarriage. It turns into our yard. Visitors. I can watch from here unseen, friend or foe, get used to the idea before I go down. The dogs rush about the yard, barking wildly. Sylvia traipses across the yard and leans in at the passenger window, smiling in a familiar way. Friends. Then the people in the car get out, little figures with no features but unmistakable movements and ways of being, instantly recognisable. My heart steps a step higher and begins to beat too hard. David and Lisa walk into the house, hauling bags and bedrolls. Well stocked. Ready for a long stay.

"Oh, God," I say softly, reaching out and touching Babe. "Oh, God."

Babe bleats gently and the kids take up the cry, calling their lost, questing calls over the meadow. I stay out on the mound for an hour at least. I see David and Lisa come and go between the house and the car; I see Alastair come and go, Tim and Sylvia, Kit and the dogs. They're all down there. Only I am missing. What a happy family we will be.

The shadows are lengthening. I may as well go down now.

I stand blinded in the doorway, head swimming, dark shapes blossoming in the cloudy kitchen. Noise and confusion, a dog stretching. Steam from the spout of the teapot. Then David appears in the gloom before me, grinning wildly. He looks mad to me. His teeth are dirty, that's what I notice. One eyelid droops more than the other. He clasps me roughly against him, breathing loudly in my ear, quivering with tension. Then he lets me go and stands back, taking my face between his hands and gazing at it. He looks so happy to see me. He looks well. What do I say? What do I do? I look around. Tim and Alastair sit at the table drinking tea as if nothing's happening. I don't see Sylvia or Kit.

Lisa sits by the fire, long and graceful, highly made-up, one leg crossed over a knee. She's out of context. "Hi, Glory," she says throatily. Glory. Such a good friend she calls me Glory.

"Hello," I say. I feel shy, confused, like a little girl. I pull my cloud about me like a warm cloak.

He hugs me again, then over and over compulsively, as if he can't believe I exist. I stand like a doll, getting hugged. He draws me out into the hall and through the house till we come to a patch of sunlight by the front door, and a bench, and a clump of flowery growth where bees hum. We sit down on the bench. "I've missed you," he keeps saying. "I've missed you, I've missed you." I'm somewhere else. This is some other Gloria going through with all this.

He's given up the flat in London. Mary's got the cat. He needs the country again for his work. Why put a time on things? Who knows? He'll stay as long as it feels good, and it feels good, oh, yes, it feels good, it feels good. The air! So pure it makes you high. Lisa needed a break too. "Lisa's a bloody good friend, a bloody good friend, Glory. A bloody good friend to you, too. Now you've got all that paranoia out of your system, haven't you? Had to give you time to do that. It's all right, I understand. All that weird stuff about me and Lisa. Because that's all it was; you know really in your heart of hearts I'd never do anything to endanger our relationship. Good God, you're part of my youth! Lisa's very fond of you. And anyway, even if anything had happened, it wouldn't have mattered. You and me. That's all that matters."

Why have you come? Why have you come again to disturb my peace? I'd like to rub you out like a bad drawing I've worked over and over and still can't get right.

14

He's so reasonable. I don't understand. I'm lucky I'm so far away. Here's the strange thing, though: he sees this, the only one who does. He kneels before me, holds my hands and kisses the palms, his eyelids fluttering. "Where are you?" he says. "You've gone so far away. I can bring you back. I love you. It's the one and only thing in this world you can rely on." And I think: Yes, that's funny; how come the rest of them don't see? How come no one else says Gloria, where are you? Why is there a curtain between you and us? Maybe there's something in it after all.

He thinks he's come here to rescue me.

He wants to move into my room. "No," I say, not meeting his eyes, "no, it's *mine*."

He looks hurt and patient. "I'm so sorry," he says, "so sorry you feel like this. It's my fault. I was never the easiest person to live with. But it's different now, you'll see. I mean it, Gloria. You have underestimated me all these years. You have underestimated my ability to change. I've thought long and hard these months without you. I'll prove it. I have time. Time is all we have here, and time is all we need. You'll see. You'll see."

Then he moves into one of the outhouses with Lisa. They giggle and fool about like children, sweeping it out, slapping whitewash on the walls, getting furniture from old friends of Lisa's down the valley, from old corners of the house, putting pictures on the walls, running an electric cable over from the kitchen.

"You mustn't think because of this there's anything between me and her," he says. "After all, all this time you've been here alone with Alastair, and I never got suspicious." He invites me in to see that there are two single mattresses, each against a different wall. It smells damp and sweaty. There are drippy white candles everywhere.

Lisa kneels on her mattress combing her hair, an enormous canvas bag bulging open beside her. Make-up and scissors, scraps of material, battered books, scrunched up tissues spill from it. "Hello, Glory," she says warmly and quietly, smiling up at me as if I'm a dear, dear friend who's had a hard time and needs gentle treatment. He's twenty-nine. She's forty-five and looks older when you get close. Her teeth are rotten and her neck is old. I can see what he sees in her. Something she has that no other woman has: faith in him. I lost that a long time ago.

Lisa and Alastair don't communicate. The kids treat her as if she's just any other visitor, not their mother. She flits about the place in dirty clothes, picking her teeth with a nail file. Around the fire, there they are, night after night till the early hours, David and Lisa drinking wine in the glow. Alastair goes into a coma about nine every night; his legs sprawl, the wine tilts brightly in his glass, his eyes glaze over. He rarely speaks. Around one, Sylvia comes down in her pyjamas and scolds him and makes him go to bed; she's a smooth, scrubbed, sweet-faced girl with hair like a cloud. Then I go. I lie in bed and hear the two of them down there, laughing and cracking jokes sometimes till nearly light. They always sleep till the afternoon, the little yellow curtains drawn tight over the outhouse windows so not a chink remains.

"Why are you letting him make a fool of you?" Kit asks, standing in the doorway of my room.

She spends most of her time down below now, in a large blue house in the village where her best friend from school lives. I walk past there sometimes when I'm shopping and if she sees me she comes out and stands at the gate to talk to me, or walks with me a while till it's time to find Alastair and the van and go home. "Are you coming?" I ask.

She shakes her head. "Not yet. Later. Delia's mum said I can stay for tea. You don't mind, do you?"

She practically lives in the blue house now. Delia's a nice, plump, happy girl. She has older sisters and an auntie and a brisk, friendly mum with frizzy brown hair and bi-focals, who greets me in the street like a friend now and calls me dear. I'm glad Kit's got a friend. I remember me and Mary at that age.

"Do you know how it looks?" Kit says, looming over me, hands on hips. "Do you know what people say? A funny set-up, that's what they say."

"It doesn't matter," I tell her. "They'll be gone with the cold

169

weather. Don't take any notice. After all, it's over now, all that."

"Over!" she cries, as if she wants to shake me. "Over! What's over?"

"You know. Me and David."

She laughs bitterly. "Oh, yeah!" she says. "It looks like it, doesn't it? Somebody ought to tell *him* that." She flounces out of the room. I sigh, put a vague hand to my head as if to push back the mist that's rolling down my brow like it rolls down the mountain on those queer silent days, look around and think: Yes, yes, I see what she means.

It's quite a large airy room. I have my books over there in the space between the windows, a rug on the wall, a little table with a jar of wild flowers, a desk with an angle-poise lamp, a lumpy green settee and two old chairs. David comes here every day to visit me. Lately he's here more and more. Lately he doesn't knock. Lately I come in and find him here already. Yesterday he was asleep on my bed. My books are out of their places, leaning drunkenly all over the place just as they do when he's been at them, lying face down on the floor, up against the skirting board. His coat slouches on the back of a chair, two dirty T-shirts lie discarded on the floor at the foot of the bed. The desk is covered with his papers – work in progress. He says the light in the outhouse is impossible to work by. I don't mind, do I, if he just pops in now and then – when I'm not there, of course, he wouldn't dream of disturbing me – and uses my desk?

My head aches. I lie down on the bed. I hate myself for being so tired, for this lethargy that weighs me down like a disease, sits on my tongue, says to me always: Never mind, hang on, leave it, leave it, leave it. They'll be gone soon. I fall asleep. I wake when David comes into the room. I rise through sickly layers of deep sleep: I'll tell him, now I'll tell him: take your things, clean up your mess. But he comes smiling through the dim room, his lips wide and smooth, his eyes artless and young once more the way they used to be. He smells of the cold outdoors. He carries a proud, spreading bunch of purple and yellow flowers, which he offers to me, bending his head gracefully so that a soft hank of hair falls down across his forehead.

"For you," he says.

I burst into tears. He lays the flowers down and puts his arms

170

around me without a word, rocking me backwards and forwards and crooning, "There, there, there, there, there. Oh, my little love, I'm here; everything's all right." I try to wriggle free. I can't.

"I'm OK," I say. "I'm OK, I'm OK." I look over his shoulder. The sun is dying on the wall.

He loosens his grip and kisses me wetly on the mouth. I don't want it. He kisses me again, trying to prolong it, but I turn my face away. He sits up and gathers the flowers gently in his long nimble fingers, his face in shadow. "It's all right," he says softly. "Take your time. When you're ready, I'm here." Then he stands and carries the flowers away. I hear him down the corridor, filling something with water.

When he returns the flowers rise from a sunflower-yellow jug, nodding before him with delicate, drooping necks. He places them on the desk amongst his papers then comes and lies down on the bed beside where I sit, locking his hands behind his head and regarding me steadily with a fond half smile.

"I know you," he says after a while. "I know you better than I know myself. I know we've had hard times, I know how unhappy you were; I know everything. But it's over now, all that. All you have to do is see it. If you knew how much I really love you. I loved you before you were born."

Then he sits up, suddenly eager, leaning towards me. "Let's get under the covers!" he says gleefully, like a child, eyes shining. "Let's get right under like we used to and pretend we're in a womb."

"No," I say, shivering. Goose flesh rises on my arms.

Winter comes, winter closes in, one long night that goes on and on. Kit likes to come into my room in the evening, bringing her homework and her portable TV. She isn't here because she likes my company: she wants to annoy David.

I draw pictures, sit in my cloud, which grows thicker day by day. Their voices go tit, tat, tit, tat, tit, tat; they slam in and out. I'm just waiting for a sign to tell me my leaving time has come.

"You promised," she says. "You said he'd go. He's not going. Is he? Is he?"

He touches me obsessively, my shoulder, my head, my back, as if to convince himself I still exist. He brings me more flowers, yellow tulips made of some stiff gauzy material, puts them in the yellow

171

jug and watches me anxiously. "They're lovely," I say. He leans against me so hard it hurts. He jumps up and paces.

"I can't write," he says brokenly. "You're driving me mad and I can't write. Oh, God, I'll never be anything! I'll go soon. I won't inflict myself on you any longer." He covers his eyes, heaves great sighs, hates me with his looks.

"You are responsible," he says. "Whatever becomes of me, you are responsible. Never forget that."

Then a night of rain comes, hissing coldly at the black window that rattles slightly in its frame. Kit's been nagging me all night. I don't feel very well, there's a steady ache in my left arm and shoulder and my fingertips tingle. She's brought her TV in and sits watching it, sprawling, eating crisps, crunching and crunching. Heart, I think, flexing my fingers and finding them numb, worrying in a detached kind of way. I look over the top of the TV, where a woman is getting stabbed, to the lovely deathless heads of the yellow tulips. The room is in chaos, everything scattered everywhere. On the rug in front of me my latest picture lies, the back yard and the outhouses, curling up slightly at either edge. The ache goes nag, nag, nag, Kit goes nag, nag, nag.

"You know, don't you?" she says. "You know. He's doing it right now, he's having it off with that scrawny bitch."

I don't care. "Don't talk like that, Kit," I say. "You're too young to talk like that." I just want to sit very still and stay very calm so that my heart won't stop. I want to fall asleep.

"When are you going to throw him out? He's useless. A poet? Hah! You. You're just so passive and pathetic. I can't stand all this silent martyr stuff . . ."

"Shut up, I'm tired."

"What did I do?" she says bitterly, screwing up the crisp bag and letting it fall to the floor with all the other mess. "What did I do to deserve you for a mother? And *him*."

I shut my eyes, shut out her, shut out the cars screaming through San Francisco on the screen. The door opens, my eyes open. David stands in the lurid glare of the landing light, striking and skeletal, something rather frantic in his eyes, mouth moving, constantly exploring its own dryness.

"Here he comes," Kit says. "The big bastard. The playboy of the western world, ha-ha!"

He comes in and closes the door. "Can't you shut your foul-mouthed daughter up?" he says, sitting down beside me on the settee and handing me a brown paper bag, stained wet at one side, crumpled at the neck.

I look in and see a small buoyant cluster of fat green grapes. "Thank you," I say. He's carried them round with him all day. I imagine him in the village, going down the road and into the shop and asking for the grapes, for me.

"Oh, what a day, what a day," he says, yawning, then gets up and stumbles about the room, wrecking it still more before settling down like a child on the floor with a heap of old cardboard from one of his boxes. He starts twisting and twisting the cardboard into incredible shapes. He'll play all night now, good as gold. Kit sneers and turns away, folding her arms and draping her legs over the side of her chair.

I drift away. The pain in my arm is quite intense. I listen to my heart.

"Make me a cup of tea," David says to Kit.

"Make it yourself," she replies.

I gaze at the flowers, thinking I might be going to die. I feel interested, but I hope it won't happen. So silly and sad after all these years, to die with fake yellow tulips blooming in the wreckage of this poor old room.

"Make me a cup of tea," he says again, flicking his Zippo lighter. "Go on. I've had a rotten day, really shitty. I've had to walk all the way up the hill twice. Out of common decency you ought to make me a cup of tea."

"Fuck off," says Kit.

"You and your mouth." He scowls.

"Both of you," I say, "don't start."

"Who's starting?" He looks up, aggrieved. "She's unnatural, she is."

"I'm not making nothing for you," says Kit. "You're nothing to do with me, I don't have to."

"She's growing up selfish, your daughter," he says.

I jump up. "Oh, for Christ's sake, *I'll* make the bloody tea."

"No!" she bellows.

He winces. "Keep your voice down!"

I hate them both. Kit jumps up and pushes me back on to the

173

settee then flounces out on to the landing to plug in the electric kettle, leaving the door ajar.

"Leave her alone," I say.

"*Me* leave *her* alone!" he cries. "Oh, that's good. That's very good. Ha-ha-ha-ha-ha!"

"You're an adult," I say. "Behave like one."

"Yes, Mum," he says sarcastically. "No, Mum. Three bags full, Mum. You treat me like a child and I'll act like one."

"Oh, don't," I say. "It's boring."

Kit appears in the doorway with the kettle, white steam billowing from its spout.

"Life's boring," he says.

"Then don't make it any more so."

"I don't."

I rub my arm. I'm so tired, the world is over-bright. "Please," I say, "do we have to have a scene every time the two of you are in the same room?"

"Looks like it," he says carelessly.

Kit runs forward with the steaming kettle, her face shocked and horrified. She tips it with a strange delicate motion over David's back as he sits on the floor amongst his bits of cardboard, and the lid falls forward, steam gushing forth like an explosion, burning her hand so that she drops the lot on to him: kettle, lid, boiling water and all. He screams, a terrible harsh curtailed scream, falls forward, rolls himself into a ball, stretches convulsively, eyes screwed tight, teeth bared. He clutches uselessly at his steaming jumper, unable to get a hold. Kit leaps back, knocking into the jug with the tulips, which falls on to the floor and spews ancient green slime from its depths in a clot on to my picture of the yard.

This is my sign.

I fall to my knees beside him. He's crying, whimpering, mouthing the carpet, his face white and sweaty. I pull the jumper from his back, burning my hands, then his shirt, all steamy and sodden and sticking to him. Somehow I get them off him. He makes little noises with his throat, pants for breath, grips my hand and holds on for life. His back is cooked from neck to waist, moist and red like a ham. It will blister soon. My hands shake.

"Quick," I say calmly. "Call the hospital. This is bad." I look up. Kit stands crying, fingers in her mouth. The TV blares.

174

"Anything wrong?" comes Lisa's voice up the stairs, a bit drunk.

Kit just stands there and cries. Her face is so young and desolate and terrified that I want to go to her and put my arms round her. But there's no time now for that.

"Cold water," I say, "quick." I try to free my hand from his rigor mortis grip. "Quick, Kit."

She says, "No." She stops crying. "No, no, no, no, no." She walks out of the room.

I run to the bathroom, soak a towel in cold water, run and lay it on his blistering back, kiss his head, tell him everything's going to be all right, run downstairs towards Lisa's upturned face. "David's scalded," I say. "Take some cold water and help him." I pick up the phone in the hall and dial. Tim appears.

"David's scalded," I say. A voice comes on the line and I speak to it. What drama this is. It has nothing to do with me. Tim stands listening then goes into the kitchen to tell the others. The house hums with shock.

I get ice from the fridge, answer questions, run upstairs, kneel beside Lisa who's bending white-faced over David. "Please," she's saying, "please try and drink it." She holds a glass of water to his lips. The TV sings. I turn it off.

"Ice," I say.

"Jesus Christ," she says.

"Listen," I say. My voice is stiff and clipped, like a telephone message. "An ambulance is coming. This is what you say when they ask you at the hospital what happened. You were bending down to pull out the plug when the cord snagged and the kettle fell down from the top of the cupboard. It was an accident." I look hard at Lisa. "It was an accident. She tripped over. She feels bad enough, as it is. I don't want anyone giving her a hard time over it. Right?"

Lisa says nothing, her lips are hard.

"It was an accident, David. Do you understand?"

His open eye is fixed on the carpet, his lip distorted. He breathes oddly.

"It's all right, my baby," Lisa says. "Maybe we should take him down ourselves," she says to me.

"No," I say. "He's in shock. Wait."

I go into Kit's room to find her gone, her school bag gone, the

175

wardrobe open, the drawers raided. I can see her fleeing down the twisty lane in the dark, hood up against the rain. What now? What end is dawning? Running downstairs to grab my coat from its hook in the hall I hear the radio playing in the kitchen, silly songs, cosy and normal. Music from another dimension. She's taken the torch. Outside is all black and bitter. I take the van, pass the ambulance at the bottom of the lane and drive on to the village, watching out for a bobbing light, a rushing figure at the verge, but no one's out on a night like this. Hedges glisten in the headlights, the village hunches like a goblin. The gate of the blue house is open, the front window glows yellow.

Delia's mum answers the door. "She's here," she says before I can speak, "come in." And she stands back, a nice, solid woman in brown trousers and old jumper, something in her mouth that she's sucking, wiry hair clipped back on her neck. She has a sympathetic, sensible look that judges me still. You poor thing, her eyes say. The way you people live. Poor Kit. I could have told you it would end in tears.

She shows me into a room with a flowery three-piece suite and a piano; turns on an electric fire and goes off to make tea, which Kit brings a few minutes later and sets down before me with a plate of ginger biscuits.

Then Kit sits opposite, pink-faced and damp-haired, smiling nervously. "Will they send me to prison?" she says. "I'm not sorry. I'm just not. Only I don't want to go to prison." She speaks defiantly, voice trembling, eyes moist and scared but overlaid with a feckless humour.

"Of course they won't send you to prison," I say. "It was an accident."

"No," she says, shaking her head. "It was a terrible thing, wasn't it? Really. I didn't know I was doing it till I'd done it. I'm not sorry. I'm not coming back." She stops suddenly, as if someone's jammed a hand in her mouth, then laughs, a high, faintly hysterical laugh.

"Kit," I say, "nothing's going to happen. He's going to be all right. It was an accident." I lean forward and take her hands. "It was an accident." If I say it enough times it will be true. She looks back at me with the same nervous smile, shaking her head. "I'm going back to London tomorrow," I say, surprised to realise that this is true. "You can come with me. We could stay at Mary's at first. No more David. I promise."

But she goes on shaking her head. "No. I'm not moving any more. Really! Sleeping on the floor at Mary's! Back in the old routine. Not for me, I've had enough. I made my mind up a year ago. You and him, though, you won't leave me alone, you follow me about. You and him can do what you want, but I'm not moving again. It's OK, Delia's mum said I can stay as long as I want. I'll stay here till he's gone – and her – they won't stay long after you go, they don't stay long anywhere. Then I'll go home. I mean it. I'm never going anywhere I don't want to again just because of what other people do. I'm all right. I don't need looking after."

She's grown up. I've done it, I've done it, I've finally got rid of them all. We just sit looking at each other, holding hands.

"I didn't know the lid would come off," she says. Her eyes fill with tears.

I return to the wreck of my room and stand there looking around. David and Lisa are at the hospital, everyone else in bed. I see twisted cardboard, spilled yellow tulips, my picture with the green slime stain all over the yard, a wet bag of grapes. If he comes back he'll see these things and remember me. I stand for so long the sky at the window changes from black to blue and the rain stops. Then I realise my arm isn't aching any more. I'm not going to die this time. And the cloud lifts and I give a start, as if someone's just ripped a plaster off a wound.

It will never be any easier to leave than it is now.

I take a little bag with some money, my ocarina, my lucky fish, Shep's collar and Kit's red ribbon, steal past Joseph and his brethren and set off on foot down the hill through the dawn, wide awake, heart pounding. The loch glitters, the sky is wild with rushing clouds reflected in the puddles in my path. The grass is wet and fresh, standing up in quivering ranks. I feel clean and bright; truth washes through me.

It's true. It's true. I'm all alone. Always was. Don't be scared.

PART THREE

PART THREE

15

After two years I'm still amazed at my luck. I'm safe. I've settled like a tree: my roots are all these things on shelves and in cupboards and drawers. No one will take these things away from me. I have a phone. I have an alcove full of plants, leaves that cascade about me. Sometimes I just sit alone in here feeling happy. No one tells me when to eat, when to sleep, what colour to paint the walls, what I can listen to or watch on TV. I never get nagged, except when Esmeralda decides her dinner's late. I walk in the park, see my friends, go to parties, draw pictures, take in typing, work three days a week. Sometimes I go to Scotland on a visit. I am a rich woman. I have a stereo and nice carpets on the floors, I drink wine often and I eat well. I've been lucky, after all.

And yet, sometimes, with unfair suddenness, a feeling of intense self-pity falls over me like a veil, as if the whole room and everything in it becomes a callous presence at my shoulder. And then I prowl about the flat, the skin tight on the back of my neck, look in the cupboards, under the bed, behind the settee. I don't know what I'm looking for. I stand very still, listening. My stomach is a knot. The place where my heart is spins like a whirlpool, pulling things down. The hairs along my arms quiver and stand erect, straining towards something unseen, something coming back after so long. Then it's gone and I sit and think about it. I don't know what to call it, so I call it strange like I did before – then I laugh and say it's all right, just Gloria going off her rocker again. And life goes on.

I never felt better. I never felt stronger and prouder when I walk down the street. I know what I look like now. I have a great Medusa cloud of red hair, scarlet lips, a pale face, eyes all dark and smudgy. From the neck up I'm like a consumptive Victorian beauty, but I like to wear tough clothes and they're always peppered with cat

181

hairs. That, or something terribly elegant, depends on how I'm feeling. I love dressing up and walking sassy. I'm very sure.

Being like this means I can do anything I want. Any day now I'll strike with my long sticky tongue at Christian, wounding him fatally. Serve him right for just appearing the way he did out of the blue, breaking the evenness of it all. Because I'm so secure that even romance is an intrusion – I don't count the old friends wanting a quick roll between the sheets, or the drunk faces at parties wanting to take me home and slobber in the back of a cab. This one's different. This one's the only flesh and blood character in a world peopled by cartoons.

I'd come home from work in the afternoon. It was very hot; I drank iced orange juice and opened all the doors and windows, watered the plants, took a big honeydew melon and a knife and plate from the kitchen and went to sit on the balcony in the shade. The melon dripped everywhere when I cut it. Esmeralda lay sprawled in the grass at the top of the steps leading to the lawn, back legs wide open. The sky was tense and blue, without a blemish. I leaned back against the wall and closed my eyes and when I opened them again this young fellow was standing on the iron steps below me. For some reason I wasn't surprised. The strap had fallen from my right shoulder and hung down my arm, so I lifted it back up. See how casual I am. He looked uncertain but then smiled, a wide, thin, big-toothed smile. "Someone gave me your address," he said. "You do typing?"

I saw that he carried a yellow folder. "That's right," I said.

"I've got something I need typing. It's not very long, about eight thousand words. Can you do it?"

Peanuts. Hardly worth my while. "I can do it," I said, "but not till after the weekend."

"That's all right." He shifted his weight and passed the folder to his other hand, looking down. A heavy, childish, slightly Neanderthal cast informed his features, vanishing again as soon as he looked up. "Only I'd like to point out one or two things, bits where it might not be too clear . . . do you have time now?"

I hesitated, not from doubt but because my stupid body was doing all those funny things it does when it fancies someone – changes in the throat, in the chest, so pleasant I wanted just to sit

182

and enjoy them – but he must have taken it as annoyance. "I'm sorry," he said, "I should have telephoned."

"That's OK," I said, and smiled. It was nice, him down there looking up, me on the balcony like the caterpillar on the mushroom. "Bring it up. Hang on, I'll open the door."

So I let him in and fetched another cushion and we sat on the balcony with the melon between us. A soft breeze moved the leaves on the old elder tree at the end of the garden. Esmeralda sprang up beside us and stalked proudly by. I could feel my hair tickling my arms, see it from the corners of my eyes. He took a sheaf of scribbly A4 pages from the folder and started leafing through them and I saw that his handwriting was appalling. "Here, this bit here," he said, pointing to a scrawl in a margin. "This has to go up there, not where it looks as if the arrow goes. Do you see? I put another arrow in, but it's confusing."

He had a soft, low voice.

"OK," I said, feeling pleasantly shy. He took out a green pen and started to write something at the top of the page, whispering to himself, while I looked at him. I could see him following the plough in some old woodcut. There was a rough-featured peasant look about his face: hair straight and yellow, eyes blue and dreamy, the bridge of his nose high, whitened by a slight scar. I thought he looked about twenty-five. He wrote quickly, his hand smooth and brown; he wore a big gold ring and a flashy gold watch though his clothes were nothing special. Then he looked straight at me with a clear frank look, then away, smiling vaguely.

There was that confusing, indefinable something and nothing between us, so that I was suddenly relaxed, very happy, unable to make a wrong move or say a wrong word even though that funny light feeling was still in my chest. I offered him a slice of melon and he took it, eating fastidiously, hardly dripping at all. We sat and talked for about ten minutes. He waved a hand over the scruffy papers and told me they were an article he'd written and was going to send up to a psychology journal. He'd just finished a course in social psychology. He should have been clumsy from the size of his shoulders and hands and feet but there was a certain elegance in the way he sat: hands loose, head tilted, body slightly lopsided.

"So what does a social psychologist do?" I asked, and he grinned.

183

"Picks olives," he said. Then he said he had some more studying to do, but not yet. He was going to hang about in London for the summer then go to the South of France where his sister had a bar, work in the bar for a while, do this and that, start another course the following autumn in Paris. Yes, he spoke the language. His mother was French. He'd grown up half here, half there. The hand with the big gold ring stroked Esmeralda, long, total strokes that gave her visible shudders.

I told him to call me next Tuesday or Wednesday, I should have it done by then; and led him inside where the shadows blinded us. We stood awkwardly.

"I have your number," he said. Then he pulled a little pad from his pocket, tore a sheet off and bent over the table, writing something. "In case there are any problems," he said, and left.

I read his name, address and phone number. Christian Hooper. Lived just the other side of the park, not ten minutes' walk away. Why not? I thought. I smiled and wandered aimlessly about the flat. "Well, well, well," I said to Esmeralda. "How about that, then?"

A diversion. It's been a very long time since I had one worthy of the effort. Funny how you suddenly notice someone. He must have been around the district all along but I never saw him before. Now I see him everywhere. That week I saw him three times. First in the off-licence buying a bottle of red wine. We stood and talked for a few minutes about nothing at all before he had to dash off because he had someone waiting. Then in a baggy grey T-shirt with sweatstains under the arms, kicking a football in the park with some big kids. Then walking along on the other side of the road with his head down, counting money in his palm. There's a nice gentle feel about him.

I typed his article, which was good but pedestrian, called him up and told him it was ready and he was there within the hour, looming shyly in my doorway. We drank coffee and talked about politics and the press. He looked at my books and borrowed one then asked me if I fancied a drink; so we strolled around the corner to the Dog and Gun and sat in the beer garden at a spindly white table. How solid he is, I thought, etched there against the rose bushes and garden wall.

"How did you get the scar on your nose?" I asked.

He said it was from coming off his bike when he was fifteen.

Then we couldn't think of anything to say. Better get drunk, I thought. So I did, and began to feel afraid – I could tell from a hundred invisible signs, from a certain warmth in his eyes, from the way the muscles in his jaw moved when he drank, from the way he crossed his legs and picked his nails, that this one would take away from me everything I'd built over the last two years if I wasn't careful. He'd leave his things in my place, give me new habits, different expectations. Some of me wanted it, some of me didn't.

We talked about where we'd come from. He'd grown up in Portsmouth, and Troyes, near Paris. His father had been in the Navy. I told him I had a sixteen-year-old daughter in Scotland. He didn't say I didn't look old enough to have a sixteen-year-old daughter, just nodded as if it was quite expected.

"What's she doing in Scotland?" he asked.

"I used to live there. When I came back to London she decided she wanted to stay."

"With her father?"

I shook my head. "Her father's dead." And I told him the old, old story: father, motorbike crash, years ago. Then I told him about where I'd lived in Scotland. My voice spoke and my mind raced. Once in my bed, he'll never get out. That's what I thought, and I panicked, watching the sky grow dark behind his big, solid head, his big, solid fist lifting his big, solid pint to his lips. He drank, and his face was once more that sweet, childish Neanderthal. He'd leave his dirty socks stuffed behind the cushions of my settee and turn the TV on at all the wrong times. I couldn't stop him, I couldn't stop him, I knew. He looked at me and smiled and there it was, practically visible, the little ray between Venus and Mars throbbing crude neon. I smiled, panic beating in my breast.

"Well," I said, cool and collected, looking at my watch, "I'd better go now."

He looked surprised and disappointed, said he'd walk with me.

"No, no, it's OK," I said. "You stay and finish your drink. It's out of your way. Well, good luck with the article. See you." And I went, leaving him alone and uncertain at the shaky white table, wondering how come he'd read the signs all wrong and if he'd said something stupid.

I almost ran home – drunk, furious with myself or something

else, I didn't know what; found myself lying sulking on the settee with a dizzy head at nine in the evening. How stupid. Not fair, why can't I have fun like everyone else? Now, Gloria, come on, this other voice said, you know you don't really want all that. You're an independent woman. Think he'd be fobbed off with any old thing? He'd want the lot.

So I fell asleep angry and woke calm. What was all the fuss about? For heaven's sake, he's just some young fellow you had a drink with. Want to make something of it? Anyway, he's going away in the autumn. No harm, whatever you do. And, by the time I'd washed and eaten and walked through the park to buy my paper and a pint of milk, I knew once more that I was strong and powerful and could have whatever I wanted, just so much and no more. So I will if I want to. So there.

Today I work till three in the Red House, a pleasant, sunny bar-cum-restaurant with lattice chairs and round tables, a bowl of fresh flowers on every one. I take my turn in the kitchen, sweating in the heat and steam, preparing corn salad, rice salad, pizza, meat stew with thyme, fresh fruit salad, banana split, picking at the food and listening to the radio. Then I go out and lean on the smooth dark expanse of the bar, drink iced water and talk to Toshinari who's lolling on a stool in front of the chalked-up menu, reading the *Daily Mirror*. Tosh comes from Tokyo. He was a student but he dropped out. He's very bright in an immaculate blue-and-white-striped apron and yellow T-shirt, his thin shoulder blades protruding like the tips of wings.

"Your friend was here," he says, "the one with the mandolin. She said she'd come back."

I nod. There's nothing much doing out here but one coffee and one toasted cheese sandwich with Perrier. The door to the street stands open. Heat shimmers on the glaring white pavement.

Tosh folds his paper closed and comes over to me. "Do my nails," he says. He's obsessed with them. This has become a ritual over the past year. I take a little manicure set from its place under the counter and pointlessly pamper his already faultless nails, while he leans back and sighs erotically. Then he leans his head against my breasts, closing his heavy-lidded eyes. "Mummy," he says, smiling faintly.

"Son," I say.

It's a game we play. We laugh softly.

After the lunch time rush Tina returns. She buys coffee and carrot cake, sits at a table by the door with her mandolin up against the wall. She's been back in London six months trying to earn some money to buy a place in Northumberland with some people she knows. She says she hates London. She busks doggedly and seriously six days a week, starting at seven in the morning and finishing sometimes late at night. Now she's on her coffee break. She saves her money diligently in a Building Society, makes thirty pounds on a good day, playing any old thing: "Honeysuckle Rose", *Captain Pugwash*'s theme, "Show Me The Way To Go Home", "Always", "I'm Forever Blowing Bubbles". All, no matter what, become high melancholy under her slow, thin fingers; she can't play them any other way. You hear her as you wander through the tunnels down below, a desperately wistful sound, all the pathos of a mouth organ round a lonesome campfire.

I take my coffee and go sit with her. She wears a leather jacket and jeans; her hair's still short and spiky, her face tiny and white. She never sweats in the heat. Nothing changes with Tina. You'd never think she was thirty-three.

"Guess who I saw?" she says flatly. "Your ex-old man. And Lisa." She laughs. "Things don't change much, do they?"

I laugh too. A fly buzzes in the door then buzzes out again. Tosh washes glasses in front of a glittering array of bottles. "Where were they?"

"Walking down the platform on the tube station. Him in these big black shades, her in this old jumper down to her knees. Both really dirty, I mean *really* dirty. It's how they walk. Kind of like: Look at me, look at me, I'm not ordinary. So they get to the end of the platform and squat down in all the muck and get out their ciggy papers and baccy and start rolling up, looking round with these disdainful what-are-you-looking-at-type looks. You know. They didn't see me."

They left Scotland, moved here and there, finally ended up back on the old manor in a tower block called Aristotle Point. Now and again I see them. Lisa drinks too much and gets stupid. It's all dear old friends now, no hard feelings, what we three have seen, all mature people, that kind of thing. He's taken to wearing an old black leather cap and looks fierce and striking under it, doesn't write poetry any more, or, if he does, no one gets to see it.

"Kit's still threatening to come," I say.

"I don't see it," she says. "She never liked London."

I shrug. "People change as they get older." I look out of the window and fiddle with my hair. "I don't know," I say. "I hate the thought of living with someone again after all this time, even Kit. Someone's stuff all over the place. Going home and things not being as you left them. Eating with someone. Can't even make a cup of tea without having to say Do you want one? Am I unnatural?"

"No," she says simply. "Tell her she can't come if you don't want her to. She's not said anything definite, has she? Anyway, I thought she had a job up there."

"Only for the summer. In a café."

"Well, then . . ."

"Murmurings," I say, "just murmurings."

"Well . . ." She gestures.

My own daughter. I should want her. "Am I unnatural?" I say again.

She smiles at me, not answering.

"I have this dread of intruders. Sometimes when I go home I stand outside the door for a minute thinking someone's inside. I don't know what I mean. I think I'll open the door and all my things'll be gone or some other person's stuff'll be there. As if someone's taking over. Sometimes I'm scared to look in the mirror in case there's another face there."

She takes my hand across the table and squeezes it. We've come a long way together.

At three I walk down with her as far as the tube station, where we hug and part. We always hug these days, two survivors of a long, strange journey. I think we are surprised to be grown up and hug for reassurance.

I walk on, post a letter to Kit, get home, feed Esmeralda, turn on the TV and let it burble away in the background while I trim my split ends, look out of the window, walk about, pick up a book, put it down, yawn, stretch, get undressed because it's so, so hot, stretch out on the settee naked and watch some rubbish on the screen. I scratch myself all over luxuriously. The TV gets really boring so I start to make love to myself. I'm the best I ever had. First I just squeeze and stroke, then I put the pressure on down there, never too hard or too weak, totally considerate, anticipating my every need. I keep it going for a long time before the explosion. Then I put my arms tightly about myself and give me a loving hug. Then I'm sleepy and still for ages and the TV dribbles crap all over the place till I get up and turn it off.

I lie dreaming in the moose's antlers.

The phone startles me.

I roll over on to the floor and lie there holding the phone. It's a reverse charge call from Scotland. Kit. She's always doing it, the phone bills are enormous. "You'll have to stop doing this," I snap at her before she can speak. "What do you think I am, made of money? Do you know what my last phone bill was?"

"Sorry, Mummy," she says.

Then I feel guilty and tell her not to worry, I know she hasn't got much money. I'm always feeling guilty about Kit. "I've just written to you," I say. "Just this minute posted the letter."

"Oh, goody gumdrops," she says, then takes a deep breath. "Well," she says momentously. "I have decided."

"What?"

"At the end of the summer. I'm coming to London. This time, really."

"Oh." I go blank. "Are you sure? You keep saying . . ."

"Oh, I know, I know." She talks rapidly, fading in and out like someone with a wonky microphone. "I've been changing my mind every five minutes. But this time I've *really* decided. I mean, I know you've only got a little place and I can't stay there too long, but don't worry, Delia's coming and we're getting our own place; if we can just stay there for a little bit, just till we're sorted out. I mean, you're right, you're right, I do love it here but I need a change; we both do and now we've made up our minds absolutely not to go back to school . . ."

"Kit . . ."

"Alastair thinks it's a good idea. Live a bit, he says. Don't end up like me – it's too easy to take root here. I've got my head screwed on, Mummy, I really have, far more than you ever had. Don't you believe me? I'm going up the wall here. Sylvia's in Edinburgh. Tim, oh Tim, he's gone horrible. He's got this horrible girlfriend that's here all the time. *You* know what it's like, sometimes you just have to get away . . ."

"Kit, listen," I say. "I'm not saying don't come. I'm saying think . . ."

"You don't want me to come, do you? You don't want to see me."

I grit my teeth and sigh. "Don't you start this old game, Kit. Of course I want to see you – I just want to be sure you know what you're doing. You're sixteen, you throw up school, head for bright lights, big city – what do you expect me to say?"

She laughs, not amused. "Oh, the concerned mother," she says. "Oh, that's very good, that is."

"Kit," I say sadly, "you come. Just you, without Delia. You just stay here for a while and have a break and then . . ."

"All on my own," she says. "No fun on my own. Delia's my best friend. I've promised. I can't leave her in the lurch."

"What does her mother say about all this?"

"Oh, her mum's all for it."

I don't believe it. "Well," I say, "there's lots of time yet. We can all think some more. Of course you're welcome here but we have to be realistic. That's all."

So we make a truce and talk of other things, the heat, some disaster on the news, Alastair's health. I see the old place as it once was, gone for ever.

"Well, I'll go then now," she says. "Look forward to getting your letter."

"OK," I say. "Take care, Kit. Love to everybody. Bye."

"Bye, Mummy."

I put the phone down and sit on the settee with my knees drawn up, seeing her as I last saw her playing in the lane with a little dog. She looked stocky and brisk, tall. She had a friendly pink face, high sensible voice. Her hair was bright and streaky and spiky, she wore red leather and ribbed tights, Doc Marten shoes. My daughter. I don't want her to come. Everything will change. She'll stay and stay and stay. I won't be able to sit around like this, naked.

I jump up and pace about the room. The plants, my jungle, are a backdrop of undiscipline. The clock says quarter to five. I dress, check my bag for keys, money, lucky fish, practically run out of the place and down to the tube station, where I take a train half a dozen stops, get off and walk through the balmy summer afternoon to Aristotle Point. Why I'm here I don't know, unless it's just that I want to tell someone who knows her well, someone who was there – anyway, they owe me money. I take the lift to the tenth floor, ring the bell and wait, ring again and shout through the letterbox that it's me. They're very paranoid.

There's a kind of shocked look about him when he opens the door. He's like a washed-out hawk, pale and drawn, thin lips ageing more than they should, cheeks falling in on themselves. His hair sticks out in disarray from under the eternal leather cap. "Gloria!" he cries dramatically. "Oh, come in, come in. This is a surprise!" His upper teeth are out.

He walks ahead of me down the hall, which smells of cat shit from the open door of the toilet where the litter tray's kept, lurches into a door and bangs it open. We go into the living-room. At the big window I see blue sky and fluffy white clouds. A hatched partition leads to the kitchen. The room is in a state of flux, as if the contents of a junk yard have been involved in a game of airborne musical chairs and simply dropped down wherever they were when the music stopped. A TV burbles. The hideous carpet is covered in crumbs and fluff and the odd dropped match or cigarette paper. David and Lisa love one another because of their mutual desire to live in chaos.

"Hang on a minute," he says, goes into the bedroom and reappears with his teeth in. "Lisa's out. Sit down, Gloria, sit down."

I sigh as I look at him. I want to take him by the back of his neck and shake him till his bones rattle. I don't know what he's on. I never bother to ask any more. Dope, of course, given the nature of Lisa's business, but something more.

He goes behind the partition and I watch his torso moving about as he makes the coffee. He starts to tell me about the sore glands in his throat. He's had them for ages. He's been to the doctor. "They don't know what's the matter with me," he says proudly, eating a biscuit, his voice full of it. "They keep saying nerves. Bullshit. That's what they say when they don't know." He ducks his head and looks at me through the partition with those scared pale eyes, that too-serious face I can't take seriously. His mouth is a mess, wet and covered in crumbs.

191

"Wipe your mouth," I say.

He does. He brings the coffee in dirty mugs and we drink.

"Kit's coming back," I say. "She wants to stay with me."

He snorts into his mug. "Sooner you than me."

"Is that all you've got to say?"

"Well . . . it won't affect me. She certainly won't spend all her time round here, will she? I mean, she's not exactly my greatest fan." He reaches down to roll another cigarette, chuckling. "She's all right. I don't really mind old Kit. Hell to live with, though."

How tolerant we all are now, how we have matured. It was all so long ago.

"You make me angry," I say flatly, leaning back and looking over his head at the sky. "I can't even talk to you about it. I just wanted to talk about how I feel about her coming back, and I can't even do that. All you can talk about is yourself."

He shakes a match lethargically and is wreathed in a blue cloud. "Gloria," he says, "I take no responsibility for Kit. I don't even feel obligated to talk about her. She's not mine and she never was. I feel no responsibility whatsoever."

"You never did," I say. And there you have it. It means nothing now, nothing at all.

"I'm sorry," he says, "it's true. I never did. She was just something I had to put up with to be with you."

We sit for a while drinking coffee. I ask for the six pounds I'm owed from about a month ago and he tells me next week, there's a big deal coming up, Lisa's seeing about it now. "I've got all this tension in my back," he says. "Top of my spine, I can feel it." He wriggles, rubbing the back of his neck, his face petulant. "Give me a massage, Gloria. You're the only one that's got the touch. Go on."

"Sod off," I say wearily.

"Aw, go on," he says frowning, "don't be mean. Don't be petty. Two minutes. Don't take things out on me; it's not my fault. Come on. Don't rake up the past. What can I do?"

"I hate you sometimes," I say. I sigh. "You're a bastard, David. I don't know how Lisa puts up with you."

He grins and closes his eyes. I go and stand behind him, palpate his neck and shoulders and the knobs of his spine, and he wriggles under my fingers, giggling when I dig them in too hard. I imagine closing my fingers round his throat, crushing the Adam's apple, strangling him. I get bored very soon and refuse to go on.

Lisa comes in. "Hi, Gloria," she says, unpacking groceries into the hatch: bread, biscuits, teabags. Her jeans are very dirty, her face, half hidden by dark glasses, tanned, thin, but slack around the mouth. She's dyed her hair recently and it's very black. "How's tricks?"

"Kit's coming," I say. "She wants to stay with me for a while."

"Oh, how lovely!" she says, taking her glasses off and dropping into a chair, swinging her legs over one arm, dabbling in the mess on a side table.

"Don't be stupid," David says. "It's not lovely at all. Gloria's shitting herself because she doesn't want her to come."

"I am not!"

"Yes, you are."

"Well," says Lisa. "Just tell her she can't. Say it's not convenient. They have to learn."

I don't know why I came here.

"Well," I say, "I've got to be off," and I go into the kitchen to rinse my cup. The cat's dish looks and smells revolting. The sink's half full of dark grey water with orange grease and bits of slimy vegetable matter floating on top.

David follows me out into the hall. "Hang on a minute," he says. "I'll come down with you, I've got to get some fresh dirt." Then he keeps me waiting ages while he tips all the old crap and solid blocks of piss-hardened earth out of the cat tray into a polythene bag. The disturbance of all this causes the stink to intensify.

"Oh, God, David," I say, putting my hands over my nose and mouth, "that's vile, that's really vile."

He grins, gets a little trowel from somewhere and is ready to go. On the landing, he chucks the foul bag down the rubbish chute. We wait for the lift then give up and walk down the stairs. At the bottom we stand talking in the sun for a while by a little patch of earth where he's going to dig with his trowel. He holds the tray before him like an offering; it is indelibly stained with countless fillings of earth and smears of dried cat shit that have created a fuzzy piebald effect on the white plastic. Then he squats down and scoops earth into the litter tray, rocking on his heels, prodding gently at the earth, turning it over and over carefully.

193

"Some of these little whatsits," he says. "Incredible."

"Little what?"

"Little things that live in the ground." He rises and comes over, holding one hand cupped in front of him. "You've got to be really careful," he says, "don't want them getting in the tray." He smiles suddenly and his eyes go warm. "What a way to go: smothered alive in cat shit." A fat, grey, segmented thing lies curled in his palm.

"That's a leatherjacket," I say.

"Is that what it is?" He turns and squats again, laying it gently back in the earth. There's a kind of deep familiarity about him that amounts to a kind of indelible fondness you could almost call love. But it's very tired. I walk away, catch the bus instead of the tube. It goes down his road, past Aristotle Point, and I see him there in the sun, continuing his pleasant, lazy examination of the soil, a smile on his face.

Getting off at my stop, I walk along by low walls, little gardens, yards. African rhythms well into my ears as I come level with a window, ebb as I pass. I walk across the park towards my street, grow suddenly vague and stand by a little pond, letting the late sun on the water hypnotise me. I feel myself drifting into another space and pull myself back, drift, pull back, drift, pull back, drift. I sit on the ground and wallow in drifting. A moorhen struts by me, sweet creature. I am a child sitting in the mud on the banks of the pool where I used to live. The moorhens make their nests on little tufty islands. Mist drifts. The old wooden bridge rattles. A woman walks to her execution.

"Hello," someone says.

Of course. Must be fate that I am here at this moment and so is he. Who am I to buck fate? I look up. "Hello, Christian," I say. Won't you come into my parlour? I'm dangerous. I stand and smile, we talk. He carries a sack, he's been doing his laundry, he says, grinning foolishly. And then we walk along together very slowly, looking away in opposite directions, not speaking. I'm sweating. I wipe my upper lip surreptitiously. Two boys on skateboards zoom past us down the path. We come to a spot where a beautiful old tree lies on its side, its great leafy boughs forming green caves where children sometimes play. Here we sit on the horizontal trunk, listening to the sound of rackets hitting balls in the tennis courts.

I'm going for him, yes, I am. I don't care. Because I know I can. He has long, strong cords in the side of his neck, his thighs are apart. I don't care. I'm not even bothered about timing or subtlety or playing the game. We don't speak for so long that the silence becomes a tension in the space that separates our bodies. His lower lip hangs prominent, soft, dry, delicately creased. Heat generates between my legs. Suddenly I smile, very happy, excited. Today was so bland and now it is not. I'm going for him.

A yellow-and-black-striped caterpillar walks along a branch over his head. I watch it, fascinated. It makes me think of the mushroom field. I reach up, my slick exposed chest coming closer to his eyes as I stretch over him, pluck the caterpillar from its creeping walk and place it on my palm, settling down again. It tickles, walking on my palm. I am the hand of God. That was the right move. Every move I make is the right move. He's looking at me and I can read his face. I have him, I've plucked him like the hand of God.

"That's an alder moth," he says.

The tension goes.

"Is it?" I say. "How do you know?"

He shrugs. "I know a bit about insects," he says. "It's called an alder moth but you get them around oaks too. Plenty of oaks around here."

I smile. "You weren't one of those awful little boys who pin butterflies on boards, were you?"

"Oh, no," he says immediately. "I just liked looking at things. I had my spotter's book, you know. And I had some things in glass jars, but I took good care of them. I love insects." He leans forward, animated, telling me about a caterpillar that has red tails and an awful face, a green beetle that turns red when you pick it up, a yellow ladybird. I forget about the caterpillar on my hand till he reaches out and lifts it gently, curling, puts it back in the tree. "I think he's happier there," he says.

I think he's delightful.

I tell him about the little black thing on the mound at the back of our house in Scotland, the glyph of Neptune on its back. "What would that have been?" I ask.

He shrugs again. He shrugs a lot. He says it sounds like some kind of bug to him. I laugh. "I could have told you that," I say. Then I stop thinking, lean forward into the smell of his face and hair and kiss him on the lips, which smile as mine approach, opening to let me in. He's going away in the autumn. I don't care. I'll have some fun now. He puts one hand behind my head, his sweet tongue glides, my own sweet tongue glides, his eyes roll back under their lids and the lashes quiver. He's warm and tasty. Some little hairs curl in front of his ear. We move closer till my breasts flatten against him, hold each other and rest our two heads, each looking away across the other's shoulder, breathing slowly, rising and falling together. He strokes my back kindly, I stroke his.

"Now we have to get to know each other," he says. Suddenly I see Esmeralda walking down the centre of the path, firm and steady towards the gate, and I hear the sound of tennis balls. A great weariness seeps into me. I don't want to get to know him. I want to bite his lip, stoke the heat, stroke his back, rub against him like one stick against another making fire. I was skinned once. Do I really need to put on another skin, tentatively, little by little till it sticks invisible, just over my own? Only, little by little, to be skinned again, made bloody and raw all over?

What have I done?

We draw apart and look at each other. He smiles. Then he draws his eyebrows down and says, "What's the matter?" I don't know what he's seen in my face. For the first time I notice how mobile his brow is.

"Nothing." I'm lightheaded.

He holds my hands, then lifts them and kisses them in a courtly gesture.

"What shall we do?" he says. "I want to come home with you, stay with you all night. But I can't. I have a meeting. Shall I come later?"

My ears are muffled. "Tomorrow," I say.

"Tomorrow. When?"

"Tomorrow night. I'll be in."

He smiles and pulls me close, hugs me fiercely and kisses me again. I can't shake it, I can't shake it, the muffler pulling tighter and tighter round my ears, my face, my entire head. I can't breathe. I kiss him, eyes closed, hiding it all. I *will* have fun.

"Tomorrow," I say, pulling away. "I have to go now." I stand.

"Gloria," he says.

"What?"

"Tomorrow night," he says.

I walk away. After all, this is nothing. A snog in the park. I go home, flustered, bang my hand against the side of my head to clear it. Esmeralda's there before me, she mews under the iron steps. A meeting, I think. What meeting? What kind of people go to meetings? Tomorrow night. Fun.

I get this awful feeling as I come in, just for a second as I enter. It's almost panic. As if I'm coming in on someone else. Oh, go away, feeling, whatever you are I can't be bothered. I have enough on my plate. I hate this, I will not have it, the worm of fear. Feelings that creep up and touch you slyly, like a paw, on the back of the neck.

I check the wardrobe, the cupboards, the kitchen, under the bed. Everything's normal.

16

After work I go to the South Bank and wander in the sun, the heat burning my arms. I buy an ice-cream that splurges like pink and white diarrhoea out of a machine, a fluted spiral with a peak on top, lose myself amongst the tourists walking along the embankment. Bright in their summer clothes they stroll, dark glasses, cameras, paunches, sandals, ice-cream. I sit down on a bench and watch them go by, thinking about Christian. I've slept with him three times now. In the mornings he brings me tea and kisses my toes. I'm not seeing him till the weekend. We're being very sensible. I've told him I won't get too involved and he says OK, what's the rush, we both have plenty to do. He studies in the library and works a couple of days a week in a big house full of disturbed kids, sometimes staying the night there. I see him playing football with them in the park.

I like Christian. I think about him a lot, and when I do I end up smiling stupidly.

I walk on. On Hungerford Bridge a stocky black man plays "Stormy Weather" on a saxophone. Clink! go the coins from time to time, as now and then a figure stoops and drops something into the cap that lies before him on the ground. I stand watching the river. Must be the heat, suddenly I feel funny, all foggy and lost in it all — the silver on the water, the wake of a pleasure boat heading for Greenwich, the soulful breathy notes of the saxophone, the summer air. Clink! Clink! go the coins. Nothing so melancholy as a saxophone. Silver on the water blinds me. I'm going to faint. Stop it, stop it. I'm like a dot getting smaller and smaller, there's nothing I can do. But I don't fall down, I just go out, my empty body stands amazed looking into the Thames with nothing to tell it what to do, and the world goes by like a lethal indifferent current.

I come back. My ears sing. I think I'm going to float like a bubble away above the rooftops, away into the terrible emptiness of the sky, so I hang on to the rail and swallow and let it all back in, the clink, clink, the saxophone, the strange tongues chattering, the megaphoned voice of the pleasure boat. I wonder if there's something wrong with me, something in the brain maybe. I turn and walk away from the river, walk and walk, then get a bus home. Going down my street I see Esmeralda coming out of the park. She sees me and quickens to a clumsy run, raising her face and mouthing silently at me. "Hello, sweetheart," I say, "my little pussy cat. Who's a lovely little pussy cat?" She walks along home beside me like a dog till we reach the house, then stalks away to vanish into the long grass and shadows under the elder tree, heavy with Motherdie. A full moon rises in the light blue sky. A little breeze comes from somewhere. I think there'll be rain. It will be welcome.

I go in and open the window to let in the fragrance of the garden, make salad and omelette and eat it at my table by the window, then sit looking out as the evening comes on. Christian's working tonight. What happened by the river? Was it the heat or something else? No, no, nothing else. I'm perfectly healthy. The sky deepens. A small shadow, my dear Esmeralda, moves from the base of the elder tree at the end of the garden, disturbs the grass and springs gracefully for all her bulk to the top of the wall. Her silhouette against the deep blue sky is like a cat in a child's picture book, perfectly symmetrical. I pick up my ocarina and play something short and plaintive, repeating and repeating it till everything is a mingling of twilight and sound, feel suddenly afraid and stop, thinking: My God, what is happening? The silence is unnatural for the city, some illusion, some deafness. I look around, uneasy. It's quite dark out there now. The moon hangs enormous. I call Esmeralda in and close the window. The garden is bluish in the moonlight which etches the tree and the lovely bough that stretches towards me as if offering something, picks out the distant faces of wailing men and women in the bricks of the high back wall. Above is the flat, starless sky. The moon hurls silence at me. I feel a tension in the soft blue scene. The two little steps leading to the lawn are the approach to an empty stage, I am the audience. The appearance of the players is imminent. Offstage, a soundless laugh. I watch, transfixed. It's so quiet I can hear the faint whooshing sound of a million empty miles coming together inside my head.

Then the rain starts very softly, pinpricks of light on the window, making a tiny sound like hundreds of opening mouths. Something cold rubs itself like a paw in the hollow at the base of my skull.

Fear.

Here it comes again.

As soon as I turn my back, something will invade the garden, something I do not want to know. But I break away, close the curtains, turn away, saying Nonsense, stop this, pull yourself together. It's all in the mind.

I go upstairs to the bathroom and splash cold water all over my face and shoulders. Coming back, I see that the door that leads to the upper house stands open. Looking through, I see a thin woman in a long silver dress ascending the broad stairs in the dark. The moonlight through the window on an upstairs landing gives enough light to see her by. I close the door and go back and sit in the chair by the fire.

I start to tremble. Esmeralda stops washing herself and looks at me as if I've somehow changed. I tremble all over, look down at my trembling in amazement. There's a kind of vibration in my ears as if something's shatteringly loud but just beyond my senses.

I can't get it out of my head that I've seen a ghost.

The phone rings and I grab it and listen.

"Hi, Mummy," Kit says. "How's that for a surprise? Me paying for a call?"

The trembling fades and stops. "Hello, Kit."

She's all sunny. She's dying to see me. She's going to work in a hairdresser's when she gets here, there's this girl Delia knows who's got a friend who works in a top salon and reckons he can get her in as a trainee. "It's all right here," she says, "but me and Delia, we're both ready to move on. After all, you can't stay all your life in one spot. *You* didn't." They're going to get a flat somewhere like Pimlico. Pimlico's nice. Yes, of course she realises it's not that simple, but nothing venture . . . positive thinking, that's the way to do it. It'll be all right. She's really looking forward to the big city. She's ready for it now. Then she's gone as suddenly as she was there, like a quick burst of some loud programme on the radio.

I sit back and take a deep breath. She's coming, that's a fact. And if she's coming, she'd better be with me. I look around. The room is plain and flat, normal. I've been stupid today, easily panicked.

All I have to do is carry on as if nothing's happened. I put on the TV and watch something brash and banal till it's time to go to bed, then dig out a night light from the back of a drawer. I haven't used one in ages, but tonight I will. Not because anything's wrong, it isn't. It's passed, whatever it was. The people upstairs have a visitor, nothing strange about that. I lie and drift then think about Christian. I wonder if he's asleep in that big house full of delinquents, or if he's lying awake thinking about me. I toss and turn, remember the two of us sweating and striving together in this bed, how it felt to dig my fingers in his flesh, stick my tongue in his ear and feel him squirm, and how his fingers felt, gently probing.

For a long time I lie in the moose's antlers. I forget about the strange and the passing strange. The forest soars above me like a cathedral, the moss is soft, the great beast paces down these long lush tracks where even the shadows are green. I fall asleep to the steady, swaying rhythm of his walk.

I sit in front of the mirror covered in a fine sheen of sweat, wondering how to look, getting ready to go out with Christian to this party at some friend of Tina's. I clean my face, put heavy make-up around my weary, rather bloodshot eyes, thinking of last week when I went down for my father's funeral.

I didn't feel very much. I remembered the way his false teeth clicked, walking with him on the cliff path, hating his moped, handing him his dinner as he sat in front of the telly. I remembered him telling me to stop whingeing. As the coffin was lowered into the grave, I suddenly remembered him grinning at Pearly the Mouse through the bars of her cage. The church bell rang, an echo from childhood. Afterwards we had tea and sandwiches and wine. And then I went gladly away, past my old house with its usurped windows and the hedge where I hid Pearly's cage, past the pool, past a thin strip of no-man's land at the side of a modern housing estate, all that is left now of the mushroom field. Never to return.

He left ten thousand pounds for me, nothing for Kit. I never knew he had that much. I'll give her a thousand, some when she gets here, some when she's older. Of course, she's coming. Of course, she'll stay as long as she wants. I owe her that much.

I walk out into the summer night, go to Christian's place and stand there on the doorstep with my dress sticking to me. He lives at the top of an old terraced house with a row of bells framed by peeling wood, in a room full of piles of books and papers that rise up from the floor like a city of skyscrapers. He calls out of a window for me to wait, then comes down, and we walk down to the High Street hand in hand and take a taxi to a block of flats where a party blasts sound and light into a courtyard. The party is full of studded noses, ears with multiple rings, spiky hair and black leather. Tina's there. We hang around a mantelpiece full of nuts and twiglets and crispy things and I wonder why I've come. I never did like parties. A door is open and a cool breeze comes in from the balcony.

Under the party babble I keep thinking I hear someone say my name, but it's never real. I'm wiser now. I don't call this fancy or imagination. I know it's a voice, for me, but what it wants to say I don't know. So I just keep taking my plastic cup into the tiny kitchen that's crammed like a lift in the rush hour, and keep filling it up from a bowl of reddish punch that never diminishes and changes colour every time I go back to it.

Christian is one of those people you can take anywhere; there is an innocence about him that trusts all company and does not judge. He is at home. So it is that everyone he meets gets the feeling that they already know him. I watch him now as he talks to someone across the room, full of admiration because this is something I'll never have. The light on his big friendly face makes him slightly unearthly: the beak-like swoop of his nose, the steep upward curve of his mouth. His eyes are very blue. There is a reality about him that shocks me, a little kick inside, a slight quickening of the heartbeat. He's tied to me like another self, a projection. I always know where he is even when he's out of my sight. I feel dangerous, as if I'm the cliff he's about to fall over, but what can I do? What *can* the cliff do? I'm just there.

When he looks up and sees me in the distance he smiles and lets his eyes stay on me. A deep, strong pleasure fills them. I can't remember the last time a look like that was turned upon me.

Someone says it's raining, would you believe? People are dancing. People are drumming. I've lost count of these drinks.

"Gloria," someone says, touching me lightly on the shoulder. When I turn around there's no one there.

The room is orange, a palm tree scrapes the ceiling. A woman in two bits of white lace joined by strings criss-crossing her midriff

202

struts by on high gold heels. People are roaring with laughter. The music slides and dips and soars. Christian is tying up the window curtain where someone, drunk and silly, has pulled it down. Christian's fingers coax, his hands are gentle. I go outside.

Tina stands leaning on the wall of the balcony, looking down through the fine, gently swirling rain at the lights shining in the slippery courtyard. I go and lean beside her and we stand silently for a while. Her face is lean and lucent, the little wisps of hair above her brow quiver slightly in the night air.

For some reason I start telling her about Pearly the Mouse, how she starved to death because I forgot to feed her, how she turned into a mass of maggots that heaved about in the bottom of the cage, how I carried her outside, my stomach also heaving, pushed the cage out of sight under the hedge and never went there again. Then I stop talking and just remember Pearly the Mouse and the terrible loneliness of her life. I remember the fine lilac veins in her perfect, paper-thin ears.

"A-aw," says Tina. "Oh, Gloria, how awful."

I never thought before what it must have been like.

I imagine the poor little mouse running about in her foul cage, pissing on her own piss, shitting on her own shit, good little houseproud mouse eating the last of her dutifully stored food, wondering somehow in her minute brain why the big moonfaced creature didn't come and hover again, bringing food and fresh water. The water turned sludgy and then dried up. She must have run around and around that metal box of hell, from nest to wheel to empty pots, nest to wheel to empty pots; and all alone she must have grown weaker, run slower, raised herself up against the bars on her fragile pink feet, looking out desperately into the beyond with her thin pink nose twitching. Does a mouse hope? Does she lose hope? And sometimes, in the distance, she must have seen that big moon creature pass, stuffed and blind and ignorant.

I see the very faint smudge of chocolate on Pearly's flank. Such a detail to follow me down all the years.

I'm guilty as Hitler.

I hope I starve to death and get eaten by rats in my next life. I abandon all my creatures. The courtyard blurs and sparkles. My eyes expand, then I close them and cry and cry, throat aching with the effort of silence, a hard, deep, violently suppressed crying like poison escaping from a pinprick. I try to hide it but give up and let go.

"Oh, Gloria," Tina says. "It wasn't your fault. People shouldn't give animals to children."

I cry so hard I crouch down on the balcony and lose consciousness, go inside my head where it's all dark and swirly and some presence laughs at me. *Bit late now, isn't it?* she says gleefully. She has the voice of a child, the authority of a parent.

Then I come to. Christian is peering into my face. "That's it," he says, "that's it. It's all right now." He pats my hand affectionately and smiles, then gives me a tissue. The bricks behind him are red and shiny. Tina stands watching. The leanness of her face, I see now, is because she's older. My God, I think inanely, we're all getting older. My God, we really are!

"Oh, how stupid," I say. My teeth chatter. "I don't know what happened. I don't know where all that came from." I laugh. They laugh too, relieved.

"How much of this stuff have you drunk?" asks Tina, pointing to the cup of punch which I'm still holding.

"Too much," I say, and laugh again.

Christian puts his arm around me and gives me a squeeze, treating me like a child. "Shall we go home?" he says.

I nod. I stand up, my knees tremble. We go inside and I fix my face up in front of a mirror in someone's bedroom. Two girls sit talking on the bed, taking no notice of me. How thin and white and ghostly my hands look, fluttering in my hair. I think they are quite beautiful, like small white birds, so I let them play about for a while in the dark air about my face. They keep coming together and snapping at each other, angry little birds. The girls are looking at me now. I turn and look at them to let them know I think it's rude to stare, and they pretend they weren't watching at all and go back to their conversation.

So I go out into the hall where he's waiting and we walk down to the street and move through tranced, drunk, 1 a.m. silence past closed pubs, shuttered shops, old redbrick flats. The rain is soft, the air seems fresh and sweet like country air. I am wide awake, alert, nerves stretched. On the main road the wheels hiss their cold hiss, take-aways and a club are still open, people wait at bus stops. We catch an all-night bus full of loose, inebriated people, then

204

another that's nearly empty. I look out of the window and think that everything out there is a great exhibition for me alone – lights and faces and windows and signs above shops. I lean against him and he turns his face against my hair and we go tense. Then I turn my head up and kiss him on the mouth. We sit close and still till it's time to get off.

The rain's stopped. A long black street unfolds ahead like a shiny ribbon of liquorice. We turn off it and walk home past the fragrant, mysterious mass of the park. We are different tonight. We don't speak.

Esmeralda's in a foul mood because I've left her out in the rain all this time. She yells a long moan at me from under the iron steps when she sees me, then follows us in and plods about the room snarling for a bit before settling down to wash herself, making a big wet patch on her favourite chair.

Christian stands big and awkward about the place, as if it's his first time here. I look at him and see a shadow in his face and think: How funny, how funny, he's so easy with everyone else and now he doesn't know what to say. But he starts to talk in a fast, flat tone that means he's nervous. He says this is very important to him; it's not just any old thing and he doesn't want to start it if he can't be sure it's going to last. He'd rather go home now if I'm not serious. Am I? Am I? He'd like to know. Such impossibilities he demands. I can't lie to him but I haven't the strength to let him go. So I step over to where he's standing and put my arms around his neck and kiss him.

"How long have we known each other, Christian?" I ask him.

He calculates, sliding his arms around me. "Six weeks," he says, "I think."

"Six weeks, and what do you want? Promises? I don't know the future." I kiss him again, right between his serious eyes, but he draws back and looks into my face.

"I don't want this to be casual," he says.

I just look at him. I don't know what to do. He isn't getting out of here tonight, that much I know. Then I realise it's too late for him – it doesn't matter what I do; so I relax, go soft against him and tell the truth. "I don't know," I say. "That's the truth. I want you to stay here with me tonight, that's all I know."

And that's all it takes. We go into the bedroom and lie down facing each other. Our shoes drop to the floor, my damp hair curls like petals into my face. We take our clothes off and come together. His thighs are long, his bones hard, his skin smooth as silk. I want to bite him, crush him till his bones crack. We put our arms and legs around each other and play for a long time, squeezing and stroking and licking and kissing, till I invite him in and hold him there, and we go on and on and on, looking into each other's faces. Our skin is hot and sticks together.

In the end we're steamy and sweaty and tired and full and lie peacefully joined at the crotch like Siamese twins, our hips still slowly rocking together. We smile, touching each other's faces. Then we get under the covers and snuggle up and he kisses my eyes, putting the hair back solicitously from my forehead, strand by strand. "Do you feel all right now?" he asks. "Everything's all right, isn't it? There. There."

I wake at dawn and look at him sleeping. His lips are rough and dry, the lower hanging childish and full. I study him curiously, look at the hairs up his nose, the marks on his skin, the pattern of his eyebrows. His throat moves from time to time. What does this mean? What am I doing? Pulling on a skin, pulling on another skin. I'm scared. I kiss him for comfort but he doesn't wake. I fall asleep, wake again, see him sleeping still, turned towards me, the hand with the big gold ring curled at his cheek, the sheet pulled up around his neck. The smell of his breath excites me so I kiss him again and carry on till he wakes and rolls hard against me and it begins again and goes on all morning, sleeping and waking, till the sun's high in the sky and I wake with a start from a drifting doze, alone.

He doesn't come back. I get up in sudden panic, sick at heart, wander about like a fool picking things up and putting them down. If he could walk off without a word after all that, the world's upside down. I must have read him wrong. He's not coming back, he's not coming back. I grab Esmeralda and hug her forcibly and she scratches me. My throat feels tearful. I go to the mirror. I look awful – oh God – I pull at my hair, poke at the skin under my eyes, bare my teeth and examine them. I'm nine years older than him. I walk about, stand at the window looking out at the garden. I hurt, feel old, ancient, tired, sick. I go into the bedroom, lie down in the bed in the smell of our sex, the stained sheets.

The door opens.

"The milk had gone off," he says, his arms full of a plastic bag. "Hope you don't mind – I left the door on the latch; didn't want to wake you." He tosses me a newspaper and goes off to make tea.

I feel like when I was a kid and got a day off school; want to giggle and hug myself gleefully. First I read the paper in bed, then I get up and sit with him at the round table overlooking the garden while we eat breakfast. This is a game, a lovely game.

We go out and sit on the balcony, very close, smiling and stupid, and talk about ourselves. He wants to know it all, everything about me, he says. I smile mysteriously. How can he know it all? What do I tell? I can give him a picture, leave in this, take out that. It's up to me. He wants to know what made me cry, so I tell him about Pearly and Shep and then I show him my lucky fish and my ocarina. "Play something," he says, so I do, and he laughs and throws his arms around me.

"I'm falling for you," he says. "In at the deep end, I can't help it. I say everything too soon. Come away with me in October, everything you're doing here you can do there. Have you got a passport?"

"Yes."

"Good. It's easy, then. You just come with me, it's as easy as that."

"I can't," I say, drawing away. "My daughter's coming."

He doesn't speak for a while then he says, "Can I brush your hair?"

We go inside and I sit on the floor leaning against him as he brushes slowly, thoroughly, untangling patiently with his fingers, lifting the roots of my hair from the nape of my neck so that darts of pleasure disperse like liquid through my skull. Now and again he bends forward over me and kisses my lips, his mild blue eyes filled with a mixture of kindness and desire. He seems to me absolutely lovely, strange, unlike anything I've known. I close my eyes, leaning back against him. He could have been my father in another life, brushing my hair in front of the fire before bedtime. There could have been warmth in childhood. I could cry. The brush glides through my hair, electric, the hairs flying out under it, all around my head.

He tells me about the bar his sister runs, how we can stay there;

there are rooms for tourists but that time of year there'll be plenty of room. Don't worry about money, he says, he'll take care of that, oh, yes, don't worry about it, he has enough and he can get more, his family's well-off. It's quite near Avignon, he says. On the Rhône. There are olive groves, vineyards. And then we'll go to Paris. He'll teach me the language. We can hire a car when we get over there. Can you drive? Good, but anyway the trains are good over there, not like here . . .

"Christian," I say, turning and taking the brush from his hand, "Christian, my daughter's coming. Didn't you hear me?"

"Your daughter," he says solemnly. "How long have you lived apart?"

"Four years."

"Four years. And now suddenly you *must* be with her. You aren't close. You told me so. You don't want her to come here." He looks away, blanking his eyes. "You use your daughter as an excuse not to come with me."

Very suddenly I'm angry. I jump up and cry, "It's too soon, leave me alone! What do you want me to do? Leave my daughter? My home? Everything? I only just met you! I've told you, I've told you, I'm not coming, and if I do it'll be *my* decision, not yours! Leave me alone!" I run into the bedroom and stand fuming. He will not tell me what to do.

A moment later he stands in the doorway. "I'm sorry," he says.

"Don't try and take over, Christian," I say. "Don't you dare try and take over." I sit down on the bed, exhausted.

He comes and takes my hands. "You're right," he says. "I have no right to influence you. I'm sorry."

Day after day we are together. I lead a charmed existence: someone's on my side. Sometimes when he's out and I'm alone in the flat, I stop and stand still and laugh aloud. Then I feel afraid.

I buy a new dress, a long, thin, silky thing the colour of autumn leaves. When I wear it I feel sleazy and sophisticated all at once. We walk in the park between flaming flowerbeds, me in my new dress; sit down on a bench and watch the tame squirrels under the trees. I lie back against him, reach up and touch his sun-warmed hair. We say sweet things to each other. I go to work, type, talk to my friends. "I'm not sure," I say. "I don't know what to do . . . Kit's coming."

Christian wants me to go away with him. Everyone gives me advice.

I sit in the kitchen at the Red House watching Tosh knead pastry, his bony brown arms smeared with flour. "I don't know why you make such hard work of everything," he says. "Just stick with this Christian, he treats you OK – settle down, have a few kids. Not like Kit, you were too young. You're a nice girl, Gloria; you should have a man. You deserve a good life."

Tina says, "What's the rush? Don't let him push you into anything. You don't owe anyone anything, not him, not Kit, not anyone. Now me, I never get into these situations."

Mary says it's a baby I want, not a man: I'm mistaking my emotions. Men all turn out the same anyway. "Get pregnant but don't tell him," she says. "He's going, anyway, so he'd never know. No skin off his nose. I manage with Josie, don't I? We could pool our resources, mutual support, that's what it's all about."

Christian sleeps considerately, giving me room. His face changes, as faces do when you get to know them. He says he loves me. What does this mean? What exactly is it that he loves? Is it my new dress, this summer's tan, the way I make coffee or climb on top of him in the morning? Is it my face? What if I take my face off, tear the frontage from my head, blacken the teeth, singe the hair? Who'd love Gloria if she was ugly? Who'd love sick, old, tired, weak Gloria?

I don't know what he means.

I panic one day. I look around: his clothes are all over the floor in the bedroom, his books creep on to the shelves, his smell is in the bathroom, the food he likes in the fridge. Who is this? He turns on the television in the morning. I never do that. He lies asleep on the settee, head thrown back, one arm trailing. A dribble crawls from the limp corner of his mouth. When he wakes, he looks bleary like a child as he grins at me, his hair standing on end.

"Christian," I say, "I need some time alone."

He considers this. "Am I being greedy?" he asks.

He doesn't argue. "Give me a couple of days," I say. "Anyone'd think we were living together."

Next morning he leaves a silence in his wake, one I lie in with closed eyes, appreciating like a hot bath. I hear the faint ticking of

209

the clock, the capable clicking of Esmeralda's tongue as she washes herself. I decide to spend the day like a cat, dreaming and dozing and meditating. I'm on a plateau. I don't care about anything. I fantasise that me and Christian live happily ever after, tell it to myself like a story that goes on and on and ends nowhere. Later I get up, eat, wash a few things for work tomorrow, hang them on the line and watch them drip into the long grass. I type someone's manuscript. It's so boring I keep making mistakes and yawning, rubbing my thighs together and stopping and thinking about last night: Christian, Pearly and Shep; Kit saying, "I hate you, Mummy," David saying, "You are responsible. Whatever becomes of me, you are responsible. Never forget that." Then I remember David at seventeen sniffing the spines of old books on the market. "When I'm rich," he says, "I'll have a library full of old books. I won't read them. I'll just go in every now and then and smell them."

I am leaning on the typewriter, gazing out of the window, my eyes full of tears. I can't go through it all again, I can't. If I could cut out of me the bit that feels . . .

I pull myself together and type, my fingers dance. Click, click, go the keys, and the sun patches on the wall move round as the day proceeds.

Someone knocks on the door that leads into the house. This is very unusual. I get up and open it and there's no one there. The hall is flat brown, the stairs run down to the bathroom. "Go away," I say loudly. I listen.

After a moment, just as I knew she would, she speaks. The voice I heard at the party, child-woman. I know it's her because she speaks in two places at once, here in my head and there in the hall of the house below.

Are you coming? she says, and then she laughs in that way she has, controlled and rather tired.

She can't fool me. I know who she is. Little Gloria. She won't lie down and die. I hate her. I'm angry and eager, want to see her face to face, the little horror, grab her and shake her till she's all blurred, till her teeth rattle and her bones break, till she's all gone. I'll get her yet.

So I run out of the room, down the stairs, push open the door that leads into the main body of the house and step into the hall. It's empty and the house creaks peacefully. Some flies buzz around the front door, up and down the window panes. The door opens. A willowy secretary woman who lives upstairs comes in carrying a Debenham's bag. She's very shiny and tanned and her make-up is too thick and makes her look older than she really is. She smiles, wondering what I'm doing down here.

"Hello," I say, smiling, feeling silly, and pretend to be looking for mail on the hall table, though everyone knows I get my mail delivered through my own entrance round the back.

"Isn't it lovely and cool in here?" I say foolishly.

"Yes, it is," she says, and tells me about the crowds in town.

I go up and sit in my room, listening. Esmeralda comes and sits on the arm of my chair, purring and watching me with what I like to think of as fondness. I go rigid with listening but nothing comes so I start to cry with irritation. Esmeralda moves very slightly, as if she thought about coming nearer to me but thought better of it, makes a soft little sound in her throat, never taking her eyes off me. We sit like this, companionable, till the sun fades. Then I jump up and grow brisk again, eat, watch TV, sort out my clothes, feed Esmeralda, water the garden and my plants.

There is a stumbling and a mumbling outside, then a prolonged ringing of the bell.

"Who is it?" I call through the door.

"Me!" comes David's voice, and Lisa giggles.

"Shit," I whisper, opening the door. They burst into the place, crude and intrusive like a very bad quiz show, dead drunk, reeking, laughing. David's cap is askew, his face dirty with one black eye. Lisa wears some terrible old fur that smells like a wet animal.

"Glory, Glory!" cries David, flinging his arms around me and trying to kiss my lips with his wasted ones.

I pull away. "For heaven's sake," I mutter.

"Whoops!" shrieks Lisa, falling into a chair, laughing and laughing in a thin, high, uncontrolled way, pulling a quarter bottle of Scotch out of her handbag.

"Don't be like that!" David yells in my ear. "Aw, come on, now, Glory, don't be like that." He strides over to Lisa and shakes her by the arm as if trying to wake her up. "She's not even pleased to see us," he says. "We come to see her and she's not even pleased to see us."

211

Lisa thinks this is very funny, goes weak with laughter. "Where's the glasses?" she asks. "Come on, get them out."

Both of them shout. Esmeralda escapes through the window.

"I'm not getting you any glasses," I say coldly. "I don't want a drink. I don't want you here like this, drinking and acting stupid. What have you come here for?"

"Right!" says Lisa, uncapping the bottle. "Right! I'm not too posh to drink out of the bottle!" She does, then passes it to David, who's watching me very closely. The skin under his eye gleams shiny blue, like an insect's back.

"You're a misery sometimes, you are," he says. "A right bloody misery."

"Oh, I'm not in the mood," I say. "What do you want?"

They never come unless they want something.

"You, my dear," Lisa says, jumping up and going to the record player, long legs graceful. "To see our old friend, Gloria. Our dear, darling little Gloria." She puts on a record and turns the volume knob to maximum.

"Turn it down!" I tell her.

She ignores me, dancing drunkenly through the room. Her lipstick has bled into the lines above her mouth. I turn the volume down. She giggles and turns it up again.

"No, Lisa." I turn it down. She tries to turn it into a game, she turning it up, me turning it down, her face wide with laughter.

"No!" I yell.

"Boring old cow!" she says, throwing herself down in the chair again.

"Shut up, Lisa," David snaps, sitting beside me on the settee and offering the bottle.

"What have you done to your eye?" I ask, refusing the bottle.

"*I* haven't done anything to it," he says, aggrieved. "It's what this bloke did to it. Real heavy geezer." He wipes his face with his hand and launches into some rambling tale about how he owes some money to someone somewhere, some bloke hit him, he was in real danger, really, I mean if he'd had a knife . . . He grows angry and sulky, looks down at his feet.

"True, true," Lisa says, reaching for the bottle. "He could've been killed. My angel could be dead by now. I'd *die, die* without my

212

angel. You know, I'd hate me if I was you, Gloria. Give it *here*, you bastard!" she bellows at David, who isn't passing the bottle.

"Piss off," he says. "You've had more than me anyway."

"NO, I haven't! NO, I haven't!"

"For Christ's sake, shut up!" I yell.

She jumps up and stands over me with fists clenched.

"Oh, sod off, Lisa," says David, putting a hand against her midriff and pushing her hard so that she totters backwards and falls down on the rug. She lies there on her back, laughing weakly with her knees in the air. "She's drunk," he says.

"Never," I say.

"I owe money," he says to me again. "I'm scared to go out. This," he says, pointing dramatically to the bruise under his eye, "this is nothing. Just a warning. I mean, I'm really scared. Next time it could be shooters. Or a knife in the gut. Or in the face. I mean, these people don't play, it's for real . . . Gloria, do you understand? Do you?"

I feel tired. "What do you want?" I say.

"Lend us twenty quid," he says.

"But you already owe me . . ."

"Please! Please, Gloria! You may be saving my life."

"Why?" I say. "What about the business? Take it out of that."

"Tell her," he says to Lisa, "*tell* her, for God's sake."

Lisa turns her head on the carpet and smiles at me. "Business is bad," she says simply.

"Wow," I say dryly, "that's a turnaround. I thought you were up for businesswoman of the year." I mimic her. "Oh, yes, I treat my customers good. I don't do no bad stuff. They know me. Treat 'em right, they treat you right. This is a good business, this is, so long as you got your head screwed on right. This time next year we'll have enough for the holiday of a lifetime. You ought to get in on it, Gloria, save yourself all that boring typing . . ."

"It's dry," she says loftily. "Everywhere's dry. You'd know that if you paid attention to the news. Everyone's lying low for a while."

"Gloria," David says, "please. Do you *want* me to get done in? Because that's what we're up against here. Don't you read the papers? People are getting killed for less all the time. The whole scene's gone mad. You've got it. Please. Please. It's only for a couple of weeks."

"How?" I say. "How can you pay me?"

"Lisa will," he says, "out of the business."

"But business is bad."

"Oh, things'll pick up again in a couple of weeks," she says, "they always do."

David bursts into tears. "How *can* you?" he cries. "You can't be like this! What have you turned into? You were so lovely once. It's money, money that does it. Money corrupts. You got thousands of pounds sitting in the bank and we've got nothing, and people are starving to death and sleeping in boxes, and you sit here in your posh yuppie little flat, thinking you're so fucking superior . . ." He jumps to his feet, paces the room, stepping round Lisa, who has started to laugh where she lies, that awful high, weak, endless laugh, ". . . but you're not, you're not, you're stupid and blind and you've lost your soul. We've got nothing and you've got it all but I'd rather be me any day rather than you cos I know what I am, I know what I'm made of and it's better than you . . . You'd see an old friend, someone you're supposed to love, *killed* rather than part with a penny, you selfish bitch. Well, I'd rather *die* than take your filthy money and I hope you feel very proud when you hear of me lying dead with a knife in my gut; you're a pile of *shit*, that's what you are, a pile of old *shit* . . ."

Lisa leaps to her feet, slaps his face, he slaps her face, then turns away with his face in his hands. "You're hysterical!" she screams.

"Get out, both of you!" I cry, jumping up. "I'm not having this." I run into the bedroom, open a drawer, grab a twenty pound note, run back and thrust it into his face. "Take it!" I yell. "Take it and piss off and don't ever come near me again."

He takes it, his face wan and shamed, holds it delicately between two fingers, head hanging. "I'll pay you back," he says, "every penny. Two weeks. Two weeks at the most. I swear by all that's sacred, I'll pay you back."

"There!" says Lisa. "Now we're all friends again."

I flop down on to the settee. "Just go," I say, my throat constricting. "Just go."

David sits beside me. "Sorry," he says, staring into my face. "Oh, I'm sorry."

"Nicey-nicey-nice," says Lisa, swinging her foot.

214

He puts his hand up my back and gooses my spine. I shudder, repulsed. "Don't you dare!" I hiss, jumping away from him.

"Why?" he says and does it again. I jump up and stand near the door.

"I said go," I say. "Go. I mean it. I mean it, David."

"She means it, David," Lisa says.

"Does that mean we've got to go?" he asks bleakly.

She screams with laughter.

I open the door. "Go!" I say. "Go!"

"Go!" cries Lisa theatrically, striking a pose and flinging the back of one hand to her brow. "Go! Go! Go!"

David stands. She shimmies towards him with drunken grace, takes him in her arms and hugs him, laughing, hauls him towards the door. At the door they stagger and weave. A paw falls from her awful fur, somewhere in the neck region. It swings as she moves, limp and pathetic.

"When's Kit coming?" she asks.

"I don't know."

"She's our little girl," says David sentimentally, "whatever she's done, she's our little girl."

"Yeah, yeah, mine too," says Lisa. "I seen her grow up . . ."

". . . and we've got to do the best we can for her. Remember that, Gloria. Don't fail her."

"You'll love it," says Lisa, "having her back, I mean. I know. Same blood, see."

Oh, yes, I think, what about you? What about your own scattered tribe?

"I'll never forget this," David says dramatically at the foot of the iron stairs, holding up the twenty pound note. "Never. You have saved my life. Two weeks. Two weeks at the outside. I swear it, I swear."

"Oh, stop waving it about," says Lisa, leading him away into the darkness.

I close the door and lock it, turn off the record player and lie down on the settee. My heart is pounding and my eyes sting. I'm going to cry. No, I'm not, I won't cry because of them. I lie still, close my eyes, breathe deeply for a long time.

Peace returns.

I get up and call Esmeralda in, close the window and the

215

curtains, go to bed and try for the moose's antlers. But they don't come. Sometimes they just don't come.

I wake up afraid in the dark, reach for the light cord and, of course, can't find it, panic, reach and reach, grasping handfuls of darkness before I find it and flood the room with light. There sits my room, flat and stark. I sleep again, wake as the first light's coming up at the window, lie on my back drifting pleasantly. The light makes a bright sword on the wall; it shrinks and twists as the curtains move slightly in the morning air.

And a voice speaks, shockingly real, from a point an inch or two above the carpet in the centre of the room. *Help me*, Little Gloria says, shrill and terrified.

The sword bulges, fat and intensely bright, blinding. She gurgles in panic, choking. Her voice grows stronger and more brittle, accelerating, rising in pitch, rattling like loose vertebrae on a skeleton's back, full of air and moisture. It travels upwards from its spot above the carpet and rushes me like an approaching siren till it reaches a spot an inch or so above the top of my head on the pillow and there reaches its peak, shouting atrociously across my upturned face.

Then it's gone.

I just lie there staring at the ceiling, licking my dry mouth with my dry tongue. I don't know how long I lie there. I can't move. Something stirs inside me like a mountain shifting its roots in the earth, something much bigger and more profound than the familiar little seed I usually assume to be me. The seed trembles. The mountain watches. This was not like my other voices. This was not a bell inside my brain, vibrating there. This was outside me.

Morning rises, full, clear, light. I am released. I get up and throw back the curtains. I feel all right. I mean, my head doesn't feel like it's demented or anything like that. I know nothing. Absolutely nothing. Beneath my feet is the salt marsh, with every step the possibility of quicksand. The tide throws inescapable arms around me.

17

Long forgotten, autumn returns.

Christian leaves the day after tomorrow. We walk on a warm clear evening down the long, elegant sweep of the crescent where Phyllis and Roy live.

She called me up last week and invited us for dinner. "We really must make some sort of an effort, you know," she said. "I never seem to see you at all these days. I saw Mary the other day. You know Sam's at the same school as Josie, don't you, the class above? She says you've got a new man." She wants to get a good look at him. Ah, she thinks, about time too.

The air is heavy with the scent of night flowers. A bird sings in the magnolia tree on the front lawn. They've painted the house beige. There is a Neighbourhood Watch sign in the window, an iron grille across the front door, bars across the downstairs windows.

Phyllis opens the door. "Come in, come in," she sings, and leads us along the sea-green hall. A rich roast meat smell drifts from the kitchen at the back of the house. "It's such a lovely evening," she says, "we're in the garden." She leads us out there through a long, bright, piney kitchen full of primary colours, where Radio 4 talks to itself. The garden is long and svelte. On a patio near a weeping willow that trails the ground like some beautiful tragedy, they've set up garden chairs and a folding table laden with wine glasses and an opened bottle of Beaujolais.

Roy rises to greet us, smart and pink and shiny, paunchier than he was, beaming. "Gloria!" he says, squeezing my shoulders and kissing my cheek.

"Hello, Roy."

He shakes hands with Christian. "Oh, wonderful, wonderful," he says when we hand him a bottle of wine. "Will you have a drink now?"

"Of course they will," says Phyllis, throwing her heavy body into a chair and lighting a cigarette. "Don't mind if I smoke, do you? Too bad if you do. Don't say anything. I've tried and can't." She wears a loose flowery dress and big, flat sandals. Her bare legs are brown, covered in long fair hair.

We sit and drink wine and talk. Roy tells us about his trip to New York. He was stuck at the airport for six hours waiting for his colleague. He says New York's a wonderful place.

"Have you been?" Christian asks Phyllis.

"Oh no," she says. "Turkey's my big adventure."

We talk about travel and the government and films and TV and how hard it is for kids growing up these days compared to when we were young and everything was so much simpler.

Then Phyllis gets up and pads towards the kitchen and I grab my drink and follow her. "Need any help?" I say, coming into the heat.

"No, no," she smiles, bustling, "it's all done." She turns off the radio, opens the oven door, draws out a sizzling joint of meat and bastes it. I sit at the pine table and sniff at a pretty cluster of purple and yellow flowers in a vase. My wine tastes bitter. "He's nice," she says. "Dishy. You never said, you sly bugger."

I smile and go to the fridge to look for fruit juice or Perrier to mix with my wine. The door is covered in Mr Men stickers and brightly coloured magnetised letters. There is a bowl of taramasalata, some green olives, cold potatoes, cold custard, cold soup, all covered in Clingfilm. The cold is wonderful on my hot skin. I sigh exaggeratedly. "I could climb right in," I say, opening the freezer. "Good God, how many tons of ice-cream do you get through every year in this house?"

She laughs. "It's for the kids," she says.

I reach out my hand for a carton of orange juice and a sound like static turns on in my head. "S-s-s-s-ch-sch-ch!" it goes, rising to a peak.

Little Gloria speaks out of it, somewhere to the right, a little above and behind my head. *Gloria!* she says, *Gloria!* as if offering something wonderful. I freeze. I feel like a bursting pulse.

Phyllis talks, sitting at the table chopping an avocado. "It was worth it," she says. "A lot of upheaval, but worth it."

"What?" I ask weakly.

218

"The patio."

I turn, a little dazed. I thought she'd gone, the little pest, but she's like a recurring virus: each time she goes, you think that's it till the next time.

"Good heavens," says Phyllis. "You look pale. What is it? It *is* hot in here. Sit down." She jumps up and pulls out a chair. I sit. "What did you want?" she asks. "Couldn't you find it? Gloria?"

"Orange juice."

She brings orange juice and pours it into a glass, then brings ice, plonk, plonk. "There," she says. "It *is* hot." She talks about the heat in Turkey, the patio, a summer house they're planning. There's a kind of sweet innocence in the way she witters on. She's an alien. The meat smells strong and brings a bitter pain under my tongue.

Don't you know? says Little Gloria. *Don't you* know? *Get ready. I'll tell you when.*

I gulp orange juice, ice clacks against my teeth. Phyllis watches me closely. "What is it?" she says. "You're not remotely interested in the summer house. What is it – what is it, Gloria?"

I can't speak.

"You know," she says, "you know, don't you, that you can always come to me if you're in any trouble."

A tear rolls out of my eye, surprising me.

"Now, now," she says softly and briskly. "It's never as bad as it seems." She reaches out and pats my shoulder awkwardly. "Is it Christian? Is it because he's going away? It's not the other side of the world, Gloria."

I shake my head. I have to say something. "It's Kit," I say. "I'm not sure I can live with her."

"When's she coming?"

"Oh, God knows. Soon," I say, surprised to hear my own voice sounding so normal. "She could turn up any time, I suppose. I don't know her any more. She might not even let me know. She wanted to bring a friend. I have awful visions of my flat turning into a flophouse for Kit and her friends."

"Oh, it'll be all right when she's actually here," says Phyllis, "you'll see. Thinking about it's much worse than the real thing. Anyway, it's not for ever." She leans back and sighs. "Children are a pain. One has to act sane and stable for their sake, I do it all the time. In actual fact, I'm a quivering wreck half the time." She stands and goes out of my sight.

Kit phoned the other day. "Christian!" she said scathingly, "Christian! What a pretentious name."

"He's French," I said, "well, half . . ."

She did a joke French accent, insultingly. "Robbing the cradle, are you, Mum? You wouldn't be stupid enough to go with him, would you? Wouldn't you be worried that he might go off with a younger woman when you got there? What would you do, stuck all on your own in a foreign country?"

Later, she said, "I keep thinking you don't want me to come."

"Of course I do," I lied.

Phyllis returns with a round metal tray full of dips: pale-green, cream, pink, white, lilac. "Try that one," she says, putting a plate of sliced pitta bread in front of me, "mmm, delicious." I eat obediently. The food *is* delicious.

"Not too much," she says. "Don't spoil your appetite."

But I eat, I eat; I feel that I can eat and never be filled. She sits at the end of the table, legs spread wide across the Indian rug, head thrown back, fingers fiddling with something in a bowl. "You shouldn't be too discontented with your lot," she says. "It's not so bad. What do you want, Gloria? What do you really want?"

"I want to be normal," I say, scooping seafood dip on to the thin bread and stuffing it in my mouth.

"Normal!" she laughs. "Normal! What's normal? Look at you. You look kind of – kind of – I don't know, a little different, just a little, dare I say, weird? People look at you. Now me, me, I walk down the street and nobody bats an eyelid. Who's normal? Me or you? I don't know. I know I can't be anything other than what I am, and neither can you. Should we question it too much? You think *you* have problems." She laughs. "Do you think because I have a pretty garden and a nice little car to run around in, life's a bed of roses? Hmm?" She jumps up, grinning, acting her words out as she speaks. "Sometimes I think I'm invisible. I sit at the table, Roy sits there where you are, the children sit on either side, the little darlings. And I speak, I articulate, I request, I utter nouns, verbs, adjectives, whole sentences – they even make sense. And I swear my words fly out into interstellar space, bounce off the moon and are deflected into a great black hole somewhere, never to

220

be found. That's what it's like. That's how I communicate with my loved ones – my spouse, my offspring. It's true."

Our eyes meet and we laugh.

"You always had a way with words," I say.

"Yes, well," she says, sitting down again.

"You edited the poetry magazine when I first knew you. You wrote. You stopped."

"Yes, well."

"And you took photographs."

"I did," she says, smiling at the huge lamp that hangs down over the table, "I did, indeed. Still got them. Hang on." She dashes off and reappears with a big brown envelope, spreads pictures on the table in front of me. Slums and rains and urchins. Big eyes stare into mine.

The poor are always with us, whispers Little Gloria. Her icy breath stirs the fine hairs at the back of my right ear. Fifteen years roll back like a curtain.

"Do you remember," says Phyllis fondly, "the time I emptied a pint of beer over David's head in the bar?" She laughs. "What was it for? I can't remember now. Oh, well, I'm sure he deserved it."

I pull a face. "He called me up," I say.

"When?"

"Oh, couple of weeks ago."

" 'Gloria! Gloria!' David's nervous voice.

" 'Who else?' I said.

"I couldn't make out what he was on about, some big mess of trouble – he'd ripped someone off or someone'd ripped him off, they were after him, he was innocent, innocent . . .

" 'Do you mean you can't pay me what you owe me?' I said. 'Just say it, David, we don't need all the drama.'

" 'Please, don't ask me about that now, please, don't you understand? These people are nutters. Shooters and all that . . .'

" 'This sounds familiar . . .' I said.

"He groaned. 'Oh, God, I don't know what to do, oh, God, I'm in a state, Gloria, please come through for me! You, of all people. Don't be hard on me. I need to talk to you. The phone's no good.'

" 'No,' I said.

" 'For fuck's sake,' he was gasping. 'I'm cracking up, I'm cracking up, don't you understand? *Please*, I need to talk to you . . .'

" 'No. Not right now.'

" 'Why?' he shouted. 'Is your boyfriend there? Do you think I don't know? Your young stud? Has he got it in you right now? Is that why you're too busy to help an old friend? You've changed, Gloria, oh, you've changed!' Then he wept and apologised, said he was in such trouble, such deep trouble . . ."

"Oh, God," says Phyllis in disgust. "You don't need this, Gloria. Don't get involved with these people and their tragedies. Life's hard enough."

"I know," I say. And I tell her how he begged and pleaded, said Lisa wasn't there, he was all alone and dying for want of someone to talk to, how he cried long and deep, how in the end I relented and went round and Lisa answered the door. " 'Oh, hi, Gloria,' she said, 'come on in.' She seemed surprised to see me. She crouched in the middle of the dusty floor cutting her toenails, her long hair sweeping the floor. 'He's out,' she said. 'What!' I shrieked, 'he phones me up and drags me all the way over here and he's out!'

"She said she didn't know; she'd just got back and someone called and he said he had to go out. 'You know what he's like.' She made a cup of tea, standing half asleep dropping ash into the sink, then started picking at her teeth with an old nail file, plucking out bits of tartar and flicking them on to the floor. She said he was up all night drinking strawberry wine and this morning he was puking like a pig."

"Good God!" says Phyllis.

I've grown angry with the telling. I hate him. I hate them both. Under the table my knuckles are white. I could smash his stupid face in. Cry wolf. One day he'll call and it will be true – he'll really need help, and I won't come. And, if I do come, he won't get sympathy. Oh, no! No sympathy, no sympathy, not any more.

Little Gloria cackles. *He'll get more than he bargained for*, she says. I brush her from my shoulders like dandruff.

We return to the patio.

"You simply can't run a country like that," Roy is saying, twirling the stem of his glass. "You can't run a business and you can't run a country."

222

"Talking long term," says Christian, "but in the short term you can, and that's where the problem lies."

"Dinner in a jiff," says Phyllis.

Roy pours wine, emptying the bottle. "You didn't bring another bottle out, darling," he says, mildly peeved.

"Oh, no. Oh, damn. Oh, well, we may as well go in now, anyway, I suppose. It's all ready."

But we sit for a while draining our glasses and listening to a fat late bee droning in the bell of a flower. When finally we go inside, Christian hangs back. I look from the back door and see him down on his haunches looking intently at the surface of a little white wall that skirts the lawn.

I hear a cork pop in the kitchen. "Now," says Phyllis, "one, two, three, four."

The garden is quite dark.

"What are you doing?" I say, stepping out and leaning over him.

He looks up, excited. "Look," he says, pulling me down beside him.

In the light from the kitchen window I see a chaos of microscopic red dots hurtling here and there on the wall, frantic, purposeful. I put my finger into the middle of them and they divide to run about it. "Spiders," I say.

I put my arm around him and he leans into me like a dog, butting me gently with his head. "I can't believe I'm going away," he says.

"Dinner!" calls Phyllis.

"Spiders aren't insects," he says as we go in. "Did you know that?"

"Of course they are."

In the dining-room we are placed at a big round table set with candles and flowers, gleaming silver, basketweave table mats. Roy lights the candles.

"No, they're not. Everyone thinks they are but they're not."

Phyllis serves prawns and avocado in bowls like little green leaves.

"Neither are slugs," says Christian. He's a bit drunk, his face shines, the scar on the bridge of his nose is distinct. We're all tipsy. Christian eats avidly, leaning across the table and talking with animation about slugs and centipedes, neither of which, he assures

223

us, are insects. Phyllis and Roy exchange a look. They're thinking he's young and silly. I don't care.

"Please," Phyllis says, smiling and frowning at the same time, "not while we're eating."

"Sorry," he says.

Everyone laughs.

Their tipsiness flows out of their tongues, gleams mellow in their eyes, glows on their skin. Mine simmers in my brain and locks my tongue. They don't notice. Another voice speaks behind their voices, like a radio talking to itself in another room, quite calm and constant. I can't catch the words. She turned it off, the radio, she did, I saw her. What a mess of sound – four voices, not mine, the babble of cutlery, crockery, the dripping of water somewhere, the revving of a car engine in another street. All too bright, too true, too present. I wish I was home, curling up in bed, the sheet pulled over my head.

Ceramic dishes with gold and blue designs cover the pure white table-cloth. The feast is served.

"More wine, Gloria," Roy says genially, pouring into my glass. The liquid lies there, glittering like a jewel.

"You're very quiet," says Christian softly.

I smile.

There is a great haunch of dripping meat, its skin the colour of some dreadful wound. An eye in the middle of it gleams at me. There are roast potatoes, roast apples with cloves stuck in them, glazed carrots, courgettes and corn, gravy. Roy chews solidly, his jaw clicking. Phyllis grinds pepper from a mill. Christian talks about the psychology of cults. He isn't young and silly any more, he's a stranger: sophisticated, articulate, entertaining. He is quite at home here, far more than I am. He says something witty, looking at me out of the corner of his eye to see if I'm noticing. Phyllis and Roy laugh gaily. It's going well, they like him.

I'm cold under my burning skin. I drink wine and forget. I see in the darkness at the window a gabled house on the side of a mountain, a meadow, three mounds, me and my dog in the lane, Alastair with his gun, my daughter feeding chickens in the yard. *Where is Little Gloria?* There she is, there, peeping round the curtain of an upstairs window, smiling knowingly.

There is lemon mousse, cheese and biscuits, After Eights, strong coffee. In the lounge we sit around and talk, drinking brandy. All stuffed and loose and sprawling, we talk about politics and house prices and crime and blood sports. Roy's chins are very pronounced. Christian sits beside me, holding my hand. The guru smiles down on us. Mozart plays.

He's only twenty-five, I think. What if he goes awful in a few years' time and I'm stuck with him? He could. How shiny he is. I look at him and see his chins spreading, his sweet Neanderthal face coarsening, becoming commonplace, his body thickening like dough left to rise.

David was beautiful once.

"You OK?" says Christian. "You falling asleep?"

It's nearly midnight. Roy offers to drive us home, but we say no, we'll get a taxi. And the cab comes and we go home to my place, Christian talking to the driver while he plays with my hand. How funny, I think. I'm so cold, so strange, and he didn't see. All he saw was a nice night out. I wonder, was I really there at all?

When we get home I go into the bedroom at once, lie down on the bed and close my eyes. I could go with him, even now, leave here and step into a different life. My head spins. Yet another different life. There were so many. I tore up all my roots, not once but many times. Am I to tear them up again? Here is my home. Here's where I live with Esmeralda and my plants, out there is the garden where I grow herbs. I know the sounds the pipes make. I know the time of day by the sun patches on the walls. I have friends and some money. Let someone else tear up roots this time.

I feel him sit down on the edge of the bed. "You were very quiet tonight," he says.

I open my eyes and stare at the ceiling.

"What's the matter?" he asks.

I look at him. His eyes are drunk and tired and droop at the corners. I think his mouth is beautiful, full and firm and serious. "Do you believe in ghosts?" I ask.

"Yes," he says at once.

"What do you think they are?"

"I've no idea. Why?"

"Nothing." I reach out and stroke the small of his back, closing my eyes.

225

"Something's wrong," he says. He lies down beside me and we turn towards each other. "Come with me," he says, trembling slightly. I feel my way along his spine. "I get scared," he says.

"Scared?"

"I get scared. I think I'll never see you again." His eyes, close to mine, are troubled. Our mouths keep banging together and kissing. "Sometimes," he says, sliding his thigh between mine, "I think I don't know you at all. I think you're an alien."

I laugh. "That's funny. I thought Phyllis was an alien tonight." They were all aliens.

"You're cold," he says, and his brow furrows. We kiss softly and tenderly for a while and he starts to cry. His forehead sweats and his nose runs. I wipe his face and stroke his hair. His skin exudes a kind of sweetness to my senses; he's like some delicious food I want to nibble slowly, consume bit by bit. "Come with me," he says. "Come with me."

I have to give this up for Kit. Who says, "I hate you, Mummy." Who says, "God, you're so stupid." Who says, "You don't want me, do you?" Who flings her hair back continually, sniffs wetly, looks a mess, thinks she's ugly, watches me with hurt eyes just like mine. I could have dumped her on the salt marsh. I could have put her in a home. Maybe I should have, better for her, better for me. But I didn't. Instead I pulled her by the hand through years of floating fortune, said Oh, kids are adaptable, said After all, *I* had a stable home life and look at me, said Oh, she'll be fine, said So what if she doesn't like David? I can't let a child rule my life.

Here she comes again.

"I can't," I say, "not yet."

"When?" he says. "When?"

"I don't know."

"Oh, God, you!" he says. We roll about, make love drunkenly.

"Do you realise I'm leaving tomorrow?" he says. "This is ridiculous."

"Shsh," I say, dog-tired.

"So I'll go without you, then," he says. "And I'll be all alone. And you'll be all alone. And that's how it is."

"Shsh," I say.

"When, Gloria?"

"Shsh."

"Gloria."

I jerk upright, making him jump. "Shut up!" I scream. "Shut up! Leave me alone!" God, they never do, do they? They keep on at you all the time. Might as well be David – rub my back, Glory, Glory, I *need* a massage, the country, the town, a screw, a cup of tea, a fuss. I burst into tears and he pulls me down beside him and holds me.

"Sorry," he says, "I'm sorry, I'm sorry, I'm sorry." We rock each other for comfort.

"One of these days," I say, "I'll turn up on your doorstep."

He smiles.

In the early hours I watch his face drift towards sleep. Now he breathes deeply, evenly, his mouth falls open. His eyes move behind his closed lids.

"Little Gloria!" I whisper. "Little Gloria! You can come out now."

18

Christian flies away.

I grow thin. I live on wine and fruit and yoghurt and green olives.

One morning I get a call from David. "Can I come and stay with you for a few days, Glory? Only a few days, no hassle, I promise. Go on."

"Don't be ridiculous," I say, "of course you can't. Anyway, Kit's coming on Sunday."

"For Christ's sake! You don't give me a chance to explain. Listen to me, listen to me . . ."

I want to be free of him.

"I'm all alone," he says.

"Where's Lisa?"

"Oh God!" he groans. "They've got her in Holloway."

I nearly laugh. "What for?"

"Thieving," he says forlornly.

"When did all this happen?"

"Case came up yesterday. My God, I never thought . . ."

"What, out of the blue? You never told me anything about this."

"Didn't I? Well – I suppose not." He babbles nervously. "Probably didn't seem worth mentioning; I mean, it just seemed so stupid and trivial; I mean, she's had her nose clean for years. All for a few crappy bits of jewellery – I can't believe it; I didn't even bother going to court, for Christ's sake, I never thought . . ."

"Oh, come on, David, with her previous? How long did she get?"

He groans. "Six months."

I sigh and make sympathetic noises, say all those things you say, she won't do that long, time will fly, soon be over, but he cuts across me and his voice is urgent and hushed, as if someone in another room might hear. "Gloria, I've got the creeps. This place.

I'm all on my own. How about if I come over just for a couple of days?"

"No."

"Oh, come on!" His voice drops still lower. "I can't explain. I feel bad. Don't laugh, please. I feel as if . . . as if . . ." He sighs, gasps weakly. I see his lost gaping eyes wander about the room, and when he speaks again there are tears in his voice. ". . . as if something terrible's going to happen – something's coming to get me – it's a nightmare, a nightmare, Gloria. I don't want to be here on my own. I'll never sleep tonight. Every time I hear a noise I jump. It's like a premonition – please, Gloria . . ."

"No."

He growls like a dog. "How can you be so hard?" he shouts.

"I don't need this, David," I say. "I'm busy. Anyway, I told you, it's impossible, Kit's coming on Sunday . . ."

"You rotten bitch," he says bitterly, "thank you so much," and he slams the phone down.

I get up and prowl restlessly. I won't even think about him. I dig out all my old photographs from their nooks and crannies, spread them all out on the bed and gaze at the past. There's me and Mary at school: what knobbly little knees we have, how neat are our white ankle socks. There's Kit in her push chair, my mother grinning over her. Kit has fat cheeks and a bonnet that pushes her lips forward, my mother's in her old red coat. There's David walking out of the sea at Filey, his wet hair hanging in his face. Fat people wade in the shallows behind him. There's me and Tina in the doorway of the house in Scotland. Esmeralda sprawling in the yard. Alastair in shadow at the kitchen table. Shep on the mound.

My God, I don't want all these people looking at me. I flurry them away. Still restless, itchy, little eddies of strange, bored excitement skirl through me, as if something's in the air, something's coming, something . . . I play my ocarina, then go and sit at the mirror and think how weird and awful my face is, peer with concern at the poor dear old thing, make it up elaborately, lips purple, eyes yellow.

She speaks, a parasite in my ear. *Hurry*! she whispers, *hurry, hurry*!

I take the make-up off, start again, eyes black, lips crimson. *Hurry*! *Hurry*! Not right, I make and remake myself obsessively.

Then I take all the make-up off, every bit, take a hand mirror to the window and stand in the harsh light studying the wrinkles and pores and blemishes. There I am, eternal Gloria. I still love her. I still love her so much.

I go to work and waltz in the kitchen with Tosh to the music from the radio.

"Mummy," he says, putting his sleek dark head under my chin. His hair fits him like a cap.

"Son," I say.

He smiles and we sway together. He's as thin and healthy as a hound.

"What about your own mother?" I ask him.

"Dead," he says, "since I was seven. What about yours?"

"Dead," I say. "My mother was mad. Mad."

He raises his head and smiles into my face, then his tongue darts out and runs swiftly the round of my lips. We laugh, the music changes, we dance on, round and round the kitchen in the strong smell of baking and the steam of coffee. Life is full of endless possibilities.

There, I think, walking home, another one. And this one's only eighteen. There's life in the old bones yet. I feel good. I clean my flat, water the plants, eat olives and drink coffee, watch the moon come up in the deep blue sky, play my ocarina, sing to Esmeralda "Que sera, sera", whatever will be, will be . . . What will I be? The wife of a social psychologist, a lonely ageing woman in a little flat, a long-term inmate in a mental institution, a bag lady, the lover of a young Japanese boy, a woman who works in the Red House and takes in typing. I am a woman who works in the Red House and takes in typing. I can make a bouquet, draw a picture, make a living, grow herbs. I have a daughter.

I talk to Esmeralda. She listens, looking wise and blinking in all the right places. "You old crab," I say and tickle her between the eyes. I move my hand away. She looks at me and after a few seconds reaches out and places her paw on my hand. It rests there for a moment, warm and friendly, before she removes it and folds it away with the other one. This moves me so much I weep.

It grows dark. I turn on the lamp and the fire and watch the shadows of my plants in the alcove. It's very quiet. I shiver in anticipation. I don't know what it is that's coming, how it is I know it's almost here, inevitable, implacable, like destiny, this something on a collision course with me. It's a singing in the blood, a pricking of the pores, a mote in the eye, a quickening of the heart. I wake at times knowing there was a sound, surely, a voice, perhaps. I listen. I watch.

The clock ticks. The shadows are still. I am so silent in my chair that the room does not know I'm here. The moment is like a falling chord of music, perfectly in tune, slowly plucked across strings.

Someone knocks at the door, tense and furtive.

I sit on, it comes again, I get up and go to the door. "Who is it?" I call.

"Me. David."

I swear softly, open the door. He stands there with a locked cash box in his hands, his wasted white face rising gaunt from the neck of a long sinister coat that falls past his knees.

"Take a walk with that," I say.

"I only want to come in just for a minute," he hisses. "Honest. I need some kind of – like a pair of scissors or something might do . . ."

"Are you crazy?"

"Look, I can't walk the streets with this. Use your head. Ten minutes – then I'll be out of your sight." He speaks the last words through gritted teeth.

"No."

He strikes his forehead. "I don't believe this!"

"No."

"I'll split the cash . . ."

I close the door, lock it, put on the bolt. He rings the bell endlessly. I walk about hugging my elbows. It goes on and on like a fire alarm.

Then he pounds on the door. "Gloria!" he yells. "Gloria!"

I run to the window and put out my head. "Are you mad? Are you mad? Go home. Don't stand there yelling and drawing attention to yourself with that thing. Do you *want* to end up inside like Lisa?"

"I hate you!" he cries. Tears glitter in his eyes. I close the window, draw the curtains, pace the room. He rings the bell, hammers on the door, yells, "Gloria! Gloria! You cow!" His voice is loaded with poison. "Think you're so fucking good, don't you?

231

You're pathetic! Lost your soul. Lost your *boring*, *stupid*, *petty* little soul, Gloria!"

Oh, my God, the whole street can hear. I flop into a chair and cover my face.

"Your boyfriend left you, you cow! What happened? Saw the light, did he? Ha-ha-ha! Fucking *cow*! Thanks a lot! Thanks a fucking lot! All those years, all those years and you leave me on the doorstep! I hate you! Do you hear that? I *hate* you, I fucking *hate* you, you bitch!" His voice chokes itself. He pounds on the door, rings the bell. I start to cry. I hear him weep on my doorstep, a soft miserable whimpering. Then there is silence.

A moment later he pounds on the window.

"Go away, please go away," I whisper.

"Scared what the *neighbours'*ll think, Gloria?" he shouts. "Eh? Don't want to upset the *neighbours*, do we?" He roars with laughter. "I'll break it! I'll break it! I'll huff! and I'll puff! And I'll *blow* your house down!" Pound, pound, pound.

I run to the window and shout, "I'll call the police! I'll call the police, David! Think!"

"Fuck off!" He laughs. "Fuck off, my sister, my spouse!"

"I'm calling the police!" I run to the phone and lift the receiver.

"Call them! Call them, you bitch!" he yells, but he stops banging on the window. I hear him weep. The dialling tone purrs in my ear. "I'm going," he calls forlornly, "I'm going. *Keep* your ivory tower. It's all a load of crap anyway."

I put the receiver down. His footsteps descend the iron stair. Then only silence. My heart knocks against my chest: Let me out, let me out. My hands tremble. I sit down and wait for calm, lift Esmeralda to my breast and hold her there.

I want to be free of him. Oh, how I want to be free of him.

Next morning I tell Mary all about it as we sit at the window overlooking the garden. It's a fine crisp day, Josie wanders about the garden with her hands behind her back, her pigtail tied with a little pink bow. Her sandals are incredibly loose and old and flop about like boats on her small brown feet.

"Oh, men!" says Mary. "They all turn out to be babies in the end. Serve him right if he *had* got nicked." She pushes the sleeves of her jumper up her big freckled arms, drains her coffee with a gesture of scorn. "Men, I've had it up to here with them. Think with their dicks. Can you really name me one couple you envy, one couple who've actually stayed together, come to think of it? Apart from Phyllis and Roy (and they're as boring as a bus stop).

"I had this guy once, used to wait outside when I was getting off work and make a big scene in front of everyone. Pathetic. Mummy, Mummy, look at me! I'll drum my heels and hold my breath till I turn blue if you don't! Your trouble is you take it all too seriously. Heard from Christian, by the way?"

"Called me up Tuesday night."

"Mmm, very devoted," she says, lightly sarcastic. "How much did that cost him?"

"I don't know."

"Still, his folks are in the money, aren't they? What did he say? Gloria, Gloria, I can't live without you?"

"Shut up, Mary."

"Sorry. You know the best thing you could do? Have a casual fling. Something totally trivial and disposable." I watch Josie play, absorbed, her feet soaking wetness from the grass, her mouth forever moving. "None of these bleeding hearts. Tell you what, why don't we go off somewhere, a nice holiday, go to the sun and get out of all this." She waves at the still white sky, the still autumn garden. "Laze about. Drink wine. Pick up a couple of blokes, couple of handsome waiters . . ."

"I don't want a waiter!" I say, laughing but irritated. "What do I want with a bloody waiter?"

"Oh, there's all sorts of things you can do with them," she says, then scowls, screwing up her nose. "There's no fun any more. AIDS. Paranoia. Everyone's too serious." She leans back, rocking in her chair.

Josie swings on the overhanging bough of the elder tree and it creaks wearily, very loud, as if the stillness of the air has magnified sound. I shiver, a single involuntary shudder that makes my throat catch. Playing children are possessed. I remember it well. "Josie!" I call. "Leave the branch alone." It's old, it might break.

"Want some tea?" I say. "Something to eat?"

Mary follows me into the kitchen. "Are you all right?" she asks.

"Oh, yes. What do you mean?"

"I don't know." She looks puzzled. "I don't know. You're very pale."

"Oh, I'm OK." I smile. "A little bit up and down maybe. Probably hormones or something."

Josie comes in. Something comes in with her, cold air, a faint gnat-like hissing in my ears, nothing more. I am a little breathless. Josie hangs around Mary's knees, whining, pouting. "Want to go home," she says, "want to go home, Mary. Want to go home, want to go home, want to . . ."

"Shut up! Can I put the telly on, Gloria? Keep Her Majesty amused."

"Sure."

It comes on in a burst of laughter, then there is music. I make tea, shake a long red cloth over the round table by the window and lay out ginger biscuits, bread, peanut butter, shiny red apples.

"Don't *want* any of that," says Josie.

"Don't have it, then," I say.

Mary puts her feet up and her hands behind her head and complains that all the videos are crappy. On the screen a woman rolls around singing on the floor. I sit at the table looking out into the garden, pour tea, shake my head a little as if to shake water out of my ears. "Oh, go on outside," I hear Mary say, "you pest, go out and play."

Go out and play, you pest, leave me alone.

Mary talks about how fat her arms are getting, how her therapist doesn't understand her. She thinks she might take up weight training, nothing extreme like some of these women you see, just enough to tone it all up. I close my eyes and drink tea, feeling very peaceful. When I open them the screen is zapping cartoon images at me, the garden is a whiteness in the corner of my eye. "I wonder how much dumb bells cost?" says Mary.

I lean back, crumbling a ginger biscuit in my lap to give to Esmeralda. A dirty little hand comes up from under the red table cloth, cupped, begging. I tap it lightly. "You little beggar, Josie," I say. "You said you didn't want any. Come and ask properly."

The hand withdraws.

"What?" says Mary.

And in a lull in the sound from the screen I hear the steady, weary screak, screak, screak of the poor old elder tree; look out of the window and see Josie swinging on the bough at the end of the garden, the ridiculous boatlike sandals hanging loose on her tiny feet.

I go cold.

My chair goes back against the wall, screeching. I'm on my feet. Biscuit crumbs fly everywhere. I stand stupid and limp, stoop with a quick, awkward movement, flip the table-cloth up and look under. Of course, there is nothing, nothing but a few crumbs on the carpet and dust undisturbed on the branching foot of the table's single central leg. I gape.

"What's the matter?" Mary says.

I stand upright, stare out of the window, swaying a little. A siren sings in my ears, stops. "Josie!" I shout shrilly. "You get off that branch *now*!" Then I turn and walk out and go down to the bathroom and sit on the closed lid of the toilet with my hands clasped tightly between my knees, trembling all over. My teeth chatter, I wipe sweat from my forehead and it is cold.

"Are you all right?" asks Mary softly at the open door.

"Faint," I say, "feeling faint," and I swallow.

"You're really shivering." She comes into the room and bends down over me, peering into my face, and I notice how all the red veins in the whites of her eyes are too bright and stylised to be real. They look as if they'll start to crawl.

"How do you feel?"

I breathe out and straighten, laugh stupidly. "Just went a bit dizzy," I say and it lifts from me as I speak. "I'm OK now." True, it's gone, I'm fine. Only my hand still shakes a little. She fills the toothbrush mug with water and dabs some over my forehead with her fingertips and it runs down my face like tears. "Thanks," I say.

"How do you feel now?"

"Better."

"I know what it is," she scolds, sitting on the side of the bath. "You're not looking after yourself properly, probably not eating the right things. What have you had today?"

I think. I can't remember. She doesn't give me time.

"There you are! Nothing, probably. Silly twit. You're making yourself ill. I'm glad Kit's coming; give you someone to think about apart from yourself. I don't know, she's probably got more sense than you – *she* won't let you starve. Has this happened before?"

235

"Oh, no."

"Well, once is too often. You go to the doctor's. Get a blood test or something. Probably anaemic."

When I stand my knees don't shake. They carry me perfectly well up the stairs, Mary scolding all the way, into my room where the TV squawks and roars and Esmeralda sits on the arm of a chair and Josie sulks and the whole world is right and sane and ordinary. Nothing happened. Of course nothing happened. So we sit and talk and drink more tea, and when Mary and Josie go home I think: That was funny, what was it? What was it now? And my brain is misty.

"*You must get ready*," says a voice on the TV.

I turn the TV off and put on the radio. Someone talks about wine and someone else, far, far way across the airwaves, is laughing and joking in French. A little breeze blows in from the garden. It's turning cool. I rummage through drawers, sit on the floor with all my sacred objects around me: lucky fish, Kit's red ribbon, ocarina, Shep's collar. My protectors.

"Come what may," I say, "come what may," and a rush of excitement goes through me. A different time is coming, I feel it very close now. I'll get money out of the bank. Be ready for anything.

David calls me up on Saturday. "I'm sorry," he says.

"Yes," I say, "I know."

"You're not angry with me?"

"No." I'm not angry, I'm calm.

"I need to see you." His voice is reasonable but tinged with urgency and a weary slurring at the edges. "See how good I'm being? I could've just come round but I wanted to check with you first."

"No. Don't come round."

He sighs. "I am truly sorry," he says, "believe me."

There is a long silence.

"I don't want you here," I say. "Anyway, Kit's coming tomorrow, I have a lot to do."

More silence. "Is it all gone?" he says sadly. "Everything? All I ever was to you? And you to me? That's not gone."

I don't speak. I'm watching a flight of birds in the white and grey sky wheel this way and that, cheerful, ragged, unformed. Why am I smiling in this thin, simple kind of way?

236

"I am eternally sorry for having offended you," he says. "I wanted to speak to you. I wanted to tell you." He pauses, breathing audibly. "I'm ill, Glory. I'm ill."

Cry wolf.

"I'm scared. I'm all alone. I've got the creeps so bad. I don't expect you to understand; it's like I'm waiting all the time for something to happen, something to come and get me. Ever have a premonition? I could die, just fade away and no one would ever know. You don't believe me, you don't believe me, I don't deserve you to believe me. Oh, Glory!" His voice fades as if he's holding the phone very far away from his face. "I want to see you one last time," he says. "I'm going to die."

"You're not going to die." Mother knows best. "You're just being melodramatic. Of course you're not going to die."

The leaves are falling everywhere. They tremble in the sky. Everything's beginning to move. He laughs, a long, slow, creaking kind of a laugh. "Listen to me," he says.

"What's the matter with your voice?"

He laughs. "Something I took," he says. He laughs. "I'm going out like a candle, flicker, flicker." He laughs, fainter and fainter.

"Liar," I say. "You're strong as an ox. I know you."

"You're right!" His voice is loud and clear again, close to the phone. "Only this time's different. This time I'm not fooling. Of course there's no known reason on God's earth why I should die. But there's this premonition, this feeling, this . . . this . . . what? It's like nothing else I've ever felt. I *know*. I *know*, Gloria, sure as anything I'm going to die. Maybe you'll hear of me shot dead. Maybe I'll get run over. Maybe anything, I don't know. But I'm *sure*. This time I'm right."

Silence. On the lawn a blackbird forages. The leaves are deep in drifts that have blown around the side of the house, soft and cold, every shade of autumn. I might be deaf. All the little voices of the world are mute. In the silence my blood runs cold.

He's right.

"I'll come," I say. "I don't want you here. I'll come to you."

"Oh, Glory," he says, his poor voice breaking, "oh, Glory . . ."

I put the phone down, get a coat and walk straight out of the house. I'm not worried about David. I smell autumn as I walk past the park where gardeners sweep leaves into lovely russet pyres the colour of my summer dress, the one I wore with Christian. I reach the station, catch a tube, am swallowed by darkness. In the darkness all my people come to me, Kit, Christian, David. A palpitation starts inside, a swelling and an ebbing of an ache. Little Gloria whispers in my head. I put my hand to the place where it hurts and rub gently and soothingly. Sometimes I wish I were made of stone. Sometimes I think it would be nice to get it burned away, this bit that hurts. It doesn't know where to go. It's like the Boll Weevil, looking for a home.

Aristotle Point is cold and dingy, its faces grey and insulting. I get a slightly sweet pain when David opens the door. It is so sad, these ageing freaks hanging on to the old dispensation till they die, clutching the security of what they were: Lisa in her cell, David in his room. What poor leftovers they have become. This man is thirty-three. His face is white and sweaty, his hair falls into his heavy, troubled eyes. His teeth are out, his formless lips smile uncertainly. He's had a nosebleed; dark, crusted blood still lines his nostrils. He wears a jumper that's too long for him. His hands, nervous and still beautiful, fiddle with the sleeves that droop over them. "I didn't think you'd come," he says, anxious and subdued, afraid I'll leave if he puts a foot wrong. He stands for a moment before turning with an awkward movement and leading the way down the stinking hall to the living-room.

As soon as she's inside, Little Gloria jumps awake, nervous too, hissing like a snake.

"The cat litter needs changing," I say. "That poor creature must be desperate for a clean corner to pee in."

"He's gone," he says.

"Where?"

"Don't know. Just gone. I'm going to throw the tray out." His voice whistles on the s's.

"Where are your teeth?"

"Got to get some new ones," he says.

He hangs around the living-room uncertainly as if it's not his. His eyes are dead.

"What happened to your nose?"

"Nosebleed." He falls down into a chair, I sit on the settee. Blood-stained cigarette papers lie scattered in the hearth. I smell long-dried cat shit, cat pee, dirty dishes, dust, neglect.

"So," I say, "what's the problem?"

"Huh?"

"The problem. Why did you want to see me?"

"Oh," he says, looking puzzled, "do I need a reason to see my oldest friend?" Wetness gathers in one loose corner of his mouth. "I thought we could just sit and talk, two old friends together." His eyes close. I look around, tired and infinitely saddened by him. I can think of nothing to say. "So," he says, opening his eyes, "how's things with you, Glory?"

I smile. "So-so."

He smiles too, that thin smile, eyes warm and crinkly, the once sweet lips folding in upon the dark empty mouth. So we sit, smiling uselessly and mysteriously at each other. He gets up to cross the room, stumbles against the furniture, puts a record on a turntable with agonising slowness, forgetting several times during the act what stage of the proceedings he's at, unable to match his hands and his brain when he tries to find the arm and place it on the record, scratching it horribly. Finally he gets it.

"For God's sake, David," I say as he buckles at the knees and falls back heavily into his chair, "you're a maniac, you know that? You're getting worse. You're not safe on your own."

He grins, closing his eyes.

I will never forgive him for what he has become.

"Remember this?" he says fondly. "Remember, Glory?"

Same ancient record that played the night I visited him, end of term, fire glowing in the dark, blood in the coffee. The Doors. It clicks and crackles and jumps. I see him sitting here in this smell, day after day, night after night, playing ancient records and never going out.

He talks of that night lovingly, then he talks of the cathedral gardens and the cobbled market full of old bookstalls where we used to go when we were kids. "I thought you were the most beautiful person in all the world," he says tenderly, putting his hands behind his head and stretching his legs. I don't want him to talk like this, the poor fool reaching over the years to the lost boy he was, gone now. But there's no stopping him and I sit there trapped, lamenting the lost boy, while he remembers the way the blades cut the ice that night at the rink when this girl came skating near him and he couldn't believe his eyes, his luck – she was so lovely and he

239

knew then, beyond all doubt, she was the one. And the café where they used to go, hold hands across the table and talk about their lives, the young boy behind the counter who stared at her, and how they'd leave and walk and stand in a doorway and kiss; and her room where they lay on the bed and listened to the rain, and the cats padding in the corridor, and the cold that drove them under the covers, and the way her hand felt on his spine.

I don't want to hear any of this. They walk like legends at the end of a long tunnel of time, the lost boy and lost girl, forever young. I want to seize them by the scruffs of their necks and fling them face down in this smelly room and cry Look! Look! Cover your faces and crawl away.

"So what was it all for?" he asks.

I don't know. I say nothing.

"I'm ill," he says. Then, very seriously, staring straight into my eyes, he says, "You don't believe me."

This time I do. "What is it?" I ask.

The record sticks, just the way it did that night years ago. I remember, I remember, it goes: "This is the end, beautiful friend, the end, this is the end . . ." over and over again. His face begins to crumble, turn naked like a child's.

Oh, please don't, please don't, I can't bear any more of this.

"I'm frightened," he says. No tears come. "I'm frightened." This is plain terror, worse than all his games. I get up and kick the record player and it moves on.

"Tell me," I say, "you have to tell me."

"I'm ill," he says again, covering his face with long, beautiful, trembling fingers. They are still there, eternal, three rings on his right hand – a big gold square, a thin silver band, a snake with its tail in its mouth. "Be my friend," he says.

"David!" Angry, I crouch before him and pull his hands from his face. "You have to tell me."

"I don't know," he says. "I'm sick all the time. I can't eat anything. I shit blood. I have nightmares. My head hurts, my eyes hurt. I'm all alone . . ." His voice trails off and his eyes wander.

"Have you seen a doctor?"

"Yes. He said it was nerves."

"Bullshit. He wouldn't say that. I don't believe you."

"He did!"

240

"What are you eating? Crap, I bet. And taking all kinds of other crap too. Drinking. Speeding. And you wonder why you feel bad." I shake him, his lips draw back, I can't abide his mouth. The record ends. Click. Click. Click. Click. I stand and walk about the room in anger, berating him. He listens forlorn, eyebrows raised in self-pity, eyes helpless, mouth drooping.

"Don't get at me," he says, "don't get at me. I'm ill, I'm really ill." His nose runs, water and blood. A tear trickles from the corner of one eye. He stands groggily, staggers a little. "I have to lie down," he says, "I have to. Please, don't go yet. Stay just a little bit more and talk to me; I don't care if you tell me off, only, please, don't leave me alone just yet." A hand flutters towards his head. He sniggers tearfully. "The horrors," he says. "The old horrors keep coming back – soon as you go they'll come back." He moves towards the room next door. "Come and sit with me, please." He vanishes. I hear the creak of bed springs, a long wavering sigh.

Click. Click. Click. Click.

"Gloria!" he calls weakly.

I turn off the record player, go and stand in the doorway. The walls are bare, the light crude. Darkness looks in the window over a sagging pink and grey curtain. There is an old wardrobe with a door standing open, clothes strewn about the floor, dustballs on the carpet. A thin pink coverlet of Indian design falls from the foot of the bed where he lies on his back, eyes closed, head on a crumpled blue pillow. Next to it is another, Lisa's, with a grease stain where her head used to rest. The covers are awry.

"Just sit and talk to me," he says.

I sit down on the edge of the bed.

"So," he says again, "what was it all for?"

"I don't know."

He smiles. "Maybe we'll never know. Maybe it doesn't matter. Meanings. Huh." He laughs. "It might be that the last five minutes of your life are all that really count, all that you were born for."

He comes out with these things sometimes.

There is a squat black radio on a table cluttered with stains and hairpins and Lisa's lipstick at the side of the bed. His languid hand reaches out and turns it on. It plays Country and Western quietly, sentimental stuff. He cries softly. His empty mouth gapes. I watch him, fascinated.

"Hold me," he says.

I recoil.

"I'm dying," he says brokenly. "Hold me."

I will not lie down with him. I make him sit up, then hold him stiffly, suffering. My teeth clench above his head. Jim Reeves comes on the radio singing "Golden Memories and Silver Years" and it is so ridiculous that we start to laugh. "My mum used to love Jim Reeves," he says, and the voice croons on and we laugh so much I nearly cry too.

"I love you, Gloria," he says. "You know that, don't you? It's the one true thing in my life." I cringe. My flesh doesn't want him near me. "Gloria," he says, rubbing his damp white face into my neck. His breath is hot, his lips are too close, too close, he smells sour. I move away but he comes after, heavy and feverish, clinging persistently.

"I'm going now." I push him. "Really."

"Don't leave me," he says. A hand touches the side of my breast. I want to scream.

"Oh, come on, now," I say. "You must be joking." And I push, push, but he clings, clings, sticks to me as if by suction. I hate this, I hate it, a squid is cleaving to me, there are suckers on my neck, tentacles wrapping me round. My lips draw back. Little Gloria hisses. Then she laughs but it's hard to hear her through the panting of his breath, the struggle, my own voice saying, "No! No!" I push and writhe but my arms don't move.

"Please!" he says. "Please!" His gums sink into my neck and suck there; he weeps, "Gloria! Gloria!"

I can't bear it, can't bear this ancient stinking baby with his mad, grotesque dependence laying claim to me. I get a hand free, grab his hair and try to yank his head away but all it does is jerk, the features distorting like a rubber mask, then swims towards me again like a nightmare. Tears burst from my eyes. I can't breathe, my head's exploding.

Little Gloria laughs helplessly. *You've got to*, she says, *you've got to*.

I heave and strain against him and his face changes, floating close and far before me in a sea of cruel light that flings into high relief each dirt-clogged pore, each crease and crack, the slimy whites of his slitted eyes.

I hate him.

His piggy little eyes, slitty mouth, face of a priggish middle-aged boy of six. The hot fat slug of his tongue gets in my mouth. I choke. I spit. He wants to eat me alive, chew me with his terrible carnivore gums. Fury crashes in me, a delivering wave that drowns the whole world. My hand comes clear into the cool air of the room, grabs the squat black radio with its melancholy voice singing "I, I could be warm, lying in your arms, healing my scars", lifts its great weight high above his head, and he moves, our eyes meet for one second and say, bewildered: This is getting silly.

NOW! cries Little Gloria.

All the rage I ever felt flies out at him. The pounding pulse, the thrill of hate, the power and glory and joy of smashing his head in. This is what I was born for. The radio crashes over his left ear, makes a cracking sound, metal on bone, comes down again on top of his head, again in my small white hand, knocks itself off the station into some lost place between the airwaves where it settles into an eternal interstellar whispering, where Little Gloria hides. My hand opens and the radio drops on the floor.

He falls on me. I heave him over till he rolls back with his head upon the dirty blue pillow. A trickle of blood comes down the side of his face, another drips into the shiny, pink convoluted shell of his ear and pools there, dark and gleaming. His eyes, half closed, sleepy and surprised, look and look at me. I smile at him. See? It was me all along. You really *did* have a premonition. For once you were right, David. He looks through my skull, through the hollow heart, through and through and through. His lips move, faintly smiling. He closes his eyes and sleeps, deep and heavy, bleeding slowly into the pillow. After a time I pick up the other pillow and place it gently over his head, the greasy stain where Lisa's head used to lie covering his face. I press. He doesn't move. I press harder, then lie right across it, belly down, for so long I fall into a half sleep where I hear a sound like breathing, a very fine sound just on the edge of hearing. It stops, then starts again, louder and deeper, becomes heavy and steady and full-throated, moves across the room towards me and takes up a position at the back of my head. There it stays, falling sadly till it's barely perceptible.

Not much worse than drowning a puppy, really, it says. I fall asleep. When I wake I've lost track of time. I take the pillow away, replace it neatly where it belongs, sit up and sigh. My blood sings. I stand and stretch. David's Zippo lighter is on the floor by the bed. I arrange his arms neatly, hands upon his chest, pick up the thin pink coverlet from the floor and cover him neatly from head to toe. Then I walk around the bed and very gently lift it, climb under, draw it up close over our heads to make a cocoon, and lie down by his side. The light comes through rosy on us. I take him in my arms once more, just for old time's sake.

Let's play a game.

What?

Let's play we're in a womb.

We lie together for a long time, just like before, me alive and you dead, here in the womb. *I killed you once before we were born, you didn't have to come back for more.*

It's time to go. I get up and fold the coverlet down to his waist so I can see him. He's old. His looks have gone. He had nothing to live for. He deserved to die for what he did to himself. I am calm and efficient. There's blood in the bed, blood on his pillow, blood on the greasemark of Lisa's head, blood on me. I'll wash it all away when I get home. I pick up the radio from the floor, turn it off and wipe it very carefully with a part of the pink coverlet before replacing it on the table at the side of the bed. This won't come as a surprise to anyone. There were so many ways he could have died, he said so himself; you heard him, didn't you, God? The things he took, the life he led, the people he knew, the enemies he made. Nutters, heavy people, one bad debt after another, I'm not kidding, shooters, knives, you heard, you heard . . .

Just some sordid little underworld murder.

So he lies there, a young dead man; his hands touch each other timidly on his chest, rings on three fingers. Oh, the poor love, with his rings on three fingers.

I leave quietly, closing all the doors softly. It's late. I'm going away – free, free at last. I am the ultimate power. I am she who gives birth and she who destroys. I am the Grim Reaper, my bone head gleams, my awful smile glitters. There's blood on my scythe.

I walk by night and I eat the souls of men.

19

Kit's coming today. I lie in bed in the very early morning, Esmeralda at my feet, at peace. I look into my mind and seem to see there distant worlds, a multitude of them no other human being could ever know, and all the people in all those worlds also have minds full of worlds. They teem and multiply, a vital wave flowing from me. Someone in one of those worlds suffers, thinking she's real. Don't worry, I say to the woman in the distant world, it's all right, you're not real. You're out of me. Whatever happens you'll be OK because you're not real. I promise, you fade back into me when I reach the end of the story. It doesn't hurt. That's all it is, an endless fading back. But the woman can't hear. She suffers in the distant world in the mind of some person in a world in my head.

But I don't suffer. I'm cured of all that. I drift into limbo, run round and round the mushroom field with my invisible twin, playing out some desperate adventure. When I reach the Africa tree it's chopped, dismembered, headless. A lopped torso. I wake with a start and hear rain coming down outside, gentle and kind. What strange dreams I have had. And here I am; here I am, alive, sane: the real world holds me in its comforting arms. All my things are around me. I am perpetual, wonderfully pointless; I'll move, rest, stick things in me, out of me, up me, fade in, out, on and on and on, an erratic line that nothing can stop, the head of every comet, the eye of every storm. Still alive.

There is no anger left in me. My nerve ends do not tingle.

I get up, stretch, have a bath, dress, put a little make-up on, do my hair. I cook mushrooms and eggs, singing to myself, eat at the round table looking out on the wet garden. I pick up Esmeralda and she scratches me, draws blood on my hand, runs away from me. "You old crab," I say affectionately. "You old crab."

I make phone calls, arrangements. I call France. Christian

sounds near, pleased and surprised. He'll meet me. I clear the breakfast things away, wash up, go out to the shop that's always open on Sundays. I hear the sound of bells being rung well and it takes me back to my childhood. Something else I dreamed. I buy all the things I know Kit likes then go home and spend all day sorting out laundry for her bed, sorting through my clothes, laying things softly in a small case, moving here and there, touching up the flat.

I'm excited, impatient. Soon it will be time to go. I thought this place was my home. It is not. These roots: these things on shelves, these rows of books, these records, these plants, this stereo, this typewriter, these are not my home. I'll take it with me like the tortoise takes its shell. I'll take a time machine. I can be in another world. There's still someone who is on my side. I have money. I'll get by. I always do.

Kit comes in the evening with Delia and a little black dog on the end of a lead. "Delia's staying for a bit, Mummy," Kit says. "It's OK, isn't it? You said it was OK. Mummy, this is Timmy. Isn't he gorgeous?"

Timmy leaps and yelps and licks my face. Kit and I hug and kiss. She has spots under her chin and hair that she keeps pushing back and back and back and back. She wears black leather trousers that are too tight for her, and her legs are bulky. She sniffs too much. My heart goes out to her. She's just a young girl, and I think of me and Tina talking in the hospital grounds when we were her age. Tina lived here and there and everywhere and her mother was crazy.

"How's Alastair?" I ask. "How's Babe?"

"Babe's an old granny," she says. "Everyone sends love."

Delia smiles at everything, sitting on the settee with a headset on. I make tea and cook food. Esmeralda sulks in the bedroom. Timmy barks wildly whenever he hears a door close. Kit stands in the kitchen doorway and talks, leaning, assured, arms folded. She tells me she's a virgin. But anyway, she doesn't care about AIDS, she thinks it's all exaggerated. She's going to get a job in a hairdresser's.

She has this boyfriend, he's coming down in the spring. She shows me a photograph. "He's a traveller," she says. "He plays in this really good band." There he stands, eighteen or so, dark and brooding, holding the reins of a big black horse. Oh, Lord, can't you just see him heading off into the sunset? Poor little Kit.

I take her into the bedroom and we sit on the bed. I take her hand and hold it, not letting her go while I tell her my plans, my decision, the when and the where of it. I leave in the morning, early. The rent's paid for the next three months. She gets the flat, Esmeralda, some money. First she sulks, then she laughs, shakes her head, turns up her eyes. She just thinks I'm impossible.

"You're mad!" she says. "Mad!"

I laugh. "Oh, no, Kit. No, I'm not."

I run to the kitchen to stir the food and she follows.

"How's David and Lisa?" she asks.

"Lisa's in Holloway," I say.

She goes off into shrieking fits of laughter and stumbles about the room, finally collapsing on to the settee where Delia is sitting. They sit and giggle privately together, passing the headset backwards and forwards. Whenever I walk in the room they look up and smother laughter.

After we've eaten she runs into the bedroom and returns with Esmeralda. "Esmeralda!" she cries. "My old puss! Oh, my lovely, lovely old puss!" Her little dog is jealous, so I make a fuss of him. Esmeralda gives me filthy looks. Life is complicated.

"Do you remember Shep?" Kit says.

We smile.

We go to bed very late, she on the settee, Delia on cushions on the floor, me in my room. Esmeralda comes and lies with me, purring in the darkness, staking her claim. Finally, I sleep. I dream I'm walking with a child on my shoulders, Kit, on and on and on in the fog across miles of cracked khaki-coloured mud. There's a tide coming in from somewhere. We have no chance now. We know it. We aren't afraid. We just go strolling, on and on and on, towards the fog line. Me, and Kit with the red ribbon in her hair.

I wake while it's still dark and lie watching the dawn come up, listening to the birds sing. I remember the dawn chorus when I was a child. I remember walking all night. I remember running down to the pool, remember the moorhens and the ducks and the big swans.

I get up, trembling with excitement, dress quickly and quietly and go through to the kitchen, not waking Kit and Delia. The little dog jumps up, smiling and wagging his tail. I pet him, quiet him, finger to lips. He pads after me, tongue lolling, sits with me while I drink my coffee. They sleep on, deeply breathing heaps of

247

blankets, the girlish contents of their bags strewn all over my room.

For a while I look out of the window at the garden under a heavy grey sky till it's time to go, and I turn, go into my bedroom and get my case, my passport, my money. I have an envelope, it says "For Kit, with love from Mummy". I want to take my ocarina, Shep's collar, Kit's red ribbon, my lucky fish, but a small voice beside me, sterner and sadder than all the rest, commands: leave it! as I reach out to touch each one. So I do. I tremble to leave them, but so be it: Gloria's through with this bit. It's over.

I go to my clothes chair, lean down, kiss Esmeralda and say goodbye. She takes not a blind bit of notice of me. "Oh, you horrible animal," I say. "Where's your heart?"

I wake Kit gently, give her the keys, the rent book, the envelope. "What's this?" she whispers.

"Only some money. And my address."

I kiss her. She smiles, falling asleep again.

And then there's nothing left to do, so I leave. A rising wind soughs in the high trees in the park as I walk down the road. Leaves skitter and swirl in my path. I see the tree where I kissed Christian, the path where we walked, me in my new dress, the bench where we sat. Summer is so far away. Everything I have, Esmeralda, my green alcove, the elder tree, the iron stair, my clothes chair, my mirror, all are crumbling, buckling like crushed tissues, vanishing for ever. I'm filled with high elation, brightness glows through a patch in the dark sky above the trees. Little rushes of glee burst through me, rushing like the windblown leaves, suddenly swirled. My heart pounds. I'm going to seek my fortune. I'm going to Africa to find this plant that only grows on the rainforested side of an active volcano. Come what may. Me and Christian, happy ever after.

Or a knock at the door – yes, yes, I'll tell them the truth, the whole truth, nothing but the truth, everything, everything. If they come. I'm perfectly happy. I'm letting it all fall from my shoulders. Gloria forgives herself her transgressions. Gloria forgives herself: Pearly the Mouse, Shep, Kit, David, her dead twin, hearing voices, bringing Motherdie into the house, getting drunk one night and taking a lift from the devil.

In the end, there is only this: she is the little girl in the moose's antlers.

She is the little girl in the moose's antlers.

A NOTE ON THE AUTHOR

Carol Birch was born in 1951 in Manchester. After spending some time in Ireland she now lives in London. Her first novel, *Life In The Palace*, won the 1988 David Higham Prize.